Dealer's Choice

Dealer's Choice

by

Mayo Lucas

Emerald Books Bend, OR

ISBN: 978-1-954779-94-5
First Edition

23 24 LSC 10 9 8 7 6 5 4 3 2 1

Dedication

For my Great Aunt Evelyn Cochran, whose dedication of my first book, *Matters of the Heart,* was lost somewhere in the printing bowels of my first publisher. You have my undying gratitude for believing in me as a thirteen-year old writer—to the point of bequeathing me years later—your desk, chair, and your old Royal portable typewriter on which you wrote your short stories, and on which I wrote *Matters of the Heart.*

For Terry—again—who suffered with me through every re-write of this book that is my baby. You're the best friend a body ever had . . . as Miss Scarlett surely would have said.

To Keith, because a) I promised; and b) you stirred my desire to write again.

And to the love of my life, Joe. I still miss you.

Life is only a game of poker, played well or ill
Some hold four aces, some draw and fill
Some make a bluff and oft get there
While others ante and never hold a pair.

—Pat Hogen, gold rush gambler

ONE

Northern Mississippi, December 1872

It was sleeting. Tiny seeds of ice pecked at the glass and bounced away. Caroline had been smelling it—that or a rare snow—in the air all day. Luckily, she'd already gathered her pine boughs to do some Christmas decorating later.

Huddling deep into her shawl, she used the side of her fist to wipe the fog from an upstairs window. By habit, her eye swept across the once-lovely front lawn to the scars made by Grant's troops nine years ago. Most had long since blurred beneath the scraggly growth of weeds and grasses, but the deepest ones remained. For years her brother had promised to restore it all—house, lawns, everything—to its former splendor. She no longer believed it.

She'd heard him come in last night, but he'd never come upstairs. No doubt he'd spent the night on the couch in the library again. Ever since she'd made him promise to quit his gambling, he'd done nothing but sulk and try to avoid her.

Pressing the tips of her fingers together, she winced at their soreness as she rehearsed her oft-made argument. Her sewing could only bring in so much. They simply could not afford his gambling losses any longer. He was nothing like their papa, who rarely came home— even in the early days of the war—without the heavy jingle of gold in his pockets. However, he was also tipsy. In this, her brother was very *much* like their father.

The clock downstairs struck one, leaving a backwash of silence so complete it was suffocating. Oh, how she longed to break free—but to go where? And do what? Beyond her skills with needle and thread, she had no talents, only unnamed yearnings. Once upon a time, she'd assumed marriage was her future, but the war had bled a staggering number of their young men into the battlefields at Shiloh and Vicksburg. There were precious few left of marriageable age; thus, she'd made her peace with spinsterhood.

Of course, in these shriveled days of postwar depression, she knew she should count herself lucky just to have a roof over her head. Still, she missed times past with its constant stream of people, the rich smells of roasting meats and baking bread wafting in from the kitchen.

She swallowed the sudden pool beneath her tongue. She couldn't remember the last time she'd eaten her fill—which reminded her . . . She'd have to find something to fix for the midday meal before her brother finally put in his appearance, surly with hunger.

Before she could head for the stairs, a movement out the window caught her eye, and she cleared the glass again to see a rented hack come bouncing down the overgrown drive. It halted next to the veranda steps below.

Dark, straight brows snapped into a *V* over the bridge of her nose as one of her brother's favorite oaths hissed past her lips. *Another creditor!*

Twisting the ends of her shawl into a quick knot, she raced out of her room, around the gallery and down the curving flight of bare steps, ribbon-caught hair bouncing across her back. Who the devil could it be this time? Hadn't they all been taken care of—at least for this month?

She was barely to the bottom step when a demanding knock resounded through the wide entrance hall.

Grabbing the pistol from the top drawer of the hall commode, she concealed it in the folds of her skirt and yanked open the front door.

The man, whoever he was, was eyeing where their once-graceful fanlight had been patched with brown paper and paste. Sleet glittered across his shoulders and atop the crown of a derby slanted so far forward she could barely see his eyes. The velvet collar of his Chester-field was turned up, and everything about him—from striped trousers to silk neckcloth and pearl stick pin—said *dandy,* yet his stance was much less elegant. Elbows locked, shoulders hunched against the cold, and hands jammed in his pockets, he looked as ready for an argument as she felt.

Keeping one hand firmly on the doorframe, she lifted her chin. "Who are you and what do you want?" Words and tone designed to put herself in charge from the start.

He looked her up and down just as blatantly as she had him, a pencil-thin mustache drawing attention to the curve of his mouth. "Your parents home?"

The drawl told her at least being a Yankee wasn't one of his failings, but Southerner or no, the abbreviated question was rude. Plus, he failed to remove his hat. Clearly, he was no gentleman. "My parents are dead, and *I* am mistress here, so I repeat: What is it you want?"

"Is this the Cooper place?"

"It is. And you are?"

"You related to a Wendall Cooper?"

"He's my brother." She angled herself behind the door to stop the chilled air sneaking up under her skirts . . . and to keep the pistol hidden. "Now please provide your name."

"Transomb. Jack Transomb." Briefly, he lifted the brim of his derby and she caught a glimpse of dark eyes.

"Well, if you're here about that last load of feed," she began, launching her offensive, "I *told* your man he'd get his money the first of the year, and he will—but if you're here for that nasty Mr. Jessup, you can turn right around and go back where you came from. That's the worst job of tailoring Wendall's ever had done. I could've done better with my eyes closed."

The mustache twitched. "Bad debts all around, eh?"

She didn't answer.

"Place needs work," he commented, eyeing a split floorboard just beyond the threshold.

She covered it with her foot.

Returning his attention to her face, he pushed his hat brim up an inch with a single, straightened finger.

Blue. His eyes were dark blue.

"Well, I ain't here from the tailor's," he was saying, "or the feed-lot."

Suddenly, he pushed through the doorway, forcing her to drop her arm and back up.

"Now see here—!"

Striding well past her, he stopped and pivoted, sharp gaze sweeping the hallway, the gallery above, probing every doorway, every shadow. "I'm here 'cause your brother owes me money."

Icy wind gusted through the doorway. She pushed it closed as he pulled a slip of paper out of his coat pocket and shoved it toward her face. "I waited in town this mornin' like we agreed, but he never showed up."

Caroline saw only her brother's signature before knocking the hand and its offensive paper aside.

"A man shouldn't oughta wager what he can't afford to lose."

Her eyes narrowed. Gentleman, no, dandy maybe, but those words—plus his watch fob, two ivory dice stacked snugly in a little golden cage—told the bigger story. *Professional gambler,* that's what he was. She wrinkled her nose. She should've known from the start. Nobody except Yankee carpetbaggers and southern sharpers could afford to smell that good these days.

"Do you even know how to use that?"

She felt a flutter of nerves spring to life in the pit of her stomach even as she feigned innocence. "Use what?"

Oddly enough, it was his response—the dismissive flick of an eyebrow—that drained away her nervousness and replaced it with the bravado she'd come to rely on ever since her parents died and left her to overcome or make do as best she could.

"You mean this?" Without so much as a tremor, she raised the pistol straight out, aiming squarely at the middle of his chest. "I surely do know how to use it. Just point and squeeze. We get a lot of varmints out this far from town, so I get plenty of practice."

When she put her thumb on the hammer, he arched away.

"Now hold on, sugar. No need for that. I ain't here to cause trouble. Just a man lookin' to collect what's owed him."

The visible bob of his Adam's apple satisfied her immensely—so much so that she didn't even mind when he reached out a single finger to carefully nudge the gun barrel to one side.

"I don't like guns. Especially aimed at me."

"Then I suggest you leave."

"And I'll do just that—soon as I get to talk to your brother."

As their eyes locked, Caroline calculated the consequences of bloodshed over truce.

Truce, she finally decided, lowering the heavy pistol back to her side. *Cautious truce.*

"So—is he home or not?"

"Not."

She'd never know if it was an inadvertent glance that betrayed her or the fact that the library doors were the only closed ones in sight, but he was already reaching for a knob.

"I *told* you he's not here!"

She tried to dart in front of him, but he was quicker. A twist of the knob, a push on the panel over her head, and one of the doors swung inward. Jammed together in the opening, they both froze in place.

Fancy leather boots dangled on a level with their faces.

He's had them resoled, she thought inanely. Then, like a locomotive hurtling out of a dark tunnel, the grisly truth slammed into her, crushing her. The world tilted and she fell to her knees. If the gun fell from her hand, she wasn't aware of it, never heard it hit the floor. No sound came to her ears, no thought to her mind—just spots before her eyes as she pitched forward into the void.

Two

Caroline came to with a gasp. She was in her own room, in her own bed—she knew this from the tester overhead and the wardrobe looming between the two naked windows on her right. But for a space of several seconds, she was puzzled. Why was she in bed, fully dressed, quilt thrown over her, shoes and all?

Then the memory of Wendall hit her. She sat bolt upright, flung the quilt aside, and dashed to her washbowl, sure she was about to be sick. She gagged and coughed until her nose and eyes ran, but her empty stomach had nothing to give.

When the violence settled, she waited a moment longer, then poured water from her rose-painted pitcher into the bowl and washed her face. Using an old lace-edged towel, she pressed it hard to her eyes. But everything that had happened was all there in horrifically vivid detail. Numb, disbelieving, panicky, she wondered what would happen if she simply gave in to the overwhelming weakness that sucked at her, if she sank to the floor right then and there. Could she just stay there until death came to claim her as well?

It was her very practical nature that answered. *Of course not.*

Aware suddenly of an odd sound repeating itself at regular intervals somewhere outside, she turned her head. There it was again.

She went to the window, but there was nothing to see—except a dramatic change in weather. The sleet had stopped, the wind had kicked up, and the sky had cleared. Had she slept through to the next day? *Surely not.*

And there was that sound again.

Snagging her shawl, she stumbled downstairs, moving like an invalid who'd been abed for weeks. She paused at the bottom.

Both library doors were open. Reluctant as she was, she made herself go look . . . and the severed cord told her it was all true.

Her knees wobbled, so she moved away, counting on momentum to keep her upright.

Out on the veranda, she followed the rhythmic *shush . . . shush . . . shush* around the side of the house.

It was the gambler. He was inside the iron-fenced family plot, wielding a shovel.

It was as if her whole world had been picked up, shaken hard, and put down somewhere else. Everything was out of place, and nothing made sense. *Why was he still here?*

Despite the cold, his jacket and hat lay on the ground nearby. The same breeze that laid the grasses over rippled through the back of his white shirt as he paused to draw a sleeve across his forehead . . . then lift his face into the wind like an animal scenting prey.

Only then did it fully register what he was doing. He was digging. *Looking for buried treasure?* "What are you doing?"

He glanced up without surprise. "I'm digging your brother's grave."

Her mind was as sluggish as her body. Only then did she notice the raw wood coffin on the ground beside her, painfully bright in the weak winter sunshine. "But why?"

"'Cause it needs doing, that's why."

"No, I mean—"

Abruptly, he straightened and thrust out the shovel. "You wanna do it? Here."

When she didn't move, didn't speak, he jammed the spade point back in the ground. "Just so you know, I'm used to strong women—grew up in a brothel—but even the strongest, most independent of 'em needed my help from time to time. There's no shame in it, so I'm just doin' what I can to help. If you don't like it, if you don't want my help, that's fine. Just say so an' I'll be gone 'fore you can say lick-ety-split."

Still unable to find her tongue, all she could do was stare at him.

"That's what I thought. Now go back inside. I can see you shiv-ering from here. Either that or sit down somewhere. You look about ready to faint again, and if you do, you're gonna have to lay where ya fall 'til I finish, 'cause once I stop, that's it. Except for back-fillin' it later, I'm done."

With a mental shake, she forced herself to speak, to take back some ownership of the situation. "Where'd you get the coffin?"

"Undertaker's in town."

She winced. "I can't afford that."

"Me neither."

"Then how—? Oh, *no* . . . you didn't *steal* it, did you?"

After the barest pause, he continued digging. "Weren't nobody else usin' it, and there was three of 'em leanin' up out back. Just hope I picked one long enough."

Her legs gave way and, with a hard thump, she dropped to sit on the very item under discussion. *My brother's going to be buried in a stolen coffin . . .*

It was a couple more shovelfuls before he spoke again. "I'll be done here in a bit, then I'll help you load him in."

"I have to get him ready for his laying out first."

"Wouldn't do that if I was you. I didn't exactly get outa town unnoticed—what with a coffin tied to the back of my buggy 'n' all."

"You think you were recognized?"

Still digging, he slanted her a look. "Been in town playin' cards for nigh on a week now. I'm sure folks what saw me knew who I was—and probably where I was headed. There was plenty o' people around when your brother gave me his IOU last night, and again when I was tellin' the undertaker what happened."

A slight nod. "I suppose people *do* tend to remember your kind."

He didn't respond to that, but began grunting with each bite of the shovel as he dug deeper into harder packed earth.

"Where is he? Where's Wendall?"

"In the parlor on the big table—had to move some sewin' stuff first—on a sheet I took off the settee."

Absently picking at the coffin's rough, raw splinters, it took her a bit to sort through the mud in her head to formulate her next question. "Why'd you carry me all the way upstairs?"

"Didn't want you comin' round while I was cuttin' your brother down."

She blinked. *Kindness. He'd done it out of kindness.* She wasn't sure how to feel about that from this person.

"How'd you know which room was mine?"

"It was the only open door."

Her thoughts wheeled. "I can't pay you, you know. There's no money."

"Already figured that." He lofted another shovelful out of the hole.

"His IOU . . . How much is—*was* it for?"

"It *is* for one hundred and one dollars."

She closed her eyes. Six months of sewing wouldn't bring in that much. "Why the *one*?"

"Your brother bet me I couldn't catch a silver dollar off my elbow. He lost that, too." At her blank look, he volunteered, "Here, I'll show ya."

Laying the shovel aside, he mopped his brow on his sleeve before digging a silver dollar out of a trouser pocket. Bending his arm up level with the ground, hand back almost on his shoulder, he balanced the coin on the middle of his forearm. With a sudden, downward whip of his hand, he captured the coin cleanly in his palm before it could fall to the ground. "See? Like that."

"Is that my brother's silver dollar?"

"Was." He put it back in his pocket.

"Then his IOU is only for one hundred dollars *even*."

"Well, if you wanna be *persnickety* about it, *today* it's one hundred and *five* dollars—*un*even. Spent five on the coffin."

"So you *didn't* steal it."

"Neah. I was just havin' you on some is all."

For reasons she couldn't name—perhaps it was the frivolousness of betting hard-earned money on stupid child's play—the fog in her head suddenly evaporated, but the rage that rushed in behind it left no room for grief, only bitterness that her brother would abandon her like this.

When she didn't say anything more, Jack went back to digging. Nearly finished, he paused and looked around, his eye following the line of skeletal hedges across brown, barren lawns. Its columns were rough with peeling paint, the sills stained dark from gutters no longer able to carry away the rain. A shutter on the second floor hung crazily from a single hinge.

He started squaring up the edges of the hole. "After we bury your brother, you oughta leave here."

"Such a comforting word—*we*. Makes one feel less alone," she murmured, picking at the coffin lid again. Then she looked back at him with a tiny shrug. "Where would I go?"

"No family?"

"No."

"Not anywhere?"

"No. How about you?"

"I don't got folks."

"Everybody's got folks."

"Then you're lucky if you know who yours are."

"You're not lucky?"

"Only at cards."

A sudden gust of wind whipped up. She turned her face out of it while the ribbon holding her hair fluttered across her thin, cotton-clad shoulders . . . and finally around to annoy her cheek.

Jack's glance caught it all, even the way she pulled her shawl tighter and hooked a strand of dark hair away from the corner of her mouth with a little finger. "Go inside. It's too cold out here."

When she didn't answer, didn't move, he tossed the shovel away and climbed out of the hole. Bent at the waist, he slapped dirt off his trousers. "Any chance you got somethin' close to coffee? I could sure use somethin' hot in my belly about now."

Still tangled somewhere behind her eyes, it took her a moment to rouse herself, to get to her feet and walk around the back of the house—all without a word or a glance in his direction.

Despite the lack of invitation, he snatched his jacket and hat off the ground and followed. Settling his hat back in place, he punched his arms through the sleeves, then spread his palms to scowl at the blisters—the first he'd earned in years.

Trailing behind her, he picked his way through weed-clotted flower beds and broken pickets as she cut a path toward a separate structure in back, its red tin roof just visible above a hedge of winter-dead honeysuckle. Past a scatter of split firewood near the covered walkway, she lifted an iron latch out of the way and pushed open the door.

The low-beamed kitchen was dank and dark. Jars of vinegar lining the deep windowsill blocked much of the daylight coming in. Onion braids and dried herbs hanging on nails across the top blocked still more. Pewter plates lined a mantle of thick oak above a cavernous fireplace, but below that there wasn't an ember in sight. The nearby wood box sat open and empty.

"Oh, hey—almost forgot." Reaching into his coat pocket, he pulled out a muslin-wrapped bundle about the size of his fist and trussed up with a crisscrossing of cotton string. He plunked it down on the worktable in the center of the room. "One of your neighbors drove by earlier. Asked me to give ya this—along with his condolences.

She stared at it.

"It's a ham hock."

"I *know* what it is, but it—it needs to be cooked long and slow to be tender." She chewed her bottom lip. "Guess we'll just have to slice it thin."

He didn't realize he'd been holding his breath until that moment. "I'll go get us some water and wood. Be right back."

When he returned, she relieved him of the water bucket and some smaller pieces of wood before pointing to the wood box. "Dump the rest in there."

Doing as he was bid, he let the logs cascade with a rumble. Brushing himself free of dirt and splinters, he ended up frowning down at his reddened hands once again, engrossed suddenly in the tips of his fingers. "Christ," he muttered. "If I've ruined my touch because of all this . . ."

She'd already tied a cloth around her waist and was kneeling to start the fire with a bundle of pine needles and a knuckle-striker. As soon as it caught, she put the fry pan on the grate to heat up and started the coffee.

In fairly short order, they were both sitting in small, spindle-back chairs at the little table under the window with mismatched cups of black coffee—more chicory than coffee really, but at least it was hot. There was also a plate of the fried ham with white gravy, and some potatoes that had been so shriveled, he'd doubted they'd ever turn back into anything edible . . . but they had.

Dropping his derby over a vinegar jar on the windowsill, he pulled a small silver flask out of a jacket pocket. Wordlessly, he held it up in offering. When she shook her head, he poured himself a healthy draught, then splashed a dollop in her cup anyway.

After that, they both tucked into the sparse but extravagant-feeling meal, spearing the gravy-covered meat and potatoes from the platter between them without ceremony.

That's when he noticed the small mend on the edge of her cuff, and another on her collar. The neat little stitches in the threadbare cloth were so earnestly made they were painful to look at.

"I'm grateful for your help," she said when they finished eating, "but why'd you stay—really? If you think there's money hidden somewhere, there isn't."

He wiped the corners of his mouth with a thumb and forefinger. "You wouldn't be the first to survive off silver stashed in the attic or buried with the turnips."

She sniffed. "Well, if you find any turnips, be sure to let me know so I can cook 'em up for you."

Taking that small bit of sass as a sign she'd eventually be fine, he nodded and took a sip of his liquor-laced coffee, amused that—despite her initial frown at his doctoring—she was drinking hers as well.

"Tell me something," she began. "Where will you go when you leave here?"

"California," he answered without hesitation.

A sharp intake of breath. "*Really?*" She sat back. "I once read where somebody said the streets there were paved with gold. You don't believe that, do you?"

"'Course not, but I *do* believe it's where a man can make a new start for himself."

"That does sound nice," she murmured.

He looked up at the wistful tone, his gaze locking unexpectedly with hers.

He could tell the liquor had already begun to work on her. Her bones didn't seem to be made from sharp sticks anymore. She looked rounder, softer, her mouth less pinched . . . and her eyes . . . they were the color of cattails.

He scowled down into his cup, swirling stray grounds. "So, what'll you do now?"

She just shrugged.

"Much land come with this place?" he asked.

"Used to. Most of it's been sold off. The rest is mortgaged. And taxes are due soon."

They were quiet for a spell, both drinking their coffee and lost in private thoughts.

Finally, she got to her feet, gathered their dishes, and took them to a small, galvanized tub of water already heating on the grate. Untying the cloth around her waist, she hung it precisely on a peg . . . and turned to face him, white-knuckled fingers laced together in front of her. "I hate to ask this, but—but would you mind helping me get Wendall ready for his laying out?"

A nod. "Already figured to."

Grabbing his hat, he followed her outside, his own cooperation setting off alarm bells in his head. He was not a man who involved himself in other people's doings. He was usually a lot more practical than this. Knowing when to cut his losses, he was never one to run a puny pair down to the last call, carried away by emotion, or worse, wishful thinking. He knew there was no money to be had here . . . and digging her brother's grave should've been enough to stave off any sense of guilt, so why was he still here, traipsing along behind her like some stray pup?

By all rights, the girl could've taken to her bed, and he wouldn't've blamed her, but she hadn't. Because she had *grit*. She wouldn't've survived out here otherwise. Still, he admired her for it . . . as well as for the sway of her hips, he thought, suddenly distracted.

The wind was still buffeting about, slinging sleet again, yet he hardly noticed as he tilted his head for a better view of her slim, rounded bottom as she walked ahead of him.

Throwing open the back door to the central hallway of the big house, she left him to close it and follow her across the wide, neglected floorboards.

They worked well together, speaking only when necessary. They removed her brother's clothing, using the sheet to cover his private parts. Jack shined Wendall's shoes, while she bathed his body with a soft, tender touch. They both helped to dress him again in his best clothes she'd brought down from upstairs. The last thing she did was comb her brother's hair very neatly into place. The last thing Jack did was adjust the man's collar to hide the telling mark around his neck.

"You want me to go get the coffin now?"

"Yes, please." She offered to help, but he declined. "You'll get splinters."

As it turned out, Jack was the one who got splinters—a big, fat one in the web between his thumb and palm, and another on the inside length of his ring finger.

Removing the big pieces was no problem, but the smaller ones required she get out a sewing needle. He hissed and flinched as she worked. "Don't be such a mewly babe," she scolded quietly.

"My hands are my livin'. I can't afford to let 'em get hardened with callouses."

"Your hands are smooth as a woman's. Most women's. Mine are tough as a hostler's in winter." She blushed. "Not much of a lady, am I? Showing you my rough, working hands."

"They're shaped pretty."

That seemed to make her even more uncomfortable, so she pinched the finger she'd just finished with.

"Ow! Whadja do that for?"

"Just checking to make sure I didn't leave any pieces behind."

"Coulda just asked," he grumbled.

After that, they each grabbed a side of the sheet to lift Wendall into his final home, rolling the sheet up all around him . . . like he was lying on a cloud. Together, they tucked the soft-needled pine boughs around his body she'd collected for Christmas.

"There. That's nice." She glanced up at him. "Thank you. I hated asking, but I couldn't have managed without you—and you've been very respectful. I appreciate that."

"No woman should have to bury kin by herself and, at my age, I've buried a fair number of folks, so I know how it's done."

They were standing side by side next to the coffin, in the vigil pose—hands folded together, attentive.

"How old *are* you?" she finally asked without turning her head.

"Thirty-one," he answered without turning his.

"Oh."

"Oh?"

"You don't look that . . . old."

"Oh." Then, "How old are you?"

"Two and twenty."

"Hm. You seem . . . younger."

Again, they were quiet for a spell.

"It's already dark out. I'll finish the digging tomorrow. Mind if I sleep here tonight?"

She hesitated for no good reason and felt guilty for it. "No, I suppose not."

"You expectin' a lot of callers tomorrow?"

"Truthfully, I don't expect any."

Caroline was wrong. People did come. The new preacher showed up, along with some others, only one of whom she recognized as a neighbor—probably the one who'd brought the pork, she decided—and offered the only thing she had for refreshment, heavily watered cider. Everyone there returned the next morning for the burial service.

The Cooper family plot was on a slight rise, and the small group at graveside stood braced against the wind. It tugged at their clothing, making them appear queer and misshapen. Heavy skirts billowed and snapped, trouser legs molded to muscle and flesh. Bonnet strings and hat brims, lapels and coattails shivered under the constant onslaught, and whatever words of comfort that came from the preacher's lips were stolen, whipped away by the same force that ruffled the pages of his Bible.

There, laid out at her feet, was her entire family. First Papa, then Mama, and now Wendall, who'd embraced his eternal sleep as eagerly as if it wouldn't come soon enough on its own.

"And give light to them in the shadow of death. Let us pray."

Staring at the empty space beside her brother's grave, the space reserved for her, she knew—she *vowed*—she would never lie there, a cold prisoner of the earth, until she'd lived at least some part of a life, any kind of life as long as it was different from this one. The very wind whipping through her clothing whispered of a different destiny, and that, more than any prayer, was the comfort Caroline sought.

She pulled the edges of her cape closer and hugged herself beneath its folds. Seconds later, a man's coat dropped around her shoulders. The gambler's.

He'd been waiting for her in the parlor that morning—presumably where he'd slept—his clothing neat and brushed clean, before walking beside her until they'd reached graveside where he hung back and took up a position several feet away. Soon, he would move on. To California. She should've felt relieved at the prospect, but knowing she'd be alone again—truly alone this time—made a kind of panic rise up in her throat.

California . . . The name alone conjured heard-of-but-never-seen images of San Francisco, gold mines, and the mighty Pacific.

Dipping her head slightly, she sneaked a peak at him. A string tie fluttered beneath his jaw. Hatless and coatless, suspenders starkly striping his white shirt, dark gold hair raked this way and that by the wind, he was staring straight ahead, his expression unreadable. Perhaps that's what he was thinking about right now—*California*. She looked away with a pang of jealousy.

"Amen."

"Amen," came the answering murmur.

The young preacher, his baby face reddened by the cold, waited for the trickle of people to finish their parting words of sympathy before coming to Caroline's side. "Truly a tragedy, my child," he began, striving for the rounded tones of profundity. "But some of us are weaker than we realize when it comes to battling the evil influences in our lives. It's why we must seek God and lean on Him for strength."

The use of "my child" from a man scarcely older than herself annoyed her almost as much as the ill-disguised judgment of her brother. Still, she thanked him. With a perfunctory nod of acceptance, he jammed his hat firmly on his head and hurried to his waiting rig.

After saying her private goodbyes to each of her family members in turn, she closed the wrought-iron gate behind her and winced at the cold clang of metal meeting metal. It was such a final sound.

"How're you holding up?" the gambler asked.

Ignoring the tiresome question, she slipped his coat off her shoulders and held it out. As he whipped it on and flipped the collar up, they fell in step to pace back toward the house together.

"Miss Caroline! Miss Caroline—wait!"

They both looked around.

"Mr. Fox," she acknowledged as the man hurried forward, surprised she hadn't noticed her brother's friend before this. "I didn't see you here."

He grasped her hand. "I'm afraid I didn't arrive in time for the service. I was a bit detained. The Mercantile gets so busy during the holidays—but I couldn't *not* be here. You know how close Wendall and I were."

Indeed, she thought. His influence was a major factor in how her brother spent most of his evenings.

"How are you?" he asked.

She moved her shoulders. "A bit numb perhaps."

"Understandable. Perfectly understandable."

His gaze flicked toward Jack, a thunderous frown following a visible jolt of recognition. "I'd heard he was here, but I didn't countenance it. Caroline, what on earth were you thinking to allow this man on your property, much less to attend your brother's funeral?"

She blinked, startled at the criticism. "I—I don't know, he just—"

"You should've come to me!"

"Seems to me," Jack drawled, "that road runs both ways."

"What is *that* supposed to mean?" demanded Fox.

"It means she didn't see *you* hot-footin' it out here to help, now did she?"

"You, suh, are interferin' in a private conversation and I'll thank you to stay out of it. Caroline, I was with Wendall that last night, and this man is nothing but a greedy swindler. Not a shred of decency. He saw Wendall was in too deep and did nothing to stop him. I wouldn't be at all surprised if he cheated."

Jack sucked a tooth. "You were his friend, why didn't *you* stop him?"

"I, suh, do not interfere in another man's wagering."

"Well, *suh*, neither do I."

Daryl's nostrils flared and he turned back to her. "Get your things, Miss Caroline. You're coming with me."

At twenty-five, Daryl Fox was everything he thought a southern gentleman ought to be—deliberate, mannerly, and more than a bit pompous. Dressed with the same natty air her brother always affected, he wore his yellow striped waistcoat and tall beaver hat well; still, she felt the handkerchief flopping out of his breast pocket would've been more effective if it was cleaner.

Tiredly, she shook her head. "I'm not going anywhere, Mr. Fox."

"Well, you can't stay here—people will talk. I can't understand why you didn't come to me. An unmarried lady with a reputation to protect—you should never have remained here unchaperoned. People will think—and who could blame them—that you've become a—a *whore*."

She gasped, shrinking back as the word rolled out of his mouth, round and wet and slimy. Before she could even think of a suitable response, Jack stepped between them.

"You shouldn't oughta said that." His fist caught Fox square in the mouth, put his teeth through his lip, and knocked him backward in the dirt.

In an equal and opposite reaction, Jack bent double, spun back upright, his hand jammed into an armpit. "*Ay-eeee! Gawd . . . durnit!*

That hurt!" Planting a foot in Fox's backside just as the man was gaining his knees, he shoved him flat again.

Moments later, Fox was allowed to re-mount his horse and leave, spitting blood and epithets over his shoulder at them both.

In a decidedly unladylike—but very satisfying—moment, Caroline cupped her gloved hands on either side of her mouth and called, "*And don't come back, you scalawag!*"

Jack was still stumping around in circles, cradling his wrist. He looked a little wild-eyed. "Is he? A scalawag?"

She nodded emphatically. "Best friend a northern Republican ever had. Convinced Reconstruction'll help his business."

Jack's hand was visibly swelling. She tried to take a closer look, but he held it away.

"You should go soak that in the creek for a bit. The cold water'll help. It's down the hill over there," she pointed.

With a grunt of acknowledgment, he stalked off in the direction she indicated, cursing under his breath in far more vile terms than he'd limited himself to initially.

Returning to the house in measured steps, head down, she put Fox and everything else out of her mind. She needed to ponder the *what now* of her situation, her future . . . but it was like peering into a thick fog. In her own defense, she couldn't remember the last time she'd nurtured a dream or hoped for anything beyond making it through another day with body and soul still tethered. Somewhere along the way, survival had become her sole focus. The gambler—a total stranger—had been right. There was nothing left for her here. She really should leave . . . but this place was all she knew. Where would she go?

California, came the whisper.

It soon became a chant in her head—*California California California*—as she began packing her meager belongings in her father's old carpetbag, her decision made. The last item to go in, wrapped in a bit of silk, was her small, japanned jewelry box, with its few trinkets and her small-but-treasured savings—eighteen dollars and sixty-three cents. She transferred the money to her reticule with a sense of pride that she'd ever managed to save anything . . . along with the fear that it wouldn't get her very far at all.

Downstairs, she collected scattered pins and needles and returned them to her beloved rosewood sewing box. This would go with her of course. Perhaps she could start her own dressmaking business.

With that possibility locked in her mind, the next logical step was figuring out how she would *get* to California. If the gambler was, indeed, going there, it was only logical that she could ask him to escort her, yet that seemed wrong on so many levels. Not only was it unseemly for a woman to travel with a man she wasn't married to, it felt far worse to have to *ask* . . . like she was some pride-stripped beggar. Absently, she chewed a thumbnail. Mightn't he be cajoled into asking *her*, she wondered.

Before war had turned the world topsy-turvy, she'd been a child concerned only with childish pursuits. The impression that her mother and the women around her somehow, subtly, commanded the men was always there of course, but the details on how this was accomplished were sorely missing. All she had were jumbled images of women giggling and fanning themselves as they swirled around in huge, frothy dresses. Nothing useful in the lot.

When the hall clock *bonged* three sonorous notes, it suddenly occurred to her that the gambler hadn't yet returned. She could see the creek from the upstairs hall window, but he was nowhere in sight. She looked out her front window. Not there either. *Maybe he's digging for turnips . .* Downstairs, she checked the library and parlor to see if he'd left anything behind. Nothing.

Her heart began to race. Thinking he'd done all he could, had he simply left? It would be dark soon, so perhaps she should just wait. *For what?* came the rebuttal.

Finally, she could stand it no longer. If she didn't make her move now, she might never do so—dying alone and lonely, strangled by the quiet. So, in wool cloak, crocheted scarf, bonnet, and gloves, and with no more plan in her head than the imperative to *go*, she decided to set off by herself and hope to catch a ride—or a series of them—putting herself in the hands of Providence.

No sooner had she set bag and box down by the front door than she heard carriage wheels out front. The gambler was just winding the reins around the brake handle and stepping down. It wasn't until he was on the top step that he looked up and saw her framed in the open doorway.

"You're leaving," she said, anxious to speak first.

To her surprise, he removed his hat and nodded. "It's time."

"How's your hand?"

"Much better." Opening and closing his fingers, he demonstrated. "The cold water helped."

"I'm glad—and I-I thank you kindly for all you did." She heard the annoying quaver in her voice.

He answered with a single nod, his mouth set in a determined line. "Sorry to leave you like this, but—"

Then don't! she wanted to cry.

Pulling out a flat leather wallet, he counted out several bills and thrust them at her. "Here—buy yourself some decent food."

When she didn't move, he took her gloved hand, laid the money in her palm, and closed her fingers over it.

"Take me with you!" she suddenly blurted, all but unaware of the money.

His head came up. "*What?*"

"I'm already packed—see?" She moved aside to show her sewing box and bag on the floor behind her.

He scowled at the items as if they'd committed some personal offense.

"You said I should leave here."

"Yeah, but I didn't mean—"

"I know you didn't, but it's the only way I'll ever be able to go."

He was still scowling when he met her eyes, but when he spoke, the words were softer than expected, and not unkind. "You . . . you should wait for somebody better'n me to come along."

"Besides creditors, you're the first person, the first stranger I've seen in nearly a year." *And the first person who's going somewhere else.* "I won't be a bother—*promise*. Just take me as far as the river and I'll go from there."

"Go where?"

Not expecting the question, she stuttered over her answer. "I—well, *you*—you made California seem awfully appealing."

"You got money?" he asked the fanlight over her head.

"Some—but I can earn more by mending for people along the way."

Looking aside, he tugged on an earlobe. It was something her father used to do when he was deciding something. Wavering.

"*Please.*"

"You just buried your brother," he reminded her with an accusing glare.

She met it squarely . . . and the seconds that followed in silence seemed like the longest in her life.

Suddenly, he was all movement—glancing left, glancing right, hat getting screwed back on his head, neck stretching as if his collar was suddenly too tight; then a loud, deep exhale before looking down the length of a single, stiffened finger pointed at her face. "Just to the river—got that?"

Heaving a sigh of relief, she nodded and grabbed up her carpet bag.

"After that," he went on, "well, that's up to you. You can decide that once we get there."

She nodded again, struggling to scoop up her sewing box with her free arm.

He turned away, stopped, and turned back to pluck the ignored money still sprouting from her hand. In a deft, one-handed move, he had the bills folded and out of sight almost before she could blink. "There, now you can pick up your box."

Knowing a doffed hat did not a gentleman make, she couldn't have cared less at that moment. She was getting what she wanted—a way out.

"Should be at the river by morning," he volunteered without prompting.

Again, she nodded. She was nodding so much she felt like a rag-doll in the hands of a toddler.

After he grabbed the carpet bag from her and tossed it into the rear boot with his own, she handed him her sewing box.

He frowned at its noisy rattle. "What's in here?"

"Thread spools."

"*Christ.* Noise'll drive me plum crazy," he muttered, wedging the box as tightly as possible in between his leather bag and her cloth one. "Maybe that'll muffle the racket some."

Handing her into the buggy, he vaulted up beside her, handed her the lap blanket from under the seat, and unwound the reins. "Ready?"

She nodded, then forced herself to say the words. "I'm ready."

As he drove them down the long drive, she allowed herself to look back exactly once—briefly—just as they turned out onto the road.

At last. As fearsome and blank as her future was, she felt tremendously relieved at leaving this part of her life behind . . . even as she had to ignore the imagined cry of protest from her family.

Jack set the horse to a sedate pace, one that would last them through the night and all the way to the river. Except for the clatter of wheels, the clop of hooves—and the rattle of wooden thread spools—they rode in silence. Even in the open carriage, sitting this close to him felt uncomfortably intimate, and she could sense the previous ease between them ebbing away. They had returned to being strangers.

Finally, she fell asleep and slept until he nudged her awake.

"We're here. We're at the river."

THREE

The mud levee just north of Robinsonville was small and unimposing—just a couple of warehouses, a livery, the dockmaster's house, and a ticket office. Their whitewash was thinner than Caroline remembered, but little else had changed in the years since she'd been here as a child. It still smelled of river, wet hemp, and animal dung.

The day promised to be a bright one. The sky was cloudless, and the air was mercifully still for the first time in days. In the absence of wind, the world seemed quieter, the *clip-clop* of horse's hooves unnaturally loud on the hard-packed road as Jack threaded them next to the levee.

They used to come here with Papa when he shipped his cotton. She and Wendall would run back and forth like wild things. He'd pull her pigtails, then run away laughing—

She yanked herself up short, banishing the rest of that memory. Self-exile, that's what her brother had chosen for himself, and so be it. She had turned a corner and could not afford to look back. Not now. Not yet. Maybe not ever.

She glanced over at Jack. He looked haggard, eyes red-rimmed from no sleep and driving through the night. Beard stubble shaded his face and blurred the neat line of his mustache. He reined them in at the hitching rail nearest the ticket office and stepped down stiffly. After handing her down to the ground, he lifted out their belongings. No longer cocooned in the blanket, she shivered.

The levee wasn't as crowded as she remembered. It was Christmas Eve, she realized with a jolt, and the division between rich and poor not as sharp as in the days before the war. Of course Blacks were still the ones who hefted bags and bales while whites oversaw the process . . . but the faces were similar now in thinness, moods all linked by the common goal of survival.

A young boy, his green corduroy coat patched in several places, hawked a variety of services to those converging on the levee. "Shoeshine, sir? Stable your horse, mister? Carry your bags, ma'am?"

Jack flipped him a silver dollar, instructed him on caring for the horse and rig and getting them both back to Coldwater before week's end. Then he turned to her. "Well, what's it gonna be? We partin' ways here or not?"

We. Again that comforting word. "California," she answered, feeling a frisson of excitement.

"Okay." He picked up both their bags in one hand as she took her sewing box, its spools tapping rhythmically with each step as they headed for the ticket window.

"How—how long will it take to get there?" she asked, trotting beside him.

"The way I'm plannin' on goin', it could take weeks, maybe months. There's a lot of games, a lot of money to be had between here and there," he answered without slowing. "If you're impatient, you should find a faster way to go than taggin' along with me. Nothin' says we gotta travel together, but if we do—" here he swiveled a sharp glance at her "—I expect you to earn your keep."

Her pleasure dimmed at this new phrase, and suddenly—for the first time—the pitfalls, indeed the *dangers* of traveling with a strange man leapt to mind. Standing here now, literally on the edge of a new life, she realized her place in the world had shrunk to the ground beneath her feet, and she was much less sure of her decision than she'd been moments ago.

"Why you stoppin'? If you've changed your mind and want to go back, tell me now, so I can find that boy and—"

"No, I do *not* want to go back!" The spools rattled with her vehemence. "There's nothing to go back *to*—but I need to know what you mean by *earn my keep*?"

A careless shrug. "Nothin' really. Just don't want you thinkin' you can mooch off me is all."

With an indignant huff, she stalked past him and arrived at the ticket window first, placing her box on the ledge that protruded out past the wrought iron grille.

The old man behind the grille had a face like a dried apple. "Where to?"

"California."

"You'll need to get off at St. Louis then."

"Which boat is headed there?"

"Both the *Sultana* and the *Quincy* are headin' north. The *Natchez*'ll be up later."

Shading her eyes, she looked toward the river and the boats moored there. The *Quincy* was the better looking of the two. It was a double-decker, the name painted on the housing of its giant stern wheel in red-and-gold letters. Although big, the boat was nothing so grand as the old *Dubuque* or *Robert E. Lee*. In the last few years, the railroad—those noisy, iron monsters—had stolen much of the riverboat's thunder, robbing her of the urge for cosmetic gilt and gingerbread, and turning her into a plainer, more practical maiden of the riverways.

"Passage for one aboard the *Quincy*, please."

"That'll be eight dollars."

She bit her lip as she pulled open her reticule.

"Here." Jack placed some bills on the counter.

"Thank you, no, I can pay. Wouldn't want to be a *mooch*," she added as she slid her own money through the cutout in the grille.

Inside the cage, the man's gaze flickered between the two of them as he raked her money off his side of the counter. He handed back a yellow paper ticket. "Cabin number's written on the side. Happy

Christmas to you," he said with a respectful touch to his round black hat.

"Happy Christmas," she returned, poking her change back through the puckered mouth of her reticule. Ticket firmly in hand, she retrieved her box, picked up her carpet bag by Jack's feet and headed for the *Quincy*.

"One," she heard Jack say behind her. "On the *Quincy*."

At the back of a short boarding queue with her baggage at her feet, she was hugging her elbows when Jack came up beside her.

"Gettin' the vapors?"

"*What?* No."

"You'll be fine."

"I *am* fine . . . and *will* be, but why do you say so?"

"Because you got grit."

A brief nose wrinkle. "Doesn't sound very feminine."

"Everybody needs grit to survive."

A quietly heavy sigh. "It's just hard to accept failure."

"Failure?"

"To hold my family's legacy in trust for the next generation."

"You didn't fail. You were dealt a crap hand. Never play a crap hand—and that back there was a crap hand, so you get credit for knowing when to fold and walk away."

It didn't matter that she didn't fully understand that, she felt her shoulders relax and could finally take a full breath again. "Well, thank you for that. You have a talent for making a body feel better."

He snorted. "Ain't nobody ever told me *that* before."

"*No one has ever* told you that before," she corrected.

"Folks? Say, folks!" Suddenly, the agent was out of his cage and jogging over to them. "Beggin' your pardon. No offense meant, but I can always spot a married couple having a spat. Been there myself a few times. Thing is, I sold my last cabins to y'all, so I'm gonna have to turn away them nice folks and their little ones—back there, see—'cause we don't sell deck passage in the wintertime. So what do you say? Any chance you two could kiss and make up? After all, '*tis*

Christmas." He held up money, his other palm up in anticipation of one of their tickets.

Before she could even sift through all that, Jack plucked her ticket out of her hand, gave it to the agent, and accepted the proffered cash in return.

"I beg your pardon!" she protested.

The clerk lifted his hat to Jack. "Thankee kindly, sir!"

"That was *my* ticket!" Glaring at the ticket agent as he hurried away, she hollered, "*That was my ticket!*"

"Keep your voice down."

"I will not keep my voice down! How dare you give back my ticket?" she demanded as the man called "Good news!" to the family still clustered at the ticket window.

"I didn't *give* it back, I *sold* it back. You might need it down the road." He held up the cash, giving it a little shake. "And we still have mine."

Her gasp was so sharp, she nearly strangled. "We can't share a cabin!"

"Why not?"

"Because we're not *married*, that's why!" she hissed.

"Who'll know? He didn't," he said, nodding toward the agent, who had just waved the family through.

"*I'll* know."

He shrugged. "There's always the *Sultana*."

Snatching the money, she jammed it back into her reticule. "I bought my ticket first, so *I* should get the *Quincy*. *You* should take the *Sultana*."

"But this is *my* ticket." He held it up, then yanked it out of reach, grinning, when she made a grab for it. "*Ah-ah-ahhh!* Oh, don't look like that. Ain't nothin'—"

"*Isn't.*"

His mustache pinched in the middle. "*Ain't nothin'* to be afraid of. I don't bite, and gamblers sleep during the day and play all night. We might never see each other this whole trip."

"Well, *there's* a blessing."

Picking up her sewing box, he tucked it under one arm, grabbed their bags, and nudged her ahead of him as they were finally waved aboard.

The narrow gangplank bowed, springy with each step, and the *Quincy's* gray painted deck was streaked with muddy footprints. Despite the early hour, it was quickly crowding with a mix of travelers—men in swirling great coats, checkered sack coats, or long frock ones and string ties, collars turned up against the cold. Deck hands, their trousers held up with lengths of rope, stamped along behind, balancing trunks on their massive shoulders. Women, dove-quiet and similar-looking in dark cloaks and bonnets, moved to walk next to the bulkhead, eager to get as far away as possible from the cold that rose off the brown, lapping water.

Caroline briefly entertained the thought of appealing to one of them for help. Surely someone would sympathize with her plight and offer to share their cabin. But before she could commit to that course, the gambler was already climbing the companionway to the middle deck. A split-second decision had her following him.

He had slowed down to compare door numbers to the one on his ticket, and she caught up to him just as he said, "Here we are."

Reaching over her head, he pushed open a paneled door to a tiny box of a room containing a plain, iron-framed bed, a washstand, a stove piped across the ceiling and out an equally small window, and one wooden straight-back chair. The place was dank and mildewy.

"Take the key out of the lock and shut the door behind you," he instructed, moving around her to drop their bags onto the bed's blue-and-white quilt. Her sewing box he put on the floor. "Christ! Silence at last!" he groused, loosening his tie. "You don't know how many times I wanted to stop last night and pitch that damned thing out on the road."

Dropping the key on the bed, she went over and picked up her box as a mother might retrieve an endangered child.

She looked around her without enthusiasm. There wasn't even a dressing screen for privacy. "This is it?"

"This is it."

He sank down on his haunches and began stoking the stove from the bucket of wood on the floor. "You're free now," he said inexplicably. "You can relax."

"*Cast off the stern line! Cast off the spring line!*" they heard the captain bawl, then felt the boat lurch as she moved out into the current.

"This ain't so bad," he said over his shoulder. "I've seen worse, and like I told you . . ." He paused to strike a match and touch it here and there to the kindling in the stove "At night, while you're sleeping, I'll be playing the tables. During the day, while I sleep, you can go to the ladies' parlor." Satisfied the wood would burn, he clanged the little iron door shut.

"And do what?" she asked, setting her box down by the chair.

"Dunno. You're the lady. It's your call."

She untied her bonnet and hung it on one of the pegs that marched in a line high across one wall. Then, trying to take up as little space as possible, she stood with her arms tightly folded as he moved around the small room, settling in.

Without removing any of it, he checked the contents of his pockets, added the key, then took off his coat and hung it neatly over one of the washstand's iron hooks. The derby went precisely over another. His tie followed just as neatly, and his boots received a quick swipe with a handkerchief before they were placed beside the bed. The flat leather wallet went under the nearest pillow. When he started to undo his shirt, a button came off in his hand. He frowned and looked around like he didn't know what to do with it.

"Just put it and the shirt on the end of the bed, and I'll sew it back on for you."

He looked faintly suspicious. "You wouldn't mind?"

"No . . . and I'll only charge you fifty cents."

He huffed air, and she was subjected to another one of his flat, unreadable stares. "I'll take it off your brother's IOU."

Her chin lifted. "No, you will not. That's my brother's debt, not mine."

His nostrils flared. "Fine." Tossing the button on the bed, he shrugged out of his shirt and tossed that, too.

Wide-eyed, she stared at his bare, muscled torso, at the butterfly of golden hair on his chest, wondering how he could be so casual in her presence.

Raised in a brothel . . .

"What are you doing?" she squeaked when his hands went to the top of his button fly.

He paused. "I'm undressing so I can go to bed, what's it look like?"

She felt her face turn as red as the long johns peeking over the top of his waistband. "You can't do that."

"Why not?"

"*Because.*"

"Don't look if it offends ya."

They stared at one another in a silent clash of wills.

I can stare just as coldly and just as long as you can, she thought.

"Women," he finally grumbled, angling his back to her by way of compromise.

She turned her head as well. When she looked again, he was kneeling to tuck and smooth his trousers beneath the mattress. "Keeps 'em pressed," he explained.

"I didn't ask," was her sulky response.

Dumping their bags on the floor, he threw back the quilt, rolled into bed, and pulled up the covers. Only his dark gold head and one shoulder remained visible.

"How can you sleep like that? Without a nightshirt? It's freezing in here."

"It'll warm up. And I don't own a nightshirt."

Seconds ticked by.

"You gonna stand there all day starin' at me? I can feel it, y'know."

"I don't know where the Ladies' Parlor is."

"On the main deck usually. Ask somebody."

And still she stood. The thought of facing one more unknown turned her limbs to lead.

"You goin' or not?"

She sank into the little wooden chair. "I believe I'll unpack instead, shake out the wrinkles."

"Suit yourself." Pulling the covers up higher, he punched his pillow into a more pleasing shape. "Just do it quietly. And don't touch my game box," he mumbled sleepily.

"Game box? What game box?" she asked, but he didn't respond, and within moments, she heard the deep, even breathing of sleep.

Picking up her sewing box again, she set it in her lap. Inside, her needles, thread bobbins, and scissors were all jumbled together, but everything was still there. Softly, she closed the lid.

Feeling an unsettling mixture of abandonment and relief, she rested her elbows atop the satiny rosewood and looked around the shabby, whitewashed room, one wall striped with firelight through the grate. The window by the door was curtained in plain, unbleached muslin over a drawn shade. A small candle lantern hung from a hook by the door. The rim of the chamber pot was chipped, and the tiny mirror attached to the washstand was spotted with age. *Like measles*, she thought glumly.

California, she reminded herself. The word alone had become a beacon, a promise that one day she'd be living a whole new life in a whole new land.

Setting the box aside, she pulled open the purse still hanging from her wrist and dug out what was left of her money. She'd done the math in her head at the time, but counting it out now reassured her. She was down to ten and the change. Perhaps she should've let him pay after all.

Nonetheless, she felt better now that they were actually onboard and moving. At least her life would have some structure until they reached St. Louis.

Returning the money to her purse, she pulled the braided cords tight and looped them around her wrist . . . twice.

As soundlessly as possible, she set her carpet bag on the chair and began pulling out her clothing to hang it on the pegs.

As she worked, all the terrible memories of the last week kept trying to intrude, but the more they pressed, the more she resisted. The past was the past, and this, the Mississippi River, was the clean break between her old life and her new.

You're free now . . . you can relax.

Yes. She *was* finally free of a life that weighed on her like a grinding wheel, and a couple of deep breaths allowed her original excitement to return. Her heart lightened immediately—*California*, she repeated to herself—and smiled.

On that, her last garment was hung.

Jack was right. The cabin had grown warmer, and she removed her cloak. Hooking it over the last peg, she shoved her empty carpet bag beneath the bed and sat in the chair again.

She stared at the shirt in need of a button.

Digging as quietly as she could through her sewing box, she found the items she needed, and was soon settled into the comforting rhythm of sewing, needle-to-cloth, needle-to-cloth, the material sliding through her fingers. It smelled of him—the sweet, spicy scent of bay rum.

She'd been carefully avoiding looking at him, but now her glance strayed to his sleeping form. As coarse as he was, she couldn't help being grateful for his presence. There was only so much a body could face alone.

Plying her needle, she listened to his quiet, even breathing and—along with the faint, steady beat of the paddlewheel—her head began to nod. She roused herself, bit off the thread, folded the shirt over the handles of his leather bag, stowed her sewing items, then attempted to find a comfortable position in which to sleep. Sitting sideways, she leaned her temple against the chair back. When that didn't work, she tried another position, and another and another, feeling half sick with weariness.

As if sensing her distress, Jack rolled over and lifted his head to gaze at her sleepily. "Come here," he ordered gruffly. Flipping back the covers, he bared the bed beside him. "Come sleep."

She stared at that oddly inviting place, her mind listing all the things a lady should say to such a shocking suggestion, even as her body yearned to accept. So she devised a compromise. Fully clothed and booted, petticoats crowding them both, she crawled gratefully onto the space he offered—albeit on *top* of the covers. She was asleep almost instantly.

She awoke to the yellow flicker of candlelight, and was staring at an unfamiliar wall. For a brief, panicky moment, she didn't know where she was. The air was tangy with wood smoke and she heard an odd *chunking* sound, a deeper *thrum* behind that.

Oh—the riverboat.

With the gambler . . . who was busy stoking the glow in the stove back to life. The *chunking* sound was him tossing wood in. The other sound was that of the giant paddlewheel still churning them sluggishly upriver.

He'd laid the candle sideways on the washstand, and every few seconds a clear drop of tallow would shimmer in its own light and drop to the bare planked floor with a tiny *tip . . . tip . . . tip*.

Rubbing her eyes, she rolled over to watch him sleepily, to watch the muscles in his bare back move and shift, skin buttered with light.

He rose, brushing off his hands. "You're awake," he said without turning around.

"How'd you know?"

"Your breathing changed."

She sat up and swung her feet to the floor.

"You always sleep with your purse tied to your wrist like that?"

Reflexively, she felt for the money inside—*still there*—and relaxed, countering with, "You always sleep with your wallet under your pillow?"

She glanced over her shoulder at the window. "What time is it? It feels late."

Pulling a gilt watch from the pocket of his coat still on the washstand, he thumbed the catch, setting the caged dice to swinging. "It is. It's nearly ten o'clock."

"At *night?*"

"Yep. Hungry?"

"Famished."

"Good. Let's get to the dining saloon and see what's left."

She watched him splash water on his face, do a quick lather and shave, wondering how he avoided cutting himself with such perfunctory swipes of the blade. While he dressed, she dug out her brush and quickly ran it through her long hair, then wound it back into a figure eight at the back of her head, anchoring it with pins and fumbling fingers. She'd never shared the intimacy of her toilette with a man before, and it made her acutely uncomfortable.

He peered into the tiny mirror as he attached and adjusted one of those new celluloid collars to his shirt. "After we eat, you can come back here and get more sleep if you want."

"What will you be doing?"

He met her eyes in the mirror. "Farming."

"*Farming?*"

"Yep. Trying to grow little money into great big money."

"I should like to watch."

He didn't respond right away. Instead, he sat on the bed beside her and pulled on his boots. "I'd expect you to hate gambling."

She twitched a shoulder. "Not necessarily, however, I *do* hate boredom, and there's nothing else to do."

"There's always the Ladies' Parlor."

"Probably nothing there but a bunch of old women talking about their rheumatism or some such."

He stomped on the floor several times to settle his heel. "Well, a gamin' parlor ain't no place for a lady."

"*Isn't any* place, and I've heard of ladies gambling—lady gamblers, too, for that matter."

"They're few and far between, and they ain't ladies, trust me."

"*Aren't*, and I still want to watch."

"Suit yourself, but—" he pointed a finger at her, "—stay out of the way."

Agreeing with a nod, she peered over his shoulder as he pulled the flat wooden box out of his bag. Intrigued, she watched as he opened the carved lid on neatly ordered rows of chips and mother-of-pearl markers, a lidded brass cup, several packs of Hart's Linen Eagle playing cards, two pair of ivory dice and—she drew back—a small pistol.

She watched him pick it up, check the cartridges, and slide it into a pocket. "I thought you didn't like guns."

He dropped the lid. "I don't. Unfortunately, they're sometimes necessary. Nothin' you need worry yourself with—but remember," he repeated sternly, "stay out of the way."

"I heard you the first time. Now I require the same of you. You'll have to finish dressing outside," she told him primly. "I need some privacy."

"It's freezing outside! What d'you—" His glance at the chamber pot made them both blush. Snatching his jacket and hat, he left without another word.

She took her time. Shaking the wrinkles out of her somber, black dress, she tied her bonnet ribbons under her chin and studied her reflection critically—what she could see of it—then remembered her mother's cameo.

"There," she breathed, looking again. *Better.*

The *Quincy*'s dining saloon was long and narrow, its ceiling snaked with wooden loops, finials, and curlicues—like an ornate birthday cake turned inside out, Caroline thought as she and Jack entered. At least a dozen doors opened off each side, the transoms above them the only avenue of natural light come daytime. Right now, six evenly-spaced chandeliers provided the light of nearly a hundred candles. There were rows and rows of padded leather chairs flanking damask-draped tables, and thick, patterned carpet hushed their steps. Despite the late hour, there were still other diners present—satisfied-looking men with port and cigars, and a handful of demure-looking women who sipped from teacups or picked delicately at their desserts.

Every few feet, a waiter in a white coat and long apron stood ready to serve. One of them held Caroline's chair for her, and she felt soothed by the attention. The heavy silver and thick, white ceramic plates were warm to the touch. Because of the hour, their waiter informed them, there was only roast pork, gravy, and grits left.

"That'll be fine," Jack said, game box on the table beside him, hat on top of that, his eyes roving restlessly around the room.

The food—more than Caroline had seen at any one sitting in ages—came quickly. She ate ravenously while the gambler chewed absently. His mind was obviously on other things, his gaze hawk-like as he assessed their fellow diners. It seemed he recognized several of them, exchanging a surreptitious nod here, a flick of an eyebrow there.

"Do you know those men?"

"You could say that."

"Do you want to invite them to join us?"

"Just 'cause I know 'em don't mean we're friends."

"*Doesn't* mean. Are they gamblers, too?"

"Maybe."

"Well, I declare!" she grumbled, slicing off another piece of pork. "Why all the mystery? It's just a *game*, Mister Transomb."

There was that stare again. "You *know* it's not. It's a living—my living—and don't you think it's time we started usin' each other's names?"

"I do use your name, *Mister Transomb*."

"Call me Jack." He motioned to the waiter while saying to her, "Go on, try it."

"I don't need to. I can say it perfectly well. I just choose not to is all." She pulled open her reticule.

"It's easy. *Jaaaacck*," he said slowly, drawing it out comically. "And I'm paying for dinner."

"No, thank you," she argued, secretly hoping he'd insist. "As I told you, I'm no *mooch*."

"Don't try to bluff a bluffer. I'll pay."

"How kind of you," she acquiesced with a small nod.

"Now say my name."

"Why on earth are you insisting on this?"

He leaned close enough that she could see the dark ring around the blue of his eyes as he lowered his voice. "For your sake. In public at least, we need to pretend we're actually married."

For no reason she could fathom, she felt herself blush, which only made her blush harder. She pressed cold fingertips to her cheeks. "I see no reason—" she began, then gave in with a sigh, but did the opposite of what he'd done, compressing the sound into as little space as possible. "*Jck*."

"You make it sound like a bird cough. It's just Jack," he said at normal speed, "and you're *Caro-liiiine*."

She saw his tongue curve around the last syllable. "That's *obscene*." He laughed.

"I *prefer* Miss Cooper if you don't mind."

"'Fraid I do mind, so it's gonna have to be Jack and Caroline from here on out."

"I suppose you think I'm silly."

"I think most women are silly."

"What a thing to say!"

He twitched a shrug, left money on the table, and picked up his box. "Ready?

Stuffing a final forkful of buttered grits into her mouth, she nodded, dabbed her lips with the napkin, and rose, favoring him with a pointed look when their waiter sprang forward to help her with her chair since he made no move to do so.

The smell of roast pork and cigar smoke followed them out on deck, and she smiled gratefully at the waiter who held the door for them.

"Good manners are so hard to come by these days," she remarked.

He ignored her, and Caroline found herself having to take two steps for his every one as they passed along the deck on their way to the gaming parlor. He was a man on a mission and obviously could no longer be distracted by anything as ordinary as conversation.

But then he informed her out of the blue that, "Gambling's forbidden on some boats."

Glad that he was at least speaking, she feigned interest. "Oh?"

"That just means there's no gambling in the main parlors where it can be seen. Keep it in private cabins n' it's fine. Luckily, the *Quincy* knows gaming's good business."

She pulled the throat of her cloak closer against the chill of the night air. "What do you play? Faro?" she asked, scraping her memory.

"Used to. Quick game, decent odds, but every man n' his mule seems to be a banker for it nowadays, so I started playing a new one—poker. Or Brag if nobody knows that one. Now remember—" he stopped in front of a door that muffled the buzz of voices and laughter inside, "stay out of the way."

She nodded as he swung open the door.

"Good Lord!" she breathed.

Under a wood-ribbed ceiling—like she imagined the inside of Jonah's big fish—there were more chandeliers, more doors, more chairs pulled up around more tables than she could count in a single glance. Compared to the serene atmosphere of the dining saloon, this place was a veritable riot of sight and sound. Cards flashed, wheels spun, people laughed and smoked and played with earnest attention to their particular pursuit, faces alive with avarice. Some sat with cards fanned out in front of them, others stood clustered at spinning wheels. Still others faced a seated man, cards lined up between them, playing something Caroline could only guess at. And above it all, like a musical accompaniment, was the constant *clink* and *dink* and *ring* of money.

A gleaming bar fortified one end of the long room where a mustachioed barkeep busily wielded bottles and glasses, bright green garters holding back his sleeves, a towel slung over his shoulder.

There were women, too—mostly of the "soiled dove" variety, she judged from their mode of dress that left a shocking amount of flesh visible.

Jack steered her toward a small table by a draperied window, and ordered her a coffee from a waiter who glided up immediately. "Order whatever else you want, give 'em my name, and tell 'em to put it on my tab," he told her, already heading away.

Within moments, the waiter brought the steaming dark brew in one of those thick white cups. "Thank you," she murmured, sipping carefully while this new collage teemed around her.

Ah! real coffee, she sighed, remembering the bitter-good flavor from when she was little. Not boiled peanut shells or that awful chicory that left a green scum at the bottom of a cup. No, this was real coffee. The bottom of this cup was clean and white, and she cradled its comforting warmth gratefully.

Studying the collective mood of the room, she began to feel a curious separation from the crowd, an aloneness enveloping her. Here it was, Christmastime, and she was in a room full of strangers. The scrawny Christmas tree squatting at the far end of the bar, a miserly token of the season with its haphazard paper ornaments, seemed a mockery. The inevitable memories of long-ago Christmases with family bubbled up—and she clamped down on them hard.

Gripping her cup, she forced herself to look around again, to find the people beneath the unfamiliar faces. She looked first for Jack, but her eye was arrested by the sight of a woman dealer. Dressed in robin's egg blue with a froth of white lace at her bosom and each wrist, she seemed out of place in this hard-edged crowd . . . until Caroline looked closer. In contrast to her dainty appearance, her movements were deft and sure as she split the deck precisely, shuffled, and dealt with economical speed. Fascinated, Caroline unconsciously flexed her own fingers in response. Despite the flirtatious, smiling eyes, the woman slanted this way and that, the stacks of coins in front of her spoke of considerable skill. The game, whatever it was, went quickly, and she was the obvious winner, adding still more money to the pile at her elbow. Her opponents—a half-dozen men—instead of being disgruntled, merely laughed, gave mock throes of despair, and remained to play again. Apparently, the charm of the victor made losing less painful, Caroline noted.

Four men sat at the table next to hers, and facing her was one in a black Prince Albert coat, his blond hair short, beard stubble glinting gold along his narrow face. He remained a small isle of quiet among his rowdy companions, who were guffawing loudly.

As Caroline watched, he laid down his hand. "I call," he drawled, an inbred grace softening his thirty-some years.

One of the others slapped down his own cards, crowing, "Ha! Beat ya again, Preacher. Three kings!"

"Merry Christmas!" chimed in another. "You jes' been beat by the three wise men."

"An' God bless 'em!" the winner chortled, raking a pile of coins toward his chest.

Caroline craned her neck to see, intrigued and more than a bit shocked at the thought of a gambling member of the clergy.

"Gold, frankincense, and myrrh . . ." the man called Preacher intoned softly, staring sadly at his losing cards. "Merry Christmas, indeed." Placing his long-fingered hands flat on the table, he seemed to debate with himself for a moment, then, as if coming to a reluctant conclusion, sighed and rose.

"My friends!" he addressed the room in a tone only slightly above normal, "I've just been reminded—in the pocket where it hurts more than usual these days—that it's Christmas, the birthday of our Lord."

Caroline looked around. Only a few people paid the man any direct attention, but a fair number of voices murmured acknowledgment. The jingle of coins and slap of cards continued.

In a graceful sweep of one arm, he scooped the winning hand off the table and held it high. "Three kings, my friends! The three wise men who came from the east—or in the case of my friend here, perhaps the south end of his sleeve."

"Hey!" the man protested, causing instant tension there and at the surrounding tables.

Waving away the seriousness of his words, the preacher's smile was gentle, and Caroline wondered if he hadn't made the accusation simply to snag attention.

"Almost two thousand years ago they traveled—as we here are traveling—but could any here say that *we* are wise men?" There was laughter and an answering murmur to the contrary. "And yet the light of God, of the Son himself, still shines within us all." He pointed a long finger. "In you . . . and you . . . and you. We call ourselves men of the world, but who among us was not an innocent child once?"

"Not Hank here—he was born in bed with a whore!" cried a raucous voice.

"Yeah—his mother!" called another.

Some laughed, some *shushed* the speaker. The tall, lean preacher just smiled and began to walk among the tables, revealing a stiff right leg. "You remember the story of the first Christmas?" His gaze came to rest on a flinty-eyed man with long, stringy hair. "Remember?"

The man nodded, his game forgotten for the moment. The preacher smiled and nodded back, speaking to him and him alone. "A long time ago, but you still do."

By now, the undercurrent of voices and clink of money had quieted as the others openly strained to hear.

"Where? Where did it happen?" the preacher prompted softly.

"Beth—" the man cleared his throat, "Bethlehem."

"That's right," he was told and beamed like a child praised in Sunday school. "In Bethlehem." The others were included again by a slight rise in volume. "Joseph led Mary from town to town, far into the night . . ." and he proceeded to tell the familiar story to an utterly quiet gambling parlor.

As he continued to talk and move among them, squeezing a shoulder here and there, she watched him reel in the crowd, his melodious voice causing hard faces to soften, games to be forgotten, cigars to hang loosely from the corners of slackened mouths. Even the bartender had stilled his ever-moving rag to lean on an elbow in rapt attention. The white-coated waiters had paused in their tracks.

Glancing over at the gambler—at *Jack*—she found him politely silent, but the mask of his face was unreadable as he studied the cards in his hand. It made her wonder what kind of Christmases he'd had growing up.

As the story wound to its conclusion of renewed hope for the world, there was a long silence, heavy with private reflection until a voice rose from somewhere, gruff and cracked, singing, "*Si-i-lent night, ho-o-ly night . . .*"

By ones and twos, other voices joined in, rich with baritones, and solemn.

Looking out the curtained window, Caroline watched the spotted reflection of the boat's lamps on the river's surface, and let her own soprano rise, thin and clear.

"*Slee-eep in hea-ven-ly peace.*"

Someone had started passing a hat, and she watched it grow heavy, some sweeping their tables clean in a joint tithe. As the felt collection "plate" came her way, she touched her throat self-consciously—and felt the cameo. On impulse, she unpinned the tiny gold catch and dropped it in among the money as it passed, satisfied with her offering. Made it feel more like Christmas.

The last notes of the hymn died away and, as if by signal, the business of gambling resumed, full-throated and noisy.

She continued to watch the preacher as he accepted the offering with a sad twist of a smile, patted a few more shoulders, and limped out one of the side doors.

She felt soothed and sated, glad the day hadn't passed unheralded after all.

Her eyes went back to Jack. Animated once again, his hat was pushed to the back of his head, mustache stretched wide over white, white teeth as he laughed at something one of his table companions said. He was, she realized with a start, quite a handsome man.

Apparently, she wasn't the only one who thought so. Just then, a woman sauntered up, garish in a red corset boned in black and a frothy skirt that left her lacquered heels and scarlet laces showing. She looped her bare arm around Jack's neck. Caroline waited for him to shrug her off, but he didn't. Indeed, continuing his deal around the table, he didn't even seem to notice the woman's presence—until the last card fell. Then he wrapped an arm around her ample backside and snugged her close against him. They grinned into each other's faces.

Caroline's brows pinched. This hadn't occurred to her—that he might take up with another woman—and that alone shocked her. It made her wonder just how far behind in life she might be. The grit required for survival was no substitute for experience in other matters, like behavior between men and women.

As she watched, the other woman draped herself languidly over his shoulder as the hand was played, gradually plunking herself onto his knee and holding his arm tight to her waspy waist.

"More coffee, ma'am?"

Her head snapped up. "What?"

The waiter smiled. "Would you be wantin' more coffee?" he repeated. "Or mebbe some of Cook's black bottom pie? It's real tasty."

"No. No, thank you."

As he nodded and glided away, her head swiveled back to the tableau in the middle of the crowded, smoke-filled room. The woman's dark ringlets bobbed with her laughter, the light catching a bit of gold dangling from each ear. Caroline's stomach clenched. So much for pretending they were married when in public.

Jack reached up just then and slipped a gold piece between the woman's indecently exposed breasts—and that was the last straw. Caroline jumped to her feet. She needed to do something and she needed to do it *now*.

One of the others at Jack's table spotted her first and rose to his feet as she approached. The others followed hastily, chairs scraping. Jack was the last to look her way. As soon as he did, he patted the woman's bottom and she slid off his lap with a pout, sneering at Caroline as she passed.

He rose smoothly, meeting her eyes with a half-smile on his face. "Caroline . . . Gentlemen," he waved a hand toward her, "my wife." One eyelid drooped. Not quite a wink, but enough to remind her to play along.

Despite the rattle the foreign-sounding introduction caused in her head, she managed to acknowledge the others with a nod, her own tight smile frozen in place. "Please forgive me for interrupting, but I'm afraid I've developed one of my megrims and I need to lie down for a spell." Then, "Jack, *dear . . .*"

He glanced down at the hand she'd laid lightly on his arm. "Yes . . . dear?"

"Could I trouble you for our room key?"

His gaze slid toward the other woman in her retreat and one eyebrow quirked in apparent amusement. "Of course." He dug the key out of his pocket and handed it over. "I'll be awhile yet, so don't wait up."

Her eyes narrowed when he leaned over to give her a peck on the cheek, but her smile remained in place. "I won't. Gentlemen, please," she gestured gracefully, "go on with your game." On a little wave, she sailed away, satisfied she'd made her point to the woman in red . . . and any others of her ilk who might be watching.

A waiter opened the door to the deck as she approached. "Have a good evenin', ma'am."

She responded in kind and stepped back out into the night, sucking in great a lungful of the damp, river-chilled air.

She shouldn't wait until she got to California to make plans. She needed to start making them *now*.

Jack tossed another coin into the pot as he resumed his seat. "I call," he said. As he suspected, the man on his right had been bluffing, and his own two pair held sway.

Scooping up his winnings, his eyes strayed to the little table by the window. Two strangers occupied it now. Perhaps she really had gone back to their cabin—or followed that preacher. She hadn't been able to take her eyes off the damn man . . . and giving that shyster her cameo—what a stupid thing to do! And *he'd* been stupid bringing her along in the first place. She'd just looked so damned pitiful standing there in her doorway, neat and tidy and prim as a schoolmarm in her black mourning, bags all packed, with nowhere to go and no way to get there.

He cut the cards for the man on his left and waited until all five cards were down before picking them up and spreading them a fraction apart, mere inches from his chest. A deuce, a seven, two jacks, and a queen. He discarded the deuce and seven, and settled back to return the red queen's heavy-lidded stare. He picked up his two new cards. Another jack, another queen. A full house. He didn't allow himself to smile, just as he hadn't allowed himself to trespass earlier.

It had been something of a shock to wake up to find her in bed next to him. Only vaguely did he remember inviting her. He'd just wanted to stop her noisy fidgeting, but when he woke to find her there—and could've reached out to twirl a loose curl around his finger—a whole new agenda sprang to mind. And body.

That's when he got out of bed. But that bold move of hers just now was—

"*Hey!*"

He jumped.

"What's it gonna be there, fella?" came the irate demand from the portly man on his left. "You gonna call, raise, or fold?"

Jack looked up, gleaned everything he needed to know in the man's change of posture, and tossed several more gold pieces into the pot. "Guess I'll have to raise you, say, twenty?" *And then I'd better do something about her,* he thought grimly, settling into more concentrated play, *before she ruins me.*

Four

On deck, Caroline's pace gradually slowed. The exercise along with the steady splash of the water against the boat had unwound her last knot of tension. As she approached the stern, the splashing grew louder, while stentorian voices, thick and strident, rose above the noise.

"Seben come eleben!" someone cried. A dry rattle of dice followed.

"Snake eyes, boy! Snake eyes!" came another voice amid groans and laughter.

"Put up yo' money, child. Come on, feed ol' Pappy *good*."

The familiar clink of coins was unmistakable, and Caroline leaned over the rail to watch. Gambling fever was rife it seemed. Even the roustabouts had fallen prey to it. That those with so little would waste it in such a fool's pursuit nettled her.

Turning away, she abruptly collided with a woman standing quietly at the rail beside her, nearly invisible in her dark cloak.

"I beg your pardon! I didn't see you."

"No harm done." The woman's features were hard to distinguish in the darkness, but her voice was mature, low, and musical, with a slight foreign-sounding lilt. She indicated the men below them with a dip of her head. "Looks like they're having fun, *non*?"

Caroline sniffed noncommittally.

"You don't approve?" There was tolerant humor in the question.

"They can't afford it."

Gems sparkled as a pale, gloveless hand ringed by white lace waved that away. "I'm sure they know that better than you. Perhaps gambling takes their minds off it, *n'est-ce pas?*"

"And what takes their families' minds off it—a poverty increased by their gambling?"

"You speak as if from experience . . . or training. Which is it?"

"I just don't believe in money foolishly spent, that's all."

"What do you consider foolish? Is dreaming foolish? Is hope? Who's to say those men aren't investing what little they have quite wisely? For a few pennies, they can buy hope, a dream, or maybe only a little distraction on a cold, lonely night away from those very families of which you speak. Gambling is everywhere, my dear. Isn't life itself a gamble? How are those men any different from, say, the girl who buys a hair ribbon in hope of catching a boy's eye? Or a settler buying a wagon and crossing the country in hope of a better life? This country was built by gamblers. Without someone willing to take a chance, there'd be no railroads, no new towns, no inventions—no growth of any kind. Where would we be without them? I, for one, am very glad there are those who choose to afford it."

Not once during this small speech had the woman's voice risen a notch or become infected with passion, and Caroline didn't know which impressed her most—her expansive outlook or her courage to speak it. "You have a most . . . liberal viewpoint, ma'am."

"Simone. Simone Jules."

"How do you do? I'm Caroline Cooper—of the Johnson County Coopers."

"Sorry, I'm not from around here," Simone said with a small shrug. "As to my liberal viewpoint as you call it, it must come from owning my own life all these years. It makes me believe others should have the same freedom."

"You're not married?"

"*Mon Dieu*, no. I take my companions when and where I choose. That way I'm never bored."

Caroline flinched. To make such a statement, that one took companions—*lovers*—was either the mark of a woman truly at ease with herself, or someone with a gauche disregard for the rules of polite society. Or both. "Isn't it frightening being alone?" she asked in spite of herself.

The woman spread her hands, sending a hint of expensive French perfume into the air. "Alone? There are over a hundred people on this boat. I'm not alone—and neither are you."

"But how do you get by . . . if I may be so bold?"

The woman's head lifted proudly. "I do not 'get by,' I *live*. I'm a dealer. *Vingt-et-un*—blackjack as you Americans call it. In fact, I'm just out for a bit of air before returning to the tables. Are you shocked?"

Compared to the statement that she took lovers, confessing to being a gambler seemed downright republican. "No. Once upon a time perhaps. But, well, no, not after tonight."

"Most people are, even if they say they aren't."

"Well, I'm not most people. My brother gambled, although he wasn't very good at it, and I-I'm traveling with a gambler," she added, driven to try out the other woman's boldness.

"Ah, so it's in your blood. I'm surprised you fight it like you do."

"Fight it?

A gesture indicated the men below them, still rattling the dice and crowing or groaning at the outcome. "I just assumed . . ."

"No, it's just that—oh, *wait!* You're the one I saw earlier—in the parlor. You were winning, too. All that *money!* You must be very good."

Simone laughed softly. "That would be immodest of me to admit . . . but you say you're here with a gambler? Who? I might know him."

Caroline hesitated, but couldn't think of a gracious way to dissemble. "His name's Jack."

"Jack—Jack *Transomb*?"

"You know him?"

"*Knew* is a better word—years ago."

Uncomfortable at the familiarity she heard in the other woman's voice, Caroline changed the subject. "Well, I want to be an independent woman of means, too, but—"

"But what? Life is short, *mon amie*. If that's what you want, chart your course and never look back. Don't let anyone tell you that you can't. Be brave. Be bold."

"But I'm not like you," Caroline protested even as she soaked up the words, aware suddenly of how much she craved advice and encouragement.

Simone tilted her head. "Are you sure?"

Caroline's fingers clenched in the folds of her skirt. Part of her took umbrage at the suggestion she could have anything in common with a creature who thumbed her nose at every decent value she'd heard extolled since childhood, yet another part of her responded with an unexpected thrill. The mix was unsettling.

"Well, perhaps not," Simone conceded with a touch of frost when Caroline didn't answer right away. "In any case, you'll have to excuse me. I must get back."

Impulsively, Caroline reached out. "Do you really think I can? Chart my own course, I mean?" The woman was probably only ten years her senior, but self-confidence made her seem far older.

"If you don't, some man will."

The oblique criticism surprised Caroline. Simone had just described in one brief stroke what Caroline believed was every woman's dream, a dream she herself once harbored—that some man would come along and sweep her off her feet, making his destiny her own. She'd been raised to believe *that*, and not independence, was the natural order of things for a woman. Unwittingly, Simone's pronouncement confirmed what Caroline had only recently learned—that, natural or not, there was danger in devoting one's life to someone else.

"The choice is yours if you choose to make it. Now I really must be going."

Following another impulse, Caroline held out her hand. "I'm very pleased to have made your acquaintance, Miss Jules. Our little talk has—well, it's meant a lot to me."

Her hand was clasped warmly, briefly, in return. "I'm glad—and now goodnight."

As she glided away into the darkness, Caroline turned back to watch the roustabouts, seeing them through new eyes. Is that what Wendall had been doing? Buying a little dream, a little relief from their bitter existence? Or had he merely been addicted to the thrill of risk? She'd never know of course, and it no longer mattered.

Caroline continued her promenade, invigorated now with new possibilities. It was as if a door never-before-seen had suddenly swung open on a whole new world. Simone Jules, she decided, had been a sign.

As she rounded the bow once again, she saw a lone man leaning on the railing. She hesitated, started to turn back, then stopped. It was the gambling preacher.

He spotted her at the same time and angled himself toward her. "Evenin', ma'am."

"Good evening." He was without hat or great coat, and the night wind plucked at his string tie, flipping it against his shoulder. "You must be chilled to your very marrow."

"Hardly." His tone suggested he suffered far greater discomforts than what mere weather could inflict.

The twenty feet or so that separated them disappeared as she moved closer, drawn by some whiff of commonality. "I enjoyed your sermon this evening."

"Sermon? Oh, that. Why?" His tone was less welcoming than expected.

"It made it feel a bit more like Christmas, that's all."

"Glad to be of service. You must be the one who gave the cameo."

She blinked. "How ever did you guess *that?*"

"It's a lady's jewelry, and you were the only lady present."

"Well, I hope you were rewarded handsomely—many times more than my pitiful tithe."

"Not really, at least not as much as I'd hoped."

The bitter words surprised her. "You shouldn't take it personally. Times are hard."

"They are indeed."

"You're an eloquent speaker," she offered.

"Glad you think so." He leaned his elbows on the railing, and stared out at the dark trees that lined the riverbank, bare branches creaking dryly as the wind soughed through them. "It's something I don't do very often anymore."

"Why not?"

"Brings up memories. Things best left behind." He gestured with one hand and lamplight glinted off a silver flask. "So I've been administering a bit of forgetfulness. No doubt why I'm not feeling the cold." With that, he tipped his head back and drank deeply—then coughed and straightened, blotting his mouth on the back of his hand. "I *beg* your pardon! How rude of me." Twisting the cork down tight and pocketing the flask, he inclined himself in a slight bow. "How do you do? I'm DeForest Atchison, known simply as Preacher these days and *not* known for tippling in front of ladies. Who might you be?"

The more conventional turn of conversation allowed her to relax. "I'm Caroline Cooper of the Johnson County Coopers—and I don't mind your drinking. My father and brother both drank. 'A good Southern vice for good Southern gentlemen,' they used to say."

"Ah, gracious as well as beautiful—but *drank* . . . past tense?"

"Yes. They're gone. Both of them," she said, realizing how close she'd come to a slippery slide into grief.

"The war?" His voice softened to the mellifluous tone he'd used earlier in the parlor.

She nodded. It was the easiest answer.

As if it were the most natural thing in the world, he reached down and picked up her gloved hand, pressing it between his own. "I'm sorry."

"You're too kind."

"Not at all. So, tell me—what are you doing here?"

She withdrew her hand. "Here?"

"Onboard."

"Oh. I'm going to St. Louis."

"To family?"

"No, just passing through on my way to California."

"Surely you're not traveling alone," he said, pulling in his chin.

She lifted hers. "Why not? Do you think it unseemly of a woman to travel alone? Or do you simply believe females are too pudding-headed to get where they're going by themselves?"

"Forgive me. I meant no offense." Leaning an elbow on the rail, he focused the whole of his attention on her. "I was actually thinking how brave and adventurous you must be."

"Don't be fooled. If the war hadn't come along and put our family in, well, reduced circumstances, you'd find nothing brave or adventurous about me. I'd be downright dull."

"I doubt that, but tell me: What will you do when you get to California?"

Ah, there it was. A simple question, but one that instantly gripped her with uncertainty.

She started to say something about her sewing, but by some trick of the mind, she caught a sudden whiff of French perfume. Indeed, so real was the scent, she turned her head, fully expecting to see Simone standing nearby, but they were alone.

"What is it?" he asked, turning to look himself.

"Nothing. I met a woman earlier. Said she was a gambler—a professional gambler."

"I see. And?"

She tilted her head. "You're not shocked?"

"Should I be?"

"Well, for one thing, I don't think one would exactly call her a lady, if you catch my meaning—and for another, well, isn't gambling a sin? Aren't you supposed to condemn it?"

"I gamble," he pointed out.

"Yes, but you do it to make a point, right?"

He shook his head. Putting his hands in his pockets, he stared out at the black landscape sliding by. "I'm sorry to disillusion you, but I do it because it's all I *can* do with any degree of skill." He glanced her way. "Oh, sometimes I feel a flash of inspiration from the Holy Spirit, but more often than not these days, I do it from the sheer weight of debt."

"Oh." It must be a night made for bold, unvarnished confessions.

Light gilded one side of a brief smile. "You're young yet. The world's still black and white. When you get to be my age, everything becomes a little muddier, a little grayer."

"You sound so sad."

"Do I? I'm sorry. Go on, tell me about your encounter with this notorious woman."

"Now you're poking fun."

"Hardly. Please—I'm very interested."

So, she did, absolving her guilt over gossip with the notion she was speaking to clergy.

"You're really not shocked?" she asked when she'd finished and he hadn't reacted.

"I'm afraid not."

Long-held assumptions about preachers, gamblers, and more were all reshuffling themselves in her head. "So you don't think what she does is a sin?"

"It's never a sin to survive."

She sniffed, faintly suspicious of such generosity. "Some people would consider her a fallen woman."

"I try to stay away from labeling people—they're rarely what they seem. Besides, I admire self-sufficiency in a woman. A woman needs to be strong in this world."

Feeling both challenged and comforted, she was perplexed. "You're not at all what one would expect from a preacher—even a gambling one."

"No?"

"No."

"I shall take that as a compliment. But make no mistake—I was once very traditional, too. There was a time I would have been shocked if a lady had confessed to going clear across the continent to create a new life for herself. The old South, my South, demanded nothing more of a woman than she be beautiful, charming, and *utterly dependent*." He leaned back, resting his elbows on the railing, and drew in an audible breath. "If I close my eyes, I can still see it, still hear it . . . the sleepy drone of bees on a summer's afternoon, the taste of cool mint tea, lawns made mysterious by dark drapes of Spanish moss."

Caroline knew well the picture he painted.

"It's a shame you're too young to remember the South the way I do," he said as if arguing with the image in her head. "Back then, life was measured and orderly, the men brave, the women soft and vibrant as the flowers in their hair." He pushed himself upright, breaking the spell of his own words. "But like I said, you're too young to remember all that. I thought—we all thought—it would go on forever." He reached over to tuck an errant strand of hair behind her ear, spiking her senses at the unexpected touch. "It's a shame really. You were robbed. I can just see you in a gown of sprigged muslin . . . flowers in your hair."

Something about all this talk of the old South, the South that would never return, bothered her. It felt as if the past was trying to suck her back and rub some of the shine off her hoped-for future.

"It's late," he said suddenly. "And you're cold. Don't deny it—I saw you shiver."

"Yes, I should be getting back," she agreed, holding out her hand. "Goodnight, Mister Atchison. I've enjoyed our little talk."

The wind ruffled his pale hair, the lamps in their brackets picking out the wayward strands, tracing the taut curve of one cheek. "I'm glad to know the pleasure was not all mine," he presented his elbow. "And I'd be honored if you'd allow me to walk you to your cabin."

"There's no need for that."

He drew her hand through the crook of his arm. "Oh, but I insist."

It was easier not to argue, so she pointed the way. As they walked, curiosity made her press, "You *really* don't think it wicked of a woman to gamble?"

"I really don't."

"What would you say if *I* decided to become a gambler?"

"You?" He glanced down at her and was silent for several seconds. "I'd say you'd probably make a killin' at it . . . and I feel for the poor, besotted souls who'll happily lose their shirts just for the privilege of sitting across a table from you. What man could resist? If he was smart, he'd deliberately throw every hand just so he could continue to sit there and bask in the light of your charm."

"Oh, you don't mean that!" She laughed, grateful for the dark that hid the hot blush she could feel in her cheeks. "Would *you* do such a thing?"

"'Deed I would. In fact, I do believe similar opportunities—with ladies not nearly so fair—explain much about the empty state of my pockets of late."

"Then perhaps that's what I shall do when I get to California—become a lady gambler."

He sighed dramatically. "Then I shall simply have to follow and place all my future fortunes at your mercy."

She laughed again. "You really aren't shocked, are you?"

"I'm really not."

"It's too bad then that I don't know the first thing about being a gambler," she said, slanting him a look from beneath her lashes.

"Hallelujah! I may be saved a bit of supper money yet."

"I'm serious."

"So am I."

"What is it you play?" she asked with calculated mildness, shortening her steps to prolong their conversation.

"Faro mostly. Bucking the Tiger, they call it."

"Sounds frightful."

"Not really. The name is the scariest part—meant to ward off willful youths, I suspect . . . and attract ne'er-do-wells like myself."

"Oh, stop. You're no such thing."

He patted her hand on his arm. "To hear you say so, I could almost believe it."

"You—you wouldn't be willing to teach me how to play, would you?"

He reared back a step. "Good God, no!"

The blunt refusal surprised her. "Whyever not?"

"For one thing, I'm terrible at it. For a game that's supposed to have near fifty-fifty odds, I manage to lose more often than most. All I could do is teach you how to lose like me, and I'd suffer terrible guilt over that. So please—try not to judge me too harshly for declining."

"Oh, all right," she grudgingly agreed.

She stopped. They'd reached her door . . . *of the cabin she shared with Jack.* "Well, here we are," she said crisply. "Thank you."

"My pleasure." He snagged her hand before she could turn away. "Before you go, I want you to take this." He folded back his lapel and there, pinned to the underside, was her cameo. Sliding it free, he placed it in her hand and curled her fingers over it.

"Oh, you mustn't give it back," she protested, shocked that he'd kept it on his person. She thrust it back at him. "I gave it cheerfully."

"Yes, and because of that I want you to keep it. I'd rather see a woman adorned in her finery. It's a rare treat these days. Please."

Left with no graceful way to refuse after that, she gave in. "Thank you."

"It's I who must thank you," he said, lingering and making her itch with nerves. "I still say you're too young to have known the South the way I knew it, but tonight—" he inclined himself briefly, "you gave a bit of its charm back to me, and for that I'm in your debt." He held out his hand. "Your key—so I may unlock the door for you?"

"Oh!" She fumbled in the soft, unwieldy mouth of her purse again. "Not necessary, I have it," she said, jamming it into the lock and twisting it with ill-advised force. "See?"

"Indeed. Goodnight, Miss Cooper. Sleep well, and perhaps—"

"Yes, you, too!" She slipped inside and all but shut the door in his face. Sagging against it, she didn't breathe again until she heard his footsteps recede, then she hung up her bonnet and cape and sank onto the corner of the bed. She felt abuzz from all the new visions in her head—past, present, and possibly future.

The tap on the door startled her. Leaping to her feet, she yanked it open only to find it was Jack, not Preacher, and couldn't help a quick glance in both directions.

"Expectin' someone?" he drawled.

"No, of course not, but you look a little surprised yourself."

"Didn't know if you'd be here or not."

"Where else would I be? Or perhaps you were *hoping* I wouldn't be here."

"Why would I hope that?" He pushed past her, dropped his game box on the bed, and sank down on his heels to re-stoke the stove.

"I don't know. Perhaps you'd rather be traveling with a different woman—like that one who sat in your lap earlier."

"What? Oh, her—*yeah*."

"Well, I *never*! Why?"

He grinned over his shoulder at her. "Because she sat in my lap."

"So any woman, as long as she sits in your lap, will do?"

"Dunno. Let's find out." Brushing his hands off, he pushed aside his game box, and sat on the end of the bed. He patted his thigh. "Come sit in my lap."

He laughed outright at her shocked expression. "Trouble with you is you spent too many years by your lonesome in that big ol' house of yours. Made you a mulehead."

"Have you been *drinking?*"

"A little. You should try it. Might leach some of that starch outa you. I mean *look* at you. Arms all folded up tight like you forgot to lace up your corset."

She felt her own neck stretch. "Undergarments are *not* a proper topic for discussion."

He was still grinning. "Just lettin' you know I've untied a few in my day, so if you ever need help with yours—I know they can be hard to reach."

"Not all laces are in the back." Her face flamed as soon as the words left her lips, and he laughed again.

With his game box once more tucked under his arm, he headed for the door, then paused.

"What are you smirking at?" she asked, arms still folded.

"See? That's what I'm talkin' about. You're awful pretty to look at, but you don't know anything about a man. You don't know the difference 'tween a smirk and a smile when he looks at a pretty girl."

She flinched when he reached out to tug on a strand of hair that had come loose in front of her ear. "Now lock up after me—and keep it locked when you're in here by yourself."

She followed and stuck her head out behind him. "Is that all you came back for—just to stoke the fire?"

His only answer was a brief, backhanded wave.

"*And I'm not a mulehead!*" she called after him . . .then quickly checked to see if there was anyone nearby that could overhear.

She shut the door *and* locked it—but didn't feel the least bit tired. More like she had bees in her blood, so she settled back against the bed pillows to ponder.

Caroline Cooper, seamstress.

Caroline Cooper, dressmaker.

Caroline Cooper, lady gambler.

She imagined herself smiling at a table full of admiring men, raking in piles of money. There was no comparison. Lady gambler was so much more exciting!

If she was honest about it, she'd always been a little jealous of Wendall—always going out to "play" while she stayed at home trying to make ends meet. She *was* better at sums than he. That's why dealing with their creditors always fell to her. Plus, she'd learned how to hold the line with them, how to act tougher on the outside than she felt on the inside. Surely there was something of the gambler in that. So, all that remained was learning the games . . . and maybe some experience.

Suddenly, she felt *behind* in so many things. Much as she hated to admit it, Jack was right. She had spent too many years alone, and many things in life had simply passed her by. Most women her age were long since married and raising families. Only now did she recognize a new hunger within herself—not of the body this time, but of the spirit—and she fortified herself for the things to come with Simone's encouraging words. *Be brave! Be bold!*

Hours later, just short of dawn, Jack knocked on the door once, twice, a third time. *"Jesus, Caroline! It's me—open up! It's cold as a witch's tit out here!"*

Finally, he heard the key in the lock and shot in, almost knocking her over as he shook himself like a dog. His steadying grab for her arm turned into a quick, exuberant hug. "Brrrr! G'mornin'! Hey— what did you do?" he asked, pushing her out to arm's length. "Sleep in your dress? Boots, too? That's how you catch cold, y'know." Not waiting for an answer, he sent his hat sailing for the washstand where it caught on a hook, spun, and stayed. "Ha!" he crowed.

She yawned behind her hand. "I just sat down to think and must've dozed off . . . but you're awfully cheerful. What's happened?"

Swinging his bag up onto the bed, he stowed his game box. "What's happened is I just won us enough to last for weeks, that's what!"

She rubbed her eyes. *So they had become an "us" now, had they?*

He considered her sleepy face. "What you need is coffee. And breakfast."

"I'm not hungry yet."

"Well, *I* can eat enough for both of us."

She yawned again and sat back down on the bed. "So tell me about the game."

With just that bit of encouragement, he launched into a recounting of the players, the strategies, the breaks—both lucky and created—and relived his victory all over again.

He watched her face as he talked, expecting boredom. It never came. The sleep cleared from her eyes, and she started asking questions, following his answers better than he expected. When she expressed confusion over a point of play, he didn't think twice. Whipping out a deck of cards, he sat down beside her. He smeared the deck across the coverlet, face up, looking for particular ones so he could rebuild the hands and demonstrate the sequence of play.

"See? I held onto the four, five, and six of clubs, threw away these two, and . . .."

She followed his hands, intent as if she was trying to commit it all to memory, but he could tell she was having a hard time keeping up, so he slowed down, indulging her interest, but the hours were starting to catch up with him. He tilted onto an elbow as he talked, then sagged onto his back, still holding his cards, feet still on the floor. "And then I—" he yawned hugely. "I knew I had him. I knew . . ." He thumbed his eyes, trying to refocus, then tucked his chin to smile up at her. "You're awful pretty, you know that?"

She looked away, then back again, finally giving in to the smile his compliment caused.

He wanted to say more, but couldn't concentrate. "Just need to rest my eyes a second. A minute, that's all. Just—"

The bed dipped as she leaned over him. "I thought you were hungry."

"I was. Am," he mumbled without opening his eyes. He felt himself already drifting away.

"Jack?"

He dragged himself back. "Hmm?"

"I need you to do something for me—a boon, if you will."

He frowned, but didn't open his eyes. "What?"

"I need you to teach me to do what you do—the gambling games."

He cracked open one eye. "Why? You that bored?"

"No, I just think it'll be a—a useful skill is all."

That amused him. "Can't say as I ever heard it described like that before."

"I need the money."

He groaned. "And *I* need sleep, so I'll buy it for you, whatever it is."

"No, I mean I need to make a *living.*"

On a huge exhale, he elbowed himself back to a sitting position and scratched his scalp. "Looks like I ain't gettin' to sleep any time soon."

"I assure you I've considered this long and hard—"

"Well, consider it longer and harder." He started to lie back. "All night, in fact."

"What about your sewin'?" he asked, eyes closing once more.

She made an impatient sound. "I'm tired of sewing. Of being poor."

"Well, I don't know any rich gamblers—leastwise not in the long run." Grouchy, but reluctantly alert, he got to his feet. Dragging his bag off the bed, he dropped it to the floor.

"I just need someone to teach me the games."

He laughed. He couldn't help it. "You think it's that easy?" He snapped his fingers with a magician's flourish. "You'll learn and start winnin' money—just like that?"

"Well, maybe not right away."

"No? How long you think it'll take?"

"A month—a couple maybe," she kept amending as he continued to laugh and shake his head.

"Amazin'. Plum amazin'!" He tugged off his tie and unbuttoned his collar. "Sorry, sugar."

"What do you mean, *sorry?* You mean you won't do it? You won't teach me?"

He flung tie and collar onto the washstand. "I'll think about it."

"That's what Papa used to say when he wanted us to stop asking. What he really meant was *no.*"

"Did it work? Did you stop?"

She waved away his question. "I'm serious, Jack. I want to earn my keep—like you said. Or are you afraid I'll get as good as you, maybe better?"

"Oh, for—! Now you're just bein' silly." He got up and stalked around the bed, pulling out his shirttail. "I been gamblin' more'n half my life and I ain't as good as you're talkin' about—nobody is. Where did you get this straw-headed notion anyway?"

She twitched a shrug. "Well, for one thing, I found the gaming parlor last night rather *exciting*, and the gambler I spoke to afterwards was exciting, too."

"Who'd you talk to?"

"Her name is Simone Jules. She was the one who—"

"Oh, I know who Simone is. We—"

"Please!" She stopped him with a gesture. "No need to share your personal life with me."

"Wasn't gonna." He scrubbed at his mustache. "All I was gonna say was we go way back, and she's hardly the kinda woman a lady should pattern her life after."

"Why? Because she doesn't need a man to survive?"

"Is *that* what she told you? Well, don't you believe it, sugar. Simone survives *because* of men. So what else did she say? Did she tell you what it was like to sit on a hard chair for hours on end, eyes gritty from cigar smoke and lack of sleep, that you need to go to the privy, but you don't dare leave the table—did she tell you any of that?"

"There's no need to be crude."

"Crude? Gamblin' ain't a tea party, Caroline! Ain't nothin' dainty or polite about it."

"*Isn't,* not *ain't,* and I sit for hours at a time sewing, don't I? It's nothing new to me."

"Sittin' with a bunch of people who *ain't* bathed in a fortnight *is.* You'll hear swear words that'll fry your ears off, feel the slime of tobacco spit under your slippers, and hope no tempers are lost, no bullets start to fly—maybe aimed at you, maybe not—but your chances of gettin' killed are the same either way. You want all that?"

"No, but I'll take my chances."

"Well, *that's* the first thing you've said that sounds like you might have what it takes."

"I *want* this, Jack."

"Do you want it bad enough to learn every game there is, every angle, learn all the odds—none of 'em very good. You wanna shuffle till your knuckles ache? You wanna know a deck of cards so good you can *feel* if even one card is missin'? So good you can *feel* the ink-weight difference 'tween an ace and a king—and that's only if you get *really, really* good at it?"

"Yes—and I'll get that good."

"You want decent women, so-called 'good' women to sweep their skirts outa the way when you pass by? To look down their noses at you—if they look at you at all? I'll bet Simone didn't tell you 'bout any of that, did she?"

"Oh, fie!" She paced away. "I'm sick to death of worrying about what other people think all the time. If everyone did that, nothing would ever get done. Why, there'd be no railroads, no new towns, no inventions at all!"

She stopped to consider her reflection in the small mirror, then faced him, fists on her hips. "Why are you acting like I'm proposing to sell my favors?"

Jack felt his ears start to burn as he looked from one brown velvet eye to the other. "Because one often leads to the other for a woman, that's why. It ain't an easy life, Caroline—and it certainly ain't no life for a lady. I don't want you endin' up like your brother."

He saw the color leave her face.

"I'm not my brother," she said quietly.

His had been a deliberately low blow, but the quiet dignity in her response shamed him. Somehow, she always managed to pull on feelings he didn't know he had. Tenderness. Guilt. Feelings he had little use for.

"I won't end up like him, I promise you. I'm smarter than that."

"It ain't always about smarts. Sometimes it's about luck—and she's a fickle bitch. What happens when you're down to your last dime, but you gotta great hand, a hand you're sure can't be beat, the one you just *know* is gonna get you that big, fat pot in the middle of the table, and the man across from you—a filthy, smelly pig—raises? Maybe you're outa cash by then, so he wants you t'put yourself, your body on the line. There's a good chance he's got a better hand than you. What then?"

"I wouldn't let myself get in that situation. I'd always keep money back or-or I'd quit."

"Well, there goes your steady income." He sat and began tugging off his boots. "Stick with sewin'. That's a job for a lady."

"Don't you think what I choose to be—lady or *harlot*—is my choice to make, not yours?"

His answer was to jump up and close the short distance between them in two steps. She backed up, but immediately ran out of floor space. When he smacked both palms against the wall on either side of her head, it startled her. But her exclamation of surprise was caught by his mouth. Her lips were all he touched, yet a small frisson of lightning shot through the rest of her, and she forgot to breathe. When his tongue traced the seam in her lips, she jerked her face away, hand pressed to her mouth.

"*Oh!*" he breathed, smile spreading. "You ain't never been kissed before, have you?"

"I have, too. Lots of times." She wouldn't look at him. "You—you just came at me like a *mauling bear*, that's all!"

He dropped one arm away. "Yeah? So who'd you kiss?" Their faces were still only inches apart.

"Well . . . um . . . Billy Sidles, for one."

"Billy Sidles, eh? When was this? When you were twelve?'

"*He* was twelve." She moved away. "*I* was eleven."

"Well, forget harlot and stick with lady. It's safer—but once I get some sleep, and ain't feelin' so *maulish*—I'll teach you how to kiss like a grow'd woman. Who knows? Knowin' how to kiss a grow'd *man* might come in handy someday."

That reignited all those lightning sparks and sent them racing again, and in what was less dismissive than she'd thought and more seductive than she knew, she unpinned her sleep-mussed hair and raked her fingers through it. With the efficiency of long practice, she twirled it back into its usual figure eight and re-pinned it in a matter of seconds.

That done, she finally looked at him to see a nakedly hungry expression on his face . . . and instinct suddenly provided what training had not. "I'll make you a bargain."

A visible swallow before he refocused on her face. "What kinda bargain?"

"If you teach me how to gamble . . . I'll let you teach me how to kiss."

One eyebrow arched. "Sounds like I'll be doin' all the work in this bargain o' yours."

"But we'll each be getting something we want out of it."

"Oh, so you think I *want* to kiss you, do you?"

She smiled. "Yes. I do actually. I also think you'll be better at it than Billy Sidles."

As she spoke, she put on her cloak and bonnet, wound the cords of her reticule around her wrist, and had her hand on the doorknob when he asked her where she was going.

"To the Ladies' Parlor . . . to start with."

She closed the door behind her, then opened it again long enough to say, "Oh—and Merry Christmas." She was gone again before he could return the sentiment.

Jack Transomb, he berated himself in the silence left behind, *you're in trouble, boy. Big trouble.*

FIVE

The air outside was brittle cold, the sky just pinking up. Lacy frost decorated cabin windows, lamp globes, and spittoon rims. Only the faint swish and splash of the river reached her ears as she quickly circled the upper decks to get warm. And to think about Jack.

Just remembering the feel of his mouth on hers, the hungry expression on his face stirred her yet again. But what on God's green earth had possessed her to accept—no, *propose*—kissing lessons? *Brave* and *bold* were fine when it came to gambling, but this—*this*—was literally asking for trouble, the kind that both scared and compelled her in equal measure. If she hadn't tied the bargain to the one thing she wanted most, she could simply tell him she'd changed her mind.

Suddenly, she realized she'd been walking this whole time with her gloved fingers pressed over her mouth—over his kiss. Feeling the heat of a blush, she dropped her hand and walked even faster.

The Ladies' Parlor was on the main deck, its simple brass door plaque plainly lettered. She poked her head inside. Empty—not unexpected on this holiday morn. Damp with musty river smell, the room was earnest in its attempt to appeal to the assumed taste of women. Every chair was upright, every arm doilied, every fabric a garden of rigid flowers. The braided rug on the floor, around which every item of furniture circled obediently, was clearly tasked with calling all to serious-minded order. Behind a screen in the corner, she found the necessary items to perform a brief toilette, then left quickly. The empty room reminded her of the years she'd spent home alone, and she couldn't help comparing it to the gaming parlor the night before. There would be no laughter in the Ladies' Parlor—nor gambling. Nor would anyone be sitting in someone's lap.

As if taking their direction from her thoughts, her feet led her to stand outside the gaming parlor. It was empty, too—or nearly so. As her eyes adjusted to the gloom, her nose to the stale, cigar-smoked air, she saw the bartender still on duty, but dozing, his cheek pleated on his fist. In the back corner was a handful of men playing cards with little animation.

One of them, a skinny, ferret-faced man dressed all in black, even to a black neckerchief knotted loosely around his sunburnt neck—caught sight of her. He looked rough and unsavory, but rose smoothly enough and nodded in her direction. "Happy Christmas, ma'am."

"Happy Christmas. I'm surprised to find anyone here—on Christmas morning, I mean."

"This is the Mighty Mississipp', ma'am. Gamblers Highway all day, ever'day."

"Yes, I suppose it is."

The others at the table exchanged glances in the beat of silence that followed.

"What are you playing?" she asked.

"Bluff. Poker some call it. Brag 'fore that."

She nodded as if she knew one from the other.

He squinted. "Is there somethin' we can do for ya, ma'am?"

"Um, no . . . thank you." He started to resume his seat. "Well, yes—actually, there is. Would you—would any of you—be willing to teach me this game of Bluff?"

Eyebrows shot up all around.

"Or perhaps you'd simply allow me to watch," she offered quickly, sensing imminent rejection even as she took another step forward. "One can learn a lot from watching."

"I don't know. This ain't—"

"Oh, let her watch," one of them said. "What harm can it do?"

"Thank you!" Without waiting for a consensus, she hurried the rest of the way forward. "I'll be as quiet as a mouse—you won't even know I'm here."

The man in black tugged on his neckerchief. "Well, I'm Del Griffith." He pointed around the table. "This is Ethan Brennan—"

"Ma'am," nodded a big blond with dark eyes and darker brows menacingly slanted.

"His brother, Shaun. We just call him Knuckles—"

Another blond with wild hair and wearing a long leather coat merely nodded and obligingly cracked said joints.

"And Paul Cochran," he finished.

"Pleased to meet you," said the older, balding man in gray plaid smoking a pipe.

A fifth man, apparently unknown by name, merely tipped his cowboy hat in her direction.

"Gentlemen," she acknowledged with a self-conscious smile.

The cowboy with no name nudged out an empty chair with the toe of his boot. "Have a sit," he offered, tossing down a couple of cards. "I'll take two."

So, she 'had a sit'—perched on the edge of the chair, prepared to flee if anything untoward happened. None were drinking currently, but all had empty shot glasses beside them, crescent amber stains in the bottoms.

She felt like an intruder. She *was* an intruder, she realized, but vowed not to let that label deter her. One *could* learn a lot just from watching, she decided, hands folded primly in her lap.

And watch she did, for a long time. She learned that playing began only after the "pot was right"—a pot, she couldn't help noticing, that contained enough money for her and Wendall to have eaten well for a month. It was a powerful realization, an insight into the lure gambling must've been for him, and an incentive to redouble her concentration.

The shuffling intrigued her, too—the visual fanfare, the careless grace and dexterity involved in making the fancy "bridge" or the spare neatness of the corner shuffle that barely made contact from one half of the deck to the other until the two halves were shoved together.

From where she sat, she caught a glimpse of Paul's hand and took note of the way he lined up his cards, and she soon learned what a "flush" and a "straight" meant.

Without warning, the deck of cards hit the table in front of her with a smack.

Del, the black ferret, was grinning at her. "Wanna cut?"

Timidly, she reached over.

"It won't bite," he assured her.

And neatly divided the deck as she'd seen it done.

"No, always cut *toward* the dealer."

"Oh." She corrected herself and sat back, prepared to become invisible once again when she saw she was being dealt cards along with the others.

"You got any money on you?"

Convulsively, she clutched her reticule. "A little. How much do I need?"

In silent conference, Paul made eye contact with the others. "After you ante up, a couple dollars'll keep you in the game for a spell. What you do after, that's up to you."

Shaun tossed two silver coins into the pot. "I'll ante for you this time. Christmas gift."

"Oh, you're too kind! Thank you." Earnestly, she leaned forward. "I'll repay you from my winnings of course." She laid two silver dollars and her change on the table beside her.

Picking up the cards she'd been dealt, she fanned them open. A four, an ace, a jack, another four, and a seven. "What now?" she asked brightly.

"For starters, see if you've got a pair—two of the same thing."

"Oh!" she exclaimed happily.

"Without lettin' on you got one."

She sobered instantly. "Oh."

A flood of instructions, ranks of hands, procedures, and vocabulary followed, all of them suddenly talking over one another.

"And now you put in some money," Ethan instructed. "Something to let ever'body know you got a hand worth playin'. Or, if you got nothin' and still wanna play, you throw in money and bluff up a storm, hopin' ever'body else'll sprout chicken feathers and fold."

Amused at the image, she wagered a single coin and handed in two cards, the seven and the jack—a totally arbitrary decision—to be replaced with two new ones, an ace and a king.

Watching the others throw in more money—all except Shaun, who laid down his cards and folded—her excitement mounted. When No Name Cowboy finally said, "Call," and everybody showed their cards, she was the winner.

"Another hand?" Del asked.

"Yes, please. This is quite exciting—and not nearly as hard as I thought it would be."

The others just grinned and exchanged glances as the cards fell again in a silent circle.

After the sixth hand, Paul threw down his hand in disgust. "She's won again!"

"Beginner's luck," Shaun grumbled, shaking his head.

Giddily, she raked the pot toward her with both arms and laughed. "I don't care what it is, I just hope it continues." She already had enough from this one game to buy herself a new dress—a ready-made one, no less! At this rate, whatever she wanted wouldn't take long at all!

Her opponents yawned, waiting patiently for her slow shuffle and even slower deal.

As she gripped the cards, dividing them carefully, she became aware that morning had arrived in full force. Pale, winter sunshine brightened the room through its bank of windows, the barkeep was gone, and sometime in the last few hours the unoccupied chairs—all but theirs—had been turned upside down onto tables. A young boy was just finishing sweeping.

Hours had gone by, yet she was feeling alert and invigorated as she dealt the more-familiar feeling cards around the table. She looked at each man in turn. It was obvious they were all bone-tired. Perhaps they were playing sloppily because of it. And perhaps that was a clue. Maybe she should keep normal hours herself and simply take advantage of those who had been up all night. It was such a simple strategy, she wondered why others hadn't thought of it.

"All right, gentlemen, read 'em and weep," she chanted, delighted to be able to use the jargon she'd learned. "Guts to open and—"

"What the hell—?"

Jack—one shirttail in, the other out, wearing boots but no coat—stood in the doorway, a thundercloud on two legs. *"I've been looking everywhere for you!"*

"Good heavens! Like that? You must be freez—"

"What do you think you're doing?"

Ignoring his fury, she beamed at him. "I'm learning to play Bluff—and look!" She indicated the pile of money in front of her. "I'm winning!"

Stalking a beeline to their table, his black scowl turned on the others. *"Not funny!"*

Del offered a lazy shrug, eyes sly with suppressed humor. "Just trying to make the lady happy. She wanted to learn, so we was teachin' her."

"Bad call, Griffith! Come on, Caroline. Let's go."

"At least give us a chance to win our money back, Transomb," Griffith protested.

Jack ignored him.

Caroline hadn't moved, but jumped when he barked the order a second time. She started scooping up her winnings, pausing to pay Shaun his original investment.

"Leave it," Jack snapped.

"I most certainly will not. I won it—it's mine. And I put my own money in to start."

"How much?"

"Two dollars and thirty-six cents."

He leaned in, counted out that amount, and slapped it down in front of her. "There. Now let's go."

She glanced at the others in mute appeal as she took her money, but no one would meet her eyes. She rose uncertainly, not understanding the sudden change in the air. "Well, thank you for your time, gentlemen," she said frostily. Kicking back her chair, she avoided Jack when he reached for her arm and stalked past him out of the parlor.

"Aw, don't be mad," Del called out. "We was just having fun! Thought you was, too!"

"Caroline, wait." Catching up to her, Jack tried to take her arm.

She shook him off, skirts churning. "Why? So you can make sport of me, too?"

The deck was beginning to fill with people on their way to and from breakfast, greetings of "Happy Christmas" on everyone's lips. Caroline only managed a thin, distracted smile in return. Jack didn't manage much more.

"Ain't nobody makin' sport of you, but what made you go there by yourself? It ain't safe. There's as many ruffians onboard as not."

She rounded on him so sharply, he had to back up a step to keep from running into her. "What was going on back there? I know you know, so don't pretend you don't."

"They were cheatin'—but did you hear a word I just said?"

"Yes, ruffians, I heard—but people cheat to *win,* and *I* was the one winning."

"That's what they wanted you to think. They were *letting* you win."

"That makes no sense. How do you cheat to let someone else win?"

"By simply lyin' or, more likely, controllin' what cards you were dealt."

Her eyes narrowed. "You can *do* that? Can *you* do that?"

"Yes, but can we finish this somewhere where it's warm?"

She didn't budge. "So you admit it? Gamblers—professional gamblers—cheat?"

"Nobody's luck holds day in and day out, Caroline, but the need to eat does."

"Is that what you were doing with Wendall—cheating?" The question was out before she knew it, before she knew if she really wanted the answer.

But he didn't hesitate. "If you're askin' did I cheat during the game, the answer's yes. If you're askin' did I cheat your brother, the answer's no. Truth is, he was a reckless player, throwin' good money after bad like it didn't matter. Never knew when to fold."

She saw the truth in his eyes—and felt a ridiculous sense of relief. Resuming her pace, she hugged herself against the cold that had finally registered.

When he gained her side this time, he tried dropping a companionable arm across her shoulders. Again, she shrugged him off, but with much less vehemence than before.

"Are you always this cranky in the mornin'?" he asked.

"Are you always this cheerful?"

"Why shouldn't I be? You're awful pretty for a man to look at first thing."

She shot him a sour look, but his eyes crinkled with good humor—*and he actually started making faces at her!*

Feeling her cheeks flush was the only warning she had before her own face cracked with laughter. "Stop that! You're being ridiculous!" but her black mood had fallen away.

He grinned. "Well, what do you know!"

"Oh, *hush!*" She continued walking.

With a scooting quick-step, he caught up and pried one of her hands away from her side just as they neared the noisy dining saloon. "Your hands are like ice. Let's go in and eat something."

"I'm not going anywhere with you like that. You look like an unmade bed."

"I can wash up," he offered, already tucking in his shirttail.

"Fine." She stopped, shivering in earnest now. "I'll wait here."

He rolled his eyes and snagged her arm. "God, you're stubborn! I'm not cuttin' myself with a razor trying to hurry because you're out here freezin' to death."

She allowed herself to be pulled along.

"Ah!" he said, spotting a uniformed porter coming their way. "I got a better idea," he said, catching the man's attention.

"Yessir?"

"Can we get some ham and eggs, biscuits, and a pot of coffee sent to our cabin?" He pressed a gold piece into the man's hand and gave him the cabin number.

The porter touched the brim of his short-billed hat. "Yessir! Comin' right up. And a very Merry Christmas to y'all!"

By the time Jack opened their cabin door and nudged her over the threshold, her anger had turned to self-pity. "I can't believe they were *cheating*." She sank onto the corner of the bed, pulling the sides of the quilt up around her shoulders, shawl-like. "Are you *sure?*"

He was stoking the fire as high as it would go in the little stove. "What were you holdin' when I came in, do you remember?"

"A pair, no, two . . . again."

"Of fours and aces?"

"How'd you know?"

"Thought so." Leaving the grate open for the moment, he sat down beside her. "When I came up behind him, Del was holdin' a seven-high flush."

"So?"

"A flush beats two pair—"

"I know that!"

"But I'm sure you'd've still 'won' again." He tucked the quilt edges closer under her chin. "You were bein' hustled—but not in a bad way. Del was right. They didn't mean you any harm, but there was no way they were gonna let you walk away with their money. They were feedin' you just the cards they wanted you to have. Aces and fours are

Del's trademark. In the end, you woulda started losin' just as steadily as you'd been winning at the start."

Her shoulders drooped. "And here I thought I was learning something."

"You were," he said, moving back to poke at the fire and close the grate. "Never put your faith in a winning streak. There's always somebody better'n you just waitin' to take you down. Maybe now you'll forget this foolish notion of yours."

"Forget it? Why should I? I want to go back there and give those *gentlemen* a piece of my mind—and a *real* run for their money! But you're right, I *did* learn some things."

"Okay." Pulling out his game box, he flipped open the lid and took out a deck of cards. "Let's see how much you remember."

"By all means."

He settled in the middle of the bed, legs folded and crossed.

Moving to the head of the bed, she propped pillows up against the iron rails of the headboard and sat, her feet still firmly on the floor.

He shuffled and dealt with spare economy of movement, the cards sliding softly across the blue-and-white quilt into two piles. She reached for one of them, but Jack's hand came down on hers, pinning it and the cards to the bed.

"What's your ante, Miss Cooper?"

Frowning peevishly, she snatched her hand free. "Can't we just play for practice?"

"No. If you're really gonna do this, you're gonna know from the start what it's like to have somethin' at stake. It's the real way or no way."

Caroline had seen a lot of sides to this man in the little time she'd known him, and this was the one who'd come to their door, demanding his money. His eyes were flat, humorless, and almost veiled behind his lashes.

"What do you suggest?"

"You have money."

"No. Name something else."

"What else you got?"

Opening her reticule, she pulled out her cameo and laid it on the bed between them.

He stared at it, picked it up, and rolled it through his fingers. "Is this your only one?"

"Of course—why?"

His thumb rubbed circles over the delicately carved profile. "I would've sworn I saw you drop this into the hat going around for that Bible shyster last night."

She swallowed a sudden nervousness she didn't fully understand herself.

After an unbearable moment of silence, he handed it back. "Save it. You might need it."

"Then what else is there?"

He pursed his lips in consideration. "Hairpins. Start with your hairpins."

"My—! Oh, for goodness' sake!" she exclaimed, self-consciously touching the coil of her hair. "What could you possibly want with my hairpins?"

He didn't answer.

"Fine," she allowed. "Now what's *your* wager, Mister Transomb?"

"What do you want?"

She looked at his game box, then slid him a testing glance. His expression didn't change. "Your dice," she announced, "or maybe one of those pretty mother-of-pearl thing-a-ma-bobs."

"Markers."

"Yes, those."

"As you wish." He tossed one on the bed, then pointed to her.

With both hands, she began unthreading the wiry pins from her hair. The chestnut mass tumbled down around her shoulders. "How many?" she asked, holding them out in her palm.

But he wasn't looking at the pins. He was staring at her hair, his eyes following the line of it as it waved around her face and flowed over her arms. "What? Oh. One. One at a time'll be fine." He leaned away from her in a half-recline, propping himself on an elbow as he scowled down at his cards. "Do you know the ranks of the hands?"

"From lowest to highest, it's high card, one pair, two pair, three-of-a-kind, straight, flush, full house, four-of-a-kind, a straight flush, and," she recited, huffing through her nose at this last to show she understood the incredible odds against it, "a royal flush."

The praise she expected didn't come. He merely nodded and told her to place her bet.

She looked from her cards to the meager pile of pins and decided. Only four pins left.

An hour passed. Breakfast had been delivered—with Jack again doctoring their coffees liberally from his flask—and they devoured it all with distracted relish, crumbs littering the cotton quilt, dishes and silverware left in precariously tilted stacks on the tray that shifted and clinked each time one of them moved. Neither could be bothered to call the porter back or place the tray outside the door. Finally, it was Caroline, annoyed by the rattle, who put it on the floor.

Her back ached, her eyes watered. She was tired, but didn't dare complain. Her ivory needle case, two hair ribbons and one stocking, had gone the way of all her hairpins, but she refused to back down. She stifled a yawn. "So what's your wager, sir?"

Jack had already bet his boots, hairbrush, and had moved on to bits of clothing himself. Snagging his string tie off the washstand, he tossed it on the bed between them. "Raise you."

As they played, he'd given her pointers like never try to fill an inside straight, the odds of making this hand over that one, and the benefit of counting cards—along with the advice to never get caught doing it.

The next move was up to her—fold or see his raise. Looking at the pile of intimate items between them, items that now included his collar and cuffs, she wondered where this game would end. Chewing her lip, she reluctantly added her other stocking to the pile. She needed to win them back. She felt naked beneath her skirts without them. "I'll see you."

She watched the muscle in his long, lean cheek work as he debated, then in a quick movement, he sat up straighter and whipped off his shirt.

"Oh, now *really!*" she protested, then looked at him in wide-eyed shock when he said, "I'll see that and raise you, say . . . twice as much." At her disbelieving look, he shrugged. "Surely a whole shirt's worth more than a stocking." He grinned at her expectantly. "Well? Want to see what I hold, or do you want to fold now and lose it all?"

"You won't keep it."

"The hell I won't."

"This is the most outrageous, *indecent*—and don't think I don't know what you're up to! You think I'll back down, claiming offended sensibilities or something, that I won't be able to hold my own in a man's game."

His grin only widened.

"No real game would proceed like this—it's ridiculous!"

"*Tsk-tsk*," he said, wagging his head. "No guts, no glory. And you got no idea the things that get wagered in a real game—land, livestock, gold mines . . . *wives.*"

After sixty seconds of silent, eye-to-eye warfare, she rocked forward on hands and knees to reach for her sewing box. "My thimble— it's silver. And I call *again!*"

His fingers wrapped around her wrist and stopped her. She looked up at him through a veil of hair, pulses spiking, but didn't resist when he tugged her over onto her back. "Jack—"

"Hmm?" His eyes were focused on her mouth, his head slowly dropping.

"What are you doing?" She watched his mouth move closer, curiosity drowning out everything else.

"Kissing lesson number one. Now pay attention," he whispered gruffly.

"I'd rather be standing when you teach me."

"Next time. Open your mouth—no, not now. When I kiss you."

"Why? So you can stick your tongue in it like you tried to before?"

"As a matter of fact . . ."

She made a face.

"If you give it a chance, I promise you'll like it."

"I don't see how."

"Who's the teacher here—you or me? Trust me."

"Oh, all right. So what do I do first?"

"Stop talking for one thing. Secondly, relax."

She flopped her arms around comically, and it was that—her own silliness—that told her she'd imbibed far too freely.

"Okay, we'll call that relaxed. Wait—don't move." Reaching down for one of the coffee cups, he rubbed his thumb through the sugared whiskey dregs. "Now close your eyes," he said, stroking his thumb across her bottom lip, "and taste."

"Mmm. Sweet."

"Yes, you are."

Kissing her cheeks, her temple, her jaw, under her ear, he then moved to do the same on the other side. "Breathe," he instructed quietly, slowly brushing his lips over hers. Once, twice. When he finally tilted his head, deepening the pressure of his mouth, she matched it.

Backing off, he touched the tip of his tongue to the corners of her mouth, first one, then the other. This time when his tongue stroked to penetrate, she opened and met his tongue with hers.

"You taste like whiskey," she murmured, "and coffee."

"So do you. Should I go on . . . or stop now?"

"There's more?"

He grinned. "*Lots* more."

"Then a little bit more, please."

Again, the trace of his tongue was hot, wet. The kiss deepened, and she knew a rising sense of wonder. The human body was such a wealth of sensations . . . the feel of his fingertips tracing along her ribs . . . her own hands drifting over his bare shoulders to the base of his neck . . . the quiver there just under her fingers . . . the slide of his leg across hers, and the sudden ache it produced in the cradle of her hips.

When he finally lifted his head and looked down at her, she was floating on arousal, heavy-limbed and pliant. "What are you holding?" he whispered.

She blinked, trying to focus. "What? Oh—uh—a full house, I think. Why?"

He held his cards up beside his face where she could see them. "Four kings," he said unnecessarily. Abruptly, he levered them both back to a sitting position. "You let yourself be distracted and you can't ever do that."

"*Oh!*" She scrambled to her feet in the middle of the bed, scattering cards, the pot, and rocking the mattress like a rowboat. "Is *that* what this was about? *Distracting* me?"

His gaze was cool even as he reached to steady her. "No. I just wanted to kiss you."

Mollified—but running on pure nerves by now—she stomped down to the floor, skirts swaying. "Well, *I'm* through." She turned in time to see the tilt of one eyebrow. "For today," she amended. "I'm tired and I'm going to sleep." She threw a pillow at him.

He blocked the pillow with a forearm, laughing. "How 'bout we go for an early Christmas dinner instead?"

"No, like I said, I'm tired." He just stood there, looking at her, so she scooped up the rest of their belongings—the pot—and dumped it all on the chair before throwing back the quilt.

"Where's my thimble?"

She looked at him in disbelief. "You really want my thimble? I suppose you really want to keep my stockings and hairpins as well?"

"No. Just the thimble."

"Fine." Digging it out of her box, she tossed it at his head. "Here!"

He caught it and rolled it in his palm a few times as if determining its value. To her surprise, he actually pocketed the thing. "A memento," he explained at her disbelieving look.

"*Hmph*!" Removing her shoes, she slid under the covers, pulling them up to her chin.

"Sure you don't wanna go to get somethin' to eat?"

"I'm sure." She thumped a dent in her pillow and settled down to the business of sleep, dismayed to feel the room whirl a bit behind her eyelids.

"What happened to our deal—that I'd sleep days and you'd sleep nights?"

"That was before I decided to become a gambler and keep the same hours myself."

"I see. Guess that means we sleep in the bed together then, huh?"

She frowned, but didn't open her eyes. "As long as you stay on your side of the bed . . . and don't touch me on my side."

The bed dipped and swayed as he got into his side, and the tug-of-war over the quilt began. *Whish* one way. *Whoosh* the other. Back and forth they went, both straining and grunting, determined to win.

Finally, she sat up and twisted 'round. "*This* is the middle!" She marked that line with the side of her hand, from headboard down to quilt.

"No, the middle's *here*," he said, marking his version of the half-way point a good six inches into her territory.

"Half means *half*—two equal parts! Where'd you go to school?"

"*I didn't.*" On that, he rolled himself up in the quilt, leaving her just enough—but only if she pressed right up against him.

After a great deal of huffing and puffing that got her nowhere, she surrendered, turning onto her side and pushing her back up against his, which was warm as a cookstove after a day's worth of baking. *Rather nice,* she admitted to herself—but gave him an elbow. Just because.

He elbowed her back. Just because.

And more content than either would've confessed, they both fell asleep.

Caroline woke alone in the dark. The fire in the grate had died to a cat's eye, but the room was still warm. Sounds of conversation and laughter filtered through as she came alert. Good. It wasn't as late as it felt.

Immediately, her thoughts strayed to her kissing lesson, but knew it wouldn't do to dwell upon, so she decided to simply consider it a bargain fairly met and let it go at that.

As she lay there now, it came to her that she had choices, for a change. Eat. Walk. Go back to sleep. Gamble. That last made her smile. Stretching, she savored the moment. Surely, she'd had choices before, but now she had bright, shiny new ones. She allowed herself the luxury of a huge yawn. Well, she happened to be hungry at the moment, so . . .

Buttoned boots . . . tied cloak, bonnet . . . gloves, and the cords of her reticule snugged around her wrist, its small amount of money verified once again. She would go to the gaming parlor after she ate, pick a table, and see how confident she felt about trying her luck. Her pulse quickened at the mere thought. She'd never before *planned* to risk money.

The early diners had gone by the time she entered the dining room and was led to a small table against a section of wall that boasted an elaborate sconce.

"Coffee first," she told the waiter, unfolding her napkin.

"Evenin', ma'am. Remember me?"

She looked up to see Del, hat in hand, damp hair giving evidence of a recent wash.

"I do indeed," she assured him coldly.

"Still fumin', eh?"

"I do not 'fume'—but if I did, I'd be well within my rights, don't you think?"

"We wasn't aimin' to offend, ma'am. We was just trying to amuse—teach you some, like you asked. If it means anything, you caught on real quick."

The waiter arrived with her coffee, and she turned her attention to it without offering to share her table, hoping he'd get the hint and leave.

He didn't. Instead, he pulled out the empty chair, turned it around and straddled it to face her. "You got a good memory. That's important. Most beginners are unpredictable—you were, too—but if you can hang onto that, especially in games where you gotta bluff, you might could do well for yourself."

"I shall endeavor to remember that."

"You're still mad."

"Only dogs get mad."

"How 'bout if I make it up to you? I could teach you to play *vingt-et-un*." He pronounced it *vanty-er*. "Blackjack. If you're serious in wantin' to learn, that is."

Blackjack. Simone's game. She was interested in spite of herself. "And how often would I 'win', Mister—"

"Griffith. Del Griffith," he reminded her. "And you'd only win when you beat the dealer. Fair and square."

She had no reason to believe him, yet she couldn't afford to dismiss his offer out of hand either. "This blackjack—is there much money in it?"

He smiled. "There's money in anything if you're good enough."

She kept her expression stony; but inside, her excitement was mounting. This might be her chance. She offered her hand. "Then I'd say we have a bargain, Mister Griffith."

If anything, the gaming parlor was noisier and more colorful than the night before, but its bluish haze of smoke was nearly too thick to breathe. An attendant came to take her cloak, then Del led them to one of the few empty tables along the edge of the room.

It took her a moment to spot Jack. He was in the crowded center of the room again with several serious-looking men, an island of quiet concentration in a sea of rowdiness.

As soon as she and Del were seated, he drew a deck of cards out of his vest pocket—cards so old the edges were fuzzed and frayed, falling together softly as he shuffled.

"If you can count to twenty-one, you can play blackjack," he told her. "Never take a hit over sixteen, always figure the dealer thinks the same—and he wins ties. Always take the split on aces and eights, never on tens or fives, and never on much else if the dealer's showing a nine or above, and it helps to remember what's been played."

With that, he "burned" a card—turned a card face up on the bottom of the deck—so they'd know when to start over, he said.

As he dealt, placing one card face up and one face down in front of each of them, she looked up to find Jack staring blackly at them from across the room. She smiled at him. *Take that, Mr. Distraction!* and returned her attention to Del.

Del was right. Blackjack was simple compared to Bluff, and she was itching to try a real game. So, when he finally suggested joining another table of players, she didn't hesitate.

She smiled at those seated around the table, but there were no introductions this time. Del sat beside her. *Be brave,* she reminded herself. *Be bold.*

With a small stake pulled from her reticule, she was offered the next deal. After winning on a gutsy split, she laughed from the sheer thrill of triumph.

Across the room, Jack saw her laugh. Her expression, usually so determined, had softened, her dark eyes shining. She was a mood-a-minute, and he was finding her damned irresistible. That "kissing lesson" earlier had been the most entertainment he'd had with a woman in a long time. Her unexpected touch on the back of his neck—a spot that tingled now just thinking about it—had shocked him with the pleasure of it.

As their round of Blackjack came to a close, Jack saw Del lean over and say something close to Caroline's ear.

She nodded, offered a polite smile to the others at the table, then began scooping her winnings into her reticule.

Rising together, they went their separate ways. Del headed for another table. She took her bonnet and cloak from the waiter and left the parlor.

Jack had watched all this with suspicion. He looked, but didn't see the preacher anywhere. Could Caroline be meeting him somewhere on deck? Surely she couldn't fall for someone like that, could she? And if not him, there were other risks out there as well.

Peeling back the corners of the cards, he assessed his hand without picking them up off the table. "Fold," he said.

He sent another dark glance at the door she'd gone through.

Maybe she'd just stepped out to breathe some fresh air and would be back in a few minutes to try her hand at the tables again. She was certainly determined enough—tenacious as a snapping turtle—and she'd already proven herself a quick study. Maybe having a woman with him wasn't so bad after all. A pretty face to distract, a little knowledge to give the setup some teeth. Not bad at all. In fact, he could think of some distinct and, um, very *interesting* advantages.

"Fold," he announced again and turned the deal over, waving himself out of the next hand. He felt restless. Maybe he should stretch his legs some.

The guy next to him nudged his elbow. He was a thin fellow with a timid manner, greedy eyes that were never still and a yap to match. "I know how you feel. Too rich for my blood, too. Just spent a fortnight in New Orleans—" he gave Jack a conspiratorial wink "—on *business*, if you know what I mean. Now it's back to St. Louis and the wife. Got her a nice present though. Set me back a tidy little sum. Wanna see?" Without waiting for Jack's reply, he pulled a small blue velvet box out of his pocket and opened it to reveal a pair of little golden bird cages—ear bobs—lying on a bed of the same velvet. "Nice, huh?"

When the box was shoved closer, Jack touched one of them with a fingertip. It flashed delicately in the lamplight. "Very nice," he said. Perhaps he should get Caroline a present, he mused, mildly surprised that such a notion would even enter his head. Well, it *was* Christmas, he reasoned in self-defense. And she'd mended his shirt. Christmas or no, one good turn deserved another.

He rapped his knuckles on the table. "Deal me back in."

Caroline cinched the neck of her cloak closer against the cold and moved to look over the railing.

"Why, hello there."

She turned to see Preacher in a curled brim hat and a swirling cloak. He was just about to enter the parlor, but joined her at the railing instead.

"Hello. Well, I've gone and done it. I've become a fallen woman," she announced dramatically.

"I beg your pardon?"

"I've been learning to gamble."

"Oh! Well, *that's* a relief. How do you find it?"

"Frustrating—but exciting, too. So many rules, so many details to remember."

"I'm sure you'll do just fine. Who did you find to teach you?"

"A man named Del Griffith—some of his friends before that . . . and this other man," she added with calculated casualness. "His name's Jack Transomb."

"Ah," he said with a nod.

"Do you know him?"

"I'd say I know more *of* him. Our paths cross occasionally, but we don't play in the same league, and he's got something of a reputation with women."

I know who Simone is . . . we go way back.

She changed the subject. "So tell me more about you."

"What do you want to know?"

"Whatever you care to tell me."

"Well, before we leave the subject of you and your new pursuit . . ." As if they'd done it a hundred times before, he pulled her arm through his and pulled her in step with him as he returned the way he came, lamplight and shadows pouring over their faces in quick succession as they passed lanterns bolted at intervals along the bulkhead. "I suggest you be on your guard with these teachers of yours—all of them. We gamblers can be an unsavory lot."

Another couple strolled past in the opposite direction, and they all exchanged greetings.

"How gallant of you to be concerned, and I promise I shall be very careful."

"I wish I could say I deserved your praise," he said as they skirted the wheel housing.

"You should think better of yourself."

"You're very sweet—perhaps that's what attracted my eye last night in the parlor. You were at the next table looking at someone on the other side of the room . . . and something about your expression reminded me of my wife."

Caroline's steps faltered, her arm sliding free of his. "I didn't realize you were married."

"I'm not. Not anymore. Helen died while I was away in the war. . ." He drew in a long breath. "Lost souls fighting for a lost cause and a lost way of life."

"I'm so sorry. What was she like?" she asked because she felt it was expected.

"Blonde and sweet . . . as fair as you are darkly beautiful."

Warmed by the flattering contrast, she asked, "Do you want to talk about her?"

He was quiet for a moment. "Not really—it was a long time ago. A different time and place," he added tiredly, turning his face into the night breeze as if the movement of the air could carry it all away.

"You speak as if you're ancient."

"Sometimes I feel ancient."

"You said you were a preacher once," she prompted, hoping to lighten the conversation.

"That was a long time ago as well."

"There you go again . . ."

He shook his head, amused "Well, Miss Cooper, I was born thirty-three years ago, in Booneville, Mississippi . . ."

Jack pulled his coat collar up as he left the gaming hall, but his expansive mood was almost insulation enough against the bitter cold that greeted him.

He drew deeply on the sweet cigar—just a small part of his winnings. He was on a roll, had been since they'd boarded. Lady Luck's pout over the Cooper boy had definitely been avoided. Surprisingly, bringing the sister along was the best move he'd made in a long time—and it was about to become a profitable one to boot. There were those in his business who said a woman was bad luck, but you couldn't tell it by him. His wallet and belly were full, he was smoking fine tobacco, and he had the pretty woman herself for company. Now where was the bad in that?

The sound of footsteps and the murmur of voices came toward him around the wheelhouse. It was the preacher. With Caroline. Jack stopped, a gesture of surprised greeting already half-made, but they were so deeply engrossed in each other, they passed him by without so much as a glance. He started after them, but stopped as the shadows swallowed them up again.

"Well, I'll be damned . . ." On a huff of mirthless laughter, he considered his half-smoked cigar, and flicked it overboard.

"What happened to Helen?" Caroline asked in the lull that followed the brief summary of his life, her curiosity genuinely piqued now.

"Well . . . I spent most of the war a prisoner at Camp Douglas."

She gasped. She couldn't help it.

"I see you've heard of it."

"Of *course* I've heard of it—everyone has. The Yankees talk about the horrors of Andersonville, but their Camp Douglas was just as bad."

"About a month after I was taken there, I was able to get a letter to Helen. I should never have done that. It would've been far kinder to let her think I was dead. When I got back home, her mother told me how she'd sold everything, bit by bit, piece by piece, to send me money to make my hell a little more tolerable. I never knew, of course, never received so much as a letter or a dime. The Yankee guards saw to that. They—" He swallowed hard, and when he spoke again, the bitterness that had crept into his words was gone, his tone neutral and dispassionate once more. "She gave up everything for me, including her health. I couldn't tell her not to, couldn't even thank her for it. She'd been dead three months when I got home."

"Oh, DeForest . . . I'm so sorry." She laid a hand on his arm. He covered it with his own, and they stood at the rail like that for a long moment, taking and giving silent comfort.

"Where are we? On the river, I mean," she began after a bit, hoping to steer him away from his sad reflections yet again.

He roused himself. "I heard the captain say we'd passed the mouth of the Ohio sometime last night. I'd say another full day and we should be in St. Louis."

"I'll be getting off there," she reminded him.

"I'll be disembarking as well."

"Oh? Where will you go from there?"

"Wherever the wind blows, I suppose."

It finally penetrated that her feet were freezing, and she shifted her weight. As if reading her mind, Preacher pulled her arm back through his and turned them around. "Heavens! Here I am going on and on while you're standing there shivering. We'd better get you to your cabin, sugar pie, before you catch your death."

The endearment, one she hadn't heard since childhood, sent a collage of forgotten memories tumbling through her head—dim ones of a warm calicoed bosom and shoofly pie. It made her smile. So did the kiss he placed chastely on the back of her wrist just above her glove as he delivered her to her door moments later. "Goodnight, my dear. Sleep well."

As she dug for her key, the cabin door suddenly opened. Caroline felt her jaw sag as Jack—derby slanted to the back of his head, mustache stretched over a thin, tight-lipped smile, said, "Ah—there you are, my dear. Atchison," he acknowledged.

"Transomb?"

Tongue glued to the roof of her mouth, she watched Jack take her arm as if seeing it happen to someone else. "Thanks for seeing my wife safely back to our cabin," he was saying.

Caroline heard a faint mewling sound . . . and realized it was coming from her.

"My pleasure," Preacher replied stiffly.

She felt her lips move, but no words came out. What could she possibly say?

He touched the brim of his hat. "My compliments to you both. Suh. Madam." With that, he turned and walked away as Jack pulled her over the threshold and shut the door.

Six

The room was dark and cold.

Jack set his hat on a hook and went to work throwing kindling into the stove as she dragged her cloak off and threw it, wadded, onto the bed. Her bonnet followed so swiftly it bounced off onto the floor. Fists at her temples, she dropped onto the corner of the bed.

"How *could* you embarrass me like that?"

He left the grate open and rose, brushing his hands together, then lit the candle. "I figure I was saving *you* bein' embarrassed. A *married* woman walkin' arm-in-arm with a man who ain't—" she started to interrupt, but he *tut-tutt*ed "—her *husband?* You know what people will think. *And* say." He snapped his fingers. "Oh, that's right—you don't care about that anymore, do you?

"Well, you *better* care. I know you think you ain't never gonna see the folks on this boat again, but you're wrong. Gamblers are like roaches—wherever settlers go, we follow. Every time a new town pops up, we're there. We get t'know each other's names, faces, and stories—and they follow us from then on. That'll go for you, too."

She felt a bit like a deflated bellows. "I . . . I didn't realize."

"I know you didn't. That's why I'm tellin' you."

He sat down in the little chair, tilting it back on two legs, and propped a booted foot on the edge of the bed to regard her with infuriating mildness. "I saw the two of you together earlier, y'know. You were so wrapped up with each other, you didn't even notice when you walked right by me. So . . . you betrothed yet?"

"*What?* We only just met!" She hugged herself on a shiver.

"Shoulda kept your cloak on."

She shot him a lethal look just as the flames caught, their orange glow giving the room an illusion of warmth.

He was staring at her from between the upturned wings of his coat collar like some mythical predator. "Was he pourin' his usual syrup? Better make sure you have all your fingers and toes—not to mention your purse. Religious types like him, the ones that make a big show of it, they'll rob you deaf, dumb, and blind if you ain't careful."

"I don't care what you think about him or why—but unlike *some* people I know, he's been a perfect gentleman."

"If you mean I don't know how to bilk people out of their money with trite sob stories, you got that right."

"Isn't that a bit like the pot calling the kettle black?"

He shrugged. "Either way, the kettle's still black. And just so you know, he ain't never got two dimes to rub together. What he don't pour down his throat, he loses at Faro and three-card Monte. A more feeble huckster you ain't never seen. Not what you're lookin' for, sugar."

She shot to her feet. "Who says I'm looking for anything—and why are you being so horrible?"

He answered her question with one of his own. "I gotta know—does he bow and scrape and kiss your fingers?"

As if Preacher's kiss might have left a visible imprint, she folded her arms out of sight. "Being a gentleman isn't like that at all—but since you're not one, how would you know?"

He dropped the chair down on all four legs and got to his feet. "I already know I ain't no gentleman. Never aim to be," he said, closing the short distance between them. She backed up, but he moved closer still, his voice dropping intimately as he put his hands on her waist. "Instead of holdin' a woman's hand, I wanna hold all of her . . . *close*." He pulled until their bodies met with surprising solidness and warmth despite their layers of clothing. "I won't pay her flowery compliments or spout poetry 'bout her eyes bein' like—" he faltered for a split second, "cattails."

Her pulses thrummed when his gaze dropped to her mouth.

"And I'll never *ask* to kiss her," he vowed, lowering his head until his mouth met hers.

At first, she endured, then a spark of primal need ignited, and she rose up on her toes, leaning into the kiss. Gone was indignation and anger, replaced by something much stronger. *Pleasure.* Pleasure that made her whole body flush with heat when he gathered her closer.

His hands stroked the length of her back, infusing warmth and making her acquiescent, moldable. Strong and insistent, his tongue explored, drawing her closer and closer to that edge of not caring what happened next. When he raised his head, she wasn't ready to let go.

He smiled crookedly. "Bet you're glad I ain't no gentleman now, huh?"

Reason settled back in place like sediment, gritty and heavy. There was too much smug satisfaction in his eyes for her liking, so she decided to take him down a peg or two. "You must have me confused with the little tart you had on your knee last night," she said, pushing him away. "She seemed to appreciate your coarse attentions. Why not go find her?"

The smile vanished, the smugness didn't. "Maybe I will. She'd prob'ly like the present I got more'n you anyway."

"Present?" The prick of her own interest annoyed her. "What present?"

He shoved both hands in his pockets and withdrew one. Holding it out, he turned it over and opened his hand . . . and there in his palm lay a tiny blue velvet box. "Merry Christmas." When she didn't move to take it, he thrust it closer. "Go on—take it. It won't bite."

"What is it?"

"Open it and see."

Grudgingly, she took the box and opened the lid. "*Well, I declare . . .*" she breathed.

"You like 'em?"

"They're lovely." She looked up. "Where'd you get them?"

The smug smile was back. "Man at my table tonight bought them for his wife for Christmas and was showing them around."

"How did *you* end up with them?"

"I suckered him in until he finally put those in the pot—I knew he would."

"In other words, you fleeced him."

"Guess you could say that."

She snapped the lid closed and tossed it to him. He caught it and dropped it back in his pocket as if it meant nothing either way. "So some poor woman isn't going to get her Christmas present because— why? Because you're jealous of Preacher?"

"*Jealous!* I ain't never been jealous of nobody in my whole life!"

He didn't just look indignant, he looked puzzled—as puzzled as she suddenly felt. She didn't quite understand how they'd come to this point. "Maybe kissing lessons were a bad idea," she finally muttered.

He frowned. "Yeah. Mebbe so."

Racking her brain for a change in subject, she went with the first thing that came to mind. "Do you know what you want to do when you get to California?"

He looked relieved at the drop in tension. "Not certain yet, but I have a few ideas. I just know I want my life to be different than it started out, that's all."

She tilted her head, realizing she knew almost nothing about the man. "How did it start out?"

"We can talk about that some other time. Right now, I gotta get back to the tables. I can smell the money from here, can't you?" His attempt at a smile looked more like a grimace as he picked up his box and opened the door.

"*Well, well. Look who we have here.*"

Two men—the captain, she judged by his dark uniform coat with its gold buttons, along with a beefy, surly-looking stevedore in rough work clothes—blocked the doorway.

The captain was pointing a pistol at Jack.

Caroline's heart lurched as Jack put his game box back down and slowly raised his hands. "Gentlemen," he said, backing up as they came in and shut the door.

A look of pleased surprise crossed the captain's face when he saw Caroline. "Looks like we got us two birds with one stone, Lou. Search the place," he ordered abruptly.

Lou reached down with one meaty fist and yanked the quilt off the bed. Caroline yelped.

"It's okay," Jack assured her, never taking his eyes off the captain. "Isn't it, Captain—?"

"Robins, Cap'n Robins, and this here is Lou. Best boiler man— and bare-knuckle fighter—on the river. And like you said, everything's just fine—as long as nobody makes any sudden moves." The gun never wavered.

Lou was being as destructive as possible, taking perverse pleasure in dumping their bags on the floor and kicking through their contents.

Caroline snatched at a pair of bloomers about to be ground under a heavy heel. Lou towered over her, looked her dead in the eye, and grabbed them back, ripping them in half with as much ease as she would use tearing bread. "Why, you—!"

"*Caroline. . .*" Jack cautioned without looking around. "Call him off, Robins. You've made your point. Just tell me what it is you want."

"Me, *I* don't want anything, but apparently *you* did, from one of the other passengers—a Mister Whitney? Seems you cheated him out of something mighty important to him, some female gewgaw or the like. Well, not on my boat, mister. Not on my boat."

Caroline squealed when Lou wrenched the lid off her sewing box, strewing pins and thread everywhere. She folded shaking arms. "Jack, aren't you going to do something?"

"Yeah, aren't you going to do something?" Lou taunted, still wrecking with glee. "So I can beat your face in?" His voice rumbled like the very boiler in which he supposedly worked.

Except for a jaw muscle jumping, Jack didn't move. "Is this what you're looking for?" he finally asked, reaching in his pocket only to freeze when the gun was shoved a little closer.

"No tricks," Robins warned.

"No tricks," Jack promised, withdrawing the blue velvet box. He tossed it to the captain, who pocketed it after a brief shake to satisfy himself it wasn't empty. "Now Lou and me, we're gonna need a little something, too."

Grimly, Jack withdrew his flat leather wallet and handed it over.

Robins took the wallet, flipped it open one-handed, and whistled appreciatively. "You been doing pretty good for yourself this trip, haven't you, boy? Good thing, too—this oughta just about cover the trouble of putting you two ashore.

"*Lou*," he commanded, and the destruction halted as abruptly as it began. The gun was transferred to Lou's grubby paw while Robins shoved the money into another pocket and dropped the empty wallet on the floor.

"Why don't you see our 'guests' ashore?" he suggested, then tipped his hat toward Caroline. "You have a nice night now." He patted his pocket. "I know I will."

After Robins left, Lou grinned at them and gestured carelessly with the revolver. "Get your stuff and let's go."

Caroline tensed, thinking this was the moment when Jack would lunge, but all he did was stoop to grab all the clothing he could reach, his and hers, and jam it into his bag. She snatched up her needle case, but when she went to pick up her thread bobbins, Lou kicked them away.

Numbly, she handed her nightdress to Jack, who met her eyes above the wadded pink flannel. "Just do as he says," he instructed quietly, "and we'll be fine."

As they were trundled ashore across a rickety, hastily placed gangplank, Lou prodded them at every step. "Awful cold to go swimming," he chortled when Caroline teetered.

It was too dark to see much of anything as they stumbled onto the frozen bank. From behind, Lou gave Caroline another push. Then, as if it just occurred to him that there were other kinds of fun to be had with a woman, he grabbed a handful of her cloak and hauled her back to him. "How 'bout a farewell kiss, honey? A little Christmas present."

There was a small, oily click and suddenly Jack was holding a knife, its blade a dull gleam in the darkness. "The only Christmas present you're gonna get is a new vent to breathe through, fella. You did your job, now let go of the lady and *get*."

Lou released her with a shove and a laugh. "Well, well. Now ain't this gonna be fun? I could just shoot you, o' course, but that would spoil it." Pivoting with a speed that belied his bulk, he drove a meaty fist deep into Jack's solar plexus, dropping him to his knees.

Caroline shrieked.

"Lou!" the captain bawled from the door of the wheelhouse. "Get your ass back on board! We ain't got all night!"

Ignoring the summons, Lou tried to grab her arm as she ran past, but she dodged him and fell to her knees beside Jack, trying to see into the shadows of his face. "Jack—*Jack!*"

"*Lou!* Onboard *now*, damnit!"

The *Quincy*'s smokestack belched orange sparks. The gangplank creaked, tilted, then dropped into the black water. The boat was moving.

"*Hey! Wait up, you sonofabitch!*" Lou flailed through the icy water, splashing wildly, screaming obscenities all the way.

Caroline allowed herself a sneer of satisfaction before returning her attention to Jack. He was still doubled over, still gripping the knife, still wheezing painfully.

She rubbed his back. "Are you all right?"

"Yeah . . . I always . . . talk this way."

She tried to help him to his feet, but he shook his head. "Just . . . just lemme be for a bit." He coughed. "Welcome . . . welcome to a gambler's life. Pretty . . . huh?"

She stood up, hugging herself against the bitter cold. "Well, of course not, not if you're going to let people push you around like that."

"He had a *gun*."

"This is all your fault, you know."

"*My* fault?"

"If you hadn't cheated that man out of his wife's earbobs—!" She leaned down. "You didn't even put up a fight!"

"*He had a gun!*"

Her mask of anger disintegrated, mouth wobbly. "I thought he was going to shoot you."

"Me, too."

"It scared me."

"*Me, too.*"

"Were you at least able to retrieve your game box?"

"Yeah." He lurched to his feet. "Surprised Lou missed it, but I got it in my bag. I'm sorry 'bout your sewing box. Sorry about everything, 'cause we surely are in a pickle."

"So what do we do now?" she asked, her teeth beginning to chatter.

Lapping his coat lapels together, he snatched up his bag, hissed with pain, then stomped his way into the underbrush. "We start walking, that's what."

"Wait!" she cried, startled at the abrupt exit. "Shouldn't we make a plan!"

"We already got one. We're going to St. Louis. We'll follow the river as best we can. Even if you can't see it, listen for it. As long as you can hear it, you'll know you're still on track." He was a dark shape moving quickly into a darker landscape.

The *Quincy's* lights were just disappearing around the bend, the river quieting to a black, featureless sheet of glass in the pale light of a crescent moon.

"Jack! Wait up!"

"*Catch* up! It's goddamned cold out here. If we don't keep movin', we'll freeze to death."

"Jack? I can't see you!"

"I'm right here!" he called back, voice already fading.

Grabbing her bag, she stumbled forward a couple of steps, but his crunching feet had faded as well . . . then suddenly, except for the *swish* of river current, all was quiet. "Jack?"

Silence.

"*Jack!*" Fear and anger were running apace now. "Damn you, Transomb! I swear—! I know you can still hear me, and if you leave me here, I'll hunt you down! I'll claw your eyes out and dance on your grave! I mean it, Jack—you snake, you weasel, you. . . *nincompoop!*"

She heard steps crunching again and plunged through the tall weeds in their direction, dragging her heavy skirts free of snags. "Say something so I can find you!"

"Nincompoop?" he repeated conversationally, suddenly at her elbow.

She couldn't see his face, but knew he was smirking. "You enjoyed that."

He grabbed her arm and pulled her along. "Come on," he drawled, kicking a path through the inky underbrush,

"How long do you think it'll take to get to St. Louis?"

"On foot?" He expelled a heavy breath. "'Bout a week—if we're lucky."

"Preacher said he overheard the captain tell someone that we were only about a day outside St. Louis."

"Well, hallelujah. God's man said it so it must be true."

"There's no need to be sarcastic."

"There's no need to bring him up."

"Fine."

"Fine."

Onboard the *Quincy*, Deforest Atchison staggered slightly when he felt the boat crab sideways across the current, but didn't think anything of it. He was busy looking for the extra bottle of rye he usually kept beneath the false bottom of his traveling case. He'd already looked there once, didn't find it, searched elsewhere, and now he was double-checking.

Empty.

He hurled it into a corner. "God*damn* it! I know I—wait."

Folding onto his knees, he swept both arms in an arc beneath the mattress. *Ah-ha!* His fingers closed over the flask, a twin to the one he usually carried on his person, and pulled it out with a shake to determine its contents. Almost full.

He was safe again. Safe from all the memories, the pictures, the faces and voices—screams mostly—that sharpened into brittle clarity whenever he'd gone too long without the vaporous fuzzing of a little rye. Or a lot, depending. Tonight they were bad, stirred from the bottom mud of his own private hell.

With a heavy sigh of relief, he took a long, hard pull. It burned all the way down, devil's brew that it was, and he squeezed his eyes shut at the hot pain.

Like fanning a deck of cards, the pictures flipped past his mind's eye. The naked child running through the autumn woods screaming, the soldier galloping behind, whooping, waving the torn shred of a calico dress, urging the steel-shod warhorse closer and closer. Young Pvt. Orrick—and the spray of blood when they'd cut off his foot . . . the maggot-infested wound days later . . . The screams and fevered prayers . . . The sunken graves . . .

Another long swallow, another grimace, and the pictures came slower, sounds more muffled—but these weren't the real ones now.

He'd never really seen these. These were ones supplied by his mother-in-law, Rosalie, painted vignette-fashion in the stark colors of Helen's last days—the gauntness of hunger, of licking gelatin from boiled leather, her blonde hair thin and dirty, the sores and hollow-eyed death. She'd called his name for days, he'd been told. When, out of pity, Rosalie finally lied to her daughter, telling her he was there at her side, Helen's small face had contorted with tears and the single question *why*. It was her last word.

All this had been told to him by a woman who sat and rocked, vacant-eyed, all day every day on the porch of the tool shed of their family home. It was the only structure the Yankees hadn't burned to the ground. He'd sat at her feet each afternoon for weeks, hearing it all little by little, lead weight by lead weight, until he'd finally curled into a ball like a child, weeping, begging not to hear any more.

He'd left that day and never returned, but then he hadn't needed to—he'd brought it all with him.

Simone Jules leaned closer to her mirror, smoothing rosewater and lanolin into the skin at the corners of her mouth, testing the firmness of her thirty-six-year-old flesh. *So*, she mused. *Jack was onboard. And traveling with a younger woman.* She squinted and relaxed, checking her reflection for left-behind lines. She would've given half her night's winnings, maybe more, to have had him come upon her and the girl talking. Just to see the look on his face—

The knock on her door startled her. "Yes?"

"It's me, Miss Jules. It's Harold Stokes."

"Jesus," she muttered, recorking the cream jar and tossing it back into her traveling bag. "Coming, *cherie*," she called in sweet contrast. She opened the door a coquettish crack. "You are early, *non?*"

His throaty reply was lost beneath the tinkling silver of her laugh.

Jack couldn't imagine how Caroline could sleep. He and the other stage passengers, two women and three men, were swaying from side to side over a road that was nothing more than a series of rocks and ruts, with an occasional hairpin turn thrown in just to keep the driver honest.

Chivalry had automatically allowed the three women to take the one bench, thereby forcing all four men to squeeze together on the opposite side. The compartment was oppressively close, and the stew offered back at the roadhouse had contained an unfortunate amount of onions.

Outside, the late afternoon sun slanted down on their baggage-laden roof, more light than heat. The window shade by Caroline's head was missing its tie-down, and with every bump it flapped open to let in a stab of cold air—which sank immediately to the floor to chill their feet without doing anything to refresh the close quarters.

Steel rocker springs whined as they hit another bump and Jack shifted on the hard bench. Caroline slept on, her head pillowed on the cloak she'd rolled up and wedged into a corner behind the window. The violet hue beneath her lashes told him how needful she was of the rest.

It had been a rough five days. Occasionally, they'd been able to hitch a ride in the back of a farmer's wagon, sharing space with livestock and feed bags, but mostly they had only their feet to rely on.

Once they'd managed to steal a ride in an empty boxcar—until a watchman discovered them. Caroline's eyes were as big as the man's buttons when he told them to jump off, that he wouldn't stop the train for a pair of rail bums like them. They were already going slow enough, he said. Before fear could take hold, Jack wrapped his arms around her and jumped, and they rolled down the embankment together. Their bags had been tossed after them, spilling their contents over the frosted ground.

He'd never forget the sight of her as she struggled to her feet, dead grass sticking out of her hair, shrieking a mixture of obscenities and dismay as she raced after their wind-strewn clothing. She didn't speak to him for a whole day after that.

He knew it was perverse, but something about her temper amused him. It was like watching Chinese fireworks. That night on the riverbank, he'd come closer to abandoning her than she'd ever know. His brain had been issuing orders like a hot-tempered drill sergeant telling him to *walk away!* And he was—just as fast as the brush would allow. Then suddenly she started blistering the air behind him with curses, and the huff of his own laughter caught him by surprise. That's when he knew he couldn't leave her behind.

Meals had been sporadic, whatever they could beg, borrow, or steal, and at night they'd slept burrowed in hay lofts or under corn cribs. While Robins had gotten the bulk of their money, he hadn't gotten the few emergency dollars Jack always kept in his boot—money he vowed to save until he could get someplace to double it in a few well-planned wagers. But then Caroline started visibly losing weight, so he'd used some of it for today's passage.

He eyed the reticule strap still firmly knotted around her too-thin wrist. They'd get to that soon enough.

For him, the hard walking had been good. It numbed the restlessness that had gripped him in recent months. There was somewhere—his eyes searched for and found a glimpse of the trees and sky beyond the coach window—somewhere *out there* he had to get to, a place he had to find or make for himself. California was part of it, but instinct told him this woman was somehow a part of it, too. The thought terrified him.

Another spine-jarring bump, another flap of the shade, and she shivered in her sleep. Shrugging out of his jacket, he leaned over to tuck it around her shoulders.

The woman sitting next to her gave him a look of disdain. *Damned biddy,* he thought, and glanced at her younger companion. *Pity, too.* If that one wasn't so starched, she'd be pretty.

Back at the roadhouse, he'd seen the two of them size him up, gazes slide to Caroline, then sidle away when it became obvious she was traveling with him. Caroline had been too tired to notice, but he hadn't.

The stage wheels hit a rock and they shuddered to one side before lurching on. Beside him, one of the men's teeth clicked together, and Jack winced in sympathy. Caroline stirred, frowned, then sank back into exhausted sleep. Her carpetbag, balanced on her knees, began to slip off. He reached to put it on the floor at her feet.

"Why don't you keep your hands to yourself?" snapped the older woman. "There are decent folk present."

They'd been riding for nearly two hours, and those were the first words spoken.

"Certainly, ma'am. Next time I'll just let the bag fall on your toes."

"Sir!" admonished the dapper fellow on his left, spectacles glittering.

Jack gave him the same stony expression he reserved for kibitzers who hovered too close during a game. "You weren't dealt into this hand, so stay out of it."

"Now see here—!"

"Gentlemen, gentlemen." It was the pudgy little dodger in the corner opposite Caroline. He held a hinged leather case on his lap. "The name's Strohecker. Albert Strohecker. Means 'straw cutter.' Hail from Ohio." He put out a plump hand.

There was a brief pause before all the men shook hands and introduced themselves.

"I'm Blair," said the dapper one. "Doctor Blair."

Strohecker nodded. "Good t'meet ya, doc. The west can always use another sawbones."

The doctor looked none too pleased with the rough moniker.

"Transomb. Jack Transomb . . . speculator."

Strohecker's friendly gaze shuttered slightly. "How do you do? And who might you be, sir?" he asked, turning to the fourth man in the far corner.

"Robert August. Bob." He paused and shrugged. "Farmer."

"Ah, staple of the American supper table. Pleased to meet you ladies as well," Strohecker added, briefly lifting the round bowler from his head.

The prim pair nodded. Caroline slept on.

"Tedium is our enemy," he continued. "Perhaps a diversion, a little amusement mightn't be amiss." Flipping open his case, he drew out three playing cards, crimped slightly lengthwise—a queen and two sevens—and placed them across the top of his case, face down. "What we have here is an example of the old question: Which is quicker, the hand or the eye? Some say the hand." He shuffled the cards in and out of several positions. "Some say the eye. But here's the true test . . . follow it, follow it," he chanted, stirring the cards around. "Where did the queen go? Is she here? Is she there? Where's the queen? Anyone care to make a guess?"

The farmer snorted. "That's easy. In the middle."

Strohecker lifted the middle card. "So she is. Shall we try again?"

This time it was the doctor who took a stab. "On the left."

"Well, I'll be . . . Right again." Strohecker appeared nervous, and as the coach slid into a curve, his cards went flying. "Sorry," he muttered, picking them up. "Now, once more. In fact," he added, shuffling the cards around for the third time, "why not make it a little more interesting with, say, a small wager? Who thinks they know where the queen reigns on this fine winter day? You sir? How 'bout you, ma'am?" he prompted at the older woman's interest.

She sank back against the seat with a sniff. "I don't approve of gambling. It's sinful."

His shrug said *each to his own* as he turned to the doctor. "How about you, sir?"

"Two bits says the queen's in the middle there," he said, extending his money with a manicured hand.

There was a general murmur of sympathy when a seven was turned up. He lost twice more before deciding his luck had changed for the worse. "That's enough for me," he grumbled.

By now, Caroline was coming around, roused more by the conversation than the rough ride. She sat up, shoulders narrowed in a confined stretch.

Strohecker's interest swung immediately. "Well, hello there, young lady. Glad to see you back from the arms of Morpheus. Can I interest you in a game of chance?"

She declined with an irritable frown, and Jack congratulated her judgment with a wink.

"When we get to Festus," Strohecker told them all, "I'm going to open a lottery for the benefit of the many fine charities throughout the great state of Missouri." He opened his case again and withdrew a handful of colorful tickets and flyers. "Perhaps some of you would care to take a look. One dollar each, six for five dollars, or for the measly sum of sixteen dollars, one may purchase twenty chances to win one of seventy thousand prizes—all while gaining the satisfaction of helping those less fortunate than yourselves."

Jack examined the small rectangle of blue paper he was handed, its many scrolls and seals proclaiming officialdom. It looked better than some he'd seen, but it was far from *The Great Legal Drawings* the Lottery King, James Pattee, had run a few years back.

"Anyone interested?"

"What'll I win?" asked the farmer.

"There are seventy thousand prizes in all, with the grand prize being fifty thousand dollars," was the reply that made the ladies gasp.

The farmer seemed impressed and dug deep in his denim overalls for a silver dollar.

"You won't regret it, sir, and good luck to you."

The doctor bought one as well. Jack declined.

"You say this is for charity?" It was the older woman, her church face brought to life.

"Yes, ma'am. Hospitals, libraries, schools, churches—we need them and they need us."

"May I?" She held out a gray-gloved hand, examining the ticket he handed her with nearsighted intensity in the gathering dusk. "One dollar, you say?"

"A small price, wouldn't you agree?"

"Oh, I would, I would indeed . . . and how many tickets did you say you'd be selling?"

"Er . . . no more than seventy five thousand. Excellent odds, if I do say so myself."

Jack bit his tongue watching the woman scrape to the bottom of her reticule and hand over a silver dollar. The number of people who gambled while telling others—and themselves—that they didn't approve of the practice never ceased to amaze him.

Strohecker thanked her, then looked expectantly at her companion who glanced uncertainly at the older woman shaking her head.

Caroline looked out the window and said, "I think we're here," just as the driver bawled "Fe-e-e-ss—*tus!*"

After a last, careening curve and a rough application of the brake, they slid to a halt and were finally, mercifully still. For a moment, they all just stared at one another in a kind of dumb weariness, then started climbing out, pausing in the doorway only long enough to be thoroughly unimpressed with the township of Festus. The driver had already unstrapped the luggage and was tossing down trunks and bags without prejudice to their possible contents.

With Jack's help, Caroline climbed stiffly to the ground.

The sun had set, and darkness was quickly obscuring a thorough view of the town. There was little to see, however—just two streets that crossed at right angles. Utilitarian structures thrown up with obvious haste made no pretense toward pleasing the eye. Some lacked windows, many lacked paint. There were few trees, and with such a blank expanse of sky from horizon to horizon, there was little to stop the bitter wind that tore down the street, carrying with it the sting of snow. It swept under skirts and down collars as they all hurried toward the two-story, raw wood structure that seemed to lean slightly. *Big Swede's Saloon-Hotel-Restaurant*, read the sign over the doorway.

Heat, light, voices, the smell of wet wool, whiskey and unwashed bodies, each a distinct and separate impression, hit the passengers all at once, subduing them. The place was papered in a tiny rosebud print more suited to a bedroom than a public house. A Christmas tree—a tall, spindly spruce stuck in a cut-down barrel—stood in the back corner wearing simple red ribbon bows as ornaments.

Quietly, by ones and twos, the passengers drifted in to take seats at the small, mismatched tables and chairs or fill in along the bar— rough planks set across barrels.

Jack took a table near the stove for himself and Caroline, then went to the bar to get food.

"All they have is rabbit stew," he said, returning.

"Fine." It could've been shoe leather for all she cared.

He nodded to the proprietor, Big Swede himself, by the look of him—slitted blue eyes and a walrus mustache above two yards of white canvas apron. "Make that two," Jack told him, and sat down. "Still tired?" he asked her.

"In spite of all the sleep? Yes. You?"

He nodded, already assessing those at the bar.

"Looking for your next mark?"

"For our ticket out of here. We're still ten dollars and twenty miles short of St. Louis."

"Another day's ride?"

"Only a couple of hours by stage."

The stew came and Caroline's thoughts of shoe leather returned. Oh well, she told herself as she blew on a spoonful of the brown grease, at least it was hot.

Hunched over their brown stoneware bowls, they ate in silence. Jack finished first, dropped his spoon back in his bowl, and scooted back his chair. "I'll get us a room."

At the bar, he handed Big Swede the bowl and paid for their food. "I need a room."

"You not gonna stay up fer de celebration?"

"What celebration?"

"It's Noo Year's Eef! Der's gonna be fireworks and lots of *la-la-la-la-laaaaaa!*" He waved a beer mug with the vigor of a band leader. "You come, ya? You and de missus."

Caroline heard the word and waited for Jack to react. He didn't.

"No thanks. We just want a room."

"Dat's all der be. Everboty sleep in von rhoom. Got von bed lef'. Fife dollar."

The back of Jack's neck turned red. "Five dollars! For one bed? In a common room?"

"Dat's it. Take it or leaf it." Big Swede leaned over the bar, walrus mustache twitching, as a dark stream of tobacco juice arrowed for the bucket by Jack's feet.

Jack moved out of range and glanced back at her. She shrugged. She knew if he'd been by himself, he'd've slept in the nearest barn again.

"Is there any other place in town to stay?"

The Swede grinned, showing large yellow teeth. "Nawp. Jus' here."

"Fine. We'll take it."

Fine was not the word that came to Caroline's mind as they climbed the ladder to the second floor. Long and narrow, sloping uphill toward the one empty bed—or cot, to be more accurate—the space was crowded with at least ten other adults and half that many children, including a nursing infant that cried in colicky distress in between pulls at its mother's breast. There was one lamp, sitting on the floor in the middle of the room, casting its yellow glow upward, streaking the rafters with shadows.

Jack nudged her in the back, and they began threading their way through the human maze. They stepped over people's trunks and bags, sometimes over the people themselves, finally reaching the one empty cot crammed under the eaves—where, to settle in, they had to maneuver like a pair of hunchbacks.

Jack, she noticed, was getting irritable, and the more he grumbled, the more withdrawn she became, uncomfortably aware of all the others in the room. Without even removing their boots, they tried to find a way to fit on the cot together.

Her petticoats, although not large or stiff by fashion's standards, crowded them, rustling and crunching, their bulk making the coarse wool blanket slip first off one side, then the other.

"I'm sorry!" she hissed when his explosive sighs reached the danger point. "I don't know what I can do about it!"

Sitting up, he swung around and dropped his feet back to the floor. "Well, I do. Get up."

"What?"

"Stand up."

Warily, she did as she was bid.

Taking her by the hips, he pulled her between his knees.

"What're you—*Jack!*"

"Be still. No one can see." Reaching up under her skirt without so much as a by-your-leave, he found the ribbon tie of her petticoat and gave it an expert yank that dropped the garment down around her knees. "Now step out of that thing and lay down—on your side."

"That was humiliating!" she hissed.

"You'll get over it."

Inch by inch, they adjusted to the narrow space, nestling spoonlike on their sides, their backs to the room, eking out the most comfortable position they could find. Necessarily, his arm curved around her ribs, but his thumb rested against the sensitive underside of her breast. She shifted away and closed her eyes.

Someone cleared his throat, coughed, cleared it again. There was the high-pitched murmur of a child's voice, a mother's admonishing whisper. In the bed directly behind theirs, a man snored raucously.

They were both still for a long moment, and her mind drifted back across the last few days. They'd been hard ones, and they'd had their squabbles, but she'd found strength from sharing the hardships.

Again an adjustment on the cot . . . and again his hand rested on her breast, but this time she didn't move away, snared by the curiosity his touch always stirred. He caressed her, almost absently at first, then with obvious purpose. Fighting the urge to push his hand away, she forced herself to acquiesce, finding she liked his gentle touch—it made her feel all liquidy inside.

He grew bolder. Individually, his fingers traced her shape, collectively they molded and weighed, making her believe that every nerve in her body ended in the nipple he alternately tugged and rolled between his thumb and finger. He continued until she squirmed, restless with agitated pleasure, her breathing regulated by his touch.

Fingers splayed, he stroked down over her belly, pressing her into the curve of his body, grinding himself against her backside. His warm breath was moist against her ear, and she was horribly, scintillatingly aware of the other people in the room. Finally, unable to stand it any longer, she twisted around. He rose on an elbow to accommodate her.

It was the first time she'd opened her eyes since they'd lain down. The lamp was out, and she was surprised to find it so dark she couldn't see a thing . . . yet Jack's lips unerringly found hers despite the inky blackness. They were soft and warm, his tongue exploring slowly . . . making her follow hungrily at his slightest retreat.

She felt the shape of his smile; but, past the point of prideful games, took it only as a sign of pleasure and smiled back. He kissed her then with force of feeling, enough to turn her bones—her previously solid bones—into hot gelatin.

She must've made some sound for he breathed *shhh* against her lips, his hand sliding up to the buttons at the neck of her dress.

Suddenly, the sounds of snoring, of murmured voices, a baby's cry, and the smell of wet wool and bodies burst in on her pleasure-fogged brain like a bubble popping, and she clutched at his hand, stilling it. "No—please!" she whispered.

Unexpectedly, he tucked her head against his chest. She could hear his thudding heartbeat as his thumb brushed her hair away and he pressed his lips to her forehead. "You're right," he breathed against her skin. "This isn't the time or place. But somewhere else—soon."

With that, he settled back, sliding his shoulder under her head and hugging her to him. "Go to sleep," he instructed softly.

With her nose in the hollow of his throat, she nodded . . . but was nowhere near sleep.

Soon. Both threat and promise, a flash of Fox with the word *whore* on his lips.

Jack's arm tightened briefly, and he dropped an absent kiss on her hair. "S'all right."

She certainly hoped so, for she hardly recognized herself these days. Hard to believe so much had changed in so little time.

Staring into the darkness, she listened to the sounds all around her, the sounds of strangers in a strange place. Catching the whiff of a soiled diaper, she knew a moment of disorientation. Surely she was meant for better things than this.

Confused and needing comfort, she closed her eyes and curved her fingers into the button placket of Jack's shirt. They'd been together less than a fortnight, but already it seemed a lifetime.

The evenness of Jack's breathing told her he was asleep, but it wasn't until well after the staccato pop of firecrackers in the street, the muffled sound of a brawl, and several increasingly maudlin and off-key renditions of *Auld Lang Syne* downstairs that she was finally able to sleep, her head still cradled on Jack's shoulder.

"Patience," he growled. They were both stiff, irritable and hungry.

"But I want to get out of here!" she whispered. It was early, and they were the first up.

"We *will*." He threw all their travel-and-sleep mussed clothing into his own bag, both having changed under the blanket. "But first, I have to get enough money together."

"I don't want to sit in that smelly saloon and watch you risk what money we have left."

He latched his bag. "Get used to it. It's what gamblers do."

"Let's split it," she suggested. "We'll both play and see who wins the most."

He snorted. "You wouldn't last five minutes. This is a small-stakes town, Caroline. There's not enough take for two players—even if you were good enough, which you're not."

Not having a valid argument for that, she followed him as quietly as possible past the other sleepers and down the ladder.

The smell of smoke and stale beer mixed with burnt coffee assaulted her nose and made her empty stomach lurch. The fire in the stove had burned out and the air was so cold they could see their breath. Several men, apparently left over from the night's festivities, sat hunched in their seats, holding their heads; or, in a few extreme cases, lying flat out on the floor, their snores disturbing the otherwise silent room. The Christmas tree, stripped of some of its bows, leaned drunkenly.

Swede was there, moving slowly even for a man of his bulk, picking up empty glasses and haphazardly wiping the tables free of crumbs and liquor spills.

Jack settled at the cleanest one and began a monotonous, repetitive shuffle of his cards, glancing around now and then with one eyebrow raised in mute invitation. He'd placed some money in front of him as bait.

Morning light brightened one smoke-clouded window, and Caroline went over to clear a spot with her thumb. There was a crust of snow on the ground and the hazy morning sun had turned the sky a milky yellow. So, this is what 1873 looks like, she mused. God willing, it would be better than '72 . . . and it could do that without even trying.

"Der's bread and coffee ofer der at de end of de bar—free for de firs' hour," Swede rumbled to the room at large as he built a new fire in the stove. "Hep yousefs."

Gratefully, Caroline did just that, cradling the blue enamelware mug for its warmth.

Swede repeated his offer to Jack, who declined, then suggested a game of blackjack. "Jus 'til de customers come, ya?"

"Ya," Jack agreed lazily, nudging out a chair with the toe of his boot.

Swede was a loud player, slapping down his cards, complaining or crowing in a booming voice that attracted attention from those outside, who began drifting in by ones and twos. Finally, he shoved to his feet. "Dat's it fer me—but I gif you 'nother viskey. Free. On de house."

Four men immediately took his place, and he winked at Jack as he walked away, his not-so-subtle mission accomplished.

Seated on a stool by the window where she could look outside, Caroline watched the men exchange minimal greetings, then settle in for some earnest play.

The change in Jack was immediate—the sudden economy of movement and speech, the focus, the sharpened gaze disguised by a languid slouch. Right before her eyes, he'd turned into the professional gambler once again. *Here we go*, she thought.

As the morning wore on, players came and went, tagging off to go and relieve themselves or grab a bite and wet their whistles at the bar. But Jack remained as he was, rarely even tasting the shot of whiskey that had been sitting at his elbow for hours.

The first coach of the day arrived at noon, disgorging its passengers in much the same shape as the evening before. Feeling a wave of pity for the poor cramped souls, Caroline watched them troop wearily into the saloon for the same bowls of greasy rabbit stew and a cheery "Hoppy Nu Year!" from Swede. But being only midday, these people still had some life left in them and they wanted more than just a bed. After a little food and drink, they were ready for entertainment. Some wanted to gamble, some wanted to do a little horse trading. By afternoon, the saloon was filled with people, and Jack's table had a steady rotation of players.

Patience, he'd said. He was the word personified, she decided, shifting irritably on the hard stool. No matter how the game was going—and she couldn't judge by him, only by the others who moaned and groaned, flopping back in their chairs or shifting nervously in their seats—he remained as cool and still as melting snow.

He looked up once and caught her watching him. She smiled, but he returned his attention to the game without so much as a blink. She found herself studying his mouth, feeling a secret thrill, a clench not unlike the one his touch had caused last night. Watching his hands, her mouth went dry. She moistened her lips with the tip of her tongue, and she shifted her weight on the stool again. Her curiosity about the intimacies between a man and woman, mostly dormant until he'd come along, was running rampant. What if there hadn't been people around last night? What if they'd had a room of their own again? She swallowed hard. Despite her vow to remain aloof, she felt dangerously out of control, as if all he had to do was crook a finger and she'd follow. She'd have to be careful. On guard. Not against him so much as herself. She was, she realized, her own worst enemy where he was concerned.

Whore, Fox said from her memory. She looked away.

Jack shifted in his chair, easing the knot of tension between his shoulder blades. He could feel the weight of Caroline's dark-eyed gaze, and he'd been aware of her every move, however slight, since they'd awakened. He should have found a way, a place to be with her last night. If he had, maybe he wouldn't be sitting there now as dry-mouthed as a boy with wet dreams and a fatal crush.

His senses were in full revolt. Instead of the lip of his whiskey glass, he felt her lips, equally smooth, the taste *her* taste. Instead of the slick-backed cards he held in his hand, his fingers felt the shape and weight of her breast. Instead of his own clothing, he felt the warm press of her body. It left him unsatisfied and restless, making concentration difficult. She was ready—he allowed himself a slight brandish as he dropped his winning hand over the pot that now belonged to him—and so was he. More than ready. *Take her tonight and get it over with*, he decided, raking in the pot. Maybe then he could get back to business—his business.

Caroline shifted on the hard stool once again, growing antsy. Jack had been playing for hours, and while patience was a virtue, his stack of money hadn't grown much in the last hour.

She took note of the other players—a skinny man in his twenties with a protruding Adam's apple and a stained cowboy hat; a small, elderly gentleman in a dark pinstripe suit, his dangling watch fob catching the light from the window every so often. All she could see of the man opposite Jack, his back to her, was a sheepskin coat and a swirling bald spot.

And his cards, she realized with a start.

He alternately closed and fanned them, constantly rearranging them. *Nervous*, she concluded. Watching his thoughts in action was an interesting exercise . . . and a satisfying one as she watched Jack rake in three pots in a row. *At last*, she thought, *progress!*

Then, astonishingly, he lost the next two. Caroline felt downright faint.

The next deal began and, as Sheepskin picked up his cards and fanned them open, Caroline's eyes grew round. A seven of clubs, ten of clubs, four—nine! Six! *All clubs!* His shoulders twitched and he sat up straighter as he realized what he held. *A ten-high flush!*

Chewing her lip, she watched every play—especially Jack's. He'd started to yawn and rub his eyes. *Wake up, Jack! Pay attention!* When he raised instead of called in what should have been the final round of play, she couldn't believe it. What was he thinking? The man hadn't taken any cards! Even a novice like herself could read the signs when a player stayed pat like that!

Alarmed, she did the only thing she could think of—she cleared her throat. He didn't notice. She cleared it again, louder . . . and again. Finally, he glanced up and she tried signaling with her eyes, frowning pointedly at the man in the sheepskin coat. He merely scowled and hunched forward in his seat, ignoring her.

As the betting continued around the table, Caroline couldn't stand it any longer, she couldn't stand the thought of Jack losing it all and them being stuck there another night and another day while he won it back—*if* he won it back. Dropping off the stool, she coughed like someone choking on a chicken bone.

The whole room looked up.

Catching something in Jack's expression, Sheepskin twisted around. "*Hey!* What's going on here? Is she with you? Who's that woman belong to?" he asked the room at large.

Everyone froze.

"I am not a cow, suh. I do not 'belong' to anyone," she retorted.

Then everyone started talking at once, chair legs screeching, people jumping to their feet as the room erupted in heated argument.

"Hey—*you* der!" Big Swede's voice suddenly cut across the commotion.

She was surprised to find herself the target of a pointing, sausage-like finger. "Me?"

"Ya, *you!*" He came over and tugged her by the arm. "You vash de glasses, ya?" He indicated a tubful of heavy, molded glassware behind the bar.

"I most certainly will not!"

"De men are hafin' fun. It's goot fer business—you doan spoil."

Behind her, she heard Jack concede the hand and the arguments sink to a simmer. Despite her protest that she had no intention of washing dishes in a public establishment, Swede pushed her behind the bar just as Jack reached it. He looked mad as a hornet and she was suddenly grateful for the planking that separated them.

He leaned toward her with a smile for everyone else's benefit and whispered fiercely, "If you ever do that again—and I don't get shot as a result—I will wrap my hands around that pretty little neck of yours and strangle you. Is that clear?"

"But he—"

His hand shot out and he yanked her around the end of the bar by her wrist, his whisper dropping to a hot hiss. "I *know* what he had! Have a little faith, will you?"

Before she could frame a reply, Swede gripped her shoulders and drew her back to his side of the bar. "You doan worry," he told Jack. "I keep her busy. She be vashing de glasses."

Jack's hard gaze swung and he considered the larger man squarely for a second, then lifted his hat in a brisk salute. "Thank you, Swede. You're a real gentleman." With that, he shoved himself upright, and stalked out the back door—presumably to use the privy.

"Vash!" Swede rumbled, towering over her.

Defiantly, she lifted her chin even as she started rolling up her sleeves. As she brushed up a lather from the swaybacked cake of lye soap and warmed the water from the teakettle, he leaned over. In what passed as a whisper, he grunted, "You do goot job, I pay you von silver dollar, eh?"

"Two," she countered.

His frown was ferocious, his fleshy lips curling around an indignant *"Harumph!"*

Stubbornly, they glared at one another.

"Ya—two," he finally conceded.

Primly, she nodded and began washing.

When Jack returned a few moments later, stamping snow off his boots, he returned to the game without so much as a glance in her direction. She shot him a glare—*bully!*—but was relieved when he was dealt back into the game without comment.

The next few hours went by in relative silence. After washing the glassware, she started on the rest of the dishes, wiped tables, and even found herself relaying orders for rabbit stew and whiskey. To her own surprise, she welcomed the work. It was something to keep her hands busy, her attention diverted from the game that would determine her immediate fate.

She was helping Swede put the clean glasses back into the stack of open packing crates he used for display shelves when she heard the scrape of chairs.

"You done?" Jack asked, coming up behind her and leaning his elbows on the bar.

"Almost." She wiped her hands on the apron Swede had loaned her and assessed his mood through long wisps of fallen hair. He seemed relaxed, affable once more. "Swede's paying me two dollars. In silver."

Swede winked at her as he hefted a case of whiskey bottles onto the bar. "Ya. She work goot. I pay."

"Well?" she prompted quietly as soon as Swede turned away. "How much did you win?"

His blue eyes held a gleam as he tapped his breast pocket. "Take off that apron, Miss Cooper, and comb your hair. We're hitching a coach ride to St. Louis."

Seven

The last stage came through at three o'clock, and they were the only ones occupying the varnished wood interior this time. Outside, the view quickly became a monotony of trees, rocks, and road, and Caroline let the shade drop without regret. It was cold enough to see their breath, but what was left of the afternoon sunlight painted the inside of the coach a warm gold.

Looking back over the hardships of the last week or so, she was aware of a new level of confidence. Maybe it was just a case of another challenge met and conquered, but whatever it was, she wasn't nearly as nervous about California now as when they'd first started out.

As soon as they were in St. Louis—before she forgot everything she'd learned—she'd find a place where she could practice her new skills. She thought again about washing dishes under Big Swede's watchful eye, and wondered if Simone had ever had to endure such treatment. Probably, she decided. It was still a man's world.

She looked over at Jack. He sat at a slant—legs stretched to one side—resting on an elbow. Eyes closed, he seemed half asleep, swaying easily with the motion of the coach.

"That one game back there," she began. He didn't open his eyes, but his facial expression changed enough that she knew he was listening. "The man who had all the diamonds—you said you knew what he had, what he was holding. How?"

"Experience."

"No, somehow you dealt him those cards on purpose—you said it could be done."

His eyes cracked open. "What if I did?"

"Will you teach me how to do that?"

He closed them again. "No."

"You say no to everything I ask."

"Perhaps you ain't askin' the right questions." The barest slit of a mischief-lit blue eye regarded her.

She rolled her own eyes and looked away. "Be serious."

"I am."

"So you'll teach me?"

"No."

"See?"

He shifted to sit upright, amusement lurking about his mouth. "You're such a child."

"I am not."

"Are, too."

"Am not," she laughed. Something here, too, had changed. They'd settled into a kind of friendship. *Partners.* A week ago, she would've scoffed at such a notion, but there it was. She and Jack were partners. Caroline Cooper, of the Johnson County Coopers, and Jack Transomb, of—of . . .

"Jack?"

Arms folded across his chest, his eyes were closed once again. "Hmm?"

"Where do you come from?"

Eyes still closed, his brow furrowed. "Mississippi, like you."

"But whereabouts in Mississippi?"

The furrows remained. "Natchez."

Ah! Caroline Cooper, of the Johnson County Coopers, and Jack Transomb, *of Natchez*, were partners. Didn't exactly have a ring to it, but it would do. "So tell me about your folks."

"I told you. I don't have folks."

"Everybody has some sort of folks—even if they're not blood."

He leaned forward on a sigh and braced himself on the heels of his hands. "I come from Natchez—from its cotton docks, its saloons, its stables. I didn't have a mother for long—if that's even who she was—and I never knew my father. I grew up in a brothel, and except for my letters, how to write my name and do sums, what I learned from them ladies prob'ly ain't what a kid should know. I'm a bastard, born on the wrong side of the blanket—is that what you want to hear? I am who I am—*what* I am—because of what I made of myself. *Me*. I weren't raised to be this or that, I simply grow'd up and made a livin' for myself best way I knew how."

She folded her hands in her lap and looked away, wishing she'd left the window shade up so she could at least pretend to be looking at something. "My apologies. I didn't mean to pry."

"An' I didn't mean to bite your head off. Just not somethin' a grow'd man likes to talk about, that's all."

"It's fine."

He swore under his breath. "No, it's not and I'm . . . I'm *sorry*." Clearly, expressing regrets was new to him.

"All right. Since I prefer friendship to fighting, I forgive you."

"Friendship, eh? Is that what we are now—friends? Haven't had many of those."

"Me, either, come to think of it. Not since I was little. Too busy making ends meet."

He tugged on his cuffs. "So, are you disgusted?"

She looked at him blankly. "Disgusted?"

His head came up and he looked straight at her. "By *me*—where I come from."

"No, of course not. If that's what you came from, I'd say you've done well for yourself."

He snorted and slouched further back, but the scowl on his face was less fierce now.

Travel noises suddenly punctured her awareness—the beat of horse hooves, the cymbal of harness, a protesting squeak of wooden parts in constant conflict, gravel chattering beneath the wheels. The air, too, had changed—heavy now with the smell of snow and a coating of river dankness. It would be dark soon, and gold light had turned to pink.

She studied him, wishing she could draw him back out. She liked the idea of their being friends. It felt . . . dependable—and Lord knew few people in her life had ever been *that*.

Wendall. The stab came—and went, by sheer force of will.

Lacing her fingers together, she stretched delicately. "How much did you win back there?"

The arch of one eyebrow was the only response she received.

"Well, if you won't tell me that, at least tell me you won enough for a steak dinner and a real bed when we get to St. Louis."

He held up fingers. "*Two* steak dinners. No more greasy stew. Or squalling babies."

Her own words rushed back on her. *Beds*—plural! *I should've said beds!* She should say it now, correct any misunderstanding, stress that she expected separate rooms, *demand* separate rooms. But the moment was gone . . . and receding swiftly with each passing second. Saying it now would only call *more* attention to it, not less. *Ooohhh!*

"What is it?"

"What is what?"

"You groaned."

"No, I didn't."

"Yeah, you did. Just now."

Maybe I'm worrying for nothing. Maybe he didn't notice. "It's getting colder," she observed for lack of anything better to say.

"There's a lap robe under your seat."

"Probably too dirty to be abided."

"Prob'ly."

"At least it's not as crowded as the last coach we took."

He grunted. "Surprised you remember. You mostly slept the whole way."

"Have you ever been to St. Louis before?" she asked abruptly, aware that she was quickly running out of small talk.

"No."

"Me either." *Well, that's it for me.*

On the opposite seat, Jack's brooding had finally lifted. His attention, wandering hither and yon, had caught and sharpened on the word *bed*—*no* s.

He studied her in the last bit of daylight. She had good blood in her. It showed in the perfection of her features. There was no line blurred, no curve indistinct—everything had definition. Like good, precisely turned wood. Even her coloring was crisp and sure, and she had that perfect "pitcher" profile between lip and chin.

Seeing the purity in her face should've made him, with his bastard blood, feel guilty for wanting her, and even more for feeling he could have her. He knew he didn't—wouldn't ever—*deserve* her, but once an upstart, always one, he guessed because he *did* want her and was determined to have her. That's all there was to it.

Her word *friendship* had depressed him a bit though. Whoever heard of a friendship between a man and a woman? Seemed like an awful waste. When he looked at her, he didn't see a friend . . . he saw her naked and arched beneath him in abandon, his lover and his alone.

Just the thought gave him that same stomach-tightening clench he got right before a big-stakes game, a combination of anticipation and excitement. He resented the rapid descent of darkness, but it didn't stop him from seeing in his head the pleasures to come. She was young, but she was ripe—and ready for him. *Yes . . . this time we'll get a real bed. A big one.*

"If you sit beside me," he said, "we can share our warmth. Or freeze together."

"Thank you, but I'm fine over here. Besides, I don't like riding backwards."

"Ain't my favorite either, come to think of it." And with that, he moved over beside her.

"*Isn't* your favorite."

"*Will you please stop that? Please?* I gave up more cussin' around you than you know, but the rest of it's just the way I talk, so just lemme be."

She sniffed. "As you wish."

"Shoulda been a schoolteacher," he grumbled half under his breath.

Minutes went by. Hoping to mend the breach he'd impulsively created, he put an arm around her shoulders and drew her closer. She stiffened, but a breath later, melted against him like sugar in a warm skillet. "Better?" He felt her nod, and he relaxed some. All was not lost.

They rode in silence for a bit, but he could sense the debate in her head. Finally, she came out with it. "Any chance you won enough for separate rooms this time?"

His hopes plummeted. "Maybe if I'd won that first big pot," he couldn't resist saying.

She poked him hard in the ribs.

"Ow!" He pushed her hand away. "We'll eat good at least, I can promise you that."

"You mustn't have done too badly then."

"Let's just say I don't give up 'til I get what I want, and leave it at that."

Suddenly, she scooted closer to the window and lifted the shade.

That annoyed him. He liked it better when she was tucked up against him.

Although there wasn't much to see in the dark, Caroline stayed glued to the window, and within the hour, she was rewarded when their iron-rimmed wheels finally hit cobblestone.

Street lamps were lit and carriages criss-crossed each other's paths over the snow-dusted streets. A dozen riverboats, gray ghosts in the darkness, lined the slanting, cobbled levee. Hotels towered several stories above the streets where a steady stream of people of all colors hurried to their destinations, noses tucked into fur muffs or behind mufflers. Everywhere she looked, there were lights and movement. Even in the dark of night, she could tell St. Louis was bustling and thriving. The place positively hummed.

The coach pulled up and let them out at the corner of Fifth and Walnut Streets, and they stood together on the snowy cobbles, stretching their legs, looking around to get their bearings.

"Where do you want to stay?" he asked her, holding both their bags in one hand.

"There." She pointed. *The Southern Hotel* its sign read.

He squinted up at the six-story, yellow stone building that gracelessly took up the entire block on that side of the street. "You sure? That one's prettier." He indicated the four-story *St. Louis Hotel* on the corner behind them.

It was her turn to squint as she considered the four-story brick building with its tall, arched windows at street level, and slender white columns supporting an iron-railed balcony. As much as she wanted to show decisiveness, that she could not be swayed, it *was* prettier . . . and probably less expensive—which could well mean Jack could afford *two* rooms.

"You're right. Let's stay there."

"Oh, what the hell—c'mon." Taking her arm, he turned them back toward The Southern.

Wondering if she'd just been outmaneuvered, she allowed herself to be towed along . . . but once inside, she gasped at the abundance of polished wood, chandeliers, carpets, and elaborately framed paintings and mirrors on the walls.

He leaned on the counter, casual as you please, and looked around. "Kinda grand, huh?"

"Yes, but let's go back to the other one."

"No, don't worry—I got this."

The desk clerk, dark hair parted straight down the middle and shiny with pomade, handed a key to the uniformed porter at his elbow before referring to the register book Jack had just signed.

"Welcome, Mister Transomb, Missus Transomb. That'll be seven dollars per night. In advance," he said, noting their meager amount of luggage.

Caroline plucked at his sleeve. "*Jack!*" she whispered.

He gave her a quelling look as he handed over the money. "We want baths as well."

"Certainly, sir. A tub can be brought to your room, and there's gentlemen-only bathing downstairs. Just there," he said, indicating a gleaming brass balustrade that swept down into a brick, arched opening in one wall.

"In the room."

"Very good, sir. We also offer a telegraph office, a Gentlemen Only parlor, and a restaurant right through that other archway there." He pointed behind them.

Jack nodded his acknowledgment. "The rest of our bags'll come on tomorrow morning's train. Can someone fetch 'em for us?"

The clerk was visibly relieved. "Certainly, sir."

At her surprised look, Jack leaned over and whispered, "Bluffing ain't just for cards."

"What happens when nothing arrives?" she whispered back.

His sigh was resigned, exaggerated. "Damned railroads—noisy *and* undependable."

She took the arm he jauntily offered her as the porter came out behind the desk and took their scuffed and stained bags. Jack acted like this was an everyday courtesy in his life. Feeling embarrassingly grubby herself, Caroline couldn't help but admire his aplomb.

After putting their cases down and lighting the lamps, the man accepted the tip Jack handed him and left.

The third-floor room—theirs and theirs alone this time—was papered in tiny, brown-and-gold fleurs-de-lis. It had a big, carved bedstead, marble washstand and folding privacy screen, a dresser with a gilt-framed mirror, and a fringed shade beneath white-lace curtains at the wide window. A narrow Grecian couch covered in pink watered silk had been placed in front of it.

Tossing his hat on the bed, Jack turned a full circle on his heel. "Not bad, eh?"

"It's lovely," she said, still taking it all in. "But far too costly. Seven dollars is outrageous. You really should get your money back, and we can go across the street."

He shrugged, seemingly unconcerned now that they were here. "Sometimes a man has to splurge. You worry too much."

"Maybe you don't worry enough."

"Mebbe. But we're here now and we're staying. It's been a hard couple of weeks, Caroline. We both deserve some spoilin', doncha think?"

Truth was, she longed for it, but suspected it would be costly in more ways than one. She removed her gloves, bonnet, and cloak. The gloves she laid on the washstand, the cloak and bonnet she hung precisely on two of its four hooks, clucking her tongue over the travel creases. Then she took her bag and set it down in the corner.

Jack hadn't moved. He simply stood by the bed, watching her, his hand curved around the carved pineapple finial of one of the footposts, saying nothing.

So she filled in the silence with movement. She checked her hair in the mirror, then turned to survey the room with the critical eye of a housekeeper about to plunge into a day's work. She flicked her fingers over the polished surface of the dark mahogany tables as if patrolling for dust. The folds of the draperies framing the bullion-trimmed shade at the window were fluffed and reshaped. Arms akimbo, the visual scan for things amiss continued.

As if struck with sudden inspiration, she marched over, grabbed one of the pillows off the bed, and took it over to the Grecian couch, patting it into place with an air of great satisfaction.

Jack had been smiling faintly, amused by this fussbudget side of her, but now he frowned. "What're you doin'?"

She faced him pertly. "You can sleep here. That way we won't be crowding each other. After last night, well, I just think what we both need is a good night's sleep."

"It's a big bed, Caroline—"

She avoided looking at the object under discussion.

"And I ain't sleepin' on that thing."

"Fine, then I will."

"What the hell! It's a little late for all this modesty, don't you think?"

"I beg your pardon! Despite our traveling circumstances, I am *still* a lady."

"I never said you wasn't, but what're you afraid of—or more importantly, *who?* Me?"

"Certainly not."

"Then why're you standin' way over there?"

With a put-upon sigh, she took a single giant step closer like a player in a child's game. "There, is that better?"

"Not really."

She took another step. Then another. "Satisfied now?"

He leaned a shoulder against the bedpost and crossed his ankles. "Hardly. I still say you're afraid." The faint hiss of the gas lamps seemed to agree.

"That's ridiculous."

"Really? Then why you got your arms folded like that—tight as a new barn door?"

She forced her shoulders to relax, but kept her arms folded as he straightened and came closer. Circling her slowly, he leaned down to speak into her ear, giving her a tingly awareness of his breath. "And why do you lean away like that?" He paused in front of her, his gaze dropping to her mouth, which parted in response . . . then he moved on. She felt his body heat as he moved behind and leaned over her shoulder to catch her eye. "Relax."

"I am relaxed."

He continued to circle and, like the walls of Jericho, her stomach began to quiver. "You're being silly—you know that, don't you? Dramatic and silly," she told him.

"I am?"

Mutely, she nodded.

"You ain't afraid o' me?"

"You're *not*—" She swallowed the correction. "No. I'm not afraid of you."

"Then it must be *you* you're afraid of. Maybe you're afraid that, if you let yourself go, you won't be able to stop yourself."

She rolled her eyes. "*Now* you're being swell-headed."

"Prove it," he whispered into her ear. "Kiss me."

Porcelain nostrils flared. "Oh, you'd like that, wouldn't you?"

"Oh, yes, I most definitely *would* like that." He stopped in front of her.

She looked from one dark blue eye to the other, then dropped her gaze to his top shirt button. "Well, I don't want to kiss you."

"Why not?"

She refused to look higher than the button. "Because you're playing games, and I don't like it. I'm tired and hungry, and you promised me a steak dinner."

"I still say you're afraid o' me, of how I make you feel." He was circling again, his tone so reasonable it was maddening. "You like it when I touch you, don't ya?"

She shivered as if he had and shook her head.

"Liar." He stopped in front of her again.

"That's—" she swallowed hard, "that's not a very gentlemanly thing to say. Besides, this is different."

"We already know I ain't no gentleman . . . but how's this different?"

"It just is." The button, probably whale bone, rose and fell with his breathing.

"Why? 'Cause it's more . . . thought out?"

"I suppose so, yes."

"I see. So only if it starts by chance is it okay to enjoy, is that it? That's not very honest." When she didn't answer, he continued. "I was watching you on the stage coming here . . . and you know what I was thinkin' about?"

She was pretty sure she knew, but denied it with a shake of her head.

"I was rememberin' how you felt last night, how you tasted. And even before that. Onboard the *Quincy*. I can't stop thinkin' about you. You're a constant distraction. I'm tryin' to play my hand, pay attention to the others, decide what I'm gonna play, *how* I'm gonna play it . . . then all of a sudden I'm thinkin' about *you* again."

"So . . ." she put a finger on the button. "Let me get this straight. You want to satisfy yourself . . . with me . . . so you can get back to what's *really* important."

Some of his predatory feathers drooped. "That ain't what I said—or meant."

Feeling she'd scored an important point, she turned away.

"Caroline—" He turned her back around and into his embrace—as simple as that—and the force of his kiss pushed her head back over the arm that pulled her closer. The bottom of her stomach dropped away, plunging with heated gravity between her legs. The shape of her, the space she occupied, he controlled completely. Expertly, he turned her and tipped her backward onto the bed, the weight of him as he followed stirring a dark excitement in her.

It was the unexpected feel of his hand on her thigh beneath her skirts that dropped her over the edge of scintillation into panic. She twisted away. He was moving too fast. "Jack—"

"What?" He started undoing the tiny jet buttons down the front of her bodice.

"Jack!" She wedged her arms between them and pushed.

He was undeterred. If anything, the space helped him gain access to the newly exposed flesh. "Hmmm?"

"I—uh—" she swallowed hard, changing tactics. "I'm very hungry. Can we go get dinner now?" She ended on a higher note than she started because he suddenly slid one arm beneath her bottom, hefted her higher on the bed and wedged his knee between hers.

He nuzzled her neck, ran a fingertip along the edge of her exposed chemise, causing her to erupt in tingly gooseflesh. "Who can think about food at a time like this?"

Wet and warm, his mouth followed the path his finger had just traveled, and she squeezed her eyes shut, forcing herself to concentrate on speaking. "*I* can! I've been looking forward to … beefsteak … and dark … red … wine!" She threaded her fingers through his hair and tugged his head back up where she could look him in the face. "Please?"

"Later."

"But I'm hungry *now*."

"So am I." He pulled loose from her grip, his mouth returning to its former path while his hands started a new campaign beneath her skirt. "For you."

"Jack—" She tried again to push out of his embrace, but he was stronger and heavier than she imagined, and suddenly she knew a moment of real fear. "*Jack—stop it!*"

One second he was there, the next he was standing as if he'd been shot out of a cannon. Breathing hard, he plowed both hands through his hair and stared down at her, a wee bit wild-eyed, like someone awakened too abruptly from deep slumber.

Clutching the bodice of her dress closed, she sat up. "Jack, I'm sorry. It's just that I—"

"Don't bother playin' the scared virgin! You say you're hungry—fine. Let's go eat." The words were gunshot hard, and she flinched with each one.

The knock on the door made them both jump.

He spun and yanked it open. "*What?*" he barked.

"You ordered a bath, sir?" Two young girls, one blonde, one dark, dressed in identical uniforms of ruffled mob caps and long white aprons over plain gray dresses, curtsied awkwardly with an empty copper tub between them.

"Oh . . . ah, yes," he said, hastily stepping aside and burying his gruffness. "For her." Without looking her way, he indicated Caroline—who was scrambling to rebutton her bodice. Catching a glimpse of himself in the mirror over the dresser, he smoothed his hair and shirtfront self-consciously. "I'm gonna take mine downstairs."

As the girls trundled in with the tub and set it down, he came back and snatched his hat off the bed. "I'll meet ya down in the dinin' room in one hour. Don't be late. I know how *hungry* you are." Turning on his heel, he left, tugging his clothing into shape as he went.

As the door clicked shut behind him, she stuck her tongue out at it. "I don't know why *you're* so angry. *I* was the one being mauled."

One of the maids looked up. "Beg pardon, ma'am?"

"Nothing." She forced a smile. "I hope you have lots of hot water and some lovely-smelling soap for me."

"Oh, yes, ma'am—lavender!"

Caroline began removing the pins from her hair. "Wonderful."

Cheeks bulging with air, eyes squinched shut, she sank back below the water's surface, risking permanent prunedom for the sheer luxury of a long, unhurried bath. Bubble by bubble, she let her air out, finally, reluctantly, surfacing. Drawing a deep breath, she wiped her streaming eyes and dunked her head back one more time, squeezing the still-warm water from her hair and twisting it into a long rope over one shoulder.

This was her third tub of rinse water, but the hotel chambermaids—Bridget and Hannah—hadn't complained once. They'd even unpacked her and Jack's clothing, *tsk-tsking* over their condition, and taking them away to brush and press. If she craned her neck, she could just see around the Japan-lacquered screen to where her black bombazine dress was now laid out, looking almost new with all the dried mud gone from its hem, its torn braid trim neatly repaired.

Feeling decadent, she lounged back and rested her arms along the tub's rolled rim. She was as clean as she was going to get, but couldn't bring herself to get out just yet. She closed her eyes on a deep sigh and let her mind drift.

Don't be late. Her half-chuckle sent a ripple through the water. She'd be as late as she pleased, thankyouverymuch. Fact was, she didn't own a timepiece and had no idea how much time had gone by. Let him wait.

Scared virgin—hmph! The water gave a choppy splash. He'd made it sound like something nasty. Anyway, what made him think she was some trollop he could tumble at will? The last time, he'd—

Her eyes popped open. *Somewhere else . . . soon.* Well, of course! He'd just *assumed . . .* and how could he not? She hadn't said a word to disabuse him of the notion. Not one. All that talk of her remaining a *lady* and not becoming a *gambler . . .* he must believe her a wanton now. A hussy!

Whore!

Water sloshed over the rim as she rose abruptly and grabbed a towel. Wrapping the rough, slubbed linen around her, she stepped over the rim and padded across the patterned carpet to peer at herself in the mirror.

She was no whore, she knew that—but *was* she wanton?

You want me to touch you, don't you? You even liked it . . .

Yes, she had, she did—and heat streaked down from belly to thighs at the mere thought. She wanted him to teach her all the things that went on between a man and woman, things still veiled in mystery for her, things she was sure he knew. It was his urgency this time—he'd pushed too far, too fast. She caught her lower lip in her teeth. If he'd wooed her slowly like before, she could admit where they might be right now—and it probably wouldn't be with him downstairs and her up here with water dripping off her chin. In a twist of irony, she supposed she should be grateful that he was a heavy-handed boor. It bought her more time to think.

But that was part of the problem, too. Her head was always full of thoughts, of worries—she was vigilant that way, it's how she'd survived. But she was tired of thinking and liked the way her head emptied out when he touched her. It was the restful oblivion of pure sensation.

So here she stood, caught between fear and desire—the frightened virgin he accused her of being. Still, she disliked his presumption, his smug confidence.

With a sound of self-disgust, she dragged the clinging towel away from her skin, bent at the waist and began blotting the water from her hair.

Why did it have to be so complicated, she wondered. Frightening and compelling, both? She'd been taught such things were wicked. Forbidden. She couldn't recall any particular words, however, so perhaps she'd just absorbed the notion from the very air in which people moved; but stated or not, the prohibition was real. Facing it now, though, looking at it squarely, she had to wonder why. Wasn't it natural? Wasn't it meant to be? Weren't men and women designed to desire each other? To want to know one another? Standing up, she looked in the mirror again, mining the depths of her own eyes, thinking that, as part of the human race, surely she must know the answers herself, must embody them somehow.

Yes, she was afraid—but of what exactly? The absence of marriage? Lack of a preacher's words and a gold ring? The word *marriage* always conjured up images of drudgery and responsibility—albeit tied up with a bow and labeled *respectability*.

Her shoulders slumped. That was it of course. She was a coward afraid of the labels, that step over moral and social boundaries that once crossed couldn't be retraced—the ostracism, not to mention the disgrace of possibly bearing a child out of wedlock. A bastard. Like Jack.

She turned away from her reflection, rubbing her forehead in agitation. Why did everything have to be so narrowly defined for a woman? A man could take a lover, be pronounced a rake and a cad, yet somehow be subtly admired—winked at—for his sly ways, while women of similar bent were condemned and shunned. She thought of her own reaction on first meeting Simone and knew it was true. Women, it seemed, were held to a higher standard and charged with holding a moral line where men were not.

Even as the inequity of that burned, Caroline knew she was no crusader willing to throw herself on the pyre for social justice. She was, in her own way, as committed to the status quo as anyone else. She simply wanted what she wanted without paying the price. She wanted to be the exception to the rules ... yet understood she couldn't afford to be. With a heavy sigh of resignation, she eyed herself in the mirror one last time.

Well, you'll just have to come up with some way to make him stop, make him want *to stay away . . . now, won't you?* She gave the image of herself a tight-lipped nod. Whatever expectations he was nursing, they were doomed. They had to be. She had plans for her future—plans that didn't include a man, or didn't include *him* at least.

Be brave ... be bold ... be *strong.* And s*tand pat,* she added, liking the gambling reference.

Don't you want me to touch you?

"No," she rehearsed aloud, firmly and with conviction.

You did before . . . You even liked it.

"Certainly not," was her vocal response. *Liar,* retorted the traitor in her body.

She threw the towel on the floor. "Oh, fie!"

Downstairs, Jack put his beer down, drummed his fingers on the tablecloth, consulted his pocket watch and scowled around the darkly paneled, candlelit dining room. Fancy, he thought, noting the potted palms, lace curtains, sideboards laden with china, and the wink of cut-crystal . . . the way the waiters hovered with their slick-backed hair and long aprons. *Snooty, too,* he decided.

If he'd been by himself, a room somewhere near the waterfront or stables, meals taken in a noisy saloon would've suited him just fine. As it was, and despite the hefty cost, he wanted to give Caroline something nicer after their hardships on the trail—and she hadn't complained near as much as he'd expected. Fainthearted she was not.

Don't bother playin' the scared virgin . . .

He winced. What did he expect? She *was* a virgin. She was young and inexperienced, and he was treating her like all the other women he'd ever known—women who knew how to play the game. He called himself all the names he could think of and felt mildly better.

He hadn't followed the skirt trail in a while, and couldn't remember the last time he put this much effort into a woman—either before or after he'd gotten her into bed. This one was a bad idea from the start of course. Everything he'd ever warned himself about was happening. He was spending too much time thinking about her and too little time looking for his next mark. He hadn't thought of California—really thought about it—since he'd put her in his buggy that day. Maybe it was time to look around for a more experienced kind of companionship. Everybody knew virgins were more trouble than they were worth.

Caroline appeared in the arched doorway just then, and he tensed, trying to gauge her mood as she paused to look around before gliding toward him across the floor. She was all neat and tidy and as prim as a schoolmarm once again in her black mourning. Only the splotches of pink riding high on each cheekbone told him she was more stirred up than she looked.

He signaled the waiter. "I've already ordered our dinner—steak and wine as you requested. Should be here soon," he said, rising and holding her chair as he breathed in the surprising sweetness of lavender.

Her arched brow took note of the unusual gesture and he ground his teeth at the blush he felt creeping up off his collar. *If she says anythin', I'll throttle her on the spot.*

But she only nodded, and sank gracefully onto the damask-covered seat. "Thank you."

He hesitated. Should he apologize now and get it over with or just let the subject drop? Unaccustomed to indecision, he felt awkward as he sat back down.

The waiter arrived moments later, bringing wine, and as he filled her crystal goblet with the deep ruby liquid, his glance seemed to acknowledge the intimacy of their relationship. Jack took it as a good sign. Perhaps the stranger's eye could see more than he could at the moment.

Caroline saw it, too, and felt outnumbered. *Who asked you?* she demanded silently. As for Jack, she sensed his discomfort and found it satisfying. *Let him stew.*

Hands folded in her lap, she took it all in. She'd never seen anything like it before. "This is nice—but expensive, I imagine."

"I told you to quit worrying about that."

"Old habits die hard."

"I s'pose—but you're livin' a new life now, right? Um . . . listen, about earlier—"

"Let's not talk about it." She picked up her glass. "Let's just have a nice dinner."

"At least let me apologize. Again. Seems that's all I do around you."

That pricked. "Then you needn't bother. Besides," she added, putting her glass back down very precisely, "I think you'll try again—that you'll keep trying."

She watched his jaw muscles work as he picked up his beer, swallowed, then replaced his glass just as precisely as she had hers. "Not unless winter's comin' to hell, sugar."

"Language, Mister Transomb—language," she scolded softly. "We're in public."

"I *damn* well know that, Miss Cooper!" he replied loudly, refusing to be scolded.

Several heads turned. Picking up her wine glass, she looked away and sipped daintily.

"Tilt that nose any higher and you'll drown." When she ignored him, he added, "And if I had a barrel of the stuff right now, I might just hold your head under."

"I'm sure you would," she agreed mildly, still not looking at him. He wanted her to lose her composure and brawl with him—he seemed to enjoy it—but she refused to give him the satisfaction.

"Where's that steak you promised?" she asked after a bit of silence. "I'm starving."

"Me, too." He scowled around the room. "I told 'em to bring it soon as you got here."

Somehow, that had a mollifying effect on her mood. She was tired of fighting with him. Looking around and noticing all the starched white shirt fronts, the glitter of beadwork, she decided this must be the place where the fashionable people of St. Louis dined. She leaned closer. "Have you ever seen so many fat people in one room in all your life? When I think of all the good folks back home barely scraping by," she went on, "it just makes me sick."

"Well, I wouldn't let them hear you say that," he responded with a tamped-down smile. "They might rise up as one and toss you out on that pretty little bee-hind of yours."

She patted the hair at the nape of her neck. "I doubt they could heave themselves out of their chairs fast enough to catch me, but," she looked at him, "I would expect you to defend me of course."

He thumbed the corners of his mustache. "Of course."

They went back to sipping their beverages, the air lighter between them now. She toyed with the tiny silver salt spoon, tapping it against its crystal cellar. *Ting! Ting! Ting!*

The material of his sleeve made a noise across the tablecloth as he reached over and took her hand. "Caroline . . . I don't like thinkin' you're afraid of me."

She looked at his face, so earnest suddenly. "I'm not." She withdrew her hand and folded it back into her lap. *Be strong . . . and stand pat.* "But I have a question for you. Why did you decide to bring me along?"

"What?"

"The day we buried my brother, what made you decide to take me with you?"

He tugged on his ear, and took another swallow of beer. "You know why. You asked me to—and we were goin' to the same place, so . . . " The smell of lavender, faint as it was, was messing with his head and making it hard to keep his thoughts—and certain body parts—in line.

"What about after that?"

"After that, well, you wanted me to teach you how to gamble. You do remember that, I hope." He made a palm-up gesture. "I guess you could say we just fell in together. I gotta tell you—after we got thrown off the *Quincy*—I started to leave you right then and there, but—"

"I knew it!"

"Well, I *didn't, did* I? So there's no use gettin' mad about it now."

"I see—well, thank you for answering my question." Her stomach felt queasy from too much wine and too little food. And she hated doing what she was doing. It felt awful. And wrong. But vitally necessary, so she took a deep breath and pressed on. "So . . . do you expect some sort of-of *payment* for bringing me along? If I'm afraid of anything at all, it's that—that you believe I owe you *liberties.*"

His face darkened as what she was truly asking dawned on him. "I never said any such thing! I never even *hinted* at it. *And you know it!*"

"But I'll bet you were thinking it."

The tips of his ears reddened. Another gulp of beer, another full-handed swipe at his mustache, then a glance around the room to see if anyone was looking before he leaned over and shoved his face close to hers. "I'm gettin' mighty tired of you tellin' me what I'm thinkin.'"

"It's not hard to figure out what any man is thinking," she scoffed. She didn't really know of course, but it sounded clever. "Why, for all I know, if I don't give in, you might try to pass me off to the first man who comes along."

He reared back, palms out. "Okay, that's *enough!*" He opened his mouth again, but nothing came out, so he started over. "Caroline, I—"

"Well, I'll be—! Jack! Jack Transomb! Is that you?"

The strange voice startled them both, and Jack's head swiveled. A man with a sweep of silver hair, in full evening dress of hammer claw tails and white tie, had paused by their table.

He clapped Jack on the shoulder. "It *is* you!" he exclaimed.

Jack's face blanked in surprise, then split into a grin as he jumped to his feet. "*Louie!* You old dog—what are you doin' here?"

EIGHT

The two men shook hands vigorously.

"I might ask you the same thing! Last time I saw you was—what? Six months ago? You were heading down New Orleans way." His bright blue eyes held an affectionate twinkle, and Jack was grinning from ear to ear.

"Good grief! Has it been that long? Here—sit down, sit down!"

"Aren't you going to introduce me to your lovely companion first?" His complexion was a startling bronze color and the corners of his eyes crinkled when he smiled down at her.

"Oh, yeah! Caroline, this is Louisiana Louie. Louie, this is Miss Caroline Cooper."

Louie sketched a bow. "How do you do?"

Caroline smiled and held out her hand. "Very well, thank you. I'm pleased to make your acquaintance, Mister Louie."

"Oh, please! Make it plain old Louie and the pleasure's all mine, I assure you." He kept possession of her fingers until the last syllable left his mouth.

"So, Mister—"

He raised an admonishing finger.

"Louie," she amended with another smile. "So how do you know Jack?"

He and Jack exchanged glances as they took their seats.

"Known him near all my life," Jack answered with a grin. "He taught me ever'thing I know, and a more ornery cuss you ain't never likely to meet. I warn you now—don't ever get in a game of blackjack with him. He'll cheat you out of your fingers and toes 'fore you know it."

"He exaggerates, my dear. I have no interest in fingers and toes. *Gold,* however . . ."

"Ah. Then you're a gambler, too."

"By avocation only."

"And by *vo*cation?" she pressed, intrigued in spite of herself.

"A ne'er-do-well." Both men laughed, but above the broad smile, Caroline noticed Louie's eyes remained shrewd and assessing. She was being evaluated.

"Whatcha been up to, you old coot?" Jack was still beaming. "Ain't this a bit far north for you?"

Louie shrugged philosophically. "A man's gotta go where the games go. Times are hard. Not too much loose money rolling around these days. But then you know that. Why, just last month, I was down near Red River Landing, and the cards were falling sweet, yet it was close to dawn before more 'n' a hundred dollars passed through that pot."

Caroline sipped her wine and watched the two of them. She'd never seen Jack so animated, so easily moved to laughter. Next to Louie's beefy stature, he seemed much younger.

"But maybe we can scare something up," Louie was saying. "Where are you staying?"

"Here at the hotel. You?"

"Same. Room four—my lucky number. Where are you?"

"We're—" Jack caught himself. "I'm in 311."

The slip sat awkwardly in the pause that followed. Jack frowned and tugged at his cuffs. Caroline dabbed her mouth with her napkin, then smoothed it back in her lap.

It was Louie who spoke first, turning the subject neatly without really changing it at all. "So tell me, Miss Cooper, how did you come to be in this scoundrel's company?"

There was no insinuation, no hint of judgment in the question, but Jack grabbed the wine bottle from the cooler by his chair and leaned toward her. "Here, have more wine."

"No, thank you, I still—" She'd covered her glass with her fingers, but he was already pouring. It splashed across the back of her hand, soaked the edge of her sleeve and stained the snowy tablecloth. She jerked back only to knock the glass over, pouring the rest into her lap.

"*Christ,* Caroline! I'm sorry!" He fumbled for his napkin. "Here—"

She stayed him with a gesture, replacing the empty glass and blotting the wine with her own napkin. Without asking, Louie simply tossed his to the task. She favored him with a tight-lipped smile of thanks, responding finally to his question.

"I'm afraid it's rather a long story." The waiter came to finish cleaning up the spill, and Jack used the lull to ask Louie to join them for dinner.

"Sure, but I've already ordered. Waiter, bring my dinner here when it's ready."

"Very good, sir."

"And bring me a whiskey while you're at it. Jack?"

"I'm fine with beer." Jack leaned toward Caroline. "Caroline, I'm sorry. Truly."

"It's nothing." She was still scrubbing at her skirt.

Louie turned the polished charm back toward her. "Well, Miss Cooper, it looks like we have all night now. Plenty of time for your long story. However, if your face turns that same color of ash again, I'm going to feel terrible for pressing you, so," he offered them both a smile, "why don't we just agree to change the subject?"

Jack looked relieved and reached for her hand to give it a squeeze. "Caroline, why don't you go see if you can get that out before it stains?"

"Stains?" she repeated, extracting her hand. "I'm wearing *black*... but then that's part of my story, isn't it?" She glanced at Louie. "You see, my brother Wendall was a gambler, too. But not a very good one. Jack, here—"

"Caroline . . ." Jack warned.

Their eyes locked in a brief test of wills, her smile frozen in place. Finally, she dropped the smile and tossed her napkin onto the table. "On second thought, I'm sure you two have a lot to talk about—and I really should go soak this out before it sours. So if you'll excuse me." She was gone before either man could rise completely.

Jack watched her sweep out of the room and couldn't help an exasperated sigh.

"Hmm. I'd say she's not very happy with you right now, son."

"No, and if history's any indication, she could very well come back here waving a pistol," he said, picturing that particular memory quite vividly.

Louie's head swiveled. "Does she *have* a pistol?"

"No." Then Jack remembered the one he kept in his game box . . . which was upstairs. *Well, not one of her own*, he thought, but decided to keep that detail to himself.

He glanced at Louie only to find himself under squinty-eyed scrutiny. "What?"

"You've changed," he said, swirling his whiskey.

"How much could a man change in six months?"

"Quite a lot it seems. You finally heading for California?"

"Yep."

"Taking the girl with you?"

"If you'd asked me last night, I'da said yes. Tonight, I dunno. Maybe."

"Her long story—the widow's weeds—you wanna tell me about it?"

After another sigh and another deep swallow of beer, Jack started at the beginning.

Louie listened without comment, but his expression grew more and more somber. The story seemed to confirm something in Louie's head. "So, it's guilt that's brought you to this."

"I didn't tie the rope around that boy's neck."

Louie's expression said *close enough,* but verbally all he said was, "Guilt's a bad thing for people like us. Next thing you know it turns us into heroes. Or tries to. So who's in room 311? Just you . . . or both of you?"

"Both. You got a problem with that?"

"Me? No, not my call. At least you're getting something out of it."

Jack snorted. "Hardly."

"No?" One silver brow arched. "You're slipping, boy."

Louie grinned into his glass. Jack scowled into his.

"The girl have any family?"

"No."

"So you just said 'I'm off to California to make my fortune, come with me' and that was that?"

Jack drained his glass. "You make me sound like one of those wildcat Forty-niners—and no, it didn't happen like that. I'd just done that Fox fella the favor of puttin' his teeth through his lip. Turns out, she was packin' her kit while I was soakin' my hand in the creek. When I come back to say goodbye—what? What are you lookin' at me like that for? Didn't feel right not sayin' goodbye."

"No, I guess not—not if you'd already stayed that long."

"Anyway, there she was, all ready and askin' me to take her with me. Since I was headed there m'self, couldn't see the harm. 'Least as far as the river. What she wanted to do after that was up to her."

"And at the river? What'd she want to do?

"Go to California."

"*Course* she did! With you."

"We were on the same boat, that's all . . . 'til I got us throw'd off."

The empty glass thumped the table. "How'd you let *that* happen?"

Jack ran a finger around inside his collar. "Just wanted to win her a little present—some earbobs—but I musta run the game a little fast, 'cause the guy went cryin' *cheat* to the cap'n . . . who showed up not long after with a brawler and a gun."

"Boy, you got a rough ride ahead of you."

"Why do you say that?"

"You've gone soft in the head, that's why. You're besotted with her."

"The hell I am."

"How many times I gotta tell you? Women—for men like us—they can't be permanent."

"Well, that's kinda the thing—she wants to be a gambler too."

Louie's glass froze halfway between lips and table. "*Really*."

"Really. She's been learnin', and she ain't half bad at it. Been gettin' anybody that sits still long enough to teach her what they know. Hell, she even got that hardtack Del Griffith to teach her blackjack. Before that, she wormed her way onto the table with him and some of his buddies. They was teachin' her Bluff. 'Course they were also puffin' her up, and she was mad as a hornet when she found out–but she stuck with it. Determined is what she is."

"And you?"

"Me?"

"You been teaching her some?"

Jack twitched a shoulder. "Some."

"Tricks of the trade?"

"Naw. Truth is I don't much like the idea of her gamblin', 'specially on her own. Now runnin' some games with her, as partners—that might be different."

"I see. You wanna keep her close."

"Yeah, but—hey, quit lookin' at me like that. It'd be a good money-makin' setup, that's all. Men get stupid with a pretty face at the table."

"Uh-huh. They sure do."

Locked into a mutual staring contest, Jack was the first one to break it off, signaling the waiter for another round. Then together, they sank into mirrored postures, shoulders hunched, shaking their heads at the wily, mysterious devils that were women.

Caroline finally returned. Louie spotted her first and rose. Jack followed suit a half-second later. She'd seen Louie catch sight of her just before Jack did, his eyes following her progress all the way to the table. The waiter arrived to pour more wine as soon as she was seated. When she was settled, a new square of white linen draped in her lap, Louie re-aimed his attention.

"All better, my dear?"

"Yes, thank you."

"Jack and I were just talking about California, how you're both heading there. But what I hadn't gotten around to telling him was that it just so happens I'm finally pulling up stakes and heading west myself. I realize we've just met—and forgive me if this seems too forward—but I'd be honored if you'd accept my protection."

Jack's head snapped up. "She's already got protection. Mine," he said with a frown and a quick glance in her direction. "Caroline, this wasn't my idea, I swear."

"No, it was mine," Louie said smoothly, "and a lady can change her mind, can't she? Change protectors if she wants?"

"Why should she?" Jack demanded.

Louie's shrug was elaborate and loose. "You never know—let's let the lady decide, shall we? Well, Miss Cooper, what do you say to me being your champion?"

His manner had changed. There was something both sly and pugnacious about him now that made her uneasy. She sensed he held a similarly unflattering opinion of her. She supposed Jack had filled him in during her absence, but now she wondered what exactly had been said. Despite his wildly inappropriate offer, it was clear that Louisiana Louie did not care for her.

"That's very kind of you, I'm sure," she responded gravely, "but I must decline."

"Ah, well." He made a careless gesture. "Nothing ventured, nothing gained."

Before anything else could be said, their dinner finally arrived—big slabs of beef and fried potatoes, corn pudding and slices of pears in a cinnamon sauce. For a few minutes, tensions eased as talk necessarily centered around the food, then Louie's attention returned to her with disquieting focus. Chewing thoughtfully, he stared at her over his whiskey glass. "So what will you do in California?"

"Didn't Jack tell you? I'm going to be a professional gambler—blackjack mostly."

"Well, perhaps on the trip there, you'll change your mind. Who knows? Maybe some rich man'll come along and marry you instead."

So, he considered her a fortune hunter, did he? "I think not," she replied coolly.

Jack fisted his utensils on either side of his plate. "Louie, what're you doin'?"

Louie was a picture of innocence. "I'm just trying to encourage her, that's all."

"Well, don't. She don't need encouragement. Besides, money ain't what matters most to Miss Cooper, is it?" He swung a flinty look in her direction. "Bein' a gentleman, that's what counts. Ain't that right?"

Feeling attacked from both sides, her jaw tightened. "Jack, what are *you* doing?"

His was an exact mirror of Louie's innocent look. "Just tellin' the truth. I'm right, ain't I?"

She eyed his glass, full once again. "I think perhaps you've imbibed a little too much."

"Actually, I don't think I've *imbibed* near enough." Hand to his chest, he turned to Louie. "You see, I ain't a gentleman . . . and Miss Cooper likes gentlemen." He lifted his glass to her in mock salute. "She's picky like that."

"Picky? Because I appreciate good manners? And while we're at it, I also appreciate good grammar. *Ain't*—I wish to God you'd quit saying that *all* the time. The word is *isn't*."

"Speaking of taste," Louie chimed in, "*ain't* these pears wonderful?"

She glared at him, then at Jack. "Wonderful!"

Jack glared back. "Scrumptious."

Unperturbed, Louie kept things moving. "So, until you become a professional gambler, what do you do while Jack plays the tables?"

She twitched a shrug, wishing suddenly she'd never suggested dinner in the first place. "Watch mostly, and learn, but I play some, too. Jack doesn't like the idea. He thinks it's an unsuitable profession for a lady. He seems to feel I can't be both."

Jack shook a finger in her direction, but spoke to Louie. "She has this fool notion—"

"It's not a 'fool notion,' damnit!"

"*Tsk-tsk*! Language, Miss Cooper! We're in public. Trouble is, *ain't* no such thing as a lady gambler! They're all—"

"Marvelous!" Louie cut in. "I think it's a *marvelous* idea. Have you been teaching her?"

Sullenly, Jack went back to eating. "Some. Already told you that."

"Then please—permit me to offer my services, Miss Cooper. I'd be delighted to teach you everything I know."

"Not everythin', I hope."

Louie slapped him on the back good-naturedly. "What's the matter, son? Worried she'll be competition?"

Caroline's eyes widened. "That's just what *I* said!"

"Did you? Well, huzzah for you!" He laughed and nudged Jack's elbow, interrupting him cutting his meat. "A female willing to earn her keep? You can't fault the girl for spirit!"

Jack scowled at his plate, sawing with renewed determination. "Trust me, spirit is Miss Cooper's long suit."

"Excellent! Then we're agreed?"

Jack looked up and held her gaze meaningfully. "Caroline, don't."

"Why not?" Louie asked. "What else is there for her to do? Watching us old gamblers all night can't be much fun."

"I don't mind earning my keep," she declared. "I want to, in fact."

Louie was expansive. "See there? She wants to, so I say let her. I'm all for these blue stocking girls, their emancipation bloomers and all that. Good for them, I say. Let 'em pull their own weight for a change. Maybe that way they'll leave us men alone and not complain so much." He chuckled heartily, gripping Jack's shoulder. "Eh, boy?"

Jack changed the subject. "You really goin' to California?"

"I am."

"You always said you were born on the Big Muddy and you'd die there."

Louie chuckled again. "Talk is cheap, son, remember that. And so are the johnny marks left on the river these days. Not one of them risks enough to keep a man in good cigars anymore. Speaking of which—do you mind, m'dear?" he asked, producing a fat, obnoxious-looking version of that very thing.

She shook her head and the two of them were off, comparing the merits of this tobacco over that, with Jack finally challenged to try Louie's blend before making any final judgments.

Caroline put her napkin aside and rose. "Well, if you gentlemen will excuse me, it's been a very long day."

Jack lurched to his feet as well. "I'll walk ya."

"Not necessary."

"But I wanna. Don't go anywhere, Louie. I'll be right back."

"I'll be here as long as the liquor holds out. After that, you'll have to come find me," Louie answered amiably, rising and nodding at Caroline. "I'm glad to have made your acquaintance, Miss Cooper. I'm sure we'll talk again."

"I'm sure we will. Goodnight."

The walk back to their third-floor room was silent except for the swish of her skirts and the heavy scuff of Jack's boots on the gold-patterned carpet. Her life suddenly felt precarious once more.

At their room, he opened the door, pushed it wide, then blocked her path with his arm.

She looked up. "What?"

"Louie's offer—that was just Louie being Louie. I had nothing to do with it, I swear."

"I believe you."

His shoulders relaxed on a beer-scented exhale. "Good. Listen, him and me still got a lotta catchin' up to do. We'll probably be out most of the night, so take the bed." His sudden, crooked smile stopped just short of a leer. "You'll sleep better without me stealin' the covers."

"I'm sure I shall."

"Caroline—"

She ducked under his arm. "Goodnight, Jack. Try not to end up in a ditch somewhere."

He grinned. "So you *do* care about me."

He opened his mouth to say something else, but she gave him a little push and shut the door in his face. "Good*night*."

"You've changed!"

"*What!*"

"You've *changed!*" Louie shouted again over the roar of the saloon—*Mackey's Pub* said the sign above the door to this basement establishment. He and Jack had descended wooden steps to shove their way through the working-class crowd of drinkers and gamblers.

"So you keep sayin'!"

Mackey's was thick with curses and smoke, and there was a lot of rowdy jostling. But it was a democratic crowd—well-dressed men-about-town rubbing elbows with rivermen and chimney sweeps—so no one paid them any attention as they squeezed up to the bar. Ordering mugs of beer, they headed for an empty table in the dimly lit rear of the brick-walled room.

Jack raised his glass. "To Lady Luck."

"To Lady Luck," Louie agreed, and they both drank.

"Who knows?" Jack said, picking up from earlier as they hunched over the scarred wood surface so they could talk and be heard. "Maybe you're right. Maybe I *am* changin'. I suddenly want things I ain't never wanted before."

"Such as?"

"I dunno. A home maybe—settlin' down, that kinda thing."

"It's the girl," Louie declared after a deep swallow of his beer. "She's making you go soft in the head. You know better. You know what a woman does to men like us."

"Y'mean men without homes and families?"

Louie shook his head, his thick silvery hair making him look every inch the old lion. "I mean men with no illusions, no empty promises to tie them down to a life of drudgery, men without entanglements who can be gone at a moment's notice." He took another swallow and wiped the corners of his mouth. "Happiness isn't a claim you can stake, a thing you can fence in. Happiness is like a cloud, it travels on the wind. And you've got to be just as free to follow it. Otherwise, you're stuck inside that empty fence all by yourself, watching life pass you by."

Jack heard Louie's words like a man with two sets of ears. One heard the sweeping freedom, stirring his heart and feet as always. The other, some newer set, heard the emptiness that crowded behind that vision. People who followed happiness made of air traveled alone, and he was tired of being alone. He stared down into his own beer, idly turning the mug in circles. "Never knew you t'be so bitter, Louie."

"Not bitter. Experienced. You're just feeling guilty about the girl—it happens to all of us from time to time, but it'll pass." He squinted at Jack through the smoky air. "Get rid of her. Put her out of your mind. After what you did to her brother—" he held up a hand at Jack's look of protest "—whether you actually put the noose around his neck or not, that's how she'll always look at it, deep down, no matter what or how much you do for her. Keeping her around is like traveling with a snake in your saddlebag. Someday—the odds are good—she'll bite you. Give her money if you want and send her on her way. You know as well as I do how fickle a woman can be. They're pretty to look at and they've got their uses, but don't get tangled up with them. They'll cause you nothing but grief—even the ones who don't have cause to hate you like this one does." He stabbed at Jack's nose with a thick finger. "And trust me on this—this one *does*. She's no good for you, son, and if you don't listen to me on this, you'll live to regret it."

"Well, I can't argue with you about a lot of 'em, but I don't think you're right about this one. She was just upset with me tonight because . . . well, because of somethin' that happened before. I can't explain it, but there's somethin' about this one, Louie. She's different."

Louie laughed outright at that. "That's what she wants you to think—that's what they *all* want you to think, but there's not a one of 'em that isn't treacherous and conniving. They'll take you for all you're worth, then run off with the very next man who comes along. You mark my words, that one's nothing but trouble. Besides, you know a woman's bad luck." Louie suddenly grinned at him. "There's only one woman for the likes of us—"

Jack laughed and picked up his mug.

"*The Grand Dame, the Queen of Hearts, no fat old tart is she!*" they chanted in unison, clinking their mugs together before upending them in a joint chugalug.

Jack licked the foam off the bottom edge of his mustache. "Well, you don't have to worry about me, Louie. I've got ever'thing under control."

"Sure you do. I could tell that by the way you looked at her at dinner."

"And how's that?"

"Like you're falling in love."

"Now who's the one gone soft in the head? I *look* all right—you can't deny she's pretty."

"No, but so are a lot of women." Laying his finger alongside Jack's nose, he pointed across the room. "Take that one there, for instance. Now there's a cradle a man could rock away his troubles in all night long."

Jack turned his head and looked, giving a long, low whistle for the tall redhead with a spray of purple feathers in her hair. "Nothing wrong with your eyesight, old man."

"Nope. Never has been."

Curled alone in the middle of the big bed, Caroline listened to the sounds of the hotel settling down around her. The clatter of horses and buggies out in the street had quieted for the night, so had the footsteps in the room overhead. Now there was just the murmur of a woman's voice somewhere, the sporadic but phlegmy-sounding cough from the man next door.

Pulling the other pillow into a thoughtful embrace, she rolled over to contemplate the dim shape of Jack's bag on the floor.

It was past midnight. She had counted the deep-throated strokes of the tall clock in the lobby below—and Jack had still not returned. Only the presence of his bag reassured her that he and Louie were not already hours west of there. That Louie would do such a thing she didn't doubt for a moment. He'd made it abundantly clear he'd like nothing better than to separate her from Jack—offering to be her champion, indeed! Leave her by the side of the road was more like it. How addlepated did he think she was?

As she lay there in the dark, she recalled every word, every uncomfortable second of that dinner, but lingered over his offer to teach her, his praise of her ambition to become a player. Had it been a genuine offer?

She sat up and lit the lamp, then leaned over to heave the bag up beside her and look inside. Jack's usual spare amount of clothing . . . hairbrush . . . She dug deeper until her fingers found the carved surface of his game box. No, he would never leave this behind.

Reassured, she paused, giving serious consideration to the notion that had just popped into her head. Could she? *Should* she? With a small nod of decision, she put the box aside and hopped up to re-dress—nightdress flung aside, undergarments and dress pulled on, stockings rolled up, feet buttoned into her high-top shoes. A quick stint in front of the mirror and her hair was pinned into its usual figure eight.

Another glance at the box and she suddenly had to pace a bit to calm herself, the window drapes getting absently parted at the end of each turn she took around the carpet. Finally, after another deep breath, she was ready.

Dragging the box closer, she lifted the lid, aware that she was embarking on a strangely defining moment.

It was all there—cards, cup, markers, dice. *Pistol.* She took the cards, hesitated, then slipped the small gun into her skirt pocket and closed the lid.

Leaving the box on the bed, she checked her reflection one last time, snagged her reticule, and left the room, card deck secreted in her sweaty palm amid the folds of her skirt—a skirt that bumped awkwardly with the weight of the gun. Her pulse pounded and she felt out of breath by the time she descended the stairs into the lobby.

It was hushed and empty at this late hour, desk clerk gone, lamps turned low, but deep notes of male voices were coming from some-where. Standing below the extinguished chandelier, she was trying to decide which direction to turn when one of the doors on her right opened and the desk clerk returned to his post. Before he closed the door, however, Caroline caught a pungent whiff of cigar smoke, a glimpse of wing chairs, and men's trousered legs.

Ah-ha!

Still concealing the cards, she aimed herself at the door, until the desk clerk inserted himself in front of her. "May I be of some assistance, madam?"

"I-I'm looking for my husband."

He solidified his stance. "I'm sorry, but this is a gentlemen-only parlor."

Pressing her free hand to her throat, she gave a small laugh. "Well, of course it is, and I wouldn't normally *dream* of intruding, but this is something of an urgent, *personal* matter, you understand. I'll only be a minute—one tiny little minute, I promise." And with that, she scooted around him and tucked herself inside. Just before she closed the door in his blank face, she held up a single finger, smiling sweetly, repeating her words in a whisper. "Just one little minute." Clearly, he was not a man prepared for outright rebellion.

When she turned around, she made a quick assessment of the dark paneled walls, heavy damask drapes at the windows, giant andirons bracing a roaring fire, and—just what she was looking for—an unoccupied set of chairs in a corner. She made a beeline, ignoring the double-takes and harrumphing sounds of male annoyance as she sped to the chair that would put her back to the room and out of sight as much as possible.

As she sank into the oxblood leather, she held her breath and waited—for the room's occupants to rise up, *en masse*, and demand her departure, or the disapproving desk clerk to suddenly appear and evict her.

Neither happened.

After tucking the reticule into the chair beside her hip, she poured the cards out of their flimsy paper wrapping onto the small table between her and the chair opposite. She forced a deep breath, divided the deck evenly, and began shuffling—just loud enough to be heard—and waited, bottom lip clamped between her teeth.

She didn't have to wait long.

"Quite the rebel, aren't you?" remarked a voice just over her head.

She twisted in her seat to see a broad-faced young man with heavy mutton side whiskers and a bemused smile, peering down at her over the back of her chair. Before she could frame a suitable response to that despised label, he came around to plop himself in the chair across from her, scooping his formal tails out of the way first.

"What do you play? Monte? Brag?" His sherry-colored eyes, the same color as the hair he pushed back off his forehead, regarded her with conspiratorial merriment.

Mutely, she shook her head.

"What then?"

"Black—" she swallowed and refound her voice, "blackjack. Twenty-one."

"Ah!" His square jaw pushed at the tipped corners of his collar and the hair got another shove. "Love it! Well, what are you waiting for? Deal, m'dear, deal—before we're discovered and there's the devil to pay."

Nodding, she shuffled again, then invited him to make the cut. "And you are?" she prompted, instinctively knowing the distracting value of small talk.

"Henry," he said, cutting the deck. "Henry Baskins. And who are you? You sound like you're fresh from Dixie."

"Why, I sure am!" She gave him her prettiest smile as she began the deal.

His eyes lit up. He barely glanced at his bottom card before he started peppering her with questions, all of which she answered in her best honey-drip. The more she spoke, the merrier he became. He was such a jolly, earnest fellow. Clearly, the small wagers he was making—and steadily losing—meant nothing to him. Apparently, the pleasure of her company—and perhaps the slightly illicit conditions under which he was enjoying it—more than made up for it.

She was halfway through another deal when her turned-up card appeared—the signal to reshuffle and start over—but before she could do so, a large hand clamped onto her shoulder.

Henry's mouth sagged open. "Oh, fiddlesticks! Jig's up."

It was the desk clerk, his face stiff with disapproval. Standing behind him was a burly fellow who, despite the perfection of his evening wear, reminded Caroline of Boiler Man Lou. Swallowing hard, she rose as the clerk jerked his head in the direction of the exit.

"Can't say as I see the harm," Henry complained, handing Caroline her winnings.

The clerk snagged her forgotten reticule out of the chair. Daintily, she plucked it from his grasp, deposited her money, then waited for the burly fellow to stand aside so she could pass. Before she did so, she favored Henry with a final smile and offered him her hand. "Thank you, sir, for your company."

Henry shot to his feet and bowed over her hand, his unruly hair falling forward again. "Oh, I assure you, ma'am, the pleasure was all mine!"

With her most regal posture, she swept past, leading a small parade of men—Clerk, Burly, and Henry—out of the gentlemen-only lounge.

Once in the lobby, she headed for the stairs without a backward glance. Behind her, the men began arguing in hushed voices, and for the first time since she'd put the pistol into her pocket, she felt comforted by its presence. Luckily, no one followed or tried to stop her. Still, it took her hours to settle down into a fitful sleep after that.

It was early morning, and she was just pushing the last of the pins into her hair when she froze at the sound of the doorknob rattling. "Jack?"

"Yeah. Open up."

He sounded strange. Did he know? Had someone stopped him on his way through the lobby and told her about her late-night venture? Shoulders back, she opened the door.

He snapped to attention—a posture at odds with his appearance. Coat hanging askew, collar loose from its button and arching away from his neck like bird wings, tie gone and hat crooked, he was a mess. Hiding something behind his back, he greeted her with blowsy good humor. "Hullo!" Then he looked over her shoulder at the mangled bedcovers. "You slept in the bed without me," he accused. "If I'd only known, I'd've come back sooner."

She returned to the mirror. "Don't be so sure of yourself. Besides, you told me to."

"Yes. I did. I do. You're right. I'm sorry. It won't happen again."

He was loose-limbed and breezy, the night's worth of beard stubble giving him a rakish look. Shutting the door, he presented her with the flat, ribbon-tied box from behind his back.

"Someone else have a run of bad luck?"

"Uh-uh." He shook his rumpled head. "Bought it fair and square. For you. Open it."

"It's early. What shop's open this time of day?"

"None of 'em." He grinned. "I just banged on the door 'til the lady stuck her head out the window above and yelled at me to quit my awful racket, that she was closed."

She twisted her mouth to control her own urge to grin. "But you didn't quit, did you?"

"Nope. Convinced her the easiest way to get rid o' me was to open up and sell me this." He gestured with the box. "It was in the window."

"I see," she said, sparing a bit of pity for the beleaguered, unknown woman.

"Go on. Take it."

Relenting, she sat on the sofa and untied the wide blue ribbon, fully prepared to dislike whatever it was. The tissue paper crinkled as she pushed it away from folds of deep green velvet, pooled like a summer lake. It was a dress, its neckline low and square and edged with a snowy inch of ruffled white lace. She stroked a hand over the nap. Under that was a new corset—with back lacing.

The dress's hem and side seams were still pinned, awaiting a fitting, but she could do that herself easily enough. She hadn't had a dress made by another's hand since childhood, and it was a fine gift that touched her immensely. "It's lovely, Jack—really—but I'm still in mourning."

"It's dark enough," he argued wistfully, "ain't it?"

Despite her eddies of rebellion, convention had been a lifelong companion and chafed her sorely these days. In truth, she longed for a bit of color. "Perhaps."

He was standing beside her and suddenly she wrinkled her nose. "Maybe it wasn't so much your charm that persuaded the woman as it was the need to sweeten the air beneath her window. I can't decide if you smell more like the inside of a beer barrel or a spittoon."

Instead of being insulted, he just grinned and made an elaborately goofy bow that told her he was still several shades less than sober. "I'll wash up."

There was a decided twinkle in his muzzy eyes and his manner so expansive, she feared a display of sloppy affection was next, so she headed for the door. "You might want to wait for water. I'll go order you a tub."

Hand on the knob, she paused. "Only because I don't want you hearing it from someone else," she said without turning around, "you should know that I dealt blackjack last night. In the gentlemen-only parlor...before I was asked to leave."

When he didn't say anything, she looked around. He'd sunk onto the side of the bed. Dragging his collar free, he squinted at her through one eye. "Ju win?"

"I left with more than I started with."

"Tha's my girl!" Sketching her a sloppy salute, he fell backwards across the bed and was asleep before she closed the door.

Afternoon sunshine streaked through the open curtains, lighting up their room. Caroline sat on the sofa with yards of green velvet spilled over her knees. She was just finishing the last of the side seam stitches when Jack called out, "Hey! Come wash my back, will ya?"

She eyed the painted screen, behind which he'd been splashing as happily as any child for the last half hour, regaling her with stories of Louie the whole time.

"You know I can't."

"Why not?"

"Because you're not decent, that's why."

"Oh." Water lapped noisily and his next words were strained, as if he was reaching for something. "There. Now come wash my back."

"What did you do? Get dressed?"

"Yep. Sittin' here—in the tub—in m'shirt, coat, and britches. Come see."

Smiling at his tomfoolery, she shook out the velvet and held it up to look in the mirror.

"Caroline?"

"All right, I'm coming."

Laying the dress aside, she gave it a last admiring glance, then peeked around the screen.

He was lounging against the tub's high back, knees poked up through the suds—a towel draped modestly, from tub edge to tub edge, across his midsection. His water-darkened hair was plastered close to his head in a series of curls and spikes. He was grinning at her. "Am I decent enough for you?"

The little towel was so at odds with his large-boned frame, she had to laugh. "Hardly. And if that towel slips, you'll have no way of drying off."

"Hmm. You're right." He made as if to rise. "Perhaps I should—"

"No! Stay where you are. Just give me that sponge so we can get this over with."

She knelt down beside him. "Lean forward so I can reach." She scrubbed vigorously at first, but the longer she applied the lumpy sponge to his bare, water-glistened back, pushing him slightly forward with the pressure of each stroke, the slower . . . and more tender her movements became.

"Mmm," he murmured, head bobbing near his knees. The towel, bunched between thighs and chest and sealed to the tub edges beneath his forearms, was quickly soaking up water.

"You like?" The abbreviated question came out softer than she'd intended.

"I do." He turned his head and squinted at her. "The dress still please?"

She sank onto one hip, black skirts billowing, the sponge now trailing creamy suds over his shoulder and down over his chest, his arm. "Yes. It's lovely . . . really. Thank you."

They smiled at each other.

She continued cleaning down the length of his arm without really thinking about what she was doing until she got to his wrist, and he turned his hand over to capture hers. "Join me?"

"I think not."

His eyes never left her face as he removed the sponge from her hand and left it to float. One-handed, he twirled the cake of soap, then applied the lather to her palm and between her fingers oh-so-slowly, kneading her hand until it was absolutely limp in his grasp. "Feel good?"

She couldn't help the sigh that escaped her. "Yes," she whispered, eyes closing.

He bent her wrist and pressed open her palm to massage it with both thumbs.

"Mmm. Where did you learn how to do that?"

"I invented it. Just now. For you."

Her forearm rested on the edge of the tub as he worked the same magic on the back of her hand. Gently, he milked her fingers and, as he finished with each, let them drop against his upraised knee. Sensitized, she could feel the wet, coarse hairs, the hardness of bone beneath. She cracked an eyelid. "Your towel's wet."

With a grunt, he tossed it to the floor. "We'll get another. Caroline?"

By now she had her other arm folded along the tub edge, head pillowed there. "Hmm?"

She felt him lean close, smelled the clean-soap smell of him as he lightly kissed the place just behind her ear. "Let me love you," he whispered. "All of you."

She buried her face in the crook of her arm and spoke to the floor. "I can't, Jack. I'm sorry—" She broke off, trying to pull her still-captive hand away, but he kept it long enough to lave away the suds. "I don't want to fight with you."

"Me neither." He laid his wet cheek briefly on top of hers. "But I am cold. How about handin' me the robe the hotel sent up? I'm turnin' into a prune here."

She sat up, rubbing the damp spot he'd left behind. "This place sure does know how to put on the dog, doesn't it?"

She retrieved the brown-and-gold robe done in the same fleur-de-lis pattern as the wallpaper and carpet—apparently the hotel's trademark. Holding it wide for him, she heard the splash of him rising and the knock at the door simultaneously. "Just a minute!" she called.

Jack was belting the robe closed when she came back with a message in her hand.

"Who was that?" he asked, the material already darkening with water in spots.

"The desk clerk. He gave me this."

"What's it say? Read it." At the mirror, he was applying a brush to his damp hair.

But she'd already read it, and now the hand holding the paper sagged at her side. She felt vaguely sick with dread she couldn't explain. "It's from Louie. He wants to meet us downstairs for dinner tonight—at seven—as his guests."

Jack met her gaze in the glass. "That Louie—ain't he somethin'?"

"He is that."

Her tone made him look around. "Hey—don't tell me you don't like him!"

There was such disbelief in his voice and on his face that she merely shrugged and moved without thinking into the arms he held wide.

"When you get to know him, you'll like him."

She heard that with deep dismay. It meant they wouldn't be parting company with the man any time soon.

"Now I don't know about you," Jack was saying, "but I need some more sleep."

"Me, too. I didn't sleep very well last night. I kept waiting to be thrown out."

Laughing, he hugged her closer. "Wish I could've seen you." He stroked her back. "How about if we both take a nap?"

She put a sharp finger in his ribs. "No shenanigans."

"None," he vowed, and pulled back the covers while she laid her new dress on the sofa. Then they both crawled in together—she fully clothed, he in the robe.

Pulling her into the curve of his body, he snaked an arm under her pillow. "Don't you think you should take off your dress? It'll wrinkle."

"No. It'll be fine. Besides, I have a new green one to wear tonight."

He huffed air and muttered, "Bad timin', Transomb. Bad timin'."

She smiled, settling more comfortably against him, but she was already thinking about the evening ahead with Louie. She had the strangest feeling that it was all a trap somehow.

"Jack?"

"Hmm?"

"This is an expensive hotel. Can we afford to spend another night here? Perhaps we should move on."

"I told you to quit worrying." He kissed her hair. "Besides, Louie lent me some money."

Her heart sank. For some reason, this made her even more leery of the man. It spoke of a deeper relationship between the two men than she realized. Jack, for all his determination to collect a debt, didn't seem the type to borrow or accept a loan easily.

She nestled closer to him, feeling horribly vulnerable.

"You cold?"

"No."

"You sure? I just felt you shiver."

"Maybe a little." She shifted onto her back to look at him.

He returned her look with both meaning and question in his eyes. "I can make you warm," he offered softly. "If you want."

Twisting further, she pressed herself close, wrists crossed and tucked between them. Mutely, she buried her head beneath his chin and nodded.

She felt his chest hitch, his heart knock under her cheek. She held her breath as he tilted her face up for a gentle, testing kiss. Allowing herself to flow against him, she let the kiss carry her—carry them—wherever it would.

She told herself she was only doing this because she had to, because she was slyly being forced to do it to ensure his continued protection. She told herself this as she met his open-mouthed kiss with her own, and again as she twined her tongue with his. And she remembered to tell herself this one last time when his stroking hand parted her thighs, touching her, stroking with his fingers . . . then her mind emptied and she forgot reasons for everything.

Only once, when he entered her much, much later with a slow, steady thrust against her virgin flesh, did she remember Fox's face, his mouth opening to condemn her . . . but the image dissolved beneath the rising waves of pleasure from Jack's deep, rocking rhythm, leaving her vision filled only with his face, his blue eyes gazing into hers as he instructed her body with his own. "Stay with me," he urged, raggedly. "Stay with me."

Locked with him mind, body, and soul, she could do nothing else . . . and let go with cries so primal she didn't know them as her own.

The gaslit lobby of the hotel seemed the center of traffic that night, with well-dressed couples crisscrossing this way and that, heading for dining rooms and downstairs shops. The trail of perfumes and pomades lingered, tantalizingly diverse in the coal-heated air.

Caroline waited while Jack did some business at the front desk, and caught sight of herself in the huge, gilt-framed mirror on the one wall. She turned slightly. Resting her hands on her exaggeratedly small waist—the result of urging the hotel maid to pull her new corset laces tighter, and tighter yet again—she swayed slightly to set her skirts in motion so she could watch the light silver the nap, the way the dark green made the lace at wrist and décolletage glow in startling contrast. She'd done her hair more elaborately than usual and now she touched the dark, gleaming coils, pleased with the effect.

Amazing, she thought dreamily. Despite the restrictive laces, she felt totally relaxed, both in mind and body. She couldn't remember ever feeling like this. Languid . . . boneless and floating. Satisfied. No thought of sin or sacrifice marred her mood.

Suddenly, her eye was caught by the reflected figure of a man who'd paused on his way past her toward the dining room. They stared at one another in the glass for several seconds until recognition startled them both into turning.

"Miss Caroline!"

Her fingers convulsed in the pure white of her lace. "DeForest— Preacher!"

NINE

As Preacher came toward her, tall and handsome in his dark frock coat, blond hair gleaming in the lamplight, Caroline's heart pounded so hard she was sure he could hear it. She'd seen his initial step toward her falter, the light of his smile leave his eyes if not his lips.

"Mister Atchison." She forced her own lips into a smile, but inside, her stomach clenched on a wave of remembered embarrassment. "It's good to see you again. I never thought I would."

Dutifully, he caught her fingers, bowed briefly over them and released her. "Nor I you. It was two days before I learned that you and . . . you and your husband had been put ashore—"

The word *husband* didn't exactly roll off his tongue, but it struck her with velocity. He saw no carnal sin, no fallen woman, just a wife willing to play her husband false.

"But here you are. Safe and sound." He stepped back, folding his hands behind him.

He was thinner than she remembered, and distant and rigid in contrast to the man she'd strolled with on the *Quincy*. Regret over a never-intended deceit clogged the back of her throat.

His brow pleated with concern. "Is something wrong?"

"No, it's just that—well, if you knew the truth, you'd despise me."

"Don't say that. Don't even think it. Whatever it is, I wouldn't despise you for it. I couldn't."

Her vision blurred behind tears of relief and gratitude. Without thinking where she was—the fact that they stood in the middle of a very public hotel lobby—she reached to put a hand on his arm.

Hastily, he handed her his handkerchief. "Here. Wipe your eyes."

Obediently, she dabbed her lashes, her smile wobbly.

And that's when she spotted Louie. Once again in formal evening clothes, a cigar stub clamped in the corner of his mouth, he was leaning in the arched opening to the dining room, ankles crossed, arms folded, regarding them steadily. How long had he been standing there?

She thrust the handkerchief back at Preacher and started to say something, but saw his eyes suddenly lock on something over her head. She turned.

"*Jack.*"

"Caroline." His gaze brushed over Preacher and dropped back to her. "Is something wrong? You look upset."

"No, not at all. You—you remember Mister Atchison."

A small muscle worked in Jack's jaw. "Preacher."

"Transomb."

There was a loaded pause where a handshake might have occurred but didn't.

"You been crying," Jack said flatly, looking at her again. "Why?"

Her lips parted, but before she could decide how to answer, Louie startled them all by gliding up and clapping a fatherly hand to Jack's shoulder.

"I'm sure it's nothing, son," he said, taking the cigar out of his mouth. "You know women—they get emotional at the drop of a hat. I think she's just a bit overwhelmed running into her old friend here." He waved the cigar from Preacher to Caroline. "You did know these two knew each other, right?"

"Yeah. They met onboard the *Quincy.*"

Louie leaned in and thrust a hand toward Preacher. "I'm Louie—Louisiana Louie."

Preacher shook his hand. "DeForest Atchison, sir. At your service."

"A pleasure, Mister Atchison. I do hope you'll join us for dinner." He ignored Jack's grunt of protest, her own sharp inhale. "I've already reserved a table and we'd appreciate you rounding out the party, wouldn't we?" His glance slid over her and Jack without pause.

Preacher's face was mobile with indecision. "I hardly think—"

"Oh, nonsense! Any friend of Caroline's is a friend of ours, right Jack?"

Jack's nostrils flared and Caroline shot Preacher a pleading glance, but he missed it. Bowing, he gave a stiff-armed *after you* gesture, and the three of them fell in line behind Louie as he led them to the dining room.

Caroline's feet dragged. She felt downright ill at this turn of events. Waiting for Louie and Preacher to get farther ahead, she inclined her head toward Jack. "I really don't—"

"Me neither, but we ain't got a choice." None too gently, he dragged her hand into the crook of his arm. "Besides, you look like you could use a glass of somethin' fortifyin'."

She pressed her free hand to her forehead. "But I—"

His grip tightened. "Don't you even *think* of swoonin' on me," he warned too low to be overhead as they passed through the archway. "And smile—folks are lookin'."

Anger stiffened her spine if not her limbs. "What if I *do* faint?" she hissed, eyes flashing over a too-brilliant smile at a dining room filled with the blur of faceless people. "Will you make a spectacle of us by dragging me over the carpet and tossing my limp body into a chair?"

"You already made the spectacle," he said through lips stretched into his own grimace of a smile, "but I like your idea better."

"I'm just called Preacher these days," they overheard.

"A man of the cloth, eh?"

"Only when the Spirit moves me."

"Or the spirits move you," Jack muttered under his breath.

Louie was eyeing Preacher narrowly when she and Jack caught up. "You seem familiar to me, sir. Have we met?"

"I don't think so. I doubt we play in the same league, you and I."

"Ah, so you're a fellow punter—I knew it!" Louie crowed, slapping him on the back hard enough to put a hitch in his step. "There was just something about you—ah, here we are! This is our table. Waiter! Another setting and a whiskey for our friend here."

He glanced at Jack, waited for Caroline to be seated, then parted his tails and dropped into the chair directly opposite her, favoring her with a toothy smile as he snapped open his napkin.

A long-aproned waiter glided up and made short work of adding another place setting, pouring wine for her and whiskey for the men, then taking their dinner order.

Not at all hungry, she went with the first thing he suggested. "I'll have that, thank you."

"Same for me," Preacher said without much interest.

"Well, aren't you two just two peas in a pod?" Louie remarked heartily.

Caroline fought the urge to look at either Jack or Preacher—but Louie had already moved on with the statement that he was a beef and potatoes man himself. He gave Jack's arm a backhanded swipe. "How 'bout you, son? Big, juicy steak sound good again tonight?"

Jack scowled down into the crystal glass corralled between his hands. "Sure, why not?"

"Good! Make that two," he told the waiter.

Caroline studied her own wine glass with undue interest. It was going to be a long night.

Louie, however, didn't let the pace lag, nor a wedge of silence settle. He leaned forward as soon as the waiter was gone, his large hands clasped loosely on the table in front of him, and stared bluntly into Preacher's face. "I keep feeling like I've seen you somewhere before," he said. "I know—that big poker game in Natchez. Lost your shirt—and a bit more as I recall."

Preacher blushed to the roots of his blond hair, but responded smoothly. "Wasn't me—sorry. I'm strictly a small-stakes fellow, faro mostly."

Louie stared at the quieter man in narrow-eyed assessment for several seconds, then abruptly swung his attention to her. "So, Caroline, Jack tells me you grew up on a plantation."

Caroline felt her cheeks grow hot. A gentleman never confessed to having discussed a lady, not her background nor anything about her. A glance at Preacher, at the frown line between his brows, confirmed his reaction matched her own. She waited for him to say something, but he remained disappointingly silent.

Louie was considering Preacher again himself. "I don't know anything about you, sir, but you seem like a gent to me, so I'm betting you did, too."

"That's true enough. I did."

"Ah! I knew it! Miss Cooper's place is near . . . Coldwater, right, Jack?"

Jack shot Louie a dark look, gave a single nod, then drained his glass and signaled the waiter for a refill.

"That's what I thought. So, where do you come from, Preacher? I don't think you said."

"No, sir. We never had that conversation."

Thinking only to save him from another sad memory of times past, Caroline answered for him. "He was born in Booneville."

Out of the corner of her eye, she saw Jack's head turn.

"Why, that's not that far from Coldwater—y'all were practically neighbors," Louie exclaimed as if this was great news. "Y'all ever run into each other?"

"No," Caroline said shortly, avoiding eye contact with everyone.

"No? Not ever? Well, I call that a shame, a downright shame! I bet you two have a lot in common. Don't you think so, Jack?"

Unnerved at this cat-and-mouse game where she and Preacher were clearly the mice and Louie, most obviously, the cat, she grabbed her glass and gulped wine.

Preacher took another swallow of whiskey. Jack just snorted before tossing his back.

If she'd been more of a religious person, Caroline might've chosen that moment to praise God, for suddenly their waiter, leading a line of other servers laden with dishes, chose that moment to arrive with their food. Attention diverted, they all busied themselves with salting and peppering and passing around a silver clamshell full of unwieldy little butter curls, its lid snapping open and clanging shut as it went from person to person, which jangled Caroline's already-rattled nerves. She wanted nothing more than to get this evening over and done with, and she could've been chewing sawdust for all she tasted of her dinner.

Jack ordered another refill.

The few attempts at general conversation failed and devolved, naturally enough, into the topic of gambling. With little to contribute to the recounting of games past, she chose silence. Preacher had already withdrawn from the conversation.

Watching the lackluster way he picked through his plate, she felt sorry for him. No doubt he was regretting that he hadn't been nimble enough to escape Louie's invitation. In this, they'd both been trapped, but instead of feeling united with him under Louie's siege, she felt abandoned outside his wall of silence. He didn't even look at her.

Like a good shepherd, Louie noticed he'd lost Preacher's attention and redoubled his efforts to bring him back into the fold; and, as if waiting for just such a moment, Jack reached over and captured her hand under the table.

He leaned close. "You're beautiful," he whispered, whiskeyed breath moist on her ear. "The most beautiful woman here tonight. You were even more beautiful in bed without any—"

She yanked her hand free. "You're drunk."

With a mirthless half-laugh, he sank back in his chair and lifted his glass to her. "Not yet, sugar, but with any luck . . ." He finished it off with a flourish.

Louie seemed the only one oblivious to the tension at the table. When he failed to draw Preacher out, he turned to the table at large, regaling them with stories of one scrape or another, narrow escapes from the law or angry opponents. He made Jack his main audience, responding to his snarly remarks with an indulgent chuckle, but when Jack began to ignore him, Louie switched his attention back to Caroline and Preacher once again, treating them as a set.

That clearly annoyed Jack, and just brewed more trouble. Every time it filtered through his sullenness, he made a point of reaching for her hand.

Louie redoubled his efforts to drag Preacher back into conversation. It was like some strange tug-of-war, and it annoyed her. They all did after a while—Preacher with his morose silence, Louie with his overbearing monopoly, and Jack with his grasping possessiveness.

"Caroline—" Jack was leaning over again, this time trying to pry her hand out of her lap.

Louie saw and suddenly raised the stakes. "Say . . . I have an idea!" He pushed his plate away. "Why don't we all move on together come morning, up the Missouri to Kansas City? From there we could head up to Omaha and catch us a ride on the Union Pacific out to Sacramento. All of us—you, too, Preacher." He smiled expansively, ignoring Jack's dark stare. "What do you say? It'll give us all a chance to get to know one another better."

Preacher roused himself. "I'm afraid I must decline."

"Why?" Louie pressed rudely.

"I wouldn't want to impose."

"Stuff and nonsense! You wouldn't be imposing—the more the merrier, I say."

"You're too kind, but still, I must decline."

"If it's a matter of money, I'd be happy to make you a loan."

Preacher's pale face suffused with color. "I assure you I'm in no need of funds. Even if I were, I could not accept such . . . largess, but thank you."

"Are you sure? It's no trouble, no trouble 't'all. In fact, I—"

Preacher raised a slender hand. "Let us speak no more about it."

Louie glowered and harrumphed a bit, but finally turned his attention back to Jack. "How 'bout you, son? You in?"

Jack was staring down into his whiskey. "No river pilot's crazy enough to run a boat up the Missouri this time of year and risk runnin' into a freeze."

"Call 'em brave or call 'em foolhardy—all I know is there's a packet that leaves here tomorrow morning." Louie tapped the side of his nose. "Always pays a man to know his escape routes. So, you in?"

Jack tossed back his drink and jammed the empty glass back down on the table with a thump. "Sure, why not? I'd love nothin' better, old man."

Ignoring the disrespect, Louie hailed this with a crow of satisfaction. "Wonderful!"

From there, he slid into more tales of games past and rumors of ones to come. "There's even one tonight right here in this very hotel—sorry, but ladies forbidden of course," Louie made a point of telling her. "But don't you worry, m'dear. You'll get your chance. I'll see to it—and I'm sure there's a faro table for you, Preacher."

Jack stared at Louie with barely concealed hostility, and Caroline's frayed nerves couldn't take it any longer. "Let's all have some dessert!" she suggested. "Something to sweeten everyone's . . ." She started to say *temper*, but substituted "tongue" at the last second.

"An excellent idea!" Louie agreed and called for the waiter. "They've got a pie here so dense with chocolate, you could drive cattle across it."

"None for me," Jack said bluntly and threw his wadded napkin on the table.

Caroline forced a smile for the waiter's sake. "I'd like those cinnamon pears from last night, if you still have them. They were delicious."

Preacher sighed and waved a languid hand. "I'll have the same as Missus Transomb."

"There you go again! You two—" Louie's eyes rounded as the words fully registered. "*What?* What was that?" He looked to Jack. "You didn't—you're not *married*, are you?"

Caroline froze as Jack swung a belligerent stare in Louie's direction. "Who says I'd tell you if I was? My business is *my* business, my things are—"

"*Things?*" she repeated, instantly ruffled.

Jack's glare flicked in her direction. "I didn't mean it like that."

"It's what you said."

"I know, but that's not what I meant. What I *meant* was—"

"You consider me a *thing*—a possession! Yes, I know—I heard you."

"Hold your tongue, damnit! Let me finish."

"Here now!" Preacher finally roused himself.

Jack jabbed a finger at him. "You stay out of this! You already caused enough trouble!"

It was Louie's voice that cut quietly across their rising volume as he leaned forward. "Okay, son, let's keep this civilized, shall we? What's done is done. I'm sure we can fix this—"

Caroline's temper snapped. "Oh, stop it! There's nothing to fix. We're not married, we just—"

She saw Preacher's head swivel, and suddenly everything in her stilled at the realization of what she'd just done. Her head buzzed. She lurched to her feet—and whether it was the wine or too-tight corset laces, the blood left her head in a rush, and she felt herself tilt. From far, far away, she heard a shout and the muffled clatter of dinnerware. Aware only that Preacher was very slowly reaching for her, she tipped into darkness.

Jack shot to his feet and yanked the table aside all in one motion. He caught her behind the knees and swung her up into his arms. Her face was bone white, head lolling limply.

"Out of my way!" he snapped at Louie, Preacher, and the small gaggle of people quickly gathering, plowing through them without apology. Ignoring their clamor, he carried her from the dining room and through the lobby to the stairs, her dark velvet skirts spilling over his arms. Just as he reached the first step, she made a small sound and tried to lift her head.

"DeForest?"

He hitched her higher against his chest as he started up. "Sorry to disappoint ya, sugar, but it's jus' me."

Her head dropped onto his shoulder. "Jack? What-what're you doing? Put me down." Turning her head, she looked over his shoulder to see a small knot of people gathering at the foot of the staircase. "Put me down—you're causing a scene."

"You already done that. Twice."

Mortified, she buried her face against his neck, but squirmed, hoping to force the issue.

He merely tightened his grip, his long legs eating up the stairs. "Keep it up and we'll go backwards down these steps. As you said earlier, I ain't exactly sober—so if I fall, you fall, too. An' your petticoats'll get tossed over your head. You want that?"

That image stilled her more than any thought of injury, so she endured the rest of the trek in stoic silence.

At their door, he dipped his knees and stood her on her feet so he could open the door. She clung to him. "I-I'm still a bit lightheaded."

He scooped her up again, kicked the door closed, and dropped her onto the bed. Without ceremony or so much as a by-your-leave, he rolled her over and deftly flicked open the long row of covered buttons down her back. Spreading the placket apart, he yanked the knot of lacing free and dug the upper crosses apart with economic speed.

"Oh, *God!*" she breathed. It was her first lungful of air in hours. "Where'd you learn how to do that?" Face smashed into the pillow, she lifted a hand briefly and let it fall back. "Ne'r mind. I don'wanna know." With a groan, she pushed herself over onto her back.

Fists braced against the edge of the bed, he was regarding her with obvious fury. "*Why?* Why didn't you let me handle Louie? Why can't you ever trust me? Or was it more important—more than your pride or your reputation—for Preacher to know we ain't really married?"

She pushed up onto her elbows. "You're a madman if you think I did that on purpose."

"Then *why?*"

"You made me angry, that's why! The whole lot of you—you're insufferable!"

Their faces were only inches apart. When he focused on her mouth, she knew what was coming next. Instead of trying to stop or avoid him, she raised up and met him halfway in a kiss that was raw with frustration and anger equal to his own—but that fast, it turned. The taste of whiskey on his tongue, the heat of his mouth flashed fire to every part of her body, tightening her belly and making it hard to breathe all over again. She hooked an arm behind his neck as he feasted from her mouth down the side of her throat, as she rubbed her lips over his ear. His deep sound of pleasure pulled a similar one from her.

Suddenly, the arm behind his head became a demand as she sought his lips again with purpose. His arms, in turn, became iron straps around her ribs as he twisted, twining them into a whole-body embrace. With a primal growl, he rolled, dug his knees into the mattress, and with the single command, "Hold on," he dragged her across the bed with him. He was tugging her skirts up, running hard fingers inside the top edge of her stockings, face buried in her throat, mustache leaving sparking streaks she felt all over. She was framing his face with both hands, exploring his mouth with her tongue, opening her legs to invite, to accommodate, to urge. She felt her own slick burst of wetness in the crotch of her bloomers when his hand cupped her there. They were both making noises—hungry, impatient noises. He crushed green velvet and stripped it down to her waist, knees driving hers apart with his own, ripping at ribbon ties to free her, at buttons to free himself. She'd lost one slipper, kicked off the other, rising, arching, meeting his every thrust with spine-jarring need. Locked together, piston breathing in ever-harder cries of pleasure ending in one final, sustained note of sheer, mindless, crash-of-heaven's-gate *bliss!*

This was no tender lovers' tryst. This was pure, animal lust. *Wonderful, stunning lust*, Caroline thought shakily as she lay panting, sprawled beneath him, forearm thrown across her eyes, completely spent.

He rolled off her with a groan, then rolled back a moment later to curl himself around her.

With her dress bunched around her waist and sweat-slicked skin already chilling, she was grateful for his warmth.

"Mmmm," he hummed.

"Mmmm," she agreed.

What was it about this man that all he had to do was touch her and nothing else mattered? What was it about her that no matter how angry she was with him, he could make her not care?

His fingers stroked softly down her arm. He leaned to kiss the top of her shoulder. "Caroline, my Caroline," he breathed.

The tenderness of that swamped her. Without warning, the tears came, the force of them distorting her mouth and pulling her knees up as the sobs shook her.

"What?" he demanded, drawing back. "What is it? What's wrong?"

Unable to speak, she could only shake her head, face buried behind her hands.

He pried them away. "Caroline, what's wrong? Why are you crying?"

"I-I—" She hiccupped and gulped air. "I don't know. Maybe Fox was right! I *am* a-a whore, a strumpet, a—"

"Stop that! Stop it right now. Y'hear me? Y'ain't no such thing!"

"But I *am*," she argued, tears still streaming. "When you're with me—" another hiccup. "When you kiss me, I can't think of . . ." and another, "of anything else. I'm a-a *wanton!*" she wailed.

"Oh, for—" He looked around like he didn't know whether to laugh or shake her 'til her back teeth rattled. Finally, he pushed himself off the bed. "Stay here. I'll be back."

"Where are you go-going?" she called on another hiccup, but he was gone, buttoning his trousers and straightening his clothes as he went, the door clicking shut behind him.

Dragging her bodice up, her skirts back down, she curled onto her side, tears and hiccups warring for the miserable lump she was. She was tired and confused, and didn't have a friend in the world she could turn to for advice, not one, she realized—and cried all the harder.

The knock came twice before it penetrated her self-pitying fog. She sat up, swiping her knuckles beneath both eyes. "Ye-yes?"

"Miss Caroline?"

She couldn't believe her ears, but when she opened the door, there he was—blond hair in spikes like he'd been raking his fingers through it. "DeForest! What on earth—?" She glanced down the hallway in both directions, but Jack was nowhere to be seen.

"He's gone," Preacher assured her. "I waited 'til he was out of sight. I just had to make sure you were all right." He searched her tear-streaked face with concern. "*Are* you all right?"

"I-I don't know," she admitted, hugging her elbows, suddenly aware that her dress was open all the way down the back. She tried to smile, but fresh tears welled. "I told you you'd despise me."

"And I told you I never could." He offered her his now-crumpled handkerchief.

She took it, blotted her eyes, her nose, and handed it back. He tucked it away.

Oh, how she loved his so-sad face, his gentle manner. "You're too kind. And I need kindness right now. I need it so badly."

He frowned. "He hasn't hurt you, has he?"

"Jack? No, of course not."

"It's just that you're crying, and your dress," he gestured vaguely, "looks all . . ."

That's when it occurred to her what she must look like, what it *all* must look like. "No, I—you just caught me in the middle of . . . changing my dress." She looked down at her sagging skirt and brushed at it. "Something must've spilled on it when I—when I fainted."

"I regret I couldn't reach you in time."

"Don't fret. I'm fine. Nothing damaged . . . except maybe my dignity."

"*Pfft.* It was too warm in there by far, and there's nothing undignified in a lady swooning from the heat."

"Again, you're very kind. Thank you."

"Miss Caroline, I'm sorry to be so blunt—especially after what you've already been through tonight—but that man, Louie, he's very coarse. In fact, he disturbs me. I don't think he's safe for you to be around."

"He's not a very *nice* person, that's for sure. However, I don't believe he presents any bodily danger. If he was, Jack wouldn't—"

"*He's* another one. Pardon my saying so, but they're both unsavory, certainly not fit company for a lady like yourself." He smoothed the sides of his hair with the flat of both hands and stood straighter. "It's why I've decided to accept Louie's loan and come with you tomorrow. It's also why I've come to offer you my protection."

She was at a rare loss for words.

"I know I'm not as successful as Jack—not as a preacher, and certainly not as a gambler, and I'm afraid I wouldn't be able to provide for you . . ." his eyes took in the room behind her, "as well as he has, but I promise," he reached for and folded his hands around hers, "I *promise* you—"

"And just what is it you're promisin', Preacher?"

Caroline froze, and Preacher's hands dropped away as he stepped back.

Jack stood at the top of the stairs holding a whiskey glass full of something pale. "To never steal another man's woman?" he suggested, coming closer.

"I'm *not* your woman," she declared with more conviction than she felt.

His eyes flicked to her, and he looked her over with such familiarity, she blushed.

"Here, drink this," he told her. "It's brandy and water. Now go back inside and shut the door. This *gentleman* and I got some things to talk over."

"But—"

"*Now.*"

Preacher didn't say a word, didn't protest at all. He wouldn't even meet her eyes.

"Fine!" Grabbing the glass, she backed up and slammed the door, then immediately leaned to press her ear to it. She strained to hear, but they must've moved away, for Jack's voice was low and indistinct—and it didn't sound like Preacher said anything. Finally, there was only the sound of footsteps retreating.

Pulling open the door, she stuck her head out. Preacher was nowhere to be seen, and Jack was just starting down the steps. Catching sight of her, he paused, still looking fierce. "Get some sleep. We leave at dawn."

"Dawn! But—"

"Just be ready," he said, continuing his descent. "I'll come get you."

"Where will you be?"

"Playin' cards. In the gentlemen-only parlor," he added with a last, forbidding glance at her through the balustrade before his head disappeared from sight.

She considered going after him, but decided she'd had enough confrontation—and enough public humiliation—for one night. So she closed the door, drank the brandy and water, and went to bed where she slept hard and dreamed wildly of Jack and Louie chasing her through the dark, deserted streets of St. Louis.

It was bitterly cold the next morning as she, Jack, and Louie stepped down onto the sloping, cobbled levee, bundled so it was hard to tell them apart.

As promised, Jack had awakened her early—jaw shadowed, eyes red, and smelling of cigar smoke. It was so early, it was still dark outside as he shoveled the few items he had on the dresser top into his leather bag while she finished her toilette. When she stepped out from behind the screen, he'd grabbed both bags, turned down the lamp, and together they'd quit the room—all without a single word between them.

Downstairs in the lobby, Louie had stood swathed in a cape-shouldered greatcoat, muffler, and top hat. He held an armload of coats for them—gifts, he said—and had a rented hack waiting outside. Nods served as greetings between them all. It was far too early for conversation.

As Jack draped the new, heavy wool over her thinner cloak and handed her back her muffler, she scanned the darkened lobby, the shadowed staircase they'd just descended, but Preacher was nowhere to be seen.

Now, as the hack dropped them off at the levee and clattered away to be swallowed by fog, all she could hope was that Preacher was there ahead of them.

"I already have our tickets," Louie told them, tapping the wool over his chest. "We're on the *J. M. White*—that one." He pointed.

It was the last one in a row of three. An older, wider boat than the colorful *Quincy*, it was another stern wheeler with one more deck, an abundance of gingerbread, and twin black smokestacks rising midship behind the pilot house.

"The ticket master assured me the boats keep running 'til the river freezes, and that we should be in Kansas City within a fortnight," Louie told them.

"If the boiler doesn't blow or we don't run into a sandbar and drown," Jack muttered.

"Relax. These boats have a shallower draft than the old ones, and the pilots are more experienced. They've learned a thing or two in the days since the *Bertrand* went down."

As they funneled down toward the water's edge, converging with dozens of other passengers, she kept glancing back, thinking to see Preacher hurrying to catch up. At the passenger gangplank, she paused one last time to look back.

Jack nudged her from behind. "You can quit lookin' for him. He ain't comin'."

Their eyes met. His were stony beneath the derby slanted low against the wind.

"How do you know?"

"'Cause I told him I'd break his neck if he did."

Her mouth fell open. "You had no right!"

"Didn't I?"

"No!"

"My mistake. Now move. You're holding up the line."

Wondering if she'd simply traded the fry pan for the fire by ever coming with him in the first place, she glared at him a moment longer, then pulled her muffler tighter and closed the gap between her and the person ahead.

Specter-like in the early morning fog, the *J. M. White*'s whitewash was chalky with age; but once they were across the small, internal footbridge arching over the center engine shaft and up the central staircase, the boat's distant glory was still in evidence.

Walking through the main parlor, Caroline felt the uneven wear in the red-and-gold-patterned carpet, but the upholstered chairs in red velvet with gold bullion fringe were still elegant despite their age. The dark mahogany paneling swallowed up the glow of ornate lamps dotting the walls beside every stateroom door along both sides. Etched-glass panels, curved to match the shape of the hull at one end, were letting in the first milky beginnings of daylight. An open saloon was set up at the same end, its bar bracketed with stepped shelves of glittering glasses and bottles on either side. Stools, tables, and chairs filled in the rest of the space. At the other end of the boat was a clear-windowed dining area crowded with linen-draped tables. Seen through the window was a sheltered deck area where more straight-back chairs were stacked for use in warm weather.

Reading names from the manifest, a porter escorted them to their assigned rooms that flanked an open parlor on both decks. As they followed their man, his starched white jacket a stark contrast to skin that gleamed like polished cypress, she heard Jack say, "Fancy, huh?"

"Miss Caroline Cooper!" the porter announced, throwing open the next door and handing her the key.

It was even smaller than the *Quincy*'s, with its green blanketed, brass-framed bed snugged tightly into one corner, an oak washstand into the other. But brighter, with a window in between, and a grate built into the side wall already glowing with welcoming warmth.

She took her carpet bag from Jack. "Thank you," she said to the porter as she passed.

As Jack started to follow, Louie put out a staying hand. She looked around, ready to hear whatever he was dipping his head to say, but meeting her eyes, he lowered his voice. Judging by Jack's scowl, it was nothing neutral. His lips thinned and he pushed past the older man. "Then I'll pay you back for mine." Louie obviously wanted to argue further, but Jack cut him off by closing the door.

In the instant before it closed, her eyes locked with Louie's. His were narrowed, but there was something there that both surprised and baffled her: worry. Simple worry. What did he think? That she was planning to kill Jack in his sleep?

"What was that about?"

Jack threw his bag onto the bed—barely big enough for two—and didn't answer. He was already testing the spring of the mattress with both hands.

Tossing her own bag on the bed, she jammed her fists on her hips. "What did he say?"

"He said he'd already booked a separate cabin for me, but where I sleep is not his call."

"You're right. It isn't." Going to the door, she opened it and stood aside. "It's mine. *Porter!*" she called without breaking eye contact with Jack.

"Ma'am?" was the response seconds later.

"Would you please show Mr. Transomb to his own cabin?"

"Yes, ma'am."

"Thank you."

Jack's lips whitened, but he didn't say a word. He just resettled the derby on his head, grabbed his bag, and angled past her out the door.

She shut the door behind him and blew out a noisy breath as she pulled the muffler from around her neck and flopped backwards across the bed. Eyes closed, she dragged her bonnet off and let it drop to the floor. Her gloves followed, falling where they would.

Arms above her head, she stared blankly at the white-washed tongue-and-groove ceiling and willed herself not to think. But soon she was seeing Preacher's face again, hearing him say he was coming, too, that he wanted to be her protector. That offer aside, she'd looked forward to his gentle, civil manner simply as a buffer between her and Louie's contempt and Jack's sudden hostility.

Sitting up, she braced herself back on her elbows and looked around the room. The coals glowed and the window sash was tight, yet the weather outside made it all feel rather bleak.

With a hitch of her hips, she dropped back to her feet and started unpacking, using the open shelves on the wall at the foot of her bed and the hooks on the back of the door to store her things and hang her clothing.

That done, she felt hemmed in. Restless.

Retrieving her bonnet and gloves, she left the room, retying her ribbons as she went.

After a quick glance at the closed doors in a row next to hers, she closed her own very, very softly. Assuming one was Jack's, the other

Louie's, she slipped by, happy not to be in danger of attention from either one for a spell.

The parlor was mostly empty at this early hour, so she didn't have to do much more than nod as she passed the few remaining souls who lingered. In contrast, the roustabouts outside were bustling, readying the boat for castoff, bawling orders over the side, unwinding ropes as thick as their arms or wielding long poles, ready to push them out into the current. The deck rumbled under her feet as unseen others stoked the boiler that would eventually engage the giant pistons and drive the shaft to the paddle wheel.

The cold quickly soaked through her woolen layers, and she wished she had a muff to warm her hands. She made do by tucking her gloved hands inside the bell-shaped sleeves of her new cloak, and stepped carefully along the slick, painted deck.

There were only a few other passengers out and about. They'd appear suddenly out of the milk-thick fog and nod a greeting before disappearing just as abruptly back into its swirling curtain. It was too cold to stand and talk, so everyone kept moving—that's why the sight of one passenger materializing stock-still at railside caught her notice. Caroline's pulse spiked, until the man turned toward her, tipped his hat, and moved past without a word. Just another stranger.

Weary with disappointment, feet numbing with cold, she returned to her cabin.

That evening, just before the supper hour, with the savory smell of meat in the air and the musical tinkle of silverware, Caroline stood at Louie's door. She hadn't spoken to him directly since their disastrous dinner the night before—but she couldn't afford to think about that now. She knocked lightly.

He opened it immediately, one hand just smoothing the collar above his black evening jacket. His hand stilled at seeing her, but there was not so much as a flicker of surprise in his cool, blue-eyed gaze. He stepped back. "Come in. I've been half expecting you."

"Only half?"

"Well, I didn't stake any money on it."

"Too bad for you then."

The twitch of an eyebrow was his only acknowledgment before he plucked a silver flask off the washstand and held it up. "I don't have a glass, but can I offer you a drink?"

"No, thank you."

She took in the cabin with a single glance. The bed was neatly made. His only luggage, a scuffed and scarred steamer trunk, was tucked into the small space between the foot of the bed and the wall, a folding camp chair strapped across the top. The two wall shelves, identical to hers, were neatly lined with some personal items. Their cabins were the exact same size, but his personality—more than his physical bulk or possessions—made his seem smaller. Even when he wasn't talking, he had a way of filling up a room.

"I never thanked you for the new cloak. It's quite warm."

"Glad it serves. Can't have you freezing when you're out strolling on deck, can we?"

There was nothing in his expression to indicate he'd seen her out there earlier, but she couldn't be sure. He was a wily old goat. Folding her hands, she faced him squarely. "We might as well be honest with each other. I don't like you and I know you don't like me. But I didn't come here for your company—or your liquor. Or even because of the cloak."

Nothing in his expression changed. "No? Then why did you come?"

"I came to take you up on your offer."

He pulled the cork off the flask. "Which offer is that?"

"The one where you said you'd teach me to gamble."

He considered her for a second. "Does Jack know you're here?"

The question annoyed her. "No, and I prefer that this conversation—and anything that might come of it—stay that way."

"I see." He took a swig from the flask, recorked it with a flat-handed smack, then returned the favor of a dead-on look. "Well, as long as we're being honest with each other, you're right. I don't much like you—don't trust you more than I don't like you. But I'm afraid I can't teach you how to gamble."

"But you said—"

He held up a finger. "All I can do is teach you how to play the games and," his lids drooped suggestively, "perhaps how to tip the odds in your favor. The gambling part—knowing when to take a risk and when to walk away—most of that you gotta learn on your own. But I suspect you already know more about that than you realize."

Not sure what he meant by that, she waited.

"One last thing." The finger was leveled at her nose. "If I decide to do this—and I say *if*—then I call the shots. All of them. Clear?"

She didn't hesitate. "Clear."

"I'm serious," he stressed. "You balk—even once—and we're done."

After a few beats of silence to let his words sink in, he retracted the finger. "It's a whole different life than the one you're used to."

"I'm counting on that . . . and you have no idea what I'm used to."

With a grim nod, he reached over, unstrapped the camp chair and opened it up to face the side of the bed. Next, he opened the trunk lid and removed a large wooden tray. He gave it a shake and, to Caroline's amazement, slender legs unfolded themselves from each corner, turning it into a small table. Placing that precisely between the chair and the bed, he waved for her to be seated. "Shall we begin?"

TEN

"Let me see your hands first."

Instinctively, Caroline hid them behind her. "They're clean if that's what you're asking."

"It's not, but without good hands, none of the rest matters. Hold 'em out."

Reluctantly, she did so, and he took them like he was assessing horseflesh. He turned them over, flexed them this way and that, pressing, pinching. "Nice palms," he pronounced. "Long fingers, flexible, with good pads. A little work-hardened, but we can fix that."

She blushed and pulled free. "Would you like to check my teeth, too?"

Ignoring that, he turned to his trunk, plucked out some paper-wrapped decks of cards—Eagles, Hart's, and some others she'd never seen before—and tossed them on the bed. "Sit. Pick a deck and unwrap it," he instructed, removing his coat, and laying it on the far side of the bed. Smoothing the fabric, he folded it very precisely, reminding her of Jack.

As soon as he settled himself on the bed across from her, he pulled out a handkerchief and tucked it beside his hip, then thumbed his suspenders into a more comfortable position. "Know how to shuffle? Good. Start shuffling."

Apparently, he'd become a man of few words, but that was fine with her. Picking up the cards, she split the deck in half.

"You're not pairing up dance partners. Make the sides unequal. Mixes better."

Correcting herself, she shuffled and shuffled . . . and shuffled again. "How much longer?"

"As long as I say—thirteen makes the best mix, but you need the practice. Keep going."

Finally, he took the deck from her. "Now watch carefully." He shuffled a couple more times himself, then dealt her five cards face down. "Did you see that?"

Her brow puckered. "Of course I did—I'm sitting right here."

"No," he said with pronounced patience, "did you see what I did—besides the obvious?"

"You didn't do anything besides the obvious."

"You sure? Turn your cards over."

"I don't—oh! How'd you do *that*?" she asked, staring at all clubs.

"I told you to watch," he said with a smirk, mopping his face with the handkerchief.

"I *was* watching, but I didn't see anything."

"Here, I'll show you again." He did it three more times, each time with a different suit.

She was stunned. Even though she'd seen it with her own eyes, she still couldn't believe it. "Well, I never—! Will you teach me how to do that?"

He just grinned and mopped his face again. "What do you know about a deck of cards?"

She ran down the four suits.

"How many cards in a deck?" he asked, shuffling almost absently.

"Fifty-two."

"Fifty-four," he corrected, still shuffling. "Two jokers. What's lowest and highest?"

"Ace through king—but it depends on the game," she added quickly. "Like blackjack."

"Good. Know how to play that? And by that, I mean the strategies, not just the rules."

"Strategies?"

"That's what I thought. Okay, let's start at the beginning."

"Wait! I do remember a few things," and she recited what Del had taught her.

"Not bad. For starters." By now, he was twirling cards between and over the backs of his knuckles. "How are you at sums—arithmetic?"

"I-I'm pretty good."

"In your head?"

He began snapping a single card between his thumb and middle finger, corner to corner.

Distracted, she didn't answer.

"Pay attention. In your head?" he repeated.

She nodded, feeling like she was back in the school room.

"Good. You need to be. You need to keep track of what's been played, to calculate what's left so you always know what your odds are. Like this," he said, burning a six and dealing them both the one card down and one card up of blackjack.

After four hands, he stopped. "How many face cards have been played so far?"

"Um . . . six?"

"Eight. That's eight out of twelve total, plus a ten. That's two-thirds of the twenty-one cards that have been played—less than half the deck. That leaves—"

From there, he ran down the rest and calculated the odds as he went until she thought her head would burst.

"Got it?"

She tried to look more confident than she felt. "I think so."

"Good. Remember, you gotta keep track. Now what other games can you play?"

"A little bluff—basics only," she added before he could ask.

"Give me the ranks of winning hands, in order, lowest to highest."

She did, and he was just as unimpressed as Jack had been on the *Quincy*.

By now, he was cutting the deck one-handed, extracting the ace of diamonds, seeming to bury it in the next cut, only to make it reappear in the next.

She was mesmerized. "What you're doing right now—it's like magic!"

"That's what a lot of this is—part magic, part skill."

"What about luck?"

He snorted. "Luck's for amateurs. Oh, you hear a lot about Lady Luck, but serious sports bribe her as much as sweet-talk her."

She pointed to the card trick he was still doing. "Will I ever get that good?"

"Maybe—if you practice. A lot. It's something you gotta build up to." He returned the ace to the deck again. "Let's start with something simple like the second deal, shall we?"

He demonstrated by dealing them both a hand, then turning them over. She had a bunch of nothing, he had a pair of aces. Scooping them back together and reshuffling, he dealt again, and again she had nothing while he held the other pair of aces.

Her eyes narrowed. "How are you doing that?"

"It's all in the dealing. And cutting . . . or not as the case may be. It's easy—a beginner's trick. Here, I'll show you how it's done. Let's start with the shuffle first."

This time he slowed his movements down, breaking down every step, holding the deck this way and that to reveal how he manipulated the cards as he dealt only from the second card, leaving the top one—an ace of hearts—in place every time. Then he did it again at regular speed, slowing down only long enough this time to show her how he plucked off the bottom card—another ace he'd been saving.

"Good heavens!"

"Heaven's got nothing to do with it, I assure you." He demonstrated again. "Now you."

"I'll never be able to do that!"

"No? Okay." He took the deck back and started to put it away.

She snatched it back, and they worked for another hour—she fumbling through the mechanics, he demonstrating them over and over, patiently correcting the position of her hold, her fingers, her timing.

Suddenly, he reached over and grabbed the cords of her reticule dangling from her wrist. "You need to get rid of this when you're dealing. Speed's important and these strings slow you down."

Keeping a wary eye on him, she unwound the reticule from her wrist and placed it carefully on the floor beneath her chair. Planting her foot on it made her feel better.

"Don't worry," he grinned at her caution, "I'm not after your money. Yet. Now do it again, but stop letting that top card click. It's a dead giveaway."

Another hour went by.

"I'm hungry," she complained for the third time, hearing the growing hum of voices in the parlor outside their door. The dining room would be filling up soon. "Aren't you hungry? If we don't eat soon there won't be anything left."

Chin on his laced fingers, studying her hands as she worked the cards, he didn't even look up. "I told you before—a full belly makes for dull wits. Besides, we don't eat 'til you get a little less clumsy with those pasteboards. Here, let me show you again."

Again became *again* and *again* . . . and yet *again*.

"Okay, that's enough for now," he said on a stretch. "We'll come back to it later."

Gratefully, she sagged forward, rubbing her aching back.

"Don't give out on me now," he said with the barest hint of humor. "We just got started."

But at least he ordered up some supper, and while they ate pork chops and stewed apples there in his cabin, he tested her knowledge of the hands and rules of poker and *vingt-et-un* as he insisted upon calling blackjack, and was gratifyingly satisfied with her grasp of both.

"Finally," she murmured on the heels of yawn. "Something I know how to do."

He grunted. "I said I was glad to see you knew how to play the games—but you don't know a whit about strategy yet."

She groaned.

"Too much? Then you're better off sticking to faro, three-card brag, and that sucker's game, monte. You won't make big money, but you'll be able to eat. Most days anyway."

Her shoulders slumped. "I don't know how to play any of those."

"No?" He regarded her almost jovially. "Well, it's all part of the package, my dear. If you aim to make a living with this, you gotta know it all." He picked up the deck again. "Tell you what, how 'bout we work on some real beginner stuff? Ever hear of Ace-Deuce-Jack? No? Well, it's easy." After shuffling a few times, he let her cut, announced that he was the bank, then turned up the top three cards—a four, an eight, and a jack. "I win—because of the jack." He tucked those to his right and plucked off the next three cards—a four, another four, and a ten. "You win." He set those to the left. He did this all the way through the deck, discarding the final, leftover card without even looking at it. "Notice anything about your piles and mine?"

"You have more."

"Yep. And I will—almost every time."

Her eyes narrowed. "What's the trick?"

"No trick. Just odds, that's the beauty of it. Want to see it again?"

She nodded.

He did, and the results weren't exactly the same, but he was right—he still had more.

"What if you did it with different cards than an ace, deuce, or a jack?"

"Ah! Now you're thinking! Okay, you pick the three cards, shuffle, and be the bank."

"Um . . . a four, an eight, and a king." She shuffled and dealt. Sometimes there were two kings or an eight and a four in a single set, but she still had more by the end.

"How on earth?" she marveled.

"Doesn't matter—but what's the difference between this time and last?"

She thought for a long moment. "I don't know . . . you were the dealer last time?"

"That's right. This is a dealer-favored game," he said, using a single card to scoop up the rest. "Invite players to put down their bets, make 'em stand, then pay all winners—even money only. That way you'll always have supper money if nothing else. Don't do it too often in the same town though—makes people cranky—but pull it out when you need to."

Her mind was reeling excitedly, but he was already moving on. "Now let me show you that bottom deal again—anybody can do it—shuffle without really shuffling, then fake the cut. You're going to practice this every night 'til your knuckles are sore and you can do it in your sleep. We'll save craps for later. Dice need a different kind of attention."

She started to protest, but he fixed her with a steely eye. "You aimin' to quit?"

She bit back a sigh. "Not at all. Deal," she said, tapping the table.

A little while later, they heard the door next to Louie's open and close—Jack's room—and they both stilled. After a distinct pause, his footsteps faded away.

Louie scowled and rapped the side of the card deck sharply against the table. "Boy's still upset with me over the cabins." He locked eyes with her. "But you're not, are you?"

She raised her chin a notch. "Despite my . . . current circumstances, sir, I'm still a lady, and as such, I find your choice of subject matter entirely inappropriate."

He sucked a tooth and handed her back the cards. "Your deal."

By dawn, she was bleary-eyed, her memory and dexterity shot, and he finally sent her off to her bed with the gruff admonition, "Better build up your stamina, girl. And here," he said, slapping a new deck of Eagles into her hand. "These are your new constant companions. You're going to become so familiar with them that—"

"I'll be able to *feel* the ink-weight difference between an ace and a king," she finished.

His stare was hard, but she detected the barest glimmer of appreciation in their chilly blue depths. "Hmph," was all he said to that, and pointed to the cards in her hand. "Practice. Oh, and take this," he added, plucking a small piece of glass paper off a shelf. "Sand the calluses off your fingers tonight and every night before bed, sand 'em all 'til they're near bloody. A gambler needs sensitive fingers."

"Whatever for?"

"I'll explain later. Now off with you."

Tired as she was, as soon as she settled under the covers, she dutifully rubbed her fingertips over the glass paper until they were dark pink and tender—like she'd been sewing all day without a thimble.

When she finally closed her eyes, her mind's eye was crowded with images of diamonds, hearts, clubs, and spades . . . face cards with their haughty stares . . . numbers flipping by . . .

And suddenly Wendall.

She hadn't thought about him, not really thought about him, since she'd turned her back on Coldwater and rode away. Truth was, she hadn't wanted to think about him—still didn't, but there he was in her mind's eye. He was laughing. She fell asleep wondering what was so funny.

She woke to the steady babble of voices just beyond her door, puzzled by the absence of motion, that subtle sense of moving with the current. They must've docked somewhere.

What time was it? Judging by the smell, heavy with beef and onions, she'd missed the morning meal altogether. But since there was still light behind her shaded window, she felt reassured she hadn't missed the noonday meal as well. Not yet anyway. She really needed to get herself one of those little time pieces she saw women starting to wear pinned at their bosom.

The porter had refilled her water pitcher and stoked the fire in the grate one last time before she'd turned in last night—only ashes left now. But there was enough residual heat that she could wash comfortably before dressing in her black bombazine.

She emerged from her room a short while later, counting on her bonnet and short cape to disguise the fact that she was only just rising. Nodding and smiling at people as she passed, she headed directly to the glass-walled dining room. It was crowded. She searched in vain for Jack, even Louie, but there was not a familiar face in sight. And the only open spots for a single diner were at the common table in the center. Although she preferred something less conspicuous, she took a seat and ordered from the long-aproned waiter, his dark mustache waxed into a long, improbable curve on either side of his mouth.

As she ate, she glanced around. Even though they were protected from the weather and it was sunny outside, the curved wall of windows framed the riverbank of bare trees, and visually brought winter inside. It was vaguely depressing. Her fellow diners seemed to feel it, too. Almost all were bundled in dark wool with mufflers and hats, and although the murmur of conversation was constant, the mood was subdued. She didn't like these people, she decided, these prisoners of daylight. She much preferred the freer, gayer, more colorful people of the night—the gamblers and the risk-takers.

Just then a tall man bumped her chair. She looked up, expecting it to be Jack—but no. She hadn't seen him since they boarded and it felt odd. They hadn't been apart for more than a few hours since they'd met; and much as she hated to admit it, she missed him.

She blotted her mouth, and left coins for the waiter. She needed to move.

Outside, the air was sharp with cold, the main deck all but empty. Wherever they were moored, nothing of a town was visible—just a wide, packed dirt path cut into the bank where two men were struggling to get a loaded pack mule up the slope.

Back on the main deck once more, she suppressed a yawn. Instead of reviving her and making her feel more alert, the full stomach and walk in the cold only made her yearn for more sleep; so she returned to her cabin. Removing her bonnet and cape before falling across her bed, she slept soundly until the porter's tap at her door woke her. It was dark outside.

"Stove wood, ma'am," he announced when she opened the door.

She stepped aside, rubbing her eyes. "What time is it?"

"'Bout half past seven, ma'am. If you haven't eaten yet, the galley's still servin'."

After the porter smoothed the sleep marks out of her bedding and left again with a nod for her thanks and the coin she pressed into his hand, she splashed water on her face, changed into her green velvet dress, smoothed her hair, then picked up her deck of cards. Tools of the trade—her trade. Perhaps one day, she'd even get her own game box. Something like her much-missed sewing box, satiny smooth and feminine.

After a while of solo practice, she opened her door and stepped out. The happy plink of a piano was coming from somewhere, and a dozen or so passengers stood about, laughing and talking now that the spirit of nighttime had descended. Whereas she fit right in before with her black bombazine, now, even in her velvet, she felt severe in contrast to the others' evening wear. Nothing overly fancy or elaborate, but she caught the subtle wink of marcasite, as well as tiny flashes of gold here and there among the women dressed in gowns of dark sapphire or burgundy or swishing, black taffeta. The men, too, were downright shiny with their oil-slicked hair, brocade weskits, and gold watch chains.

Retreating to her cabin, she opened her small, lacquered box. Clasping the gold locket around her throat, she slipped on her mother's ruby ring and wiggled her finger to make it flash in the lamplight.

Satisfied with these small improvements, she turned to leave—only to jump at the knock.

"Open up. It's me," Louie called.

She unlatched the door, and he stood there resplendent in his usual black and white, silver hair gleaming, blue eyes alight in his broad, bronzed face.

"'Evening," he said, "you been practicing?"

"I have."

"Good. Come next door and show me."

Trying not to look furtive, she swept next door and inside without meeting the eyes of anyone in the parlor. She didn't like being seen entering a man's cabin, but was counting on any observers to assume they were simply traveling kin of some sort.

Louie had the camp chair and little table already set up.

Without removing his coat this time, he settled on the bed again.

"Okay, not bad," he said after she ran through everything he'd shown her the night before. "Let's see your fingers. Good."

He pulled a new deck out of his jacket and dealt her five cards, face down, without even shuffling. "Pick those up. Don't worry about what they are, and run your fingers over them. Tell me if you notice anything unusual."

She did as she was bid. "No . . . nothing. I—oh, wait." Brows pinched in concentration, she closed her eyes and ran all the cards through her fingers once again, more slowly this time. "There seem to be little bumps here and there."

"Good." He took the cards back and put them away. "That's a marked deck—a cooler."

"What are they for?"

"All in good time, my dear. All in good time. Right now it's time to go play the tables."

"But I'm not ready!"

"Don't worry. We're not trotting out your new skills just yet. Learning to play a good square game's gotta come first. There are plenty of open games this evening and I'm going to need your help. I want you to sit across from me and feel each card you're dealt like you did just now. If you feel any bumps like that, nudge my foot under the table."

Nerves clashed with her excitement. "All right, but I—"

"Stop worrying." He pushed her toward the door. "You'll do fine."

She halted abruptly, head tilting. "Why are you doing this? Showing me all this?"

His gaze was mild. "I thought you wanted to learn."

"I did—I do, but these tricks, these *cheats* … Why are you trusting me like this?"

He gave her a hard stare. "Don't confuse trust with usefulness, m'dear. And there's nothing I've shown you here that you could use against me without harming yourself as well."

Certainly not flattering, but that's why she believed him.

"Besides," he added, "I just want you to be able to make your own way and not to have to depend on anyone else to survive."

She looked him in the eye. "Like Jack?"

He nodded. "Like Jack. Now come on. We don't want to be late."

The volume of voices in the parlor had risen steadily, no doubt with the introduction of alcoholic beverages, she thought, noticing the circulating waiters.

"It's good to see them looking so eager for entertainment," he remarked. "We'll have to do our best to oblige them tonight, won't we?"

"We?"

Suspecting a balk, he held up a blunt finger. "I call the shots, remember?"

"Of course. I was just thinking the pots might not be big enough to split two ways."

He blinked at that, then threw back his head and laughed out loud. "Jack was right," he said, still chuckling as he steered her through the crowd. "Spirit is definitely your long suit."

As soon as Caroline laid her hand on the arm he cocked in her direction, allowing him to lead her downstairs, she knew this was the true beginning of her new life, the one she had chosen for herself.

As they moved to one game after another, deck to deck into the wee hours of the morning, she soon discovered things were much more discreet onboard the *J.M. White*. There was no single gaming parlor here. It wasn't that anyone frowned on gambling—on the contrary, they literally catered to it, making sure the players' rooms were laden with trays of meats, side dishes, and sweets. Apparently, they just didn't want it out in the open, preferring that sporting men conducted their business in private cabins—in almost *every* cabin it seemed.

Soon, she came to know the layout of the whole boat, including the rabbit warren of cabins and passageways on the cargo deck where the bigger-stake games were played.

In between games, she'd watch Louie stroll through the crowded parlors, smiling, laughing, pausing now and then to exchange a low-voiced word or two before circling back to whisper a room number and sometimes the rhythm of a special knock to gain entry.

They no longer arrived together. Instead he'd go first while she waited the prescribed number of minutes, estimating them in her head, before finding her way to the designated door.

Louie always greeted her along with the others, never acknowledging he knew her. Before they'd begun this trial-by-fire introduction, he'd told her to watch, listen, do as he did, and above all, smile sweetly and flatter often.

She was nervous the first few times, but soon realized her unfailingly warm receptions were more about her sex than her skill with cards—and perhaps a healthy curiosity about the amount of gold or silver in her purse.

She bet modestly, won the same, kept her game "square," and knew when to distract. Louie would nudge her foot beneath the invariably small tables—for all the cabins, even the most richly appointed ones were on the cramped side. And by a different foot pressure, she learned when to fold, thank the gentlemen prettily for allowing her to play, and excuse herself. What she *didn't* know was what Louie was doing *while* she did the distracting. That he was performing some sleight of hand she had no doubt, but she never caught him at it, not even once. *Slick as a water moccasin*, she thought with grudging admiration.

Once she made her exit, she'd return to the parlor and wait. Sometimes he'd reappear right away, sometimes she might be left on her own for an hour or more before he'd show up again and they'd move on to another game. Knowing from Jack how gamblers most often played away the night at a single table, she understood Louie was sacrificing to be her tutor.

As she stood before each new door, she always wondered if Jack might be on the other side. While part of her enjoyed the thought of surprising him, a wiser part knew it would prove more distraction than she could handle. Louie must've known it, too, and why he always went first. Only once did he return before she could join him. With a faint frown and the barest shake of his silver head, she knew there'd been a change in plans. He never said why, but she always suspected Jack had been one of the players in the intended game. That Louie was ultimately acting in his own interests, however convoluted, Caroline never doubted; but she was satisfied that, for the moment at least, their agendas meshed.

Fact was, she and Jack did see one another from time to time—usually across the crowded dining room or out along the deck with a terse nod serving as acknowledgment, but their paths never crossed close enough to allow speech. That he was still put out with her accounted for some of it of course; however, the fact that she would fade around a corner or duck into the nearest doorway if she heard or saw him accounted for the rest.

Only once did she have no such escape. She'd just left a game on the cargo deck, and before she could make it back up one of the open-stair ladders, here he came down the opposite set, bringing up the rear behind two other men. All three were the picture of male contentment, chuckling at some joke, brandies in hand, smoking cigars.

She saw him squint through the smoke, then pivot in surprise as she squeezed past him in the tight space.

"Caroline—"

Twiddling her fingers in a wave over her shoulder, she didn't even look back. She felt both lucky and oddly miffed when he didn't try to follow her. Still, she made sure that from then on there was no sight or sound of *anyone* coming before committing herself to a passageway.

Even now, having just finished a most satisfying and mildly prosperous game of blackjack, she paused to peer into the parlor before entering to wait for Louie. It was empty, most of the serious sports having settled into a game that would take them through 'til dawn.

Somewhere a clock chimed two. By her count, she had already played in three—no, four—separate games. A yawn got past her.

"Shouldn't you be asleep at this hour?"

She spun around. "Jack! You—oh, my!" she exclaimed at the sight of his black Prince Albert coat, brocade vest, and white silk four-in-hand. "Don't you look handsome!"

Hand pressed to his vest, he rocked back on his heels to look down at himself. "Thank you. You, on the other hand, look tired— like you're about to fall asleep standin' up."

She swatted his sleeve with her mother's black lace fan she'd taken to carrying, finding it a useful distraction at the tables. "That's the most ungallant thing you've ever said to me."

He inclined himself in a slightly mocking bow. "Beg pardon."

She snapped open the fan and fluttered it. She could still feel the press of angry feelings between them, the break in trust, but didn't know how to sort it out by herself, much less how to fix it.

"Despite needin' sleep, you *are* lookin' very pretty this evenin'," he said on a softer note. "How are you?"

"I'm well, thank you."

"Ain't seen much of you—'cept for that one, um, midnight stroll."

"Yes." She fingered the cameo she'd strung on a length of velvet around her neck. "What with our different schedules, we're bound to keep missing each other."

They both acknowledged a couple strolling by, arm in arm.

"Is that it?" he asked once they passed. "We're just keepin' different schedules?"

She twitched a shrug, but said nothing.

Pointedly, he pulled out his pocket watch and flipped it open. "Hmm," he said with a hike in his brow. "It's two-ten in the mornin'. You're here, I'm here . . ."

"I just can't sleep, that's all."

"Really?" The watch was snapped shut and put away. "Tried warm milk?"

"No. I haven't tried warm milk."

"So what's keepin' you awake? Pinin' for Preacher?"

It was odd to feel relieved at the mention of Preacher, but right then it seemed more important to keep her current undertaking a secret. Waving her fan, she smiled smugly. "Why, yes, I am. However did you guess?"

His eyes narrowed, but before he could respond, she yawned in his face. "Oh, my! How indelicate of me." She smothered another yawn. "But being with you has done the trick." She tapped his arm with the fan again as she moved past him. "Goodnight, Jack."

"Caroline—"

She knew he was following her, but he was closer than she thought. Just as she reached her door, and without any preamble whatsoever, he turned her and captured her mouth in a long, slow, thorough kiss that felt more like her whole body was involved instead of just her lips. His taste and smell, the pressure of his hands framing her face, seemed both shockingly new and achingly familiar. Her bones turned to mush, and she fumbled behind her for the doorknob.

Reaching past her, he opened it himself. "Sleep well," he said gruffly.

Collapsing against the other side, she wondered for the hundredth time why he had such an unsettling effect on her, why she couldn't dismiss him from both her mind and her life.

The knock behind her head startled her, and she jumped for the second time that night. "Go away!"

"*What?* It's Louie. Open up."

"Where have you been?" she quizzed sharply, checking for any sign of Jack as she pulled him over the threshold.

"Where you left me. I realized there was another rounder at our table. That fellow with the fringe all around and bald on top—like a monk? You didn't feel anything in the cards, did you? No? Me either. He must be using some other kind of gaff, just not sure what. Took me a while to corral him and get back my own. Say, I saw Jack walking away just now. I hung back 'til he was out of sight. What did he want? Did you two talk?"

"A little."

"He's keeping a low profile this trip, but—hey, you look plum tuckered out."

"I'm fine."

"You been practicing the tricks I showed you?"

"Every night before I go to sleep, every morning when I wake up."

"Good. Come next door and show me."

As much as she wanted to sleep, she wanted this more, so she followed him.

"Much better!" he exclaimed at the end of an hour of shuffling, cutting, and dealing. "You're doing well, very well. Better than I expected."

She beamed. It felt like she'd just won a prize.

He smacked his knees and stood up. "Well, best to call it a night. Come a little earlier tomorrow evening. I've got a special game lined up with some deep pockets, but I want to show you a few things first. Just might need your help reeling in this particular fish."

"What kind of things?"

"You'll see." He plucked at her sleeve. "You got anything else to wear? Something brighter, more cheerful?"

"I'm in mourning."

"Not anymore you're not. You're in gambling . . . and a sportin' man always appreciates a little color at his table."

"I have a yellow muslin, but it's out of season—"

"Good. Wear it tomorrow. And let your hair down a little, maybe let a few curls fall over these pretty shoulders of yours."

From any other man, she might've suspected flirtation, but Louie was neither lecherous nor seductive in the assessing look he was giving her. His attention was pure calculation.

She shrugged tiredly. "Anything to keep a sporting man distracted, I suppose."

From a shadowed corner of the parlor, Jack watched Caroline return to her own cabin, her shoulders rounded with weariness, and he marked the time with a black scowl before snapping the watch closed with enough force to threaten its crystal. She'd been in there an hour!

Stalking across the carpet to Louie's door, he raised his fist to pound, when it suddenly opened and the two men found themselves eye to eye.

"Jack! It's good to see you, boy. I was just heading out for a last hand or two. Care to join me? No? Well, come on in."

Jack stood his ground. "We've been friends for a long time, Louie."

The hard tone drained off Louie's smile. "That we have. Something on your mind?"

"What are you up to?"

"You wanna be a little bit more specific?"

"You know damned well what I'm talkin' about! What are you doin' with Caroline?"

Louie's good humor returned in the form of a crooked smile. "Just keeping snakes out of your saddlebag, boy, that's all."

Jack's eyes narrowed. "Not the reassurance I was lookin' for."

"No?"

"No, but as much as I don't like the idea of you teachin' her to gamble—especially the *refinements*—that better be the only reason I keep seein' her comin' and goin' from your room at all hours. I've been watchin' you and I'm gonna keep on watchin.'"

Devilry sparked in Louie's blue eyes as he stepped out past Jack and pulled the door shut behind him. He knocked the back of his knuckles against Jack's vest front, winked, and walked away leaving Jack feeling even more confounded.

As Louie tripped lightly down the staircase leaving him standing alone in the abandoned parlor, Jack stared long and hard at Caroline's closed door. The violence with which he wanted to beat on it, demanding to be let in, bothered him as much as his own dark suspicions.

With a snarl of frustration, he spun around and took himself off to the saloon instead.

The next evening, Caroline sat on Louie's neatly-made bed, propped back against his pillow, feet on the floor, thumbing through a tattered catalog from *E.N. Grandine* in New York. Open on the bed beside her was an equally worn copy of a similar catalog from the *Will & Finck Company*, its cover declaring they were "*The Only Sporting Emporium on the Pacific Coast.*"

Doing as she was bid the night before, she'd arrived feeling uncomfortably festive in the ruffled yellow dress, but she could tell from Louie's expression when he opened the door that he was disappointed in her long, puffed sleeves and high, demure yoke of white lace.

"I had to ask a porter to find a lady who could hook me up in the back," she said, hoping this extra effort might improve his opinion, but only the last-minute rosettes she'd fashioned to anchor a cluster of curls spilling over a shoulder eased his scowl, and he waved her inside.

He was in his shirt sleeves, his coat once again smoothed neatly across the end of the bed. She removed her short cape and draped it over the back of the little chair.

Since every surface was stacked with things from his open trunk, she ignored the impropriety and took the only available space left—the head of his bed, her attention snagged immediately by the catalogs laying on the blanket.

"Why, I never—!" she exclaimed for the third time in as many minutes. "Can you believe this? Marked decks for a dollar twenty-five? '*These cards are an exact imitation of fair playing cards,*'" she read aloud. "They advertise it right out in the open!"

Louie grunted. "Not worth it. I've seen some. Too easy to detect. Best to mark your own." He was bent over, still digging through his trunk. When he found whatever he was looking for, she assumed he'd show her and that would explain all the mess he was making. In the meantime, her attention was glued in horrified fascination to the inked drawings of gambling equipment—specifically *cheating* gambling equipment—and their openly boastful descriptions.

She dropped the *Grandine* and picked up the *Will & Finck*. "Listen to this—'*Vest hold-outs...a sleeve hold-out—anyone can operate it with very little practice!*'"

She flipped some pages. "And listen to this one. They've got something called a *table bug* that—and I quote— '*can be put under and removed from any table in less than half a minute.*'" She looked up. "What's it do? Do you know?"

"It holds a few cards," he gestured, still distracted, "until you need them."

She tucked her chin reproachfully and studied the illustration again. "Well, I declare! The gall of all this—it's hard to believe."

"No gall, just business. Holdouts have their place. With the right help," he straightened, indicating the catalogs with a nod, "and enough fat sheep at your table, a man can make upwards of a thousand dollars a night."

Her eyes rounded. "A *thousand*—! *In one night?*"

Suddenly distracted by the contraption of brass rods, hinges, buckles, and leather straps he was pulling out of the trunk, she tossed the catalog aside and slid off the bed to have a closer look. It resembled nothing so much as a mangled metal skeleton. "What in the world?"

"It's called a Kepplinger harness—designed by a Mr. Kepplinger of course. I bought it a few years ago. Worst investment I ever made. I keep it as a souvenir more than anything else."

She pushed at it with a fingertip, and it rattled and swayed drunkenly. "What's it for?"

"You strap it to your arms and legs under your clothes. See these clips here? They hold extra cards, and by moving certain ways, clenching and unclenching your muscles, the cards are supposed to be released from inside your sleeves or trouser legs."

She searched his face. "You're not serious." Lightly, she tested one of the metal arms by pulling on it. It squealed in protest. "But it's so—"

"Noisy? That's the problem. Closest I ever came to being lynched was when I tried this. Damn thing jammed straight away. I hightailed it outa that saloon clinking and clanking so loud I spooked the horses. That's the only thing that saved me. Everybody was too busy running after their mounts to bother with me." He was grinning like a kid recounting a daring adventure. "Unlike more subtle skills, there's no getting around the fact you're cheating when you're caught with something like this. Simple's best," he said, dropping the harness back in the trunk with a clatter.

He pointed to the catalogs again. "And none of that stuff's worth a nickel if you don't have the hands. A sharp's best friends are his own two hands. Those and practice—remember that. Ah, here's what

I wanted to show you," he said, retrieving several wrapped decks of cards from the bottom of the trunk.

"These are club cards. See—they have plain white backs. Easy to mark—just a drop of water removes the glazing—but that also makes 'em easy to spot." He tossed them back in the trunk and opened the next deck. "With regular cards like these, dealers can add their own touches to the line and scroll work on the backs—see here? And here? I took these off a rounder down in New Orleans who was trying to cheat me." He shot her a look full of wry amusement as he repacked the deck. "Damned inconvenient when you're the one trying to do the cheating—but here, put these on," he said as he plucked out a pair of wire-rimmed glasses with blue lenses and fanned open the last deck he was holding. "See anything?"

"Just some smudges...that *glow.*"

"That's phosphorescent ink. The blue lenses make the marks show up. Ink's too messy though. I prefer a simple pin to mark my cards, and just do the aces and face cards. It increases your odds without increasing the chances of getting caught. And *that's* why you keep your fingers sanded—lets you feel your own marks...and those of others." He took the glasses back and returned them along with the last deck to the trunk.

"Every sporting man has his advantages, but for me simple is best," he repeated, reaching into his pocket and pulling out the ten-dollar gold piece she'd seen him place on the table at every game.

"Your lucky piece?"

"You could say that." Flipping it over, he revealed the other side to be burnished mirror-smooth.

"Pass the cards over this as you deal and you can see what everyone is getting."

Caroline's head spun. The flagrancy of all these devices and tricks took her breath away, but she was fascinated as much as affronted. She pointed to several small, wooden boxes that still lay inside the trunk. "What are they?"

"The one with the little guillotine blade is a card trimmer. The other two," he said, pointing, "are shavers and loaders. For dice," he explained at her blank look as he re-packed everything. "You load dice by drilling out their pips and filling them with lead or mercury, then you mend them with liquid celluloid. Crooked dice won't spin—but all that's a lesson for another day," he said, closing the trunk lid and pointing to the now-empty chair. "Sit."

He took his usual place on the bed and adjusted his suspenders like he always did. "You're looking a little flummoxed. What's wrong?"

"Nothing, it's just a bit *much* to take in. You *cheat*—blithely. Blatantly."

"I don't deny it." He took out a fresh deck of cards, unwrapped it and pushed it toward her. "But it's not just me. For every mark that comes along, there's a dozen of us professional sharpers waiting to fall on him like jackals," he confessed affably.

"That's gruesome."

"Gruesome or not, it's reality, so you better get used to it—or go knit doilies."

"One doesn't usually *knit* doilies, one *tats* or *crochets* them."

"Why have my hopes for you suddenly plummeted?"

"I have no idea. Cut."

She dealt a few hands of blackjack before her attention stalled and she blurted, "I don't think I can be like you—I don't *want* to be like you."

"Don't have to—but you do have to know about it. If not, you're just another sheep."

He had a point, a good point, but instead of thanking him, she changed the subject. "You asked me to dress like this tonight." She indicated her dress and hair. "Why?"

"Ah, yes." He took out his watch and noted the time. "In about twenty minutes, we're going down to the cargo deck for a private game—a big one. I've been trying to get into a game with this particular man the whole trip. Finally glad-handed my way to the right person and wrangled an invitation—and here's what I need you to do . . ."

Her heart was pounding by the time he finished, and they both got to their feet. "I-I don't think I can do this, Louie. I'm not ready."

"Sure you are. Trust me. I wouldn't have set this up if I didn't think you were."

He threw her wrap around her shoulders and pushed her toward the door.

"Why don't we ever play in your room?" she suddenly thought to ask.

"Always better to keep the trail from leading straight back to you."

"Oh." Her palms were sweating.

He was just reaching for the doorknob when something else occurred to her. "Louie . . . That first night—I understand how you put the cards in order . . . and the dealing part, I get that, too. But what I can't figure out is how you knew what the cards were in the first place."

"Ah!" His blue eyes lit with merriment. "Glad to see you're still thinking. Perhaps you should get yourself a nice, fluffy handkerchief, big enough to conceal an extra deck of cards," he said. "Just remember—deal good hands to your mark, better hands to yourself. Now quit stalling, and let's go."

The playing was fierce. Not fast—it rarely was—but silent and loaded with tension. There was a lot of gold on the table and a guard stationed outside the door to protect it.

The room smelled of engine oil, it was dank and lit only by the lamp that swayed slightly overhead. The only furniture was the round table and the straight-backed chairs they were sitting in.

There were times that she was sure the others—four of them besides Louie and herself—could hear her spiking heartbeat. Her smile felt false and her hands shook. Lacking a more sophisticated tactic, she simply held her cards close and tapped them with calculated innocence against her bosom.

Louie's mark was a younger man than he. Richly dressed, he carried a gold-headed cane and never took off his top hat. He remained ramrod stiff in his chair, moving only to pick up his cards, his face wooden and expressionless. His focus was intimidating.

Caroline had stuck to the plan Louie outlined for her. On loan, his shiner lay on the table in front of her. She saw the face of each card pass over its reflective surface as she dealt and would tap Louie's foot beneath the table, glancing in the direction of the receiving player whenever an ace flashed by. Exactly what he was doing with that information she wasn't sure, but there was a fair amount of gold and silver coins piling up by his elbow, so whatever it was, it was working.

Top Hat tossed in another twenty-dollar gold piece. "Call," he said quietly and laid down a full house. Aces and jacks.

Her eyes flew to Louie's face. One by one, he put down his own hand. A deuce. Another deuce. *Another.* She could tell everyone was holding their breath—*and another!*

She let out a sigh of relief and knew immediately that was the wrong thing to do.

Top Hat's hooded stare flicked to her, then back to Louie. And it was her turn to deal.

She bent her head in hopes of disguising the convulsive swallow she couldn't prevent, and her fingers were ice cold as she picked up the deck that was passed to her. She fumbled the shuffle and popped a card. Tucking it back in, she started over without meeting anyone's eyes.

The first card off the deck was the ace of spades, and she reached for Louie's foot with her own—only to have it blocked with the thrust of another . . . from Top Hat's side of the table. She froze. She didn't know what to do.

And in that terribly blank pause, Top Hat slid a thin-framed pistol from inside his jacket and pointed it directly at her. "Nobody move," he warned flatly. "We've got a cheat, maybe two, at this table, and I have a pretty good idea who—"

Suddenly, there were angry male voices in the passageway just before the door burst open. It was Jack—with the captain—who had the guard by his collar.

She was never so glad to see anyone in her whole life.

"All right," the captain boomed. "What's going on here?"

There was a beat of silence, then everyone started talking at once.

Without anyone noticing, Top Hat returned the gun to his pocket. Louie—on his feet quick as a cat—scooped up the gold and was noisily dropping coins on the table, counting aloud. "And that makes twenty dollars, sir," he said, ignoring the commotion and addressing Top Hat, who remained stiffly seated, looking at no one. Louie picked up the man's gold-headed cane and stroked the polished length. "You drive a hard bargain, sir, but I do declare it's worth every penny in this case. Nice doing business with you," he said, pocketing the rest of the money.

In all the confusion, Jack snagged Caroline's arm and yanked her to her feet. "Get out of here! Go to your cabin. I'll join you in a minute," he said, thrusting her out the door.

"But—"

"*Go! Now!*" he barked before swinging around. "Just a minute, old man," he said, catching up to Louie, who was quickly and quietly heading in the opposite direction. "What the hell do you think you're doin'?"

"Gettin' while the gettin's good. I suggest you do the same."

"You know damned well what I mean. What the hell were you doin' usin' Caroline in one of your gaffs?"

"Keep your voice down!" Louie glanced at the open cabin door where the confrontation inside continued even louder. Grabbing Jack's arm, he towed him around the corner. "I wasn't using anybody, just honoring a lady's request. Been teaching her to play the games."

"That's not all you've been doing. I saw the shiner, Louie."

"I had everything under control."

Jack's face flushed bright red. "That bastard pulled a gun! That ain't havin' ever'thing under control! You coulda got her killed!"

Louie's forced innocence fell away and his grip tightened. "Listen, son, I wouldn't—"

Jack jerked his arm free. "Don't you 'son' me, you bastard! I'm gonna remember this, Louie," he snarled and stalked off. "I'm gonna remember it, *y'hear me?*"

Moments later, he bounded up the steps two at a time only to find Caroline pacing in the nearly dark parlor, yellow skirts churning.

"I told you to go to your cabin!"

"I'm not a child you can—"

Grabbing her arm, he propelled her into his cabin with him and shut the door. "This isn't about you bein' a child, it's about you stayin' alive!"

He shoved all his stuff into his bag, then opened his door a crack and peered out. "It's clear—come on." Tugging her with him, he pushed her into her own cabin, shut the door, and leaned his weight against it. "Quick—pack your things."

"*Pack!* Why?"

"'Cause we're leavin' at the first landin' come dawn, that's why."

"But we'll be in Kansas City tomorrow!"

"We're not goin' to Kansas City—at least not on this boat."

She folded her arms and glared at him. "Well, I am not leaving another boat just so I can go tramping through the brush with you again! Where's Louie anyway?"

"If he's smart, he's busy doin' the same thing we're doin'. Now *hurry!*"

"But why? He and I were—"

"*About to get yourselves killed!*" He came away from the door, eyes blazing. "He watered at the same trough too often, Caroline, and he put you in danger doin' it! I asked around about that mark he was so keen on playin'. He once shot a man just for spittin' too near his boots!"

Seeing her face pale, her cattail eyes round in alarm, the anger left him in a rush. He gripped her shoulders, relieved that she was safe, that he could touch her like this again. "I don't know what I'd do if I lost you now." Pulling her to him for a quick hug, he kissed her hair then pushed her away. "Put on somethin' warmer, and let's go. We'll wait below. And no trampin' through the brush again, I promise. I'll rent us a buggy. Hell, I'll buy one if I have to."

"And go where?"

"I don't know yet. We'll figure that out as we go." He cracked open the door. "Still clear. Come on." He reached back behind him and took her hand.

ELEVEN

The sky was barely pink as roustabouts took up their positions to throw ropes and pull the boat in tight against lantern-lit pilings for its first dock of the day.

Once again bundled to the eyeballs, Jack and Caroline sat on barrels down in the open stern, bags at their feet. Although Jack had picked a corner protected as much as possible from the wind—and out of sight of anyone who might be looking for them—the air was frigid, and Caroline couldn't stop shivering despite the arm Jack had around her, hugging her close. "It won't be long now," he whispered.

"Aren't you going to tell Louie?" she whispered back.

"No."

"It wasn't his fault."

"The hell it wasn't." He tugged her to her feet as soon as the boat finished lurching.

She wanted to argue, but there was no reasoning with a man once he got his dander up. Besides, she was just glad they were on speaking terms again and didn't want more tension.

It was dark when they arrived in Sedalia, too dark for anyone besides the man in the livery, his lantern held high, to appreciate the red lacquered wheels and matching leather seat of their new buggy.

The neatly painted *Rooms to Let* sign above the steps of the house next door to the livery saved them the trouble of having to look for a hotel at that hour, and Jack's knock was answered so quickly, it was obvious their initial arrival had been observed.

A young man waved them inside. "Room's two dollars a night. In advance," said one Chester A. Wilcox, whose spiky cowlick seemed to reiterate the price.

Outside, the place was plainly built and neatly whitewashed, but inside, the parlor was a mish-mash of print fabrics in pinks, greens, and yellows, all of it set aglow in lamplight. It hurt Caroline's eyes even as she wondered about the eyesight of the person responsible.

Jack laid two Seated Liberties in the man's outstretched palm and received a skeleton key in return. "Upstairs, room on your left," they were told. "Fresh water's already in your pitcher."

They nodded their thanks and bid him goodnight. As they headed up the steps, Jack leaned to put his mouth close to her ear. "Musta been a yard goods sale somewhere."

Caroline covered her surprised snicker with a cough.

Much to her relief, their bedroom hadn't yet suffered the parlor's plight. It looked like any farm bedroom might—nothing fancy, just functional, well-worn, and clean, its white china lamp already lit. There was a red, white, and blue patch quilt on a bed that all but filled the room and plain muslin curtains at the window. A tall wardrobe stood sentry against a side wall, while a straight-backed chair with a sagging rush seat was tucked into the corner beside it.

With uncharacteristic abandon, Jack threw his greatcoat and hat on the chair and dropped their bags on the floor. Leaning over, he tested the spring of the mattress with both hands. "Well, at least there's no squeak," he said, his glance at her loaded with suggestion.

Ignoring him, she picked up her bag and slung it onto the bed.

He took it off again.

Ready to be annoyed, she looked up only to catch the gleam of devilment in his eyes. "Glad *you're* in a good mood," she said, putting the bag back on the bed.

He took it off yet again.

Now she *was* annoyed. "Stop that! You're acting the fool."

"So? What's so great about being serious all the time? Uh-oh! There's Miss Cooper, the schoolmarm again—hands on her hips."

When she bent to pick up her bag yet again, he planted his foot on it.

"Jack, I need to unpack and change."

It came out very close to a whine and she knew it, but she was tired. Tired and petulant. And wasn't she entitled to at least a thimbleful of self-pity after all she'd been through? It felt like fate was trying to grind her into the landscape. Wearily, she closed her eyes.

"No, you don't."

Her eyes snapped open. "Don't what?"

"Have to unpack. There's no place you—*we*—have to be." As he spoke, he stepped close, undid the ribbons of her bonnet, and tossed it away. It struck a corner of the wardrobe and landed on the floor, the ancient felt denting with the abuse. She made a mewy sound of complaint and moved to retrieve it but he caught her back to him. "I'll buy you a new one."

"You must've done very well for yourself back there—a new buggy, now a new bonnet?"

"I did well enough."

Her muffler followed the bonnet to the floor, and this sudden invasion of her personal space flummoxed her some, but she didn't have the energy to protest. One by one, he tugged off her gloves and tossed them away, then began undoing her cloak, button by button, his movements tugging her slightly forward with each one.

"It's been a very long day—and night—and day again," she protested.

"Yes, it has," he agreed, pushing the cloak off her shoulders. It puddled on the floor.

Standing there in her old cotton shirtwaist and brown cord skirt, she couldn't understand why he was looking at her the same way he had the first time she'd put on the green velvet. "What about food? We haven't eaten since that overcooked chicken."

He made a face. "That was pretty bad, wasn't it? If you're hungry, I'll go downstairs and see if they have somethin.'" Looping his arms around her waist, he leaned back to look down into her face. "Are you?"

His thighs were warm against hers, their pressure very intimate. "Am I what?"

"Hungry."

"Aren't you?"

Loose-limbed and relaxed, he started swaying slightly, playfully rocking them from side to side. "I can always eat . . . unless I have other things on my mind," he added with a crooked smile. His mustache, longer these days, blurred the top of his upper lip.

Her own lips twitched as she clutched his arms for balance. She was quickly losing the Battle of the Serious and knew it. She also knew they were flirting; in her case, flirting with danger, but he was hard to resist when he was like this. And that was the problem. Inch by inch, he'd been pulling her closer until their faces were only a warm breath apart. He stopped rocking, and his lashes threw spiky shadows over the intense blue of his eyes even as his pupils crowded out their color. He was focused on her mouth.

Her lips parted under the slide of his kiss. Startlingly warm and exquisitely tender, his tongue stroked hers with a conjurer's magic. She melted into it—into him—even as he drew back to drop kisses across her upturned face. He kissed the corners of her mouth, the tip of her nose, her closed eyes, her brow . . . until they both felt the sigh leave her chest.

"That's better," he whispered.

Scooping her up, he laid her on the quilt. His eyes never left hers as he shrugged out of his jacket, suspenders, dragged off his boots, and shed his shirt before following her down.

She knew what was about to happen, knew she should protest, but gave in to a dangerous cowardice. Physical pleasure—for that is what he always brought—was so much better than thinking about an uncertain future. Sighing at the feel of him, that female welcome of a man's weight, she relinquished her will.

Jack braced his elbows on either side of her head. "You got no idea how much I been lookin' forward to bein' with you like this again," he confessed, smiling down into her eyes. She smiled back, and like silly new lovers the world over, they lost themselves in each other. Noses nuzzled. They touched and stroked in wonder and re-discovery. Lips followed in kissing sips, the flick of a tongue, light nip of teeth, as if every sense needed to re-learn and know the other again—sight, sound, touch, and taste. Nerve endings erupted every-where with lightning frissons of heat, an intimate summer storm on a late winter's evening.

He cupped her face, his kisses still tender. Then he became more urgent, greedier. When her throat or earlobes lured his lips away, a thumb or finger became their emissary, teasing her tongue, dipping into her mouth, inviting her to suckle. It was wet, mindless play, and she heard herself moan. Coherent thought evaporated.

He dragged himself higher, grinding his hips into hers. When he slid off to the side, leaving one leg cocked across hers, she opened heavy lids to watch him, feel him stroke a hot path down her body from breast to belly, pressing his palm to the aching mound at the junction of her thighs. Her body surrendered to everything his hand claimed, but feeling smothered in her clothing, she arched against him, pleading for a release from something more than cloth.

Answering her call, he rolled up over her again, slid his hands beneath her waist, found the hooks of her skirt and released them. She lifted her hips so he could pull it down.

Suddenly, all clothing had to be dispensed with and he dragged it out of the way without thought or care for another wear. Some of it never left the bed, forgotten as soon as it was no longer a barrier. Her boots thudded to the floor. Folding back over her, he cradled her head, tipping it this way and that so he could feast at will. But that wasn't enough either, and soon his mouth explored down one side of her body and up the other even as she followed the bunch and release of his muscles moving beneath her fingers.

His hands were everywhere, molding her breast for his hot mouth, up her thighs, behind, cupping her bottom, sliding around to open her legs, teasing the slick, hard nub of her to shuddering attention, drinking the hoarse cry of pleasure straight from her lips. Her own forays ended, her limbs too limp and heavy to return the favor. He had turned her into pure liquid, without form or boundaries, flowing in whatever direction he stirred. She was a plundered flower, blooming beneath him, open, pliant, blown and scattered when he plunged deep.

With a surge of strength that came out of nowhere, she wrapped her legs over his hips, and they rocked together hard. Throats arched and straining, they rode each other straight off the cliff . . . and landed, stunned and spent.

Still locked together, breathing hard, neither one moved.

Finally, Jack levered himself up on an elbow and dropped over onto his back. "*Jesus.*"

Caroline pried open an eyelid, seeing him through her own hair plastered across her face.

He rolled his head toward her—as if that were the only part of his body still capable of movement—and a wide, lazy smile spread across his face like sunshine. "Hi," he whispered.

"Hi, yourself," she whispered back.

He held up a hand in invitation. When she laced her fingers with his, he planted a kiss on each knuckle before tucking their hands together against his chest. They lay like that for several minutes, minds empty, bodies sated.

Letting go finally, he rolled onto his side to face her. Bunching a pillow under his head, he settled down to simply stare at her and smile.

"What?" she asked, smiling too.

"Nothing."

"You're staring."

"I can't seem to help it. I—*uh-oh*. You're thinkin' somethin'. I can tell. Stop that."

"I can't help it either. So much has happened in such a short time. It used to be all my days blended together with hardly a line to mark one from another. Now . . ."

He had taken a long lock of her hair, brought it to his lips for a kiss, and was smoothing it in a spiral around her breast, working his way up to her nipple, watching it respond to his touch.

"Go on," he murmured, "I'm listenin.'"

"No, you're not. You're playing," she giggled and pushed his hand away. "And it tickles! *Now* I feel like I wake up each morning as one person and go to sleep as another."

He met her gaze with as much seriousness as he could muster. "It's been hard, I know."

"And scary."

"That, too. But it'll get better."

"Will it? I still can't believe you got the boat captain involved—not after what happened on the *Quincy*."

His mouth twitched and his gaze slid away as he propped his head on his fist. "Well, I didn't exactly involve the captain."

"I know it was him. I remember the big gold buttons on his coat."

"Anybody can wear a coat, and even a captain hasta sleep sometime." He shrugged a naked shoulder, mouth tight with suppressed humor. "And a coupla dollars put in the right hand can always produce a key."

She lifted her head to stare at him, open-mouthed with shock. "You didn't!"

"'Fraid so."

She collapsed back into the pillows. "No wonder you wanted to leave in such a hurry!"

He sighed dramatically. "The things a man has to do justa be with his wife."

"I'm not your wife—and we have to stop doing this, Jack. What if I get with child?"

Frowning, he rolled onto his back and exhaled noisily. "I s'pose you're right." A moment later, he rolled away from her, tugging the covers up over himself. "Turn the lamp down and let's get some sleep."

She should've been relieved at his agreement, yet felt miffed at the abrupt dismissal. It was at least worth a *bit* of discussion, wasn't it? She stared at his back a moment longer before she, too, wrested herself under the covers, turned down the lamp, and faced the other way.

In thick silence, they lay back to back. A moment later, his arm snaked free and he reached back behind him to pat her hip. "'Night, Caroline."

She thought about slapping him away in offended pique, but weariness sapped the impulse. "'Night." Within minutes, she was asleep.

Jack listened to her breathing become deep and even.

What if I get with child? A bastard child—like himself. Guilt and shame stabbed him. How could he inflict that on another innocent babe? On Caroline?

He scowled into the darkness. She was right. They had to stop courting danger. He knew that some women knew how to prevent a child—or rid themselves of one—but they weren't the kind he'd ask about such a matter. Nor would he ever ask Caroline to do what they did. The thought horrified him even as he was annoyed by his own squeamishness.

He sat up, hugged his knees, and looked down at her. Bits of moonlight stroked her brow, her cheek, beckoning him to do the same. He resisted.

He could always leave her . . . couldn't he? Sure, he could. He could get up right now, be dressed and gone without her ever being the wiser. He'd leave money on the washstand of course. It wasn't like he'd never made similar exits.

If he stayed, sooner or later, they'd both regret it. The knot in his chest argued with him, but it was true. Distance, not willpower, was all that could save them.

But it wasn't as easy as he'd hoped. Tiptoeing around, he was trying to identify his clothing by feel alone amid the tangled mess strewn around the bed. Finally, finding his trousers, he was just threading one leg through when he lost his balance and fell against the bed.

She stirred and he froze—one leg in, one leg out.

"What're you doin'?"

Her sleep-soaked voice scraped against his heart—and his conscience. "Just pickin' up clothes—don't want wrinkles."

She settled back on a deep sigh. Even as she drifted off again, he could hear her amusement as she mumbled, "So neat . . ."

Squeezing his eyes closed, his chin dropped to his chest in defeat.

Caroline awoke the next morning to bright sunshine already streaming through the curtains. Blinking sleepily, she was content to just lie there, mind blissfully blank. Finally, she reached back behind her for Jack, but her fingers found only air . . . and cold, empty sheets.

With a hiss of surprise, she twisted around.

Gone!

Just then, the doorknob rattled, and he walked in with a tray and a blue-and-white-striped hatbox dangling from his pinkie. Freshly shaved, he wore a crisp white shirt and brown sack coat she'd never seen before. His dark brown trousers looked new as well. "Mornin'."

She pried her gaze away from the hatbox, and with the heels of her hands, shoved herself upright as he toed the door closed behind him. "Good morning."

He placed the bed tray—made from an old picture frame and window glass—across her legs, dropped the hatbox on the foot of the bed, then sat down beside her. "Breakfast," he announced unnecessarily. "Courtesy of one Mrs. Chester A. Wilcox."

She grabbed the coffee cup to keep it from sloshing and adjusted the pillows behind her back. "You saw her? What does she look like?"

"Like her parlor, but on two legs."

A hoot of laughter escaped her before she could squelch it. "Oh, no! Bless her heart."

"Indeed." He pointed. "There's coffee, fresh eggs, bread and jam there."

"I see that. Thank you."

His eyes danced with high good humor. Clearly, he was excited about something—the hatbox no doubt—but he seemed determined to ignore it, and if he could, so could she.

She took a sip of coffee, gave a hum of appreciation, and eyed him over the rim of the cup painted with roses. "So what have you been up to this early?"

"I did some shoppin.'"

Resolutely, she kept her gaze away from the hatbox and nudged the plate in his direction. "Care to share? There's plenty here."

He shook his head. "Ain't you gonna to ask me what I bought?"

"I can see you have a new suit. You look very dashing." And he did. It was all she could do to keep from reaching out and touching.

Pleased, he smoothed a brown wool lapel, then picked up a thick slice of buttered bread and took a huge bite. "That ain't all," he told her around his mouthful.

"Oh?" She took a bite of fried egg, saw him eyeing the lift of her fork, so she offered him the next bite. After that, she started forking food alternately into his mouth after each bite of her own. He chewed but didn't seem to really notice. He was busy outlining his plans for the day, which consisted mostly of more shopping as soon as she was dressed.

"You mean it? You really want to take me shopping?"

Eyes lit with pleasure, he nodded. "Yes, but if you'd rather do something else—"

"You know I'd love nothing better. Maybe we can even find a laundry," she added, plucking at the front of her pink nightgown. "I can't smell too nice in this after all this time."

He leaned over and nuzzled her neck. "You smell just fine to me."

She pushed him away. "All right, sir. I can't take the suspense. What's in the box?"

A grin split his face. "I thought you'd never ask."

Snagging the box up by its bright blue ribbon, he swung it over as she set the tray aside.

Gleefully, she tore through the white tissue paper inside. "Oh." It was a new bonnet all right—a plain gray bonnet almost identical to her old one.

"I didn't know what you'd like, so I—what's wrong? Don't you like it?"

"Oh, no, I do. It's . . . very nice. A good, solid bonnet. Very thoughtful. Thank you."

But the light was gone from his face. "No, it ain't. You don't like it, I can tell. But why? It's just like the one ya had."

They both glanced at her old bonnet, which was still laying on the floor like a dead pigeon. Suddenly, the truth dawned. "Oh, *that's* what's wrong—it's just like your old one!"

"No, it's fine," she insisted, holding the new one away when he tried to grab for it.

"No, it's ain't. We'll take it back." He won the brief tug-of-war and tossed it back in the box. "And buy you another. They had lots of fancier ones." He twiddled his fingers above his head. "Flowers, feathers, ribbons, all kinds of what-not. I didn't know what you'd like, so I played it safe. Some of 'em looked too heavy to wear, but I'll buy you whatever one you want. Hell, I'll buy ya two."

She was pleased, but embarrassed at her lapse in manners. "No, really—"

He leaned over and gave her a quick but firm kiss on the mouth. "Yes, really. Now get dressed," he said, snagging the last of the bread off her plate.

And so they went shopping. With their scarlet wheels catching everyone's notice, Jack drove them down through the middle of Sedalia. As promised, he bought her not one, but two bonnets. One was as gray as her old one, but trimmed with pleated bands of ruby satin and a wide ribbon of the same hue that whispered through her fingers when she looped it into a big, soft bow beneath her chin. The other was dark-blue felt with pink silk roses tucked along the high side of its short, curled brim, its flat crown stuck through with a long, beaded hat pin.

Watching her preen before the store mirror, Jack shook his head in bewildered amusement. "Women like the most useless things. Neither of those will keep your ears warm."

"No," she admitted blithely, "but I don't care. They're pretty."

As she twirled before him, modeling her new finery, it seemed her lips and eyes never stopped smilin' at him, and his chest felt near to burstin' with pride and happiness. How he'd ever believed he could leave her, he'd never know. All that was left for him now was severe self-restraint. It would not be easy.

Days later, they were in Kansas City—*Paris of the Plains*, the newspapers called it—where he lavished her with two more dresses, a nightdress, soft kid shoes and gloves, a beaver fur muff, and a small trunk to pack it all in, along with a tiny bottle of perfume imported all the way from the real Paris.

From there, they went north to Atchison, further up to Omaha City, then back down to Kansas City just as spring arrived. This time he took her to Vogel's Restaurant and tried to cajole her into trying fresh oysters. When she declined with a wrinkle of her nose and the declaration she'd rather die, he just grinned, shrugged, and downed another half-dozen of the things—all at the outrageous sum of twenty-five cents each.

Taking advantage of his indulgent mood, she extracted his promise to pick up where Louie left off. So, he taught her the strategies of wagering, the nuance of bluffing, even found her a few opportunities to practice at hotel tables where the marks would be tamer than they'd be in side street saloons. When she complained that his hawk-like presence at these games made her nervous, his answer was always the same: "You're not ready to run your own game yet."

"At least stop glaring at the other players then. I'm not the only one you unnerve."

"A nervous opponent gives you the advantage. Besides, it pays to be cautious."

"That's not what Louie says. Louie says—"

"I don't care what Louie says. I ain't Louie—and you ain't neither."

Despite this minor irritant, Caroline's complaints were few and far between. Jack remained attentive and indulgent even as they returned to their alternate sleeping arrangements. The hotel games often ended early enough that they had time to return to their room and do a play-by-play of the hands themselves so she could nail down the finer points of this new level of gambling; then, he'd kiss the top of her head and set off for his usual all-night saloon games. During the day, she'd shop some. She even went back to doing a bit of needlework. The few hours they were together were pleasant and relatively uneventful. All in all, even though they hadn't made it to California yet, she was content. As the habit of constant vigilance and responsibility fell away, she found herself laughing more and worrying less.

But as spring turned into summer and the cattle herds began to arrive, it was Jack who became restless. In the early morning hours, before returning to bed and sleep, he'd begun walking the fences of the stockyards, watching the animals get rebranded for transport to buyers in New York or Chicago, absorbing the colorful talk of the wranglers.

It was still early summer when they left Kansas City a second time. On their way out of town, he slowed their carriage at the stockyards to take one last look.

The pens were crammed with cattle jostling each other for space like rebellious youths, bellowing in protest. "There's probably close to five hundred head in there . . . at twenty-five a head . . ." Narrow-eyed, he did the math in his head. "Jesus, Caroline! There's more 'n' ten thousand dollars behind that fence!" He glanced over to find her holding her nose.

"Can we leave now? It smells *awful.*"

He grinned and sucked in a noisy lungful. "Smells like money to me—the kind they call prosperity," but he obligingly snapped the reins and wheeled them upwind.

For months, they wove back and forth over old Jesse Chisolm's trail, with Caroline once remarking that if their travels had been threads, they'd've woven a whole tapestry by now. They followed the boom of every cow town, every new railhead that shipped cattle—Salina, Abilene, Topeka, Emporia. This last they left quickly upon discovering there was a town ordinance against both liquor *and* gambling. Speculation of every kind was rampant, and the very air of Kansas seemed to vibrate with excitement and the energy of rapid growth.

As Jack had predicted, they weren't the only gamblers trailing new settlements, saloons, and railroad spurs, but he did his best to keep them ahead of the pack. As soon as he'd spot a sporting man he recognized—once he ran smack into Del Griffith, another time, he thought he saw Louie just disappearing into a saloon—he'd take it as a sign of the coming rush and have them on the road again. Staying ahead of the others took a keen eye and lightness of foot, he'd tell her whenever she protested, always following with "Welcome to a gambler's life."

However, the farther away from Kansas City they moved, the rawer and more embryonic the towns became, the more prohibitions against women gamblers they ran into. *By City Ordinance*, the signs usually read. Prostitutes, on the other hand, were always welcome, it seemed. Clearly, civic fathers were more concerned with the straightness of their streets than that of their moral lines. It was this that gradually turned Caroline into the driving force behind their constant moves as she urged him to seek places where she could continue pursuing her own plans as a gambler.

"Whooo-eeeee! Here they come!"

Caroline's needle paused above her sewing as the girl's shrill call was followed quickly by the sound of running feet on the floor above.

Shutters banged open all along the side of the building facing the street. Raucous female voices and whistles punctured the air in a series of ribald speculations. The more lewd and specific invitations would come as soon as the cowhands rode directly beneath their open windows, invitations that would be accepted with great good cheer.

Caroline rose and went to her own window, pushing the shutter out of the way just enough to see without drawing attention to herself.

She and Jack hadn't been in Wichita—correction, Delano—long, but she still found the sight of hundreds of cattle, funneled straight down the middle of the street, to be a heart-pounding one. For one thing, it was the widest street she'd ever seen—and now she knew why. The Chisolm Trail ended here and, as the heat of summer increased, so did the number of herds arriving each day.

The approaching wave of stamping hooves and deep-throated lowing was deafening. The wranglers did a good job of containing the surge of long-horned animals, but invariably a few pickets of fence would go down, a porch get invaded, maybe a windowpane or two broken.

Cows were still pouring over the hill a quarter mile back in a cloud of dust, glittering like gold in front of the setting sun, but the front edge of the herd was already beneath their windows.

Caroline retreated a bit at the sudden rise of heat, dust, and pungent smell. However, the girls upstairs weren't put off at all. They crowded the sills to wave their night rails, petticoats, and bloomers over the heads of the grinning cowboys.

"Hey, honey! Yeah, you—blondie! Come see Lilah real soon, y'hear?"

The boy's dust-streaked face split into a wide grin. "Yes, ma'am! I'll surely do that!"

"But only after you wash up!" There were squeals of laughter.

"In the river!" called a different voice.

"But only at night!" called another.

"Yeah, they passed a law on t'other side—no neck-ed bathin' in the river 'cept at night!"

"Aw, shoot, ma'am! I can't—"

"And bring all your gold!" The laughter was reaching such a pitch now, Caroline worried it would spook the cattle.

Rising up in his stirrups, his job momentarily forgotten, the young cowhand shouted, "You sure are purty!"

"You ain't so bad your ownself!" was the giggly response.

"Hey, he was talking t'me!"

"No, he weren't. He were talkin' to me! Hey, honey—which one of us di'ja mean?"

He whipped off his stained hat and used it to point. "You! And you—*all* of yous!"

The girls laughed and hooted and hollered so much at this, shoving each other and jumping up and down. Caroline was surprised one of them didn't pitch right out on her head.

By now, sheer mass had slowed the herd as they bunched up at the river, and the point rider started turning them toward the stockyards.

As usual, a few cows would break loose and head down the embankment toward the water, but the swing riders had already threaded their way to the front. Past the gauntlet of girls, they followed the animals down to shoo them back up to rejoin the herd, horses and riders moving as fluidly together as if united in thought.

Across the river in Wichita, a line of men watched the end of this latest drive as they'd done with each new herd that came in, able to judge—even at this distance—how fast or slow the cattle had been moved, whether the drover had given the animals enough grazing time on the prairie to keep them fat and healthy . . . or too fast, making the animals skinny in their greed.

This herd looked good even to Caroline's unschooled eye, and she already knew they'd fetch a good price, money that would be shared with all the riders who'd babied the animals for anywhere from two to four months on the trail.

The girls upstairs had finally quieted, and Caroline heard their shutters close even as she closed her own against the hot dust curling up from the street.

She stared at her mending in the filtered light without enthusiasm.

They'd arrived in Wichita just before sunset a fortnight ago. Jack drove them straight through the middle of town, past businesses and homes facing each other squarely across an improbably wide street that led directly to the bridge that spanned the Arkansas River and connected the two communities. He stopped at the first structure identifying itself as a hotel, angling their rig in toward the hitching post out front. After securing the horse, he helped her down and they went inside the plain, white clapboard structure to register.

The place was chalky with dust, but they were greeted promptly by a big, buxom woman in wine-colored grosgrain. The high neck and tight sleeves all ended with a spit of white lace, her cheeks florid from the heat, her bun frizzy.

"Howdy! Welcome to Wichita! Where y'all from? I don't see no bags."

"Left them in the buggy," Jack said. "Thought I'd make sure you had a room first."

She looked at Caroline. "Smart man, your husband. Practical. I like that."

Caroline smiled and nodded.

After flipping to a fresh page in a large, ruled ledger, she turned the book around toward Jack and handed him the pen she'd just dipped in an inkwell.

"Where you from?" she repeated, nudging the inkwell closer.

"Mississippi—Kansas City more recently," he said, pen scratching across the page.

She held the key in one hand, the jar of sand ready to sprinkle on the wet ink in the other. "You plan on settling?"

"Probably not."

"No?"

"No." He opened his hand for the key.

She ignored him as her eyes swept over Caroline again, this time coming to rest on her left hand—which bore no ring. Her hand closed around the key as she leaned to peer at his signature. "So, what is it you do, Mister . . . Transomb?"

"Speculatin' mostly."

Her eyes narrowed. "Land? Railroad? Business?"

"Gold."

"Gold! You don't look like no prospector—and ain't no gold around here I'm aware of."

"No, I 'spect not," he agreed. "So where's your saloon? I didn't see one comin' in."

She straightened abruptly. "That's because we keep them and their kind on t'other side of the river—along with all the other kinds of riffraff we don't want here. No guns, no gamblers, no women of ill repute on this side." Her chin lifted. "And we intend to keep it that way."

She yanked the book out of his reach. "Seems I was wrong. We don't have any rooms to let after all. All full-up, we are. But I'm sure there'll be some vacancies on the other side. If not right now, just give it 'til the first gunfight and something'll come open, I'm sure."

Lest there be any doubt about her mindset, she scrunched up the page he'd just signed and ripped it out of the book, wadding it into a ball. "Better leave now, 'fore I call the sheriff." Despite her bluster, her voice quavered nervously. "And take your strumpet with you."

Caroline's mouth fell open even as a small splinter of truth pricked her, but Jack had her by the elbow and back outside before she could fully react.

"Of all the—*strumpet! Riffraff!*" she spluttered as he handed her back up into the buggy. "I oughta go back there and give—"

"It ain't worth it."

"*Isn't,* not *ain't*—and it most certainly *is*!"

"Calm down."

"Don't you tell me to calm down! That woman called me a—"

"I know. I heard—and I'm sorry. That's just the kinda talk I never wanted you to hear."

Huffing indignantly, she dropped into the seat. Back ramrod straight, she brushed at her skirt and twitched a shrug. "Sticks and stones," she muttered.

"Can hurt you—but words can hurt ya, too. *And* leave scars. Try not to let it bother you. I got used to it over the years. You will, too."

"Lord, I hope not! No one should have to get used to that kind of talk! How on earth can you, for one single minute . . ." She ran out of words and breath at the same time.

Clicking to the horse, he had them back on the road in a trice. At the river, as Jack paid the man in the tollbooth two bits to cross, she found herself looking at the glittering span of water differently than she would've before. Yesterday it would've been just a river between towns. Today it was more a life choice—and she wondered for the first time if she'd made the right one.

The horse's hooves rang and their wheels chattered over the cobblestones, but neither of them spoke until they reached the other side and rolled from stone back to dirt. Looking over her shoulder, she spotted a little structure beside the tollbooth the same size as an outhouse. Below its cutout front window was a sign that read *Check Guns Here.*

"Do you suppose it's really dangerous on this side?" she asked.

His mouth was set in a grim line. "Only one way to find out."

All the structures on this side—mostly neat, white-washed saltboxes, shuttered quietly—faced the river. Only after they checked into where they were now staying did they learn that they were no longer in Wichita, but in Delano—the home of saloons, brothels, and no lawmen, existing only to serve the needs of the pent-up cowhands who came through with each herd.

"No, sirree," declared their paunchy, balding hotel clerk. "Not a sheriff or marshal on this side of the Arkansas!" He pronounced it as they soon found many others did: *Ar-Kansas.*

As if to illustrate his point, a loud argument suddenly broke out in the street, followed by the deep-throated boom of a shotgun. Jack and Caroline both flinched.

"Oh, don't worry," the clerk assured them. "They're just blowing off steam. Comes reg'lar at the end of every herd comin' in. Rarely a serious killin' though."

"Didn't realize there was any other kind," Jack mused aloud.

The man ignored that, but spoke instead to Caroline, who was doing her best to appear unfazed. "You folks look pretty upstanding. You sure you want to be staying on this side?"

Because he'd directed the question to her—and because she could see the crowded saloon and tables of card players in the room behind him—she didn't hesitate. "We are."

With sewing still in her lap, she returned to the present at the now-familiar crack of firearms somewhere not too distant. Theirs was a nicely wallpapered room with a big brass bed between two windows, marble-topped tables, oil lamps, and a chest of drawers with a large tilting mirror on top. They even had a dressing screen. Despite the town's rough 'n' tumble nature, she wouldn't have minded staying awhile—if she wasn't bored to distraction. Little had she expected Jack to kick up such a fuss about her gambling "in a place like this"— the first place in a long time that wouldn't mind her doing so—and demand she stay put while he went out and did as he pleased.

In fact, he'd been acting odd ever since they'd arrived. Vague. More distracted than ever. Even though he still gambled almost every night, he was starting to return at unexpected times, falling into bed and sleep without explanation or conversation. By tacit agreement, they'd refrained from physical intimacy ever since Sedalia, and she could only think to blame the growing tension between them on that. In fact, she couldn't help wondering if he was spending time with other women—in a place like this, how could he not—yet he never came back with smears of paint or smelling of cheap perfume. Still, since he seemed less inclined to conversation than ever, it was hard to know for sure.

She'd done her best to amuse herself—sewing him a nightshirt, only to be disappointed when he wore it exactly once. And there was only so much bloody mayhem she could read about in the newspapers—range wars, Indian raids, and shoot-outs.

Well, fie on that! she declared to herself.

Changing into her red-and-white gingham basque and white eyelet skirt—mostly because the color and its white eyelet ruffles gave her spirits a lift—she put up her hair, checked her image in the mirror, and went downstairs to talk to the bartender.

The barroom was typical in its use of brown on brown on brown—walls, floor, and furniture—but saved from total gloom by brass lamps hanging over each table and a pair of open louvered doors letting in light and air. An upright piano against the back wall was the source of nightly music.

Several men, hats either pulled low or slanted to the back of their heads, leaned against the plain bar, their spurs jingling softly when they moved. The more high-spirited ones just arriving hadn't shown up yet.

"Excuse me," she ventured.

The bartender ignored her.

"*Excuse me?*"

Several of the patrons shifted, glancing her way.

"Jay!" one of them prompted the barkeep, who finally looked up with a scowl.

"Can't you read, Miss?"

"Pardon?"

"Outside," he gestured with the glass he'd been drying, rag stuffed half in and half out, "the sign says, 'no women allowed.' Can't you read?"

"Of course I can read—but if there are no women allowed, how is it that *she's* here?" She indicated a plump, middle-aged woman dressed in faded calico with a once-white apron pinned to her front, shuffling over to serve drinks to a table full of card players in the corner. She looked tired, her face slack with boredom.

"That's Sal. She don't count."

"Why not? She appears female to me."

"Now look here, missy, *who* I let into my bar and why—" He stopped, deciding on a more expedient tactic. "Is there somethin' I can do fer you?"

She folded her hands on the edge of the bar. "Yes, there is. You can hire me."

"Hire you!" Jay gave a queer combination of a snort and a chuckle and looked around for a similar response from the others. "Now why would I do that? You don't look like one of them upstairs girls to me."

Caroline was aware of a few more heads turning, but plunged ahead. "Well, thank you for that, but you can hire me to do what Sal does."

"But I already got Sal! What do I need you for?"

Showing more confidence than she felt, she leaned closer and silently prayed for Sal's forgiveness. "Who would your customers rather buy a drink from—somebody who looks like Sal, or somebody like me?" She raised her chin a notch and smiled into Jay's long face.

Jay gaped at her, then glanced around the bar appealing for a vote. She caught several smiles from the others, but whether they were of encouragement or amusement she couldn't tell.

But apparently Jay knew. After spitting noisily onto the floor, he gave her a nod. "All right. Pay's five dollars a week and—"

"Six," she countered.

"*Six!* That's two more'n I pay Sal!"

One of the men at the bar caught her eye and winked.

"Six," she repeated.

He spat again. "Shoot! All right—six. But you better bring in that extra two dollars of business," he said, squinting down the length of a knobby finger. "Come back about seven."

"Of course," she agreed airily. She wanted to hug herself and cheer, but maintained her dignified demeanor all the way back up the stairs.

"*What!*" Jack bellowed when she told him later. "Over my dead body!"

Instead of snidely offering to help him achieve that goal and making things worse, she stepped closer and laid her hands on his chest, pouting prettily. "Please, Jack? I shall absolutely go mad if I have to stay cooped up in this room any longer. I only leave it now for a trip to the privy."

"You have no idea what those drovers can be like with drink in 'em. They haven't seen a woman in months, and when they do, they'll assume she's for hire just like all the others here."

"Then come with me! I just need a foot in the door to set up a game." She rose on her tiptoes to kiss his cheek, deliberately over-balancing. She knew she was playing it a bit broad, but was determined not to spoil her own good mood with an argument. Things between them were strained enough lately.

He scowled. "No."

She kissed his other cheek. "Please?"

Still scowling, he pushed her away to arm's length, but there was finally some light in his eyes. "You're flirting," he accused.

"Yes." She smiled. "I am."

"With danger," he added, focusing on her mouth.

Humor wobbled on the verge of heat, so she moved to the mirror to re-pin her hair.

They heard the raspy clink of piano notes begin downstairs just as she slid the final pin in place and headed for the door.

He blocked her way.

"Excuse me."

"No."

"Let me pass."

"*No.*"

She'd been staring at his shirt buttons, determined to hold her temper, but now she looked him straight in the eye. "You brought me to this town—and don't tell me 'welcome to a gambler's life' again, for you've forbidden me from that here as well. And now you're making me a prisoner."

"I'm just trying to keep you safe."

"Safe from what? You've been gambling, why can't I? It's just a hick town, Jack."

"You can get yourself killed in a hick town faster'n any fancy gamin' parlor."

"Then *do* be careful, won't you?" she said with false sweetness, trying to push past him.

When he still wouldn't move, she clamped down on her rising temper and forced a tone of reasonableness into her next, most *un*reasonable words. "Jack . . . if you don't let me pass—this instant—I swear to you that I will start screaming, and I will continue screaming until I bring this entire place down around our ears."

His chest swelled with what she was sure was going to be a bellow of rage. However, a half-second later, he abruptly stepped aside—even opened the door for her.

"You know, you're the most stubborn, *pig-headed* woman I've ever known!" he called after her, leaning out around the doorframe as she passed. "How'd ya get to be that way? You never used t' be this way."

"I've always been this way," she tossed back, heading downstairs.

Behind her, she heard a mumbled curse and the door slam.

Seconds later, he came pounding down the steps behind her, catching up to her just as she reached the bottom. "I'm going with you."

She'd've bitten her own tongue off before admitting the relief she felt at not having to face this new venture alone, so she simply took his arm and they proceeded into the loud, smoky crush of the saloon together.

Within two hours, the colorful Upstairs Girls had drifted down on a wave of perfume and piercing laughter, and the place was packed with cowhands ringing the tables and lining the bar shoulder to shoulder—laughing, talking, arguing, shoving. The garter-sleeved piano player, cigar clamped in his teeth, banged out a steady stream of spritely jigs for anyone who managed to create a space for dancing.

With dampened curls clinging to her face and neck, Caroline wove her way through the crowd, delivering glasses of beer and whiskey. Most arrived as full as when they left Jay's hand, but as the number of bodies grew, so did the danger of upset. It was getting to be more than she could handle alone, so she was glad to see Sal had been summoned back to the job at some point.

Amid this sea of rowdiness, Jack stood alone, brooding in silence at the end of the bar, nursing his drink and watching her every move. It made her nervous at first, but as her workload increased, she gradually forgot about him altogether.

Several times, a paying customer insisted on buying her a shot of whiskey. She refused, but there were a couple of times when it just became easier to accept. And luckily, even fewer times when the buyer wanted her to actually drink it with him. The small amount she did consume had the benefit of easing the ache in her feet at least.

Suddenly, a young cowboy stepped in front of her with a crooked smile, his chin raw from a bad shave. He was saying something, but she couldn't hear him over the raucous background noise. Moving her tray aside slightly, she leaned in. "I'm sorry—could you repeat that?"

He leaned in as well. "I said you're awful pretty, ma'am. Wanna dance?"

"Oh!" she exclaimed as someone plucked the nearly full tray out of her grasp and passed it forward over several heads. "I—"

She didn't get any further. Whether the youngster mistook her response as assent or not, he grabbed her around the waist and opened up a space for them by swinging her in a circle as he gave a loud whoop of joy. She had to clutch his shoulders for balance and, despite her surprise, heard herself laugh out loud as her feet found the rhythm. Before their third revolution was complete, another man—all beaky nose and Adam's apple—stepped up and wheeled her away. Some in the crowd started clapping in time to the music and she could hear the other women laughing, see their flushed, painted faces flashing by as they joined in.

The jig turned into a reel, and someone new snagged her arm in the crook of his and spun her in a series of do-si-dos, first one way, then the other. By this point, she was laughing so hard, she could barely stand. Her partners—short, tall, young, old, some adept, some not—came and went in a blur. Beyond the first couple, she doubted she could identify any of them.

She was twirled away again, this time into the hard chest of someone who had to steady her with both hands to keep her from toppling. When he didn't immediately pull her into step with the next jig, she took advantage of the small break to catch a breath.

"*Whew!* That was—oh! Jack!" She grinned, panting. She was aware that strands of hair were plastered across her face, most of the pins gone. Patches of her basque were damp with perspiration, but at that moment, she simply didn't care. She was having fun!

The frown on his face softened and she saw him become infected with her own good humor. Turning to the piano player, he fished a coin out of his vest pocket and held it up. "Play a ballad for us," he said and flipped the coin in an arc through the air.

Deftly caught, it was pocketed with one hand even as the other began the plaintive notes of "Aura Lee." Laying his cigar atop the instrument, the piano player surprised a layer of hush from the room as he began to croon the words to the sentimental old song.

But Caroline barely heard them. To her surprise, Jack took her into a firm if not entirely proper dance posture, and waltzed them slowly around the room, parting the crowd as he went. He looked only at her . . . and she couldn't remember ever being happier.

When the music ended, he continued to hold her for a few seconds longer. "I heard some people talking earlier about something called the 'Running of the Doves' tomorrow. Maybe it's a picnic. Wanna go?" He was smiling and it was the most relaxed she'd seen him in a while.

Her own smile was broad. "I'd like that very much."

The next morning, they were downstairs lingering over their breakfast when a steady stream of the Upstairs Girls came down the steps in a froth of ruffled skirts. They knotted near the front desk in quick conference, then spilled out into the street on a wave of giggles.

A loud chorus of male voices greeted them with a cheer.

"They're here!"

"C'mon!"

"We got the wagons ready!"

Jack put down his coffee cup. "Wanna go see what all the ruckus is about?"

"Why not?" Caroline agreed.

Out in the street, sunlight winked off shiny tack and hardware. Crowds of men were gathering even as the town's brightly painted women converged from all directions. Clearly, they were the main attraction. Fat, thin, dark or fair, bland or exotic, they were dressed in every color of the rainbow; and all together they were, indeed, a sight to behold. With much kissing, hugging, batting of eyelashes and outrageous posturing, they each chose among the vying cowhands for the one to be allowed to gallantly hand them up into the waiting wagons and buckboards, grand as queens.

"They's a fine-lookin' flock of doves we got here today!" someone called out from up ahead, sounding faintly official.

Calls of bets and covers began to bounce through the crowd.

Caroline felt her eyes widen as the women's calves and thighs were squeezed amid speculations about speed or endurance "over the long haul." Even as hands were slapped and pushed away, she could tell there was no real offense taken.

She tugged on Jack's sleeve.

Without looking away from the spectacle unfolding, he leaned nearer. "What?"

"I don't think this is a picnic."

He grinned. "Me neither."

"Maybe I should—" but she got no further. The loaded wagons were on the move and so was the crowd. He grabbed her hand, tugging her in step beside him as he set off with the others.

"Wait—I forgot my parasol!"

"Too late! I don't want to miss this, whatever it is! Hurry!"

"*Hurry!*" The word echoed all around them in the throng that strung out along the road. As one, the spectators trotted upriver behind the bouncing, jouncing wagons full of women shrieking with laughter. When they were some distance beyond the center of town, just past the stockyards, the drivers wheeled their vehicles around to face the way they'd just come. The morning air was warming quickly, and the panting crowd slowed, splitting along either side of the roadway of their own accord. Jack and Caroline ended up on the high side of the embankment with the river at their backs.

The women got out of the wagons much less grandly than they'd gotten in, leaping over the sides without ceremony. Most of them were barefoot.

Caroline puzzled her memory over whether they'd entered the wagons that way—then froze on her own intake of breath. "*Oh!*" was all she could say.

Amid whoops and hollers from the spectators, the women started shedding their clothes and tossing them, willy-nilly, into the wagons, then shouldered themselves into a straggly line across the roadway just as bold as you please . . . and naked as the day they were born.

A man climbed into the bed of the center-most buckboard and stood up. He drew a pistol out of his belt, pointed it into the air and waited for everyone to silence themselves.

The line of naked women were mostly still, in various poses of readiness, staring intently back down the road.

All the wagon drivers leaned forward, reins firmly in hand.

"Alberta!" called a man's voice from somewhere on the other side of the roadway. "Remember now, you promised me you'd—"

"*Shhh!*" admonished the crowd.

Finally, the only sounds heard were the rushing river, and some deep bovine notes from the stockyards.

Bang!

The girls were off in a churn of bare knees and elbows. They passed the cheering crowd in a flash, wagons rattling near to pieces right along beside them.

As much as she didn't want to look, Caroline was transfixed by the outrageous spectacle—and vastly relieved when the last racer went by. The back view held far fewer moving parts.

When she finally found her voice again, she asked only one thing. "Jack, can we please go to California now?"

Beside her, his laughter finally subsiding, he sucked in a deep breath and let it out as one having just finished a huge meal and now faced a long digestion. "Yes . . . I think we better."

TWELVE

Caroline stood at an unpainted windowsill, looking out—not on San Francisco, or any other California city for that matter—but on yet another Kansas town at its birthing. Even through the glass, she could hear the rasp of saw blades and out-of-sync hammer blows. She also heard the puff and screech of a locomotive engine on a brand-new railhead and the occasional volley of gunshots marking the drunken or bad-tempered. She heaved a sigh. At least they were some hundred-fifty miles closer to California. They might actually get there yet.

So this is Ft. Dodge—Dodge City, she corrected herself, just as the clerk downstairs had corrected them when they arrived last night.

"Been incorporated nigh on a year now," the man informed them proudly.

A pride sorely misplaced she decided then . . . and yet again as she considered the state of their room. The hotel was so new, had gone up so fast, the floors and walls were still raw wood, lacking either paint or paper. When sunshine streamed through the un-curtained window, like now, it created a golden glare so bright it hurt the eyes. In contrast, the four-panel doors were sanded smooth, darkly stained, and shiny with varnish. As further promise to this creeping progress, bright brass oil lamps were nailed to the splintery walls—one over the bed, the other beside the door.

The furniture was fashionably carved, but so scratched and scarred—the wardrobe and dressing screen especially—they looked as if they'd fallen off the back of a wagon. Repeatedly.

Tugging up the window sash, she was greeted by a gust of fast-warming September air. With it came the smells of last night's unexpected-but-appreciated rain, new-sawn wood, turpentine, sour whitewash . . . and the fly-swarmed buffalo hides stacked six feet high at the edge of town where the frenzy of building hadn't yet reached.

Down in the muddy thoroughfare below, a steady flow of pedestrians, animals, and vehicles streamed by: buckboards, covered wagons, uncovered wagons with their arched ribs swaying, grizzled fur trappers leading mules loaded with pelts, Chinese men, their silk pants muddied at the hem, trundling past with wheelbarrows full of piglets or nails or rags, or with a brace of water buckets balanced across their shoulders. Mounted, blue-coated soldiers rode solemnly past, side arms strapped to their thighs, saddles rounded with bedrolls and sprouting rifle butts. There were workmen with picks and shovels over their shoulders, young boys carrying bushel baskets or dragging sledges of cut saplings. Businessmen wore coats and hats they had to clamp to their heads against the wind as they wobbled along the boards put down as walkways even as rough-clad workmen strode past in the mud, uncaring for their already-crusted boots.

Sight of a lone, blanket-shawled Indian, quietly riding his pony barebacked through the throng, looking nothing like the wildly painted demons depicted in the newspapers, reminded Caroline that they were in Kiowa and Cheyenne territory now, which explained the soldiers.

Across this wide, teeming expanse was a set of structures that defied all notions of what Caroline would call a city. Planked wood buildings, tall with false fronts, some with covered walkways, were snugged side-by-side with canvas tents and crude things constructed entirely of lashed-together logs. The disparities disappeared, however, when it came to their signs—huge, painted boards proclaiming the goods and services inside—dry goods, cigars, general outfitters, tin ware, groceries. Oddly enough, only the saloons demurred the obvious with names like Long Branch and Red Beard's or the slightly more direct Liberty Libations. All lined up, some with a slight lean, they reminded Caroline of a mouthful of broken teeth.

Squinting to judge the time of day by the angle of the sun, she wondered where Jack was in all this hubbub. He'd left hours ago with the promise to return "soon." Hopefully, he was scaring up a game.

Antsy to do something besides wait, she washed, raked a brush through her hair and fussed over what to wear. She finally settled on her new basque and skirt of robin's-egg blue, buttoned up her old high-tops (she refused to muddy her new ones), tied on her pancake of a straw hat, wriggled her fingers into lacy crocheted gloves, and snagged up her reticule. Satisfied with her reflection in the cheval glass, she left and went down the switchback staircase.

At the bottom, she dodged workmen to look into a side room—an older one, judging by the drunken pitch of its floor—now a dining area. Turning around, she was forced into a corner to avoid more workmen carrying in sections of what appeared to be a shiny new bar destined for the saloon next door . . . for which they'd simply cut a hole in the adjoining wall.

On a whim, she followed them through the hole, re-emerging a few minutes later to sail out the front door.

Two men walking together on the walkway halted abruptly, doffed their hats in unison, and waved her across their path.

"Ma'am!"

"Miss!"

Each earned a smile of thanks.

Immediately another man, a trapper judging by the smell and layers of grime, bounded up with a length of board to place over the mud in her path.

Another man, his bloodied apron declaring him a butcher, appeared beside her to offer a steadying hand down off the walkway. "We don't get to see many ladies in these parts, much less pretty ones—that is, if you don't mind me saying so," he said in response to her thank you.

It was like that all the way through town.

When a load of lumber tumbled off the side of a wagon, the spill got no closer to her than three feet, but several fellows nearby pounced on the poor driver, hauled him down out of his seat and over to her on his tiptoes to apologize— "or get a-thumpin'," he was told.

The young man, all brown eyes and wheat-colored hair, crushed his hat to his buckskin vest and apologized profusely.

"No harm done," she assured them all with a smile. "I'm quite unharmed."

Her defenders and the hapless driver all beamed at her as one.

Heavens! she thought as she moved on. They act as if they've never seen a woman before, which would make them easy marks in a card game, she decided. Perhaps Dodge really would be the turning point in their fortunes as Jack had predicted—his argument for stopping yet again. So, with that happy thought pushing her forward, she became less careful about her boots if not her skirts, and more adventurous about taking the rougher, less intentioned pathways, cutting between and behind structures in her hunt for Jack.

Where could he be?

She finally found him next to a large tent erected at a right angle to the main street, its walls bellying in and out with the steady wind, breathing out noxious fumes of gunpowder and rusting iron. Men in oatmeal-colored undershirts and those heavy canvas trousers with the copper rivets, were pushing empty wheelbarrows in, full ones out, spitting in the mud as they went.

Oblivious to all the activity around him, Jack sat with one hip propped on a barrel, the other leg braced against a stack of lumber, flat-brimmed straw hat slanted to the back of his head, intently reading a thin, paper-bound book curled open in one hand. His other arm hung by a thumb hooked into his pants pocket. She'd never seen him read newspapers, much less a book.

"I've been looking everywhere for you," she said, holding her skirts up out of the muck.

He roused like a man coming out of a trance. "Oh . . . hello."

"Hello, yourself. You've been gone for hours. What are you doing?"

"Reading."

"I can see that, but why here in the middle of the street—on a building site, no less?"

He uncurled the book to show her its ragged yellow cover. "Raising Cattle," he read aloud the hand-lettered title above a crude pen-and-ink drawing of a cow.

"You're reading about *cows?*"

"Cattle, not cows. Thinkin' about starting a ranch."

She felt her face go slack. "*What?*" Then she remembered all those visits to the stockyards. She didn't think anything of them at the time. "You're not serious!"

"Why not?"

"Because we're going to California—to *gamble*—that's why!" She heard her own shrillness.

He straightened with a lazy stretch. "They have cattle ranches in California, too."

"But you're a gambler!"

He gave her a look she didn't understand before shoving the book into his back pocket. The whole subject, so unexpected, made her nervous, so she changed it.

"I haven't seen any signs around here against women gambling, have you?"

"No." He took her elbow, careful of his own footing in the fast-drying mud. "Feeling up for a round?"

"Not only am I feeling up to it, I'm *challenging* you," she announced, being deliberately provocative.

"Oh? How so?"

She'd hoped for more fire in his response, but persisted. "Winnings—mine against yours at the end of each day."

"And what exactly will I win?"

There was a bit of gleam back in the look he slanted her, so she felt reassured enough for sauciness. "I'll decide *that* if and when you win, sir."

"Hm. Sounds like a rigged game to me," he said with a hint of a smile.

"So, you want to be a *rancher* when we get to California?" she couldn't help asking as they picked their way over the mud ruts together, cutting through the steady line of supply wagons with carefully gauged timing. "And give up gambling?"

"From what I can tell, ranchin's just another form of gamblin'—the long-term kind."

"You realize they're having range wars," she warned, accepting his help up to the boardwalk, which connected a few yards later to their hotel. "I've been reading about them. Sheep herders against cattlemen. Ranchers building fences and other ranchers cutting them down, people starting to murder each other over it all."

"Glad to see you're payin' attention." He stopped to light up a cheroot and stare out over the hustle and bustle. "Keepin' up, that is."

That had an ominous sound. "Why?"

"'Cause I need a change," he answered, squinting through the smoke at the structures on the other side of the street. "I think we both do."

Truly alarmed now, her next words came out more combative than intended. "Well, *I* still intend to be a gambler—a dealer."

Instead of responding to that, he indicated their choice of saloons with a smooth gesture. "So, which establishment should get our business tonight, madam?"

She considered, then pointed. "The biggest one."

"Liberty Libations it is," he said and helped her back down to the street.

"At separate tables," she stipulated. "And no glaring."

The distraction of their contest took them through several evenings of games and several less-than-serious mornings of comparing their winnings over breakfast. They'd take a table in the dining room and banter playfully, finding this part of it more satisfying than actually declaring a winner and ending the challenge. Things between them were comfortable again.

"Ha!" she crowed one such morning, perched on his knee. "Beat you by twelve dollars!"

But he hadn't finished drawing all the coins out of his vest pocket. After spilling those, he was up by over twenty dollars.

"Bah! You're such a rounder. You cheated."

He tapped her nose. "You, too. I was watchin' you. Lucky for you, your marks were too busy moonin' over you to notice." On that, he sobered. "You need to be more careful."

She tossed her hair. "Are you saying I'm on the verge of losing my looks?"

"Hardly," he said, a finger stroking the smooth skin of her arm.

Well, well! Look who we have here—finally.

As one, they looked up to see Louisiana Louie in plantation hat, trunk at his feet, leaning on his plundered gold-headed cane. More care-worn and cautious-seeming than she ever remembered, he was regarding them with a tense smile.

Jack nudged her off his knee and stood up. "Louie," he said flatly.

"Jack." He tipped the hat in her direction. "Caroline."

She nodded.

"You two staying here at the hotel?"

Jack nodded.

"Me, I'm going to have to look elsewhere—probably the rooming house I saw coming into town. They're full-up here. Care to join me for a little noonday supper after I check in . . . and accept an old man's apology? Both of you?" He held out a hand to Jack.

Caroline looked from one face to another, holding her breath in the pause that followed.

The tension left Jack like a released spring, and he stepped forward to grasp Louie's hand. She could see the relief in both their faces as they clapped each other's shoulders.

"Hell," Jack said, "let's all go together to get you checked in, then we can come back here for that supper." He turned to her, face flushed and relaxed. "Caroline?"

She smiled at him and nodded. "It's good to see you again, Louie."

"You, too, m'dear." He nodded to the table behind her where their coins were stacked in two distinct piles. "I see you're earning your keep."

She was pleased by the acknowledgment. "I'm trying."

Jack hoisted Louie's trunk onto his shoulder while she scooped up their money, and together they walked outside into the blindingly bright noonday sun, the air so baking hot it hit them like a blow. The mud of a few days before had dried hard and had already been flattened into dust again by the near constant stream of wagon and animal traffic.

In the short time they'd been there, many hasty structures had been replaced and two new cross-streets had been added—all wide enough for the three of them to walk abreast without danger of being run over.

As they walked, Louie and Jack exchanged shortened versions of their travel stories, but at one point, Louie's steps stalled. "No! You took Caroline into *Delano?* Did she faint outright?"

Jack grinned. "No, but you should've seen her face during the Runnin' of the Doves."

Louie's eyebrows shot up. "I can imagine! I've seen their, um, Sunday tradition. There're as many parts moving east and west as there are going north and south."

Caroline felt her face color. "Not exactly a decent topic of conversation. Neither of you have any manners. Don't know why I still expect any."

Jack laughed and reached out with his free arm to give her shoulders an affectionate squeeze even as Louie chuckled and touched the brim of his hat in apology.

The boarding house was on the first cross street, just around the corner. It was tall and as-yet unpainted, the inside cavernous with high ceilings and darkened from closed shutters.

Louie checked in, then he and Jack climbed the stairs to locate his room and deposit his trunk while she waited downstairs.

On the way back to their hotel, they paused in front of a large tent where a crowd had gathered. Curious, they fell in with the crush of people to see what the attraction was. Just as they pushed inside the flaps, the crowd broke into thunderous applause, with shouts of "Praise the Lord!" and amens abounding.

And there, in the middle of it all, was a tall, blond man, painfully thin in suspendered pants over a stained, oatmeal-colored undershirt and a baggy sack coat the rusty color of rawhide. He was smiling and nodding feverishly to the crowd, their arms reaching toward the hat he held out to drop in coins, their clink barely audible beneath the continued chorus of *amen, brother! Amen!*

It was Deforest Atchison. Preacher.

Caroline felt the surprise hitch in her chest. Beside her, Jack gave an involuntary grunt. He shot Louie a look loaded with accusation—to which Louie just shrugged.

Suddenly, there was a ripple in the crowd and Preacher popped free just in front of them, hat bellied out with the weight of silver and a few winks of gold. Still in motion, he swept it in an arc in front of all three of them—before stopping dead on recognition.

"Miss Caroline!" he exclaimed, a mix of emotions washing over his pale features. When she didn't respond, he had the decency to look embarrassed. "Oh," he said, just noticing Jack and Louie. "Hello."

Jack looked like he'd wanted to throttle the man. "Atchison." His lips barely moved.

Louie stuck out his hand. "Louisiana Louie. We met in St. Louis."

Preacher tucked the frayed hat under one arm, ignored the jostling crowd as they surged out of the tent now that the show was over, and shook Louie's hand. "Yes, I remember."

There was a long, awkward pause, and it was Louie who finally stepped into the breach. "We were just going to supper. If you don't mind keeping company with reprobates like ourselves," Louie touched his hat brim again by way of apology, "the lady excepted, of course—why don't you join us?" Before anyone could react, he slapped Jack on the back. "Whadaya say? Think we can encourage our friend here to join us? Sure we can!" he said heartily, cutting off Jack's obvious intention to argue.

Throwing a fatherly arm around Preacher's shoulder, he tugged him into step. "Come on, boy. You look like you could use a square meal." He pointed to the hat full of coins. "And it looks like you can afford a damned fine one—beggin' your pardon *again*, Miz Caroline—courtesy of the good folks of Dodge City." He leaned forward with a stage whisper. "Besides, it's always wise to give a little back. Never know when a kindness like that can come back around to help a man out . . . if you catch my meaning." The slap he delivered to Preacher's back caused a full-step recovery and loosened a long hank of hair over his eyes.

Preacher shoved it back with bony fingers. "Sure, why not?" He forced a smile, nodding at the last of those streaming out of the hot tent. "In fact, I-I'd be honored if y'all would agree to be my guests."

"Why, that's mighty kind of you," Louie exclaimed, flushed with the success of his none-too-subtle manipulation. "An offer no one could rightly refuse. Right, son?" he asked Jack.

Jack remained grimly silent.

Hooking both younger men by the elbows, Louie steered them out of the stifling heat of the tent and into the bright blaze of Kansas sunshine, leaving Caroline to follow. She hadn't said a single word this entire time.

In truth, what *could* she have said? *What's happened to you? You look awful—and smell worse?* Good manners prevented it of course, so now she trailed along behind them without enthusiasm, trying to talk herself out of the queerest foreboding.

Inside, the dining room was full, so they were directed to the saloon—through the hole in the wall, now widened and trimmed into an odd-shaped archway of sorts, also through which now extended twenty-two feet of gleaming, bull-nosed bar that turned a corner and reached nearly to the front door. Why the wall hadn't been eliminated entirely was anyone's guess. No one could sit at the bar in the opening without blocking foot traffic, but invariably someone would scoot his stool there, and Jimmy, the bartender, would yell at them to move their "damned lard ass outa the way!" Most complied without rebuttal, but occasionally someone would critique some portion of Jimmy's anatomy in return, moving out of the way nonetheless. It was definitely a lively and colorful atmosphere in which to take a meal.

"I do supper at seven sharp, close it at midnight," Jimmy said, speaking to her as he served them plates of chicken-fried steak, boiled potatoes, and collard greens with speedy efficiency, even managing to whip the bottle of rye from beneath his arm to top off Preacher's glass for the second time. "Never thought I'd get this busy this fast, but if you're still interested, I could use the help." He was gone before she could reply.

Jack frowned, rotating his plate to put the meat in front of him before stabbing it with knife and fork. "What's that about? Why was he talkin' to you?"

"I sought employment from him when we first arrived. I didn't know at the time if this town allowed women to gamble," she explained, trying to keep her voice low despite the din around them.

"Employment!" he barked, clearly feeling no such restraint. "Again? First, lady gambler, then serving wench—what is it this time? Scullery maid? Down on your knees scrubbin' floors?"

She blushed. "It's a moot point now since I can gamble *here*."

But he was like a dog on a rabbit. "Look around you, Caroline. This is no place for a woman. I'm serious—look around. What do ya see?" Fisting his silverware on either side of his plate, he waited for her to answer.

Chewing her first bite as if it were a mouthful of tacks, she finally was able to swallow and comply. "I see hungry, thirsty men, who—"

His mouth opened, ready to interrupt, but she overrode him.

"Who, no doubt, have some money they're willing to part with for service with a sweet smile." She offered him a free sample.

Louie burst out laughing. "Well, I'll be damned! She's gotcha there, boy!"

Jack's glower darkened and the tips of his ears grew red. "Exactly!" he retorted, ignoring Louie completely. "Men! This ain't no place for a decent woman. You can't work here and that's all there is to it," he pronounced, attacking his dinner again.

She didn't know whether to laugh or throw something, but her attention was diverted by Preacher, who'd remained absolutely silent since they'd all sat down together, when he signaled Jimmy for another refill. He was drinking a lot. More than before—and obviously much more than was good for him. Refocusing on Jack, she swept his words aside with a gesture. "As I said, it's a moot point, *but*," she pointed at him with her fork, "I'm used to earning money, Jack." She'd started to say "for a living," but history had shown that wasn't quite accurate, and she didn't care to give him a foothold for further argument.

"What do you need money for anyway? Don't I buy you whatever you want?"

Louie's attention left his plate, and he looked first to Jack, then Caroline.

"How many times do we have to go over this?" she asked. "It's important *to me* to have my own money. As Preacher once said, it's never a sin to survive."

Jack's gaze shifted hard over to the origin of that quote, and Caroline could tell—with dismay—that he'd found a new outlet for his ire. "Well, I guess he oughta know all about it—sin, that is. What with him being a man of God 'n' all. Tell me, Atchison—I don't think you've ever really said, but just how and when did you become a man of the cloth?"

Preacher shifted, uneasy at being the center of attention. Reflexively, he began touching the pads of his fingers to the rim of his glass, which now held his third refill since sitting down. "When God calls a man to serve, he knows he is unworthy, but simply follows the calling," was the evasive response.

"He doesn't feel you hafta actually *know* anything—be *trained* or anything like that?"

"Jack—"

"Are you blaspheming, sir?" Preacher inquired, rallying somewhat.

"I'm just trying to figure out what makes you the expert, by what right you call yourself a man of God and give advice to—"

"Jack!"

He looked at her stonily. "I just wanna know who—and what—he really is. If I feel the sudden need for salvation, I'd like to know who's around that's qualified to baptize me."

Preacher finished off his drink in a single swallow. "If you mus' know, I received the calling after the war." He cocked his head. "Or maybe durin' . . . at Camp Douglas. I attended a small ec—" he hiccupped, then slowed to enunciate. "Ec . . . *u*. . . men. . . ical college near my home. . . after. The war. After the war."

Jack's temper subsided some and he had the grace to look, if not abashed, at least more thoughtful, his manner less pugnacious at hearing mention of the notorious prison.

"Started spreadin' th' Gospel after—" another hiccup "—after that."

Sullenly, Jack went back to eating, but now Louie took up the cudgel. "And before the war, what was your calling then?"

"A humble . . . farmer," Preacher replied, staring down into his empty glass.

Louie looked thoughtful. "I seem to recall you saying you grew up on a plantation."

Preacher nodded.

"How many acres, d'ya think? A couple hundred maybe?"

"'Bout that."

"I'd hardly call that being a 'humble' farmer."

It seemed to Caroline that Preacher had shrunk during this exchange. He seemed shorter, smaller in stature, shoulders rounded protectively, his still-full plate virtually ignored.

Suddenly, she dashed her knife and fork to her plate with such force, the knife spun off onto the floor. "Who cares what a person was *before?* Can't a man reinvent himself? Make something better—maybe just different, more true to himself?" she demanded.

"Miz Caroline," Louie began.

"Don't Miz Caroline me! You're nothing but a pair of jackals—you and Jack both—circling, looking for an exposed throat. You should be ashamed of yourselves!"

"My dear, I didn't mean—" Louie began again.

Again, she cut him off, rounding on Jack. "And you especially—with all your rousing talk of making a fresh start!"

"Forgive me," Preacher suddenly broke in. "I seem to have sp-spoiled everyone's evenin'." With that, he rose unsteadily to his feet. "I think I shall . . . return to my room at the boardin' house." Catching his foot on the table leg, he staggered. Jack instinctively threw out a hand, but Caroline was already on her feet and grabbed Preacher's arm.

"*I'll* walk with you," she told him.

"Quite unnecessary . . . bu' I thank you jes's'same."

"I insist. I really need a turn—some fresh air. It's gotten quite *foul* in here," she added, slanting an evil look in their direction, "and I don't feel comfortable strolling by myself in this town." Her arm still hooked with his, she swept her skirt free of the chair legs. "So I'd be most obliged if you'd escort me, at least as far as the end of the street."

He patted her hand. "I'm—I'd be honored."

Louie had gotten to his feet, but Jack remained seated, face closed, looking at no one.

She didn't care a whit, not a single whit, she told herself.

As soon as they were gone, Jack shoved his plate away with barely suppressed violence. "Tell me," he demanded of Louie, "how come you both show up together on the same day?"

"Not together," Louie corrected, sitting back down.

"Maybe not, but I'd bet my last sawbuck you had somethin' to do with him bein' here."

Louie didn't dissemble. Instead, he steepled his hands over his plate. "That boy's in bad shape. He drinks too much—"

"I don't give a good goddamn if he drinks himself blind! Why'd you bring him here?"

"I didn't exactly bring him here. We ran across each other in Jefferson City a couple days after I left the boat. I've been trying to catch up with you ever since."

"And?"

"And I gave him some money. Figured I'd help him back on his feet, that's all."

"And no doubt told him where you were headed next."

"Maybe. I don't remember, but I didn't *bring* him here."

"Well, you're here and so is he. I call that close enough. And then you turn on him, go after him about being a farmer. Why? I don't understand you at all."

"She defended him, didn't she? And turned on you—I knew she would. Don't you see yet? She cares about him more 'n' you!"

"You schemin' sonofabitch."

To that, Louie just arched a brow and returned to cleaning his plate. "I care about what happens to you, that's all."

"You sure got a funny way of showin' it . . . but I know what you're doin', what you been doin' from the start. You're match-makin' and you better stop it."

"I'm just trying to get you to come to your senses before it's too late. Even you have to admit those two have more in common than the two of you."

"The hell I do—and it ain't none of your business!"

Louie's shrug said *everyone's entitled to an opinion.*

Realizing he'd gotten as much satisfaction as he was going to get from the confrontation, Jack threw some money on the table and shoved to his feet.

Watching him leave, Louie heaved a tired sigh and picked up his beer. "*Shit!*" he muttered to himself. None of this was going the way he'd hoped.

Outside on the walkway, Caroline did her best to make it look like Preacher was supporting her on his arm and not the other way around.

"DeForest, what's happened to you? You don't . . . you don't seem yourself at all."

His eyes were slightly out of focus when he looked down at her. "No?"

"No."

"M'apologies."

When he offered nothing more, she just concentrated on getting him to the boarding house—the same place Louie was staying. It wasn't easy and took twice as long as it should have. Once there, she introduced herself to the female proprietor, who helped her get him up the stairs to his room.

He fumbled for his key.

The place was tiny, a mess, and the smell of sick made her recoil. There was an empty bottle on the floor by the washstand. Nearby was a wad of clothing. There was a narrow, unmade bed right beside the door and a short wooden stool at the foot of it, on which sat a very old, very scarred leather traveling case.

She tried steering him toward the washstand, but he just tilted himself toward the bed. Too heavy to stop, she had no choice but to let him go. And he went—passed out before he ever hit the mattress.

Opening the one window, she tried to wave out some of the smell. With two fingers, she picked up the shirt from the floor along with some truly disgusting socks and draped them over the sill to air out.

Rolling him onto his back, she tugged off his boots and dropped them on the floor. At the washstand, she soaked the untouched washcloth in water from the ewer, then sat on the side of the bed to gently bathe his face and hands. He could deal with the rest himself come morning.

Somewhere in all this, she started thinking about Wendall and how she used to do this exact same thing for him after many a late night homecoming. It startled her a bit. She hadn't thought about her brother in a long time—and certainly not in the same vein as Preacher.

About an hour later, when she returned to their room, Jack was stretched out on the bed, propped on an elbow, coat and collar gone. His booted ankles were crossed insolently on top of the coverlet as he flipped cards into his upturned hat at the foot of the bed. Despite the relaxed pose, she could feel the tension coming off him like heat waves.

Foregoing a greeting, she removed her own hat, bent the straw back in shape and smoothed its black ribbon between her fingers before placing it on the dresser. She fluffed her hair in the mirror and ignored his reflection. She knew he was watching her. It was childish, she knew, but she vowed not to be the first to speak.

"Sooo," he began, the syllable ominously drawn out.

She turned around. "So?"

"Did you get your precious drunk settled?"

"He's not a drunk—not usually anyway—and you don't know what he's been through." *And he's certainly not* my *anything*, she finished in her head.

"Told ya all his sob stories, has he? All his heroic deeds while in Camp Douglas?" The cards were spinning with more energy and less accuracy now, sailing off onto the floor.

"You're being vile."

"Been pluckin' your heartstrings, too, I s'pose."

"At least he hasn't been irritating me—like some people."

Rooting through their cupboard, she plucked out her old dress of yellow muslin, gave it a shake, and held it up in front of herself as she regarded the effect in the mirror. *Too demure*, she decided, eyeing the inset of lace that filled the bodice from bosom to throat. Louie's opinion, too, as she recalled.

She went to the new sewing basket she'd put together and retrieved her embroidery scissors. Perching on the edge of the bed, she went to work snipping out the lace as close to the muslin as possible, using only the barest tips of the scissors.

The sound of flicking cards ceased and she felt the bed dip, then a warm breath on the back of her neck, replaced quickly with a soft kiss.

"Mmm," he said, nuzzling his nose in her hairline.

She turned her head slightly, but didn't stop concentrating on her task.

"We haven't been to bed yet," he reminded her suggestively. "Aren't ya tired? We could still get several hours' sleep 'fore nightfall."

"I'll admit I'm tired, but I can't sleep. Not yet."

He sat back. "What're you doing?"

"Making something old new again."

"Sounds like magic."

"Mm-hm."

With the last of the lace gone, she stood and shook out the yards of yellow muslin and held it up to herself to judge its effect in the mirror. Some time ago, she'd restyled the sleeves so they were mere puffs to cap her shoulders. Now, with its low, scooping bodice, it was more graceful and alluring—something a grown woman would wear. As she swished the skirt a bit from side to side, she smiled, imagining what Louie's reaction to this version might be.

Stepping behind the dressing screen to change, she emerged moments later and presented her back to him. "Will you hook me up please?"

He got off the bed and obliged, silent in his concentration on the tiny fasteners. His knuckles necessarily brushed along the bare skin of her spine. It sent sparks streaking to inconvenient places, so she moved away as soon as he was done to re-pin her chignon.

"What the hell!"

Startled, she looked up. They were framed together in the mirror, and he was staring at her—more specifically at the rounded tops of her breasts, now pushed into prominence over the top of her new and much lower décolletage.

"Where do you think you're going in *that?*"

"Downstairs."

He grabbed her arm and spun her around. "You will not! I forbid it!"

She wrenched herself free. "What's gotten into you? All this *forbidding*. You don't own me! You have no right to forbid me anything. I shall *dress* as I please, go *where* I please."

His face darkened. "Dressin' for Preacher?"

The question irritated her. "Why do you say such things?"

Contrition raced across his face and he reached for her again. Grabbing her by both arms, he dragged her up close to kiss her.

"Don't!" She turned her face and twisted free.

"Caroline—" His blue eyes were awash in uncertainty, mouth buttoning with frustration.

She moved out of reach. "If you don't mind," she said stonily, her back to him, "I'd like to finish dressing in private."

Tension teetered on violence, and she held her breath. Finally, he gave a noisy snort, scooped his hat off the bed, and stalked out, slamming the door behind him.

Only then did she realize she was shaking. She had to sit on the edge of the bed for a few minutes just to calm down.

Two hours later, her serving job was over, and she was dealing blackjack to a table full of eager men. Not that Jimmy was happy about it—he'd sold twice as much whiskey and beer in those two hours than any he could remember—but he'd eventually bowed to pressure from customers who clamored for her company seated across a table. Her sweet suggestion of a game of cards "to pass the time" had met with enthusiastic agreement and forced his hand.

As several of them scurried to hold a chair for her, he scrubbed his rag over the surface of his beloved bar and grumbled, "Waste of time—she won't last long."

From the far end, a new voice said, "Care to wager on that?"

Heads turned. It was Jack, who'd been standing at the bar, quietly drinking since he'd come in a while ago.

She'd been ignoring him up to that point, but pleased by the implied compliment, she smiled at him.

He frowned—but not too ferociously—and looked down into the shot glass he was rolling between his fingers.

Jimmy squinted in his direction. "She just better not come wantin' her job back, that's all I gotta say. You hear that, missy?" he called out. "I won't take you back!"

"Sure you don't wanna lay a wager on *that*, Jimmy?" asked someone else.

He spat on the floor. "Hell, Mick, if you paid your tab more often, I just might!"

The barroom erupted in laughter even as Caroline swept her skirts beneath her and sat gracefully at the hastily cleared table. Each man who took a chair earned a smile. "Thank you, gentlemen. Now what shall it be? A nice game of twenty-one?"

That had been three sets of opponents ago, and she had a decent pile of money in front of her. As much as she wanted to give all the credit to her skill, she suspected a good deal of her success came from their desire to see her lean over the table and scoop up her winnings. In this, her last-minute tailoring had been successful.

There was still a clot of men waiting to play, hovering. She refused to reveal her discomfort at this, but Jack had no such reluctance. After a while, she didn't even have to look to know the threatening glare he was fixing on whoever was sitting at her table or standing too close and working to capture her attention.

A little while later, she saw him get dealt into a game at the next table and sit directly in her line of sight. Only then did she notice he'd come without his game box. She was surprised he would play without it, but soon saw that his mind wasn't really on what his hands were doing.

In another game a few tables away, she saw Louie unhappily taking note of the same thing.

Finally aware that he was bleeding money, Jack rubbed his eyes and forced himself to concentrate. Tired as he was, he itched with irritation and something more. He wasn't just tired from lack of sleep—or even the reappearance of that damned, spineless Bible thumper. He was tired of always looking for his future in the next town . . . and the next. He was tired of the constant changes. Just once he wanted things to remain the same. Hell, he wanted to stay in the same spot long enough for his socks to dry out.

Some said you never got too old for this business—look at Louie. And there were others he could name, but *he* was burnt out. He was losing his edge, that keen taste for risk that let a man run a bluff to the very edge and still laugh, win or lose, his hands dry and steady. If he couldn't shore himself up soon, he'd be ruined. It wasn't losing at cards he was afraid of—that was part and parcel of playing the tables—it was losing the chance at a future. He had plans now and was determined to build something from the ground up if necessary—to use his head and hands for harder work than holding pasteboard chances night and day.

Before he met Caroline, he'd never really cared much what happened to him, whether he had a future or not, much less where he slept or with whom. Now he cared *a lot,* and that could be a mighty dangerous thing for a gambler. In this, Louie had been right. Since telling him about it months ago in St. Louis, the idea had grown roots, dominating his thoughts. By damn, he wanted a home—a family even. And he wanted it all with Caroline.

At the next table, Caroline could hardly lay down a card without feeling Jack's eyes on her. At first, she was aware of the resentment in his glance, but gradually she saw that soften into something else. His gaze came close to being a caress that she could feel on her bare arms, the side of her throat, her breasts. It was a different form of intimacy than she'd ever experienced, and it brought to mind all the ways they'd been together, touched and tasted one another.

Her spot under the lamp seemed suddenly warmer than before. She had to force herself to focus, or Jimmy would be right and she *would* be asking for her old job back. That helped her concentrate for a bit—until she glanced up and caught the naked look of longing on Jack's face. He was staring at her mouth, which made her lips tingle. She licked them self-consciously.

Apparently, the fellow to her right was watching and took the gesture as an invitation. He suddenly put a grubby paw on her shoulder and leaned in for a kiss.

"I *beg* your pardon!" She stiff-armed him. "Remove it . . . or lose it," she threatened quietly, determined to dispense with this before Jack came roaring over.

The sound of chair legs screeching fueled her apprehension, and since the man hadn't listened, she simply poked him in the eye. Hard.

"*Ow!*" he hollered, clapping hands over his wounded orb. "Why'd you go an' do that?"

"I warned you." She stood up, retrieved her cards, and wrapped them in her handkerchief. "I'm sorry, gentlemen, but I'm afraid our time's come to an end."

"But we ain't finished our game yet!" one of the others protested.

"Come back tomorrow," she invited, scooping her money off the table.

She glanced dispassionately at the one rocking back and forth, hand still to his eye. "But not *you*," she said, then left the room without a backward glance.

Jack had been watching all this, ready to spring to her defense, but held himself back by sheer willpower. Now he knocked his knuckles on the table in front of him. "Out," he said, and rose to follow her.

Louie stepped into his path. "Buy you a drink?"

Jack tried to go around him.

Louie stepped in front of him again and gripped his shoulder. "Let her go, son."

"I can't stomach these leering clods anymore."

"I understand, but she took care of 'em."

A smile tugged at Jack's mouth. "Yeah, she's got guts, don't she?"

A little while later, with a whiskey apiece, and sitting next to each other at the bar, Jack finished telling Louie his plans. "I been puttin' money aside, wiring it to a bank in St. Louis for a couple of months now."

Louie could only shake his head.

Reaching for the ever-present book in his back pocket, Jack handed it to him. "I know everything that's in that—read it a dozen times already—and learned more from every cowhand and stockyard wrangler willing to talk to me between here and Kansas City. And," he paused for a deep breath, "I'm going to ask Caroline to marry me."

Louie studied the liquor in his glass for a long, silent moment before looking up with sad blue eyes. "Son, you're not thinking straight—not about this and not about your game. Where was your head tonight? Never mind, I already know the answer to that—but it's not good for you, all this dreaming. *She's* not good for you."

Jack's own blue eyes turned steely as he got off the barstool. "You don't know what you're talkin' about, old man."

Louie grabbed Jack's sleeve. "Can't you see? She's not ready to settle down yet—and she won't be, not for a long while. Maybe never. Her kind—"

Jack shook him off. "Don't talk about her like that—not ever! She's not a *kind*, and like I said before—ain't none of your business. *We* ain't your business, so let's keep it that way." He walked away, leaving Louie scrubbing a hand over his face in frustration.

Thirteen

Light seeped beneath Caroline's eyelids. She could feel the heat of the day coming with the dusty air that stirred the window curtains, and she became acutely aware that she was spooned into the curve of Jack's body. They were both naked.

She dared not think about the riskiness of last night's lovemaking. Like runaway horses, there'd been no stopping either one of them once Jack came through that door. While she was past being shocked at herself, her anxiety after the fact was steep.

He roused and kissed her shoulder. "I'm a lucky guy," he mumbled, then rolled over to burrow back into sleep. Reaching behind him, he tugged her closer. "C'm here." When she obliged, spooning him, he pulled her arm under his to tuck it against his belly. "Whus wrong?"

Her cheek rested against his shoulder. "Why didn't you stop Louie yesterday at supper?"

She could feel him come alert in the small slice of silence before he answered. "Why should I?" There was irritation in his voice.

"I know you don't like Preacher, and I even understand, but Louie was just being *mean*. For no reason."

"Louie's an ass."

That mollified her some.

He rubbed his butt against her. "Mmmm . . ."

Instead of responding, she threw off the sheet and swung her legs out of bed.

He wheeled over to grab her around her waist. "Oh, no you don't!" he growled playfully.

"Jack—"

He kissed a spot between her shoulder blades. "Don't worry. I've decided that if you get with child, I'll marry you."

"A child is nothing to joke about."

"Who said I was jokin'? Now come back here. It's early and there ain't a place in the world you gotta be." He rolled over, taking her with him and tucking her back against him as before. "'Cept right here."

"You're gonna be mad at me," she said after a moment.

"Why?"

"I need to go check on Preacher. Take him some breakfast."

Again, that heavy silence. "*Need?*"

"Well, no, not *need* . . . I just feel I should."

"I don't s'pose you'd agree not to go if I asked you not to."

She didn't answer.

With a great flap of the covers, he sat up. "Fine—*go.*"

"I won't be long. Promise." She tried to stroke his back, but he twitched her off.

"Go, damnit! Go take that mealy-mouthed hangdog his breakfast."

So she got up in a huff and did just that.

"And I hope he chokes on it!" he hollered just as she was closing the door.

Carrying a plate of yesterday's ham and potatoes under a red-checked napkin she'd gotten from Jimmy, Caroline walked down to the boarding house, worrying her bottom lip the whole way. She couldn't do anything about Jack—Louie either for that matter—but

277

maybe she could convince Preacher to move on, get him out of harm's way.

Remembering her from last night, the proprietress hailed her when she walked in. With a wave and a smile, Caroline indicated the plate and headed up the stairs.

She knocked on Preacher's door. "Preacher? DeForest? It's me, Caroline. Open up."

On hearing what might've been an answer, she opened the door part way. The first thing she saw was the empty bed, so she pushed the door wider. The next thing she saw was bloodied clothes strewn across the floor—and nearly dropped the plate. "*Preacher?*"

Clad only in trousers, he was leaning on the washstand, blotting a bloody cut over his eye with one of his filthy socks. Runnels of blood branched around his ear and down the side of his neck. His lips and the one eye she could see were puffed and discolored.

Putting the plate on the bed, she went over, yanked the filthy sock out of his hand, and tossed it away. "*My God! What happened?*" At odds with her tone, her hands were gentle as she took his face between them. "Let me look at you."

"Woke up, wen' outh, playthd thum cards . . . got drunk—"

"Drunk*er!*"

He winced at his own attempt to shrug. "Drunk*er,* an' got robth."

"I need to find the cut on your head, see how bad it is." Taking him by the wrist, she led him over to the bed, moved the plate, and had him sit down.

Hands limp in his lap, he made no protest as she parted his hair with her fingers. She hissed on discovering the two-inch gash just above his ear. "Oh, DeForest. This needs a doctor."

"No money."

"We'll worry about that later, right now—" she moved the plate to the floor "—lie back while I go find some help." She pulled the sheet up over him, annoyed to see her hand shaking. "Don't you dare leave this bed. I'll be back as soon as I can."

As an afterthought, she plucked up every item of clothing she could find. Rolling it all into a bundle, she held it as far away from her as possible and went back down the steps.

"Please—I need your help," Caroline said to the proprietress, bracing herself for what was sure to be a lambasting at best or cold refusal at worst.

Immediately, the woman's freckled forehead pleated, and her brown eyes rounded with concern. "What's wrong?"

"The man upstairs, first door on the left—"

The woman reared back. "He ain't sick, is he? Sick people in a boarding house're bad news. Next thing you know, you got one of them epidemics on your hands."

"No, no, he's not sick, but he's hurt—bleeding—and needs a doctor."

"Well, you're in luck there, dear. We all are. Our first doc showed up just a few days ago. Last house, end of this street." She pointed which way, then indicated the bundle Caroline was holding. "You looking for them to get washed?"

"Or burned—they're filthy."

"*Stink,* too. But hand 'em over. I got a girl who does the washing for folks stayin' here."

"Thank you!" Relieved of that burden, Caroline dashed for the door. "*Thank you!*"

She trotted all the way down the street, and the doctor himself answered the door. He was eating an apple. Frizzy red hair, rimless glasses, and a string tie were the only things her mind registered before she launched in.

"I need your help—well, not me. A man. DeForest Atchison—at the boarding house. He's bleeding. Please hurry!"

He tossed the apple into the yard. "All right, all right. Hold on, let me get my bag."

Together, they trotted back to the boarding house, the doctor holding onto his hat the whole way.

"I'm Doc Redman!" he called to her up ahead of him.

Barely breaking stride, she did a full circle turn to look at him. "You're joking!"

"Ha! No, everybody says that!"

"I'm Caroline Cooper!" she called back.

Minutes later, after examining Preacher, he said, "Oh, this is nothing."

She'd been standing at the foot of the bed, arms folded. "Any time blood leaks out of a person's head, I figure it's something."

"Well, you're right about that, but he doesn't have any broken bones, and with a couple of stitches, this'll mend in a week or so."

Pinching a length of catgut, he threaded his needle and set to work. "There," he said, knotting and cutting off the thread with a small pair of scissors. "What he needs right now is rest, good food—" he bent down to peek under the napkin "—hopefully something fresher than this, *and*," he added, looking up at her, "no more liquor."

"I'll get some—more food, I mean."

"Good. Well, that about does it. The spoonful of laudanum I got down him should help with pain and keep him out for a bit. Just keep him quiet as you can when he wakes up, and I'll check on him tomorrow."

"Thank you, doctor."

With everything back in his bag, he stood up. "You're welcome. That'll be two dollars."

"Of course." She dug through her reticule and produced the fee.

He tucked the coins into his vest pocket without even looking at them. He was busy studying her. "Forgive me if this is an indelicate question, but does this man have any clothes that you know of?"

"They're being laundered."

"Well, if they smelled anywhere near as bad as this room does, I should hope so."

She blushed, knowing it wasn't her fault, but after walking him down to the front door, she went back to properly introduce herself to the proprietress and ask for a bucket of hot water, some lye soap and a scrub brush.

Later, as she worked the soap and water across the raw floorboards on her hands and knees, skirts tucked up out of the way and hat dangling from the doorknob, all she could think about was Jack saying, *First, lady gambler, then serving wench—what is it this time? Scullery maid?*

Apparently so.

It was well past noon when she finally dragged herself back to the hotel. She walked in the door to find Jack and Louie sitting at the end of the bar with one empty stool between them.

Jack was up in an instant, coming toward her with such fury on his face she backed up a step. "That was a damn long *breakfast!* Sure it didn't include lunch—or somethin' else?"

Heads turned.

"*Well?*"

She'd planned on telling him everything, but knowing she'd have to wade through an argument first suddenly made it not worth the effort. "I'm sorry, but I'm too tired for this. I'm going upstairs," she said, suiting action to words.

He reached for her, but she evaded him and kept on climbing.

When Caroline awoke, it was nearing sunset. She was lying on top of tangled sheets, just as Jack had left them that morning, her shoes still laced on her feet. She was alone.

Swinging her feet to the floor, she longed for a bath, but that would have to wait for morning when the bathhouse filled their tubs with fresh water again. In the meantime, she'd have to make do at the washbowl.

Shedding her clothes, she scrubbed herself in the tepid water as flashes of Preacher and that morning's events paraded through her head. Getting him dinner would be her next task . . . without setting Jack off.

Dressed once again, she chose to leave by way of the outside stairs at the end of the hall. From there, she headed around back to sweet-talk Jimmy into fixing her another plate. Luckily, he was in a good mood and only reminded her to bring back the dishes this time.

Now on a first name basis with the woman who ran the boarding house, she was greeted cheerily as soon as she came through the door.

"Hello, Caroline!"

"Hi, Sarah." Apparently, the act of asking for and receiving help had moved them past formalities to a first-name basis. It almost felt like she'd made a friend.

"I think your patient is awake. I heard him stirring a bit ago."

Indeed, Preacher was sitting up, his back against the wall, when she knocked. He lifted his swollen and discolored face at her entry.

"How are you feeling?" she asked as she scooted the stool closer and sat down.

"Like the Lord smite me. With a railroad car. How do I look?"

"Like He ran you over with the whole train afterwards."

He gave a single huff of laughter, winced, and clutched at his ribs.

"Be still, and eat this," she said, offering up a spoonful of chicken stew. "After you finish, I'll get you some fresh water to wash with . . . and some to drink."

He measured her seriousness through the slit of an eye. "Penance?"

"No. Water's just better for you—the elixir of life."

"I think tha's wine."

"Not for you, it's not . . . now hush, and eat this. I can't stay long."

When he was finished, having eaten all he could but less than she would've liked, she gathered the dishes and utensils, and toed the stool aside so she could open the door.

"They get all your money?" she thought to ask.

He nodded. "But I'm paid up here 'til next week."

"Good. I'll ask Sarah to have your clean laundry brought up, and I'll see you tomorrow. And don't," she added with a steely look just before she closed the door, "leave this room."

He nodded, looking sleepy.

"Promise me."

He nodded again, sliding back down under the sheet.

Even as she left, she had little faith his promise would hold for long.

The next morning, she awoke with Jack beside her. She'd been asleep when he came in last night, and now she hoped to return the favor, dressing and leaving without waking him.

And thus became their routine over the next couple of days, the two of them managing to avoid each other while awake, playing at different saloons and returning to sleep together, but on a staggered schedule that ruled out any conversation or confrontation. Or intimacies.

Because of this, she was startled on the third morning to return from taking Preacher his breakfast to find Jack dressed, sitting on her side of the bed, twirling his hat in his hands. Feet stalled, she tucked a loose curl back behind her ear. The day was blustery, the kind where the wind flipped collars and shredded one's hair, and she knew what she looked like. Closing the door softly, she braced herself for another blast of his anger.

Standing, he took in her appearance, but didn't say anything for a long moment, then cleared his throat and began. In the instant before he spoke—for no reason she could understand—she wanted to cry. The few feet between them suddenly felt like miles.

"My prize," he said.

"What?"

"My prize—I want to claim it. Now. This morning."

"What are you talking about?"

"Your challenge, remember? I beat you in winnin' money four days running, so now I want my prize. You said you'd decide what it would be if I won. Well, I won—and since you never named the prize, I'm naming it."

"What do you want?" she asked, steeling herself for whatever was to come.

"Take a ride with me."

"A *ride?* Where to?"

"You'll see. Just say yes, and I'll meet you out front with the buggy."

She wanted to balk, but without any reason, couldn't think how.

Apparently, the thought showed on her face. "Come on, Caroline. Don't welsh on me."

That was it—pride wouldn't let her decline now. "All right."

He leaned to kiss her as he passed, but she flapped him away. "Just go get the buggy."

"Yes, ma'am," he said. Dropping the hat on his head, he tapped it in place and left.

The wind was still brisk, the sky cloudy, and she was glad she'd brought a shawl. With that clutched closed in one hand, she hung onto her hat with the other. Jack did the same—reins in one, holding his hat on with the other—until he lost patience and shoved it beneath the seat. Looking at him like that, the wind raking through his hair, even the gray sky, reminded her of the first time she'd seen him outside, the morning they'd found Wendall. Odd how long ago that all seemed. Another lifetime.

They drove east for nearly half an hour with very little conversation between them.

Finally, just over a long, sloping rise and down into a shallow bowl of a valley, he reined them to a stop beside a whitewashed farmhouse. It looked empty.

He pulled the brake and wound the reins around the handle. Leaning elbows to knees, he took a deep breath as if the air had some restful, restorative quality.

"What do you think?"

"Of what?"

"Of that," he said, indicating the house. "It comes with about a hundred acres, from there . . . to about there," he said pointing. "Plenty of grassland, enough for a small starter herd—you need about an acre per cow. And the low point right here is a perfect place for a pond. Just need to dig it out some and re-route the road. The family who built it abandoned it about a year ago. Went back East I was told. We could have it for next to nothing."

"I can see why."

"Oh, a little fixing up and it'll be fine—good as new. Granted, not as big as you're used to, but it could be a home." He swiveled toward her on the seat and took her hands in his. "Our home, yours and mine. Whadya say?"

She looked at him blankly. "*Me?* What are you saying?"

His blue eyes fairly twinkled with excitement. "I'm askin' you to marry me. To be my wife, to settle down and start a life with me."

There was a noise in her head, as if all the nails on a tack room wall had come loose at once. And a bubble of panic closed up around her throat. Suddenly, she was back onboard the *Quincy* with Simone saying, *Chart your course. If you don't, some man will.*

"*Here?*" This wasn't the life she pictured for herself at all!

Doubt dimmed some of his excitement. "Well, if not exactly here, someplace else close to town, but yes. In general, here. Why not?" he added with a dice-throw of hope.

"Because it-it's—"

He squeezed her hand. "Maybe we could even start a family. I ain't never thought about havin' kids before now, before *you*, but I been thinkin' about it ever since we left Sedalia. Now I think I'd like that—if you think I'll make a good pa, that is. Never had one of my own, so I ain't sure, but 'least I know some things I *won't* do. I won't never abandon 'em. You neither. Whadya say, Caroline? Will you marry me?"

She felt sick. He was looking at her with such naked earnestness. She wanted to be kind, to be careful, even as a larger part of her just wanted to leap down and *run*. Nonetheless, she managed to suppress that as she extricated her hand and laid it on his arm. "Jack, I have no doubt you'll make a *fine* father someday. It's just . . ." The words, more specifically how to say them without hurting him, clogged her throat.

"It's just *what?*"

"It's just . . . this isn't the place for me, Jack. And marriage, well . . . I don't know. All I know is California's where I want to go, where I want to be."

He turned his head, eyes scanning the horizon.

She knew he was hurting. She knew it because she was hurting, too—a pain like no other—without clear reason and without any way to banish it. All of this was just so...*hateful!*

"I'm sorry," she whispered.

Without another word, he turned them around and drove them back to Dodge in silence.

They returned to the hotel, and Louie was sitting at the bar when they came through. With Caroline close on his heels, Jack headed straight for the stairs.

"Jack, wait!" She tried to snag his arm, but he shook her off and took the stairs two at a time. Embarrassed, she looked toward the bar and locked eyes with Louie. Gathering her skirts, she followed Jack.

Only moments behind, she walked in on him already shedding his clothes and shoving himself back into his old frock coat and gold-striped trousers. The birdcage of dice was put back in place, and only then did she realize he hadn't worn any of this in a long time.

"Jack?"

He didn't answer. Yanking on the lapels of his coat to settle the collar, he grabbed his derby off the top of the wardrobe. "I'm gonna have some supper, then I'll be at Red Beard's for the rest of the night."

"Jack—"

He halted in front of her, face hard as stone. "Do you love him?"

The blunt question surprised her. She didn't want to talk about Preacher, she wanted to talk about *this,* about *them.* "I *care* about him, but—"

He didn't let her finish. "Well, you'd better figure out how much and soon. There's only so much a man can take, and I'm about done with this game." He ground the derby on his head.

"*Game?* What *game?*" But he was already gone.

Left behind in the silence, she looked around her, not really seeing any of it. Somehow this was Louie's fault. Every time he showed up, her life started to unravel, become precarious. Suddenly, she needed someone to talk to. Maybe Sarah had some time to spare.

Quickly, she freshened up, brushing and re-pinning her hair at the nape of her neck.

She left by the backstairs again, and just in case Sarah wasn't available, she decided to take Preacher a bit of supper. He never seemed to eat much of what she brought, but she couldn't stop trying.

By now, Jimmy was used to finding her at his back door. Without a word, he handed her a small, napkin-covered pail with a cup of cold hash, a spoon, and an apple. She dug through her reticule to pay him, and realized she was getting low on funds. She'd have to fix that soon.

Sarah wasn't in her usual spot when Caroline reached the boarding house. She called out, but got no response, so she climbed the stairs and knocked on Preacher's door.

"S'open."

Dressed and sitting on the bed, he was propped against the wall and just lowering the whiskey bottle from his lips when she walked in.

"*DeForest!* You *promised!*"

He gave her a baleful stare, reminding her of Jack's word—*hangdog*.

It was too small a room to actually get up a head of steam, to march over, remove his traveling case from the stool, and sit, but she did the best she could to communicate her displeasure. "Give me that—right now. Give it here."

Wistfully, he regarded the half-empty bottle.

She wiggled her fingers, a silent repeat of her demand. Finally, she reached over and snatched it out of his grasp.

"I didn't think you'd be back so soon," he said as if timing was the issue.

"Clearly!" She put the bottle on the floor. "DeForest, *why?* Why do you drink so much? The doctor said no more liquor, that this constant drinking is going to kill you."

His careless shrug was infuriating.

Thumping the pail on the floor, she pulled out the cup and spoon and shoved them into his hands. "Here. Eat this."

He twisted the spoon in the hash a couple of times without enthusiasm, finally taking a bite, then a few more, chewing like a sleepy cow. Watching him eat, she wondered about the man she first met. Where was *he* in this unholy mess of a man?

"What happened to you in St. Louis?" She hadn't planned to ask that, but there it was.

He didn't pretend to misunderstand. "When I woke up, you were already gone."

"When you sobered up, you mean."

His silence was confirmation enough.

When the cup was finally empty, she handed him the apple. He rolled it between his fingers without much interest before rubbing it down the sleeve of his now-clean undershirt.

Drumming her fingers on her knees, she tried to make time go by faster with conversation. "Do you ever think about the future? Make plans?" She nudged his foot to get his attention. "You know—do something different? Raise sheep or something?"

"I'm afraid I'm not cut out for such enterprises. The only sheep I'm good with are those who might be inclined to heed the word of God . . . and let's face it," he said, glancing up with the heavy-lidded look of the not-quite-sober, "I'm not even very good at that."

"What about going back home, reclaiming your land, starting over?"

"Nobody gets to start over."

The defeated tone annoyed her. "Start something *new* then."

He was idly playing with the apple instead of eating it, so she didn't feel at all bad when she took it out of his hand, dropped it back in the lunch pail, added the bottle, cup, and spoon, and left with a clipped, "Good day to you, sir."

It had grown hot by the time she left, but the wind was still holding steady, blowing dust so hard it stung the skin and added to her irritability. Squinting, she shielded her eyes with her hand as best she could all the way back to the hotel.

Up in their room, she was standing at the washbowl in her chemise trying to wash off some of that infernal Kansas grit when the door suddenly opened.

It was Jack.

Washcloth pressed to her chest, she froze—as did he, eyes sweeping over her. Inexplicably, she blushed and reached for the linen towel.

"I forgot my game box." He pointed to the cupboard behind her.

She stepped aside, still clutching the towel.

With the box now under his arm, he turned around. "So . . . how's Preacher these days? Or should I say since you last saw him. Which was . . . what? Five minutes ago?"

"Oh, don't start this." Wearily, she tossed the washcloth back in the bowl and threw the towel over the water pitcher.

"I don't want to start anythin'. I want to stop it. I don't want ya seein' him anymore."

"Why? By what right do you even suggest it? Because you asked me to marry you?"

"No—by *this* right." Tossing the box on the bed, he grabbed her up and kissed her.

It wasn't the assault she thought it was going to be. That would've just made her angry. No, this was a kiss from the man she never thought would hold her again . . . and so she kissed him back, matching him hunger for hunger.

When they finally parted, he pulled her arms from around his neck. He looked wrecked. "How can you kiss me like that and not love me?"

"Love? Except for asking me if I loved Preacher, I don't remember you ever mentioning the word. No, I think what you and I have is lust, not love."

He set her away. "I see. So what you have with Preacher is *love?*"

"I didn't say that. What I have with him is, well, I'm not sure what to call it. We have something of a common background, so I'd call it a friendship, yet it's become too one-sided for that. But that's as close as I can come. You and I have—or did have—common goals, and we share certain . . . *passions.*" She heaved a tired sigh. "Oh, don't look at me like that."

"Ya can't rearrange people to suit you, put 'em in little boxes. Him for this, me for that. If that's the way you want it, why not just have him move in here with us? During the day, I can watch the two of you take tea with your little fingers out, discussing the glory of Old Dixie. At night, he can watch while the two of us—"

"*You go too far!*"

"Be careful you don't do the same," he said through gritted teeth. Shoving past her, he grabbed his game box and left.

She stomped her foot. That was twice he'd stirred her up only to walk away! It was infuriating—and if this kept up, she was going to be a madwoman in no time at all!

She yanked on a dress—the yellow muslin—heedless of its old seams, and jammed her feet into her white kid high-tops. She struggled to fasten them with shaking fingers, then stood up so fast her head spun, and she had to sit back down until the dizziness passed. *Damn him!*

Deciding she needed the distraction—not to mention the money—she went downstairs in search of a game, but found the saloon quiet, nearly empty.

Except for Louie.

In a coat of black broadcloth and a string tie, he was sitting at the bar just before where it turned the corner, idly shuffling a deck of cards.

Not one to hold a grudge, and thinking this might be a chance to finally settle some things between them, she took the stool next to him and put her reticule on the bar. "Hello, Louie."

Hands and cards still moving, his lion-like head swiveled slightly to give her a brief, gimlet-eyed stare, then returned his attention to shuffling.

Inwardly, she groaned. Did everyone have their tail caught in a bear trap today? It must be the weather, the constant wind, she decided. It had everyone unsettled and on edge.

Figuring her charm was up to the task, she touched his sleeve. "I'm no expert, but the woodwork in this bar seems to bear the mark of some fine craftsmanship, don't you think?"

Still mute, he finished shuffling and began laying out a hand of solitaire with unexpected care, taking time to align each card precisely with the last.

"Jimmy says he ordered it all the way from England," she continued. "Said it occupied a place near Whitehall, where the King stays sometimes," she added when he still didn't respond. "Said it cost him nearly a thousand dollars and took over a year to get here. By sailing ship," the silence continued, "then by wagon train, in sections, all the way from San Francisco."

The snap with which he turned up every card was beginning to grate, and she was just about to give up when he dropped the remainder of the pack aside and leaned on his elbows to regard her flatly. "You're playing a dangerous game, Caroline, and if you're not careful, someone could end up dead. You just better hope—for your sake— it's not Jack."

The threatening tone as much as the words startled her. She put her hand back in her lap. Why did she keep being accused of playing a game? "I don't know what you're talking about."

"Don't play coy with me!"

She shifted uneasily. "If you're speaking of Preacher, I don't see—"

"*Of course I'm speaking of Preacher! And Jack!* You're pitting the two of them against each other—and you don't know what you're playing with, what can happen. This isn't a bunch of punch-sipping swains at a cotillion. Jack's not someone to be trifled with. He's no parlor game—and Preacher's dangerous because he's unpredictable."

She forced a laugh. "Oh, don't be silly. It's not as dramatic as all that."

"You think not?" He'd gotten to his feet and was gathering up his cards, expertly scooping them up with the edge of a single card, then rapped the deck sharply on the bar and dropped it in a pocket. "Then keep it up."

He passed behind her, but stopped to lean down and speak uncomfortably close to her ear. "Mark my words. Trifling with Jack is trifling with me. And I'm not besotted with you like he is. Not even a little bit."

She leaned away, glad when he walked off, only to stiffen when he turned back.

Pulling a fold of bills out of his jacket, he dropped them on the bar in front of her. They fanned open like a rattlesnake preparing to strike. "There's a hundred dollars there, more than you're likely to make in a week at the tables. It's yours if you leave town now. Tonight."

Her heart started to pound, and there didn't seem to be enough air in the room suddenly. "He wouldn't like knowing this—you offering me money to leave him."

"No more than he'd like knowing you were in Preacher's room this morning."

She raised her head. "He already knows." Then tried to raise the stakes by adding, "did *you* know he wants to settle down and be a cattle rancher?"

Louie snorted. "He's been talking about that nonsense off and on for years. It'll never happen."

"Why not? He's been reading a lot and knows about it."

"I know a lot about whores, too, but that doesn't mean I want to pimp 'em."

Shocked at the insult, she itched to slap him—a thought he must've read in her face, for his eyes narrowed as he leaned in, crowding her with his bulk.

"I should warn you—I hit back."

Leaving the money untouched, she slid off the barstool. "You must be so proud."

He grabbed her arm. "My offer stands. It'll be the easiest money you ever make."

Pulling free, she walked away without answering, but talked to herself all the way back upstairs. *Just breathe. Calm down. You need to rest a bit and calm down before you get a game going. You'll lose everything if you don't, and you can't lose. You need the money—*

But it was hard to even think about money without hearing that insulting plop of Louie's cash on the bar. *How dare he? What made him think—? Just breathe. Calm down.*

She opened the door to the room and stopped dead. *Damnit!* Jack was back. Again.

In rolled-up shirtsleeves, hands in his pockets, he had his back to her and was staring out the window.

"What are you doing back here?"

He didn't turn around. "Couldn't concentrate."

"I know what you mean," she muttered, pushing the door closed.

When he didn't move, she went to stand beside him, curious to see what he was looking at, and was surprised when he dropped an arm around her shoulders and tucked her close. Such a simple sign of affection was disarming. She felt some of the tension leave her.

"Ain't it amazin'?"

"Isn't what amazing?"

"This." He nodded at the town, the flat emptiness beyond. "The vastness of it all?"

She hugged herself and shrugged. "It's too open and bare for me. I miss the live oaks, the tall pines. I miss Spanish moss."

"How can all this not change you?"

"All what? There's nothing here."

"Exactly! It's a clean slate just waitin' for you to write your name on it. How can you stay the same person, want the same things you did before you saw all this vastness, felt all its possibilities? Don't it stir your imagination—or ain't you got any?"

As many times as they'd argued, she'd never felt criticized by him before. It didn't sit well. "*You* call it lack of imagination, *I* call it determination."

"But—oh, never mind." His sigh was heavy. "What's the use?"

And now he was disappointed in her! *That* didn't sit well either. How could it be so wrong to simply want what you wanted?

As if reading her mind, he suddenly asked, "What is it you want, Caroline? If you could have anything?" He stretched his arms wide "Anything at all, what would it be?"

She sensed a trap, but answered anyway. "You already know what I want. I want to be a professional gambler, a blackjack dealer. In San Francisco."

He shook his head. "I shoulda took you down to New Orleans instead of headin' straight out here. Maybe there you coulda got all this gamblin' nonsense out of your head, then we coulda come west together."

"*Nonsense!* Since when did gambling become *nonsense?*"

"That's not what I meant."

"It's what you said!"

"I know I—" He stopped, sucked in a deep breath and faced her squarely. "Caroline, you say you care about Preacher. Well, I *care* about *you*. I'd give my life for you. I want you to know that—*'cause I love you*. I wanna marry you and give you a good life—a reg'lar life. Don't that count for somethin'? You say it's just lust between us, but I don't believe that. You gotta love me back—just a little. Dontcha?"

Tears sprang to her eyes. There was something . . . *sticky* about the words *I love you*. Not in a bad way, just in the way that wouldn't let you say them to someone then walk away. She was afraid to even answer his question in her own head for fear it would still bind her to him, heart and soul. If that happened, she'd never be able to leave him, and she was very afraid that walking away from him was what she was going to have to do. It was coming down to his dream or hers, but not both.

"How is it *your* dreams—" She heard the wobble in her voice and swallowed it down before starting over. "How is it that *your* dreams are important, but *mine* are just nonsense? And how is it that you being a professional gambler is—or was—important, but my wanting to be one isn't? I don't understand that at all."

"You're a woman. It's diff'ernt for a woman. Don't you want a husband and children someday?"

"Maybe—but who says that's all I ever get to want? Aren't women allowed to want other things, too?"

He looked flummoxed. "I dunno! I guess. I just thought nature made you . . . *satisfied* with those things. And maybe you can't have both. Maybe you can't have ever'thing you want. Maybe you gotta decide—so make a choice, Caroline. *Decide!*"

They were both breathing hard with a fear neither fully understood, but both knew they were fighting for something desperately important.

She glared up at him through tears. "I *have*! I'm going to California! I don't want to go without you, but I will if I have to!"

"Then *go!* I ain't stopping you! But you oughta know—the buggy's gone, so you gotta find another way to get there."

"*What?*" It came out more air than sound.

"I bet the buggy this morning and lost it. It's gone. Horse, too."

"What? *Why?* Why would you *do* such a thing? Did you think to strand me here—to *force* me to marry you?"

Eyes squeezed shut, he shook his head. "No, nothin' like that. Or maybe so, I don't know anymore. It all happened so fast."

It felt like he'd kicked her in the stomach, in the soul. "You rotten, *rotten*— How *could* you? *How could you*?" First Louie's bullying, and now this—this *betrayal!* She flew at him with a shriek, fists balled and swinging. She was an insane woman, striking blindly.

He took it at first, blocking her blows as best he could until he, too, snapped. Wrestling her down onto the bed, he tried to pin her down, to calm her down, but that enraged her more.

"Get off me! Get your hands off me! I hate you—*you hear me? I hate you!"*

He was fighting for supremacy now, using his size and strength to try and control a situation that had gone horribly, horribly wrong. She went to scream. He blocked it with a harder hand than he meant, and she went from fury to animal panic.

She bucked, twisted, and wrenched away. He grabbed for her but only caught the shoulder of her dress. Seams and fabric ripped away. Shocked, he let go and she stumbled back against the door. He caught only a glimpse of her wild eyes behind tangled hair before she clutched the torn cloth to her chest and escaped at a run.

"Caroline!" Off-balance, he lunged for the doorway. "Caroline—*come back here!"*

He could hear her tearing down the steps, the eruption of voices in her wake, and the bang of the front door.

Preacher roused at the sound of a woman crying. She was calling his name.

Helen?

He struggled to sit up, sending a bottle rolling off to the floor. He grabbed for it and almost pitched headlong off the bed. "Damnit!"

And still she cried. *Would it never stop?*

Flopping back, he covered his ears with both hands, until he realized it wasn't memory but a real person—outside his door.

Flinging an arm over his head, he struck the knob with the back of his hand. The pain of that pierced the fog in his head and jolted him more alert. Twisting around the rest of the way, he grabbed the knob and used it to pull himself into a sitting position, then stood, pulling the door open in the process.

Caroline fell into the room, into him, sobbing. He staggered and sat down hard on the floor with her in his lap. He blinked down at her, befuddled.

He patted her back, but she was hysterical and out of breath. He couldn't understand anything she was saying. All he caught was Jack's name.

He tried gathering her up in a hug, but his hand got tangled in something. He frowned at it, trying to remember what he owned that was yellow—finally realizing he was holding a piece of her dress.

At the mule-kick of an old memory, a cry tore out of his own throat. Pushing her off him, he managed to get to his feet. *Honor!* He couldn't fail to defend the girl. Not again.

Digging to the very bottom of his bag, his fumbling fingers finally closed over the oilcloth and the LeMat revolver wrapped inside.

Jack quickened his pace. She couldn't have gotten far. He was a fool for not running after her immediately. He'd wasted precious moments trying to gather his wits, to calm down. He scanned every doorway as he strode the length of the walkway toward the boarding house, eyes roving for any sign of her, ears straining for the sound of her voice. Where was she, damnit? He reached the end of the walkway and stepped off into the street.

Preacher was coming toward him, legs wobbly, raising an unsteady hand.

Jack raised his own in response. "Have you seen—"

The bullet caught him high in the chest and spun him around.

He dropped like a stone.

Fourteen

Caroline's limbs felt wooden as she stumbled down the stairs, across the street, such a long street, through doors, and across floors that tipped and swayed, pulse pounding in her ears. Her knees nearly gave way. She might have to crawl—would crawl—if only he would live.

Dear God! Let him live!

"*Jack! Where is he? Where's Jack?*" she demanded of strangers in the hallway, sobbing.

Someone took her through the crush of bodies, bodies that finally parted near the bed.

"*Oh my God . . . Oh my God! Nooo!*" She folded to her knees beside him.

He lay still and pale. His lips were colorless, his eyes ringed with bruise-like smudges. His shirt was ripped open, spread apart, a bloodied cloth high on his chest. The hand she pressed to her lips was utterly limp, lifeless. No, not lifeless! Please not lifeless! "Don't you die on me, Jack Transomb! Don't you dare, you hear me?"

No response—not a flicker—and her soul cracked open. It was pulled from her throat with a sound far past tears, her mouth misshapen by its force. Wildly, she beseeched the others.

"Do something—*please! Do something!* Get a doctor! He can't die—he *can't!*" Blind with rage and fear, she launched herself into their midst, flailing at them. "Don't you let him die! Stop it, you hear me! *You make it stop!*"

The voices, the protests, only fueled her attack until someone finally hooked an arm around her and dragged her out into the hall where she collapsed in a heap, wracked with sobs, cheek pressed into the raw, gritty floor. She didn't care. Her blurred vision took in the heavy shoes milling around her. With all her might, she prayed one of them would step on her, crush her and her misery out of existence—into bloody, unable-to-feel *nothingness.*

How much time had passed she didn't know, but when awareness finally penetrated her fog, she was sitting in a chair in the hallway, a man's coat around her shoulders. People still crowded the door of their room. She remembered seeing them ripple and part when the doctor arrived with his black bag. He was still in there.

She should be in there. She should be helping, but tears were running down her face, dripping off her chin. She was frozen with dread.

It was Louie who finally emerged from the crowd—jacketless, blood-spattered shirt, sleeves rolled up—pale, grim. She staggered to her feet. "How is he? Will he live? Please tell me he'll live! I want to see him, I—"

He took her upper arm in an iron grip and towed her farther down the hall.

"*Please! I need to see him*!"

His eyes were bloodshot, his lips barely moved. "*You! You* aren't getting anywhere near him *ever again!*" He shook her like a rag doll. "I'll see you dead first—you and that goddamned preacher!"

"Louie, please. I have to see him. *Please.*"

He dragged her up to eye level. "There's only one thing you have to do, and you *will do it, by God.* You will leave this town—right now—*tonight*, and take that snake of a preacher with you. If you don't, I swear I'll see him hanged *if I have to do it myself.*"

He let her go like he was tossing away trash. Pulling money out of his pocket, he threw it at her. It fluttered to the floor like a flock of dying doves.

She tried to grab his arm as he turned away. He shook her off with a snarl.

Dumbly, she watched him shoulder his way back through the knot of bystanders at the door, and she had no words for the force trying to suck her through the floor and down into hell.

It was difficult getting the drunk Preacher on his feet.

"Huh? Whu—why? Where we goin'?"

Shouldering most of his weight, Caroline and Sarah staggered with him all the way down to the front door, out, and off the boarding house steps.

"I told you," Caroline said again, "we have to leave."

"Now?"

"Yes, *now!* Come on DeForest, I need your help!" She had him by the lapels and was trying to get him up in the wagon she'd borrowed to get them the short distance to the train, and from there to the end of its line at the Colorado border.

"*Why?*"

She was crying again—still—and couldn't bring herself to answer. She couldn't wrap her numb brain around anything that had happened. Neither could she escape the lead weight of guilt. Louie was right—it was her fault. And she didn't blame him for hating her. She hated herself. All she could do now was save Preacher.

"It's *late,*" he was complaining—and started to sit down right there in the street.

"*No!* Oh, Preacher—*please*—I need you to *help!*"

From the doorway, Sarah stood where she'd stalled—wrapped in her shawl and her indecision whether to offer more help or not.

Preacher wobbled a full circle. "I'm goin' back i'side."

"No, you're not!" She hauled him back around and yelled in his face. "*We're leaving—right now, d'you hear me? Get in the damned wagon!*" Finally, so frustrated, she slapped him.

He blinked in shock. Silent and reproachful, he steadied himself, then slowly climbed into the bed of the wagon with the queer dignity of the offended drunk. "I'll ride here . . . in back."

She was just about to climb up into the driver's seat, when a noise made her look around.

Louie was standing on the end of the walkway. He'd dumped her carpet bag and trunk into the dirt, spilling everything. "I don't want him seeing anything of yours when he wakes up."

Relief at the word *when* weakened her knees. "Then he'll live?"

"You better pray he does." Kicking a stray glove into the mess, he walked away.

If the Atchison, Topeka & Santa Fe ticket agent gave the name of the Colorado town at the end of their line, Caroline didn't remember it. She just paid for tickets. A porter helped her get Preacher onboard and settled into a seat where he passed out almost immediately.

Sitting beside him, she stared at the scenery speeding by without seeing any of it. She made no plans, thought no thoughts. Finally, she just leaned her head against the window, letting the cool glass soothe her aching head.

"Well? Do you have a wagon or not?"

Caroline stared up at the Army Captain, only half his hard features visible in the light of the lantern hanging inside his tent.

"Are you listening to me, Miss Cooper? I've agreed to allow you and your husband—"

"Brother."

"Brother, then. I've agreed to allow you to travel with my supply train, but you'll need your own wagon and supplies. You also need to know we're taking the southern route through Indian territory. It's too late to risk snow through the mountains this time of year."

She didn't even blink, just nodded.

"Good. We leave at first light."

When she didn't move, he eyed her narrowly. "It's clear your brother's ill, but now I'm wondering about you. Are you ill as well?"

She shook her head.

"Do you have the funds for a wagon and supplies—enough to last you at least a month?"

She nodded.

He heaved a sigh and called for one of his men. "Private Quinn!"

A youngster, in full arms and uniform, dashed into the light and snapped to attention. "Yes, sir!"

By contrast to the younger man, who fairly crackled with energetic precision, the captain moved with the economy of age and time in command. He waved a hand between the two of them. "Private Quinn, this is Miss Cooper. Take her into town and get her a wagon outfitted for the trip. She'll give you the money."

The private's attention never wavered from his captain. "Yes, sir!"

He gave the boy a relaxed salute. "Dismissed."

The boy pivoted smartly. "This way, ma'am. Follow me."

Captain Clayton stared after the two of them and shook his head. "If that ticket agent sends me *one more stray* . . ."

Caroline adapted well to the military routine. There was always something to do, and the tasks were mindless enough that she didn't have to think, which was exactly what she wanted.

After hitching up the team of horses each morning, she'd pull their wagon into line and drive at a walking pace the rest of the day while Preacher slept in the back. A few times, he'd climb out onto the seat beside her; at others, he'd ride with the gate down in back, feet dangling like a child. Sometimes they'd talk, but most of the time, they just kept to themselves.

Just before sundown, the captain would order the wagons to circle up. Teams were unhitched, horses hobbled. Dinner was over an open fire.

As they moved further south, the captain picked up an Indian scout—Two Hawks, his dark, flat face chiseled and stoic—who would ask that the wagons be halted every so often so he could interpret some sort of mysterious signs on the ground. Most of the time, they moved ahead without discernible change; but every once in a while, there'd be some tense waiting, a lot of staring across long distances through field glasses and riders scurrying back and forth, rifles at the ready. Sometimes, after that, the train would double-back a bit, taking a wide loop before returning to its earlier heading.

Caroline supposed these were times she should've been afraid, but she didn't care enough.

After they'd gone south as far as intended and they'd begun their swing west, she noticed the air was lighter, thinner. It slipped over her skin like silk. Green had given way to brown, river muck to dust, and trees to stunted scrub. Even the few faces they encountered were different—the pale English look giving over to sun-creased visages, and the probe of dark eyes barely seen beneath wide-brimmed hats. It all seemed very exotic.

Most nights, Preacher turned in early. She often passed the time gambling with the men.

One evening, Captain Clayton stepped into the ring of firelight, sending the soldiers scrambling to their feet and saluting as one. He returned the salute. "Goodnight, gentlemen: Walker. Compton. Two Hawks. Dobbs." He nodded to them one by one as they melted back to their duties or their tents.

He looked down at her and touched the brim of his hat. "Ma'am."

"Captain," she acknowledged. "Care for a cup of coffee?"

"Thank you. Don't mind if I do."

He pulled a leather-covered flask out of his uniform shirt and held it up questioningly.

She pursed her lips. "Sure, why not? A small libation'll keep the evening chill off."

"Yes, ma'am. My thinking exactly." Handing it over, he sat on the bench across from her, hands wrapped around his cup. He indicated the cards with a free pinkie finger. "You seem pretty skilled with those."

"Thank you."

"Begging your pardon, ma'am, but that wasn't exactly a compliment."

"Oh. I see." After handing back the flask, she smoothed her skirt thoughtfully. "And your point, captain?"

"Well, ma'am, I don't know how much you know about the military." It was a question.

She shrugged. "Only what I saw when the Yankees came across our land."

"Ah. You'd be speaking of our recent, dreadful war then."

"*Your* dreadful war, yes."

"Yes, ma'am." He cleared his throat. "Well, my point is that in the military there's got to be discipline and camaraderie. Soldiers rely on each other. They've got to trust each other."

"Of course."

"I wasn't exactly eager to take you and your brother on—" She started to protest, but he held up a hand. "I don't say that to try and make you feel beholden, but please hear me out. Women can have—shall we say a disrupting influence—on that camaraderie and discipline. And a card sharp on top of that . . ."

Her neck stretched defensively.

"Begging your pardon of course."

Offense subsiding, she nodded.

"Understand, I'm not accusing you of anything, but it seems to me you know your way around a deck of cards a bit more than most. I don't want any trouble. Not for you, me, or my men." He set his cup down next to the fire and rose. "Hopefully we understand one another?"

"Perfectly."

He nodded, started to leave, then turned back. "Ma'am—miss?"

"Yes, captain?"

"Your reaction to the war seems awfully strong considering you couldn't have been much more than a child at the time." Again, it was a question.

"In war, there are no children, captain. I expect you would know that more than most."

"Yes, ma'am." He touched the brim of his hat again. "Good night, ma'am."

Left alone by the dying fire, Caroline hugged her elbows beneath her shawl and stared into the darkness.

Jack . . .

He was around the corner of every thought, every action. Louie's last words had offered hope that Jack would live, and she believed him—*needed* to believe him—but she'd never know for sure. Sometimes not knowing was almost worse than the fact that she'd never see him again. Sometimes she'd bargain with God. As long as he was alive somewhere, *living* somewhere, she vowed to be content with that.

Later, inside the wagon she shared with Preacher, she assured herself that all was well, all was as it should be, that she couldn't want for more as she went through the motions of settling down across from Preacher to sleep . . . even as she knew it would be a while before her mind would quiet, and that constant, cold knot of regret in her chest would ease enough to allow it.

Just before she blew out the lantern and plunged their wagon into darkness, she looked down at Preacher, remembering an earlier conversation. During a small slice of time when he was sober, he'd asked her again why they'd had to leave Dodge. He really didn't remember—in fact, most of his time in Dodge seemed little more than a blur to him—so she didn't tell him. Why make him suffer with guilt? He wasn't to blame. She was.

With the light extinguished, she lay down. Over her head, the lantern continued to swing for a bit, its handle rubbing against its hook like a metronome. *Jack . . . Jack . . . Jack . . .*

One evening toward the end of their trip, she found herself alone with the captain again. Without prompting, she began to tell him everything—her whole story, the words tumbling out.

"Not a very flattering story for a lady," was all he said when she was done.

She thought she was past the point of shame, but felt her face turn hot. "No. It's not."

As he rose to leave, he offered her a crumb she didn't know how much she needed until he tossed it over his shoulder. "The gambler, the younger one: Jack? He should recover."

Hope flared. "Why do you say that?"

"Experience. You said the wound was high up on his right side. If it had been the left, I'd say he didn't have a chance, but as it is—as long as the wound didn't putrefy . . ."

"Oh, *thank you,* thank you!"

For minutes afterwards, she couldn't slow her breathing, as if she'd been running a great distance and had finally come to a place where she could stop.

For the rest of the trip, she clung to the captain's words, repeating them to herself over and over in self-comfort.

The Pacific Ocean was a teasing flash of blue through the dark, drooping limbs of evergreens, the tallest Caroline had ever seen. The color of the water as it widened into view was turquoise—like the nugget Two Hawks wore around his neck on a length of rawhide—

deep turquoise, but muted under a layer of fog like wisps of cotton fresh from the boll.

As the supply train rumbled over the last rocky slopes, the wagons listed left and right like the bones in an old man's buckling spine. The captain had sent a soldier back to drive for her. Sitting beside him, she held onto the iron bench rails, white-knuckled against the pitch and roll, fearing a bone-crunching fling from her seat as much as missing her first sight of an ocean.

The distance between wagons shortened as they continued their precarious descent. She heard the captain calling out orders, addressing the troops, the snap responses from the ranks.

One of her wagon's wheels caught a stone and the whole vehicle stuttered dangerously sideways for a few seconds, the seat hammering her spine and forcing a groan from the back of the wagon. Moments later, the canvas parted behind her, and Preacher peered out. "Are we in California yet?"

"Have been for days, dear."

"Oh. I-I haven't helped out much, have I? I'm sorry."

Sparing a hand from the rail, she ruffled his pale hair not unlike a mother would do. "You've been feeling poorly, but all that's going to change as soon as we light somewhere. This constant motion would put anyone off their feed."

Neither of them ever mentioned the other reason for his loss of appetite—the bottles of rye he kept muffled in his bedroll—which at least eliminated their clinking, and invariably reminded her of Jack and his annoyance at her sewing box full of rattling spools.

They were moving again, distracting her from the knife edge his name always brought. She'd gone from prodding the pain, like one constantly putting a tongue to a sore tooth, to forcefully replacing every thought of him with something else. Anything else.

Twenty-four hours later, Captain Clayton bid her goodbye and, as an extra courtesy, ordered Private Quinn to deliver her and Preacher down to San Francisco proper.

"God's speed, miss." He touched the brim of his hat to both of them as one. "And since you've said you have no further need for your wagon, the U.S. Army will buy it for the return trip—at a fair price of course." With that, he dropped twenty dollars in gold into her hand.

She broke into laughter—that was less than half what she'd paid for it. "The hostiles won't have a chance if you're making the peace treaty terms, Captain."

His mouth pulled into a grim sort of smile. "Private," he said, "you have your orders. Be back here by sixteen hundred hours or lose your chance at a stripe for another month."

"Yessir!"

A little while later, Caroline could hear the city of San Francisco like an approaching horde of insects—even before they topped the last hill and it came into view, spread out like a woman's apron. Yet not even the sound prepared her for the sight of so many people—more than the town of Coldwater could produce if it emptied out every structure ten times over. Hundreds of people walked the wide thoroughfares—more and more as they drove down toward the glittering bay below—a sea of color and cultures, with faces of Blacks, Chinese, Mexican, and the occasional Indian. Feathers and beads, long braids, elaborate curls and mustaches, silks, lace, buckskin, and broadcloth, straw hats, top hats, beribboned bonnets . . . they all bobbed and dipped to a different rhythm. Voices choked the air—laughing, talking, arguing. Harnesses jingled, dogs barked, children squealed, chickens clucked, crates of fish and crabs flapped and scrabbled. Vehicles of every description—and some defying description—struggled through it all, knotting and snarling the flow. Like the insect horde first brought to mind, Caroline's first impression of the city resembled nothing so much as a swarming ant hill.

The street itself shifted and changed right beneath their wheels, from mud ruts to wooden planks to newly cobbled sections, and back again to mud. It was a relief to finally stop.

Private Quinn handed her down from the hard seat and even waited patiently for Preacher to get himself into position where he could lend him a steadying hand to climb down. That accomplished, he snagged down their bags and placed them up on the wooden walkway.

He touched the bill of his small cap. "Well, ma'am, this is it, the end of the line. It was a real pleasure gettin' to know ye," he said, looking only at her and ignoring Preacher.

Caroline touched his sleeve. "You've been the dearest boy, Sam. Thank you for everything. You and your captain made this trip bearable for me—for us," she added and glanced at Preacher, whose gaze was flicking absently over the flow of people moving past. "You'll make a fine officer someday."

Sam dropped his gaze and stubbed the toe of his boot in the dirt like the boy he was. "Shucks, ma'am. I dunno 'bout that, but thankee kindly for sayin' so." His gaze hardened as they were jostled by a clot of people moving past. "Take care, ma'am. Mind your kit that nobody lifts it. Too many shifty eyes goin' by if you ask me."

She tamped down a smile. "Of course. I shall be vigilant. And ever watchful for news of your brave exploits in the Territories."

On a final, gap-toothed grin, he vaulted back into the wagon, snapped the reins, and maneuvered out into traffic heedless of the clashing wheels and snarls every few feet around him. "Comin' through!" he bawled, as seasoned as any sergeant-at-arms. "*Ho, there! Make way!*"

Caroline followed his progress until he was entirely lost from view. It was odd to realize how attached she'd become to the soldiers, especially that one.

With a great sigh, she picked up their bags, handed Preacher his, and grabbed her trunk by its leather handle. Together they threaded through the crowd, bags bumping their knees and each other, their heads turning at the clash of harness and heated words bursting forth from the street, or raucous laughter and music slapping the air from open windows and doorways they passed.

They'd only gone a short distance when she became aware of the drag in Preacher's steps, the increasing dependence on her arm, and she realized they were wasting precious energy in walking without a specific destination. It also came to her that she would now have to be the breadwinner. She'd have to find work and a place to live—for both of them—and soon. Her bottom lip received a good chewing as she craned her neck to see down the street.

"Do you see anything that resembles a hotel?" she asked the taller Preacher. "An establishment that might serve luncheon?"

He squinted. "No, but I see what looks like a saloon on the other side of the street."

Hmph! Hardly what's needed. Out loud she said nothing, simply tugged on his arm to get him moving again.

Finally, it was the silence of one open doorway they approached that caught her attention. Inside, there were no lamps lit, but sunshine streamed in through the large front window. There were some tables and chairs, not one of them occupied. A tall china cupboard in back displayed plates, cups, and saucers, while a countertop to one side held milk glass plates of several cakes. There was the impression of doilies sprouting beneath every object. Behind the counter was a stern-looking woman beneath a large pouf of steely hair. She was wearing a long white apron.

"Pardon me," Caroline said. "Do you serve luncheon?"

The woman's stern look deepened—if that was possible—and she eyed the two of them sharply. "We serve stew, soup, soda bread, and—" She pointed to the counter. "Hot milk cake with two kinds of icing. And tea, hot or cool."

"Excellent!" Caroline steered Preacher to a table against the wall and settled him into one of the chairs. "Could you bring a portion of that—all of it—for my friend here?"

"Just him? Nothing for you?"

"No, not right now, thank you. I have some business to attend to first." She dug in her reticule for coins. "How much?"

"Four dollars."

"*Four—!* Of course," she amended, feeling a touch of panic. "Friend, you say?"

Caroline met the sharp beady eyes and made a quick decision. "Husband really. 'Friend' is just our term of affection—fast friends, that's us. I consider myself lucky in that regard."

"*Hmph*. Never married myself. Couldn't find one good enough to call to the supper table, much less 'husband.'" She was already ladling up a bowl of soup, slicing cake, pouring tea, and stirring in great lumps of sugar according to her own taste apparently. "I won't ask where y'all hail from. None of my business," she said, all the while eyeing them both with avid curiosity.

Caroline turned her attention to Preacher, snapping open the embroidered napkin and tucking one corner into his collar, smoothing it across his shirtfront with genuine tenderness.

He was watching the food being put in front of him without expression, almost as if he didn't comprehend what was happening. Suddenly, he was seized with a fit of coughing, and the woman hastily stepped back.

"He sick?"

"Just a little cough. It's nothing."

"Is he catching?"

"No, no," she reassured the woman, taking the plate of bread out of her hand and setting it down by his elbow. "We've traveled far, and he just needs some rest. Good food and rest."

He was, she realized, deteriorating rapidly. She needed to get him settled somewhere.

"Would you be so kind as to point me in the direction of the nearest—the largest and most prosperous—gambling establishment?"

"Gambling!" The woman looked her up and down. "I don't truck with such folk, not the whites, not them slanty-eyed Celestials, none of 'em—and neither should you! Filthy habit. Don't hold with them coarse, greedy gold-diggers neither." The feather in Caroline's bonnet received damning scrutiny. "You're not one of them loose women, are ye?"

Caroline managed a sweet, conspiratorial smile. "No, ma'am, but one must know the whereabouts of the devil in order to rout him out … mustn't one?"

"Amen to that—and the biggest den of iniquity I know of would be the Adelphi. Can't miss it," she said, nodding to indicate direction. "Two streets up on the corner of Kearny."

"Thank you." She turned to Preacher who was slowly lifting a torn piece of dark bread to his lips, absent as an old man. "Enjoy your lunch, dear. Wait for me—wait right here. I'll return just as quickly as I'm able." She dabbed a speck of butter from the corner of his mouth with her finger and wiped it on the napkin already speckled with crumbs. "Y'hear me?" She touched his arm and he managed to focus on her face. He seemed drunk these days even when he wasn't. It made her wild with worry.

She smoothed her stained and worn gloves and turned. "I'll settle the final bill on my return if he requires anything more." She headed for the doorway. "Just up this way, you say?"

The woman nodded. "You be careful now. There's a lot of sin out there in those streets."

We can only hope, she said to herself. Out loud, she said, "Thank you, I shall."

"And smite that Satan on the nose if'n you get the chance!"

Caroline schooled her smile. "Yes, *ma'am!*" *Old biddy.*

It was true. The Adelphi was unmistakable in its opulence of carved pillars and sweep of marble stairs leading up to a double doorway. The outer ones were held open with wrought-iron shutter hooks, the inner half-ones swinging in constant motion as gamers, punters of every size, color and mode of dress, came and went. Smells of whiskey, beer, and fry grease wafted out along with the lively tinkling of piano music, alternately tamped and amplified with each swing of the doors. The scale of the palatial structure was daunting, but Caroline felt only excitement as she looked up from the half-flight of stairs below the entrance.

Gathering her skirts, dusty hem just clearing the tops of her worn shoes, she marched up and through the doors—the crush of it all clapping down on her head so hard she was tempted to cover her ears.

The room, filled with dozens upon dozens of men and a few strikingly dressed women, was a visual riot of color and noise, stretching back in the fashion of a great hall, with a second-floor railing ringing three walls in front of a handful of closed doors. Private game rooms? Other unsavory business?

Several Faro bankers were at work, so mobbed with those placing bets they worked with assistants. There were two roulette tables and a score of others devoted to either dice or cards, but before Caroline could take it all in, a large barrel-chested man with an imposing mustache and oily, dark hair laying along his black-suited shoulders stepped in front of her.

"Ma'am," he said, but there was nothing deferential in his manner, "can I help you?"

Involuntarily, she backed up a step. "I-I'm looking for work. Employment."

Something flickered in his dark, beady eyes as he raked her with a quick, assessing look from bonnet to boots. Wrapping huge, sausage-shaped fingers around her upper arm in a manner that let her know this was his turf and his will ruled, he said, "We don't allow your kind in the front. Go around back and ask for Chen Lo."

Her face flamed. Unsuccessful in loosening his hold, she glanced around in mute appeal, but no one was paying them any mind. Swallowing down her fear, she forced herself to relax even as she forced her chin up a notch. "Unhand me! I'm here to speak to the owner. You may tell him Miss Caroline Cooper of the Johnson County Coopers—late of Coldwater, Mississippi—wishes to speak with him about a mutually beneficial business proposition. I'm a dealer of considerable repute," she added for good measure.

He searched her face for a moment, then let go. "Wait here," he instructed and, lightly as a dancer, turned and wove his way smoothly around the knots of players and up the central staircase, knocked and disappeared behind one of the doors.

Caroline drew a full breath and let it out past her bottom lip forcefully enough to stir the fringe of hair she'd taken to wearing over her forehead. *Lummox! Oaf!*

And that quickly, the lummox-y oaf reappeared and pattered down the steps as unexpectedly graceful as before. "Follow me," he directed as soon as he reached her, pivoting without further ado. She had to move quickly to keep up, and was out of breath by the time they reached the top step and stood together in front of the same door he'd accessed initially.

He rapped a knuckle on it once, then opened it to wave her inside, closing it on her heels. Immediately, the hive noises from below were muted.

She was standing in the vestibule of a large room picked out in pale greens and pinks, opulent with silks and satins, lush with plump pillows, and sparkling with lamps rimmed with dangling crystals. A brace of gilt-and-white chairs flanked her like sentries.

There wasn't a person in sight.

"I'm in here," came a lilting, French-accented female voice.

Caroline took a step and then another until she saw the room open up to both left and right. On one side reigned a pillared and paneled canopied bed rich enough in rose-colored satin to coddle royalty. On the opposite wall crouched a vast dressing table, its surface studded with cut-crystal perfume bottles, vases of fresh red roses, and jewelry boxes overflowing with gemstones, gold chains, and pearls. Dominating the wall above it all was a mirror of such proportions, Caroline could only stare in mesmerized silence.

"Mademoiselle? You wished to see me, *non*?"

Caroline blinked and refocused. So dazzled was she by the room's richness, she hadn't even noticed the beautiful blonde woman seated in front of the dressing table, the train of her frothy pink dressing gown carelessly spread across the flower-patterned carpet behind her.

Tilting her head becomingly, she gestured with a sparkling perfume stopper in one hand as she gazed mildly in the mirror at Caroline.

With a jolt of recognition, Caroline smiled back. "Miss Jules? Simone Jules? Is that you?"

Gaze sharpening, the woman turned on her tufted stool. "Have we met?" Gone was much of the accent, the lighter-than-air movements suddenly stiff with guardedness.

"Don't you remember? We met last Christmastime! Onboard the *Quincy*? Traveling north on the Mississippi," she added helpfully.

The woman's eyes narrowed slightly, and Caroline realized her youthfulness was more attitude than lack of years. "I met you on deck one night. I'd been watching you play earlier—dealing blackjack." Enthusiasm for the memory made her take a step forward, but she stopped when she saw the other woman freeze uncertainly. "You were so . . ." She searched for a word expressive enough, "*inspiring.*"

Simone laughed at that, almost without sound, but her shoulders relaxed as she shook her head. "I'm sorry, no."

"You said I shouldn't judge the men gambling on the decks below, that they were only buying a bit of happiness for themselves. You spoke about freedom for a woman in a way I'd never heard before. You told me to chart my own course before some man did. You even told me you took companions—" Caroline broke off at her own indiscretion, at the sudden darkening of the other woman's face. "I'm sorry. I should never have repeated that. Forgive me," she said as the other woman rose to her feet.

Sweeping her trailing gown out of the way, the woman walked directly up to Caroline, stopping a mere foot away to peer intently into her face. "*Mon Dieu!*" she exclaimed softly, this time with a genuine chuckle. "I remember you! The little gray, self-righteous dove!"

Caroline bit her lip, but relaxed when the woman dropped both fists onto her hips and regarded her pleasantly enough. "What in the world brings you here?" There was no trace of the French accent now. "Samson said it was a dealer who wanted to see me. That can't be you—can it? Eh?" she quizzed, tilting her head.

Caroline paused to think how she might explain her transformation, finally deciding the unvarnished truth would serve her best. "I traveled with a professional gambler who taught me."

Simone, hands still clamped over each thrust of hip bone, circled her slowly, calculatingly, eyes bright with her own private assessment. Nodding, she met Caroline's eyes from time to time, her gaze traveling over her face, taking in every detail of her figure and dress. "Yes . . . yes!" she finally exclaimed, clapping her hands. "You wish to work for me?"

Caroline's thoughts stuttered a bit. It seemed too easy. Little in her life had come to her without struggle and she almost couldn't believe her turn of luck. "I'm certainly no veteran, but I can play . . . and I can deal. "

Simone waved a hand. "Bah! You know the cards, the games, the rules, yes?"

"Yes, but—"

"Then that's enough. With the right clothes and attitude, it's more than enough to begin."

Caroline started once more to protest, but Simone stopped her with a gesture. "Technique will improve with time, but for us women, it's more about entertaining than skill." Her smile was wicked. "And it's much more fun."

Any further protest died on Caroline's lips at that. Clearly, she still had much to learn about being a professional gambler . . . perhaps even about being a woman.

"The city ordinances are starting to squeeze a bit, so we stay ready to put on a milder face with public concerts and such, but the house still banks faro, roulette, and blackjack. I own the pots and pay ten percent on table take. Be here tomorrow if you want to work for me."

"How early do you want me?"

"Early? Oh, heavens, no! We don't open 'til two. Where are you staying?"

"Well, we—"

"We?"

"A man, a preacher—he and I, we've traveled here together."

Simone tipped her head in silent command for her to answer her original question.

"Nowhere at the moment. We've only just arrived. I left him back at a little restaurant."

"I see." She opened her door, and to Caroline's surprise, Samson was still there, waiting. "Samson, who's in number eight right now?"

"Bridget and Dee."

"Oh?" Apparently, this was unexpected information.

"Dee ain't gettin' on too well with some of the others."

"Well, she better start getting on. I've got no room for belly-achers. Miss—I'm sorry. What was your name again?"

"Caroline Cooper."

"That's right. Miss Cooper and her . . . companion will be occupying number eight until I say otherwise. Have Bridget and Dee out of there before the hour's up."

"Yes, ma'am. I'll see to it."

Simone turned back to her. "So, that's settled—now let's talk about your wardrobe. What else have you got?"

"I have a few other dresses, some basques and skirts."

"Anything that shows off your bosom and shoulders?"

"I have a pretty yellow one with a bit of a . . ." She drew a finger low across her bosom "A daring neckline I created for myself." She banked all emotion before adding. "It needs repairing though."

"Good. Wear that tomorrow. We'll add from there. Like cards and dice cups, clothes are part of gambling equipment for us women—the ultimate gaff, you might say." She laughed. "And any enterprise worth doing is worth investing in, wouldn't you agree?"

Caroline nodded. "Yes, ma'am, and I'll do my best for you."

"Oh, you'll do better than that . . . but you mustn't call me ma'am. Call me Simone."

"Certainly . . . Simone."

"That's better. Now run along and collect your friend, your band-boxes, and such, and hurry back. You'll need your sleep. Samson will see you settled. Tomorrow's a long day."

"Thank you, thank you so much, Miss—*Simone!* Thank you!"

"You're welcome—now go," she said, nudging her over the threshold.

Back on the streets once more, everything seemed different. She met more smiles, noticed more doffed hats, more murmurs of greeting as she threaded her way back through the crowded streets to where she'd left Preacher.

But he wasn't there.

The woman told Caroline he'd eaten, thanked her—"so well-mannered!"—asked her to watch their bags (they were stacked by the counter), and said he'd felt overcome by his calling, that there were souls to save.

His calling to a bottle is more like it, Caroline thought.

"It's good to meet other God-fearing souls in this city."

"I'm sure it is."

"Praise be."

"Yes, praise be. Do you happen to remember which way he went?"

"Back down that way, I believe. Did you have any trouble finding that devil's den? I 'spect not. I 'spect you could smell the sin coming out of that place like the heat from hell's own oven."

"Yes, thank you. And I appreciate you watching our baggage for us. Would you mind continuing to watch it until I can find him and come back this way?"

"Not at all, child, not at all. But I'm only open 'til sundown. God bless you!" she called after her. "Both of you!"

Her joy at finding work—at finding Simone—was overshadowed by this new worry. Where had he gone? How would she find him in a city this size? *Think, Caroline, think! If you were Preacher . . . I wouldn't go far*, she realized.

She thought about the saloon he'd seen earlier . . . *on the other side of the street.* But there were more than she remembered. She stuck her head into several, receiving everything from no notice at all to polite nods of acknowledgment. Drunken invitations to come on in and join the fun were rare and were quickly shushed by fellow patrons. Women, she could tell by looking around, were a commodity in scarce supply, and, clearly, no one wanted to offend.

She finally found him, downing his whiskey neat and waxing both poetic and pious to a small, mostly attentive clientele. Preacher's gift for oratory never failed to snag him an audience.

He was both sad and glad to see her, lifting his glass in greeting. As she pulled her skirts in and wound her way toward him past the half-filled tables, she realized that was the only kind of glad he was anymore—sadly glad—as if he always saw the irony of his own life in her.

He doffed his hat with dramatic flair as she gained his side. "Darlin'," he drawled affectionately, "I see you found me—with no untoward trouble, I trust." His smile was thin and didn't reach his tired eyes. It never did anymore. She noticed he was supporting most of his weight with both hands on the back of a chair.

"You promised!" she scolded quietly, tucking herself close so he could lean on her.

"I know I did, darlin', but I'm just too flawed to be trusted." His smile became crooked with accepted defeat. "I am truly a cross to bear, am I not? Surely, I should be—"

"Oh, shush! Let's get you out of here." Taking most of his weight, she aimed them for the door. "I've found work. Do you remember Simone Jules? From the *Quincy*? She was a dealer. Now she owns her own place." His foot caught a chair leg and they had to stop while he regained his balance. "The Adelphi down on Kearny. We have a room there."

He doffed his hat and spoke over his shoulder to the room at large as he allowed himself to be towed along. "Evening, gentlemen. Mayhap our paths will cross again soon, and we'll experience the camaraderie of a hand or two of cards . . . a roll or two of dice . . ."

"And mayhap not," Caroline muttered as they reached the walkway.

A chill had come with the gathering dusk, and Preacher's lungs immediately spasmed with his first breath of damp air. Caroline staggered under his increased weight.

"We need to hurry and get our baggage. It'll be sundown soon!"

When they finally made it back, the place was closed, locked up tight. She cupped her hands around her eyes and peered through the glass. There they were, bags still stacked up in a neat pile. She knocked, rattled the doorknob, and called out, but to no avail. "Well, we'll just have to come back tomorrow and collect them."

Leaning up against the light pole where she'd left him, Preacher's eyes were closed. Clearly, he didn't have a care in the world. She wanted to kick him. Instead, she squared her weary shoulders and roused him back to semi-alertness. "Come on, let's go."

FIFTEEN

Once inside the Adelphi, she had all the help she needed from Samson getting Preacher up to their room and onto the one, big bed. Together, they moved the heavy dressing screen between that and the small, yellow brocade settee where she would sleep for now. Bidding him *adieu* with many thanks, she closed the door and sagged against it in relief.

The room was large, airy, well-furnished, and upholstered in a garden of pastel florals. Its single, tall window looked out over a side street.

The empty wardrobe stood open in silent rebuke that she hadn't made it back to the restaurant in time to collect their belongings, but all she wanted now was to wash, remove her shoes, and sleep. Thankfully, the settee was comfortable.

She woke the next morning with Preacher standing over her—in buttoned shirt, trousers and no shoes—with a tray of biscuits, butter, and jam, along with a small pot of coffee and cups.

"They fixed it for me downstairs," he told her as she rubbed her eyes and sat up.

Patting the space beside her, she invited him to sit—grateful she hadn't been awake when he left the room, sparing her the anxiety of worrying over him yet again.

As if reading her thoughts, he sat down and looked at her seriously, his eyes and manner much more focused than they'd been in a while. "Caroline, I'm going to take care of you from now on. You're not to worry about me anymore, and I want you to switch beds with me."

She patted his knee. "We'll see."

As they broke the fast companionably, she told him about her meeting with Simone.

Suddenly, her eyes rounded with alarm. "What time is it?"

"It was a little past the noon hour when I went—"

"*Noon?* Oh, no! Why did you let me sleep so late?"

"You clearly needed it, but what—"

"Never mind, I have to hurry! I've got to get back to the luncheonette and get our bags—"

"Ah, so that's where they are. I was wondering."

"—then get a bath, repair my dress, and be downstairs, ready for Simone by two." She shoved her cup and saucer at him and shooed him away so she could rise, dress, and get going.

Downstairs, people were just stirring—hair mussed, ribbon ties and braces dangling, sleepy expressions, and only monosyllabic conversations.

She went to the bartender. "How do you do, sir? My name is Caroline Cooper. I'm new to the establishment, and I'm upstairs with—"

"That fella with the charming honey-drip," came a furry, female voice behind her.

It was a tall, Titian-haired woman wrapped casually in a plum-colored shawl and an ivory night rail falling off one shoulder. Her green eyes promised trouble. "What's the name?"

"Caroline."

"Not yours, Miss La-dee-dah, *his*. The man you're shacking up with upstairs."

Caroline felt her face flame.

One eyebrow cocked. "Well, I don't see no ring on your finger, so I just thought—"

Short on patience as well as time, Caroline cut her off and turned back to the bartender. "I need to be gone for a few minutes. Can you please see that my friend upstairs doesn't leave in my absence?"

"I ain't no brother's keeper, lady."

"There's two bits in it for you if you manage to become your brother's keeper until I can return with our baggage."

"Two bits ain't much. He's a lot taller 'n' me."

"Then use your brain."

"I don't get paid to use my brain. *I get paid to pour liquor!*" he called to the swinging doors she left in her wake.

Flagging down a sturdy-looking youngster, she gave him a dollar and promised him another if he'd go with her and help her carry their luggage back.

The luncheonette was already open when they arrived, but the woman placed herself between them and the baggage while she interrogated Caroline as to the reason she hadn't returned in a more timely manner.

Enduring this as long as she could, Caroline gave serious consideration to simply announcing that she was a gambler—just for practice if nothing else. After all, it was time to embrace her new profession, wasn't it? The boy's presence was all that stopped her. Finally, she simply interrupted by pressing a coin into the woman's hand. "For all your trouble."

Leaving Preacher's leather bag and her trunk to the boy, she gathered up the rest of her things. Together they darted and dashed their way back through the throng of horses' hooves, wheels, and knots of pedestrians to the Adelphi where she handed the boy his promised dollar. "Now take those upstairs here, will you? Last door on the right—thank you!"

Activities in the Adelphi were moving at a smarter clip now, cleaning and polishing in earnest, the piano player thumbing through his music at the upright, girls in bright dresses with sharply contrasting trim setting up the tables with cards and chips. The red-haired woman she'd had a run-in with earlier was nowhere to be seen.

She glanced back at the bartender and caught his eye. He nodded toward the staircase. *Good!* Preacher was still here. She dug the promised coin out of her purse and put it on the end of the bar, then went upstairs.

In their room, Preacher was stretched out gracefully across the unmade bed. No snore crossed his lips. He was fully dressed in coat and shoes again, but it looked like the effort had worn him out, forcing him to take a nap before he could even finish tying his tie.

She looked down at his handsome-but-dissipated face . . . and felt nothing except compassion. It was almost as if he were fading before her eyes, pale and nearly ethereal. Yes, he was still handsome, but there was little vitality left in him; and he was putting her more and more in mind of her brother.

Not knowing if calling for a bath was permissible here, she decided to simply fold one of the screen panels back to shield the washstand for privacy and do her best to clean as much of the travel grime off her as possible. Washing her hair would have to wait. In the meantime, a vigorous brushing would have to do, so she bent over and brushed from the roots down, her arms aching by the time she finished. *There.* Her image in the long cheval mirror showed her face pleasantly flushed with color, her hair shiny and free of tangles. Quickly, she knotted it behind her head, then started unpacking what was left of her clothing.

And a sorry sight they were—wrinkled and stained and limp. The yellow needed some spot cleaning and re-tacking of some trim. The side seam could stand to be taken in, but, as she fingered the rent across the shoulder, she closed her eyes against the memory of her argument with Jack, of their last words to each other.

She knew he hadn't torn her dress deliberately, just as she knew she hadn't intended Preacher's drunken response. She found she couldn't use more exact words for what happened, not even to herself. The guilt would swamp her and suck her under. She couldn't afford that. Not right now. Right now, she had to make a living, and that involved finding a repair that would disguise the tear . . . and disguise her guilt.

She settled on a row of white lace rosettes she fashioned from saved scraps, and used them to cover the mended shoulder, trailing them down to the opposite side of the waist. Holding up the finished repair, she was pleased. *Perhaps that's what we all do,* she thought, *make our sins pretty enough to bear.*

That done, she set to work on the spots and wrinkles with a wet cloth, working by the window, where the only thing exciting to see outside was a man going from tethered horse to tethered horse along the hitching rail, peering into saddle bags and talking affectionately to the entire equine line as if they were all old friends. San Francisco, she decided, was a very interesting place.

Within the month, she'd settled in, and was on a first-name basis with everyone at the Adelphi—even with the redhead, the aptly named Delilah ("Dee" for short), who still called *her* Miss La-dee-dah, but mostly with a smile now. She didn't have to worry about Preacher much anymore, not about his stealing away to drink at least. He rarely left the place, apparently satisfied with what life offered within its confines.

She'd made some regular customers, always greeting them at her table as Mr. *This* and Mr. *That,* and never allowed herself to be addressed as anything less formal than *Miss* Caroline. As the men arrived for an evening of play, they'd exchange the usual, flirtatious banter.

"You're looking lovely this evening, Miss Caroline. If I was only twenty years younger."

"Why thank you, Mister Durbin. You look quite dashing yourself." By design, she always kept her hands moving—from cards to chips and back again. "The blue of your coat brings out the color of your eyes."

Mr. Durbin would smile at her compliment and pat his elaborately curled and waxed mustache. "Any room for me at your table this evening?"

"There's always room for you, sir. Ah! Mister Mooney, you're early this evening."

The men often made half-jesting remarks about how they might just as well empty their wallets then and there, so they no longer had to pretend to concentrate on the game and could, instead, do what they preferred: to simply bask in her beauty.

She'd always demure good-naturedly . . . without really discouraging them.

And so it went. She worked late, slept late, ate enough to satisfy her . . . without ever filling the emptiness she felt inside.

The noise inside the hall—a steady discordant yammer of bright piano notes, voices, screeches of chair legs, the clink of glassware and coin—often made her head ache. Her eyes and throat burned from the thick cloud of tobacco smoke that hung in the air, and it made her stomach queasy. All together, these things made her long for a bit of solitude and open air.

So great was her itch to be away that even at the zenith of her gaming hours, whenever her regulars were done for the night, she'd fold back the green baize cloth and close her table. Without a word to anyone, she pushed through the crowd, acknowledging greetings without pause until she reached the small hallway used only by staff and deliveries. There she snagged her cloak from the hook by the back door—where she'd begun keeping it just so she could make escapes like these—and quietly slip out into the damp darkness.

She wandered, occasionally catching the smell of the water blocks away, her steps aimless even as she was determined to put distance between her and the Adelphi.

Gradually, her travels widened until one Sunday afternoon she crossed Dupont Street and became aware that she'd entered Chinatown. It was a whole new world—a city within a city—chopped up with alleyways that were just as busy as the main streets. While the architecture looked mostly Western, there were paper lanterns with long, red tassels hanging from the corners of brightly painted eaves. Strange smells, strange items on display in carts and hanging from canvas canopies, the clash of bright colors and sounds—all exotic and exciting. The gambling there fascinated her, too.

The dice and dominoes she recognized immediately, but the Chinese played these while standing and with such speed and intensity, their long, oiled queues swaying, she was inclined to laugh (but didn't). *Fan-tan*, with coins or buttons tossed from brass cups into what looked like pot lids, puzzled her. Using a long stick, a man would separate them into piles of four for the circle of onlookers, who'd placed bets before the toss. Eventually, she realized it was betting on the number of tokens *remaining*—after being divided by four—that was the point. Then there was *pak-kop-pui*, or "white pigeon ticket" she learned later from Samson, which seemed to be some sort of lottery. Big leather wallets, holding bundled squares of white paper printed with columns of tiny Chinese characters, were carried over the shoulders of the game runners. The papers were sold to gamblers who marked the symbols of their choice, then returned them—presumably to be notified later if their symbols had been chosen. It was all fascinating and she could watch for hours—as long as she could abide the stony stares.

Her presence there was clearly not welcome, but she found herself drawn to that part of town over and over as time went by. She told herself it was because of this new form of gambling—sometimes she was even allowed into a game if she appealed with just the right blend of demand and deference . . . and show of money. In truth, she understood the danger, realized she was tempting fate, yet it was the only thing that made her feel alive. More importantly, it made her forget those things she didn't want to think about.

Thankfully, the back door was always left unlocked, the hinges oiled. As she slipped in without a sound and replaced her cloak and bonnet on an empty hook, she was equally grateful for the faint glow of light at the end of the dark hallway. A single lamp was usually left burning in the gambling hall—for others like herself who wandered a bit when they couldn't sleep, she supposed. Heading directly for the stairs, she was also glad tonight's venture had done its job. She was tired. It meant she would probably sleep for a change.

"Good evening."

Caroline's head snapped around. She hadn't seen Simone sitting on the red velvet sofa along the front wall, relaxed in a violet satin dressing gown, legs crossed, the embroidered toe of one slipper peeking out and bouncing to a tiny, internal rhythm. It was the lamp next to her that provided the hall's dim glow.

"Come," she patted the space beside her, "sit with me for a bit. Let's talk."

Caroline did as she was bid, pricked by a tiny needle of dread. Simone preferred to run the place and make her wishes known through Samson. Other than her nightly appearance at her own table, with her own clients—and the occasional new, handsome face she'd allow there—the owner of the Adelphi was rarely seen. She didn't usually socialize with the staff, man or woman.

Tucking her skirts close, Caroline sank into the opposite corner of the sofa.

"I'm glad you've returned safely." Simone's face was smooth, her voice pleasant.

"Safely?"

Instead of elaborating, the other woman gestured gracefully to the cut crystal decanter and glasses on the marble table in front of them. "Care to share a brandy with me?"

"Yes. That would be nice. Thank you."

Simone poured, handed Caroline hers, and angled herself into the cushions to regard her over the rim of her own glass. "You've been leaving the tables early and going to Chinatown." Before Caroline could frame a response, Simone held up a hand. "Don't bother denying it. I've had Samson follow you." She tilted her head in that manner she had. "Why? Samson says you rarely stop. You aren't succumbing to the lure of the opium dens, are you?"

Vigorously, Caroline shook her head. "No!"

"Good. I won't truck with that filthy habit. Samson says he's seen you insinuate yourself into their street games now and then, but little else. So why? What's the appeal? It's quite risky, you know. We whites aren't welcome there. Besides the danger of simply disappearing into the slave traffic, there's the unpredictability of the Celestials in general. Gangs always warring with each other over God-knows-what." She looked into her glass. "Besides the lost profits—which don't please me—I have to wonder why you're courting such danger."

"I don't think about the danger much," she lied. "Mostly I'm fascinated to realize there are so many different gambling games in the world."

"So you're bored with the games here?"

"Oh, no—not at all. I just thought learning what else was out there might be useful."

"In case I ever decide to expand our clientele to include the Celestials?"

"Well . . . yes."

"I see. And that's all?"

Caroline, uncomfortably aware of her own increased pulse, took a gulp of brandy and glanced around the room as if looking for answers. "I-I just . . . I feel restless for some reason."

Simone's heavy-lidded expression was knowing. "And you don't know why?"

"No."

"Do you want me to tell you what I think?"

Their eyes locked briefly, and Caroline nodded.

"You need a man," the older woman said, draining her glass in a single swallow.

Caroline suddenly found interest in her fingers. "But I have a man. I have DeForest."

Simone leaned, placed her empty glass on the marble with a clink, and sat back, thumbing the side of her mouth in a blunt, unfeminine manner. However, the amusement in her face took the sting out of her next words. "That's a sham and we both know it. I don't know what your relationship with him is—and I don't want to know, that's your business—but your friend upstairs isn't much good for anything except funneling whiskey down his throat."

Caroline exhaled wearily. "I know."

"We women need the attention of a man—a real man. It keeps us steady." As sudden as lightning, a grin flashed across Simone's face and was gone just as fast. "It keeps us happy, our hearts light." She tapped Caroline's knee as she rose. "Sex is good for us." Her laugh— her real laugh—was a surprisingly husky sound, rich and juicy.

But the sound died as she reached the bottom step, and she paused long enough to look back, to pin Caroline with a no-non-sense stare. "But man or no man, I expect you to pull your weight. If you want to stay here, you won't let me down again. No more visits to Chinatown."

On a hard swallow, Caroline nodded.

"Good," Simone acknowledged. "Now, goodnight. Sleep well, Miss Cooper . . . of the Johnson County Coopers."

Behind her, Caroline snorted, quickly pressing her fingers against the unguarded sound. *Wily old fox!* she thought on a wave of relief and near-affection for her benefactress.

But her mood dipped even before Simone's steps faded. She set her glass down, uninterested in finishing it. As she climbed the stairs, she became aware of her sore and aching feet. She must've walked for miles. She just hoped it was enough.

Inside their room, Preacher was stretched out across the bed again, the empty bottle he no longer bothered to hide still in his hand. She removed it, took off his shoes, rolled him fully into the bed, and covered him as best she could. He grunted once, but made no other sound. It occurred to her then that he didn't even snore. Here they were sharing a room, yet somehow it was as if he wasn't really there at all.

You need a man.

It was hard to remember him as he was when they first met. She knew he'd been attractive, but too many other images had crowded out those memories, replacing them with ones much less appealing.

He was still pleasant enough—most of the time—solicitous in the mornings when he was sober, but as the day wore on, she could see the shadows gathering behind his eyes, and he became tense and quiet . . . until he was finally drawn downstairs where he'd spend the rest of his time, rarely venturing farther. For that at least, she was grateful. Just the thought of having to hunt him down each night like she had that first night agitated her. She couldn't have faced that task day in and day out. No, this way was better. Still hard, but better. At least it was predictable. He ended every day the same way, quietly drunk.

Tiredly, she glanced about the room and sighed. All the lamps were still burning, and she went around turning the wicks down, annoyed at the waste. Their room and board, lamp oil, clothing—*whiskey*—none of it was free. It all came out of her percentage of winnings. Still, she supposed she couldn't complain. She was finally bringing in steady money, more than she'd ever earned with a needle and thread.

Washing, undressing behind the screen, settling on the settee—it was all done by rote now, and she congratulated herself on her clean mental slate as she kicked off her slippers. She'd accomplished her goal and worn herself past thought . . . yet as soon as she lay down beneath the quilt, the emotional dam cracked, and unwanted memories spilled out.

Jack.

Always Jack.

Her chest ached with the all-too-familiar rush of emptiness and loss. She'd weep if it would help. But it never did.

No more visits to Chinatown.

But it was only the distraction of Chinatown that kept her from going mad.

So the very next night she simply played out her hands, waited until most everyone was gone, and turned in her take to Reed, both bartender and accountant, before sneaking out.

The early November night was mild, much warmer than expected, and she clawed the scarf away from her neck, unbuttoned her cloak, and reveled in the cool slip of air over her skin.

She walked fast, habit more than design taking her toward the streets of Chinatown once again. Why she felt so free there, she would never know.

Everyone had been talking about the riot that had broken out there earlier in the day—Indians and Celestials fighting in the streets over some gambling game gone awry, enough money and passion to equal mayhem and—rumor had it—cannibalism. Competitors cut up, cooked, and served. A fantastic story that didn't warrant belief, and didn't deter her in the least. If it wasn't one wild story, it was always another. If there was any truth to this one, surely the police had swarmed in and restored order by now with their own brand of violence like they always did.

The dark, steeply pitched streets narrowed rapidly as she walked, cobblestone turning into hard-packed earth, lamp-lit streets into shadowed ones. The damp air coming up off the bay, kissing the skin with moisture, cool and intimate, was the same. But something was different tonight. Her steps slowed. For the first time, she felt a spark of uncertainty. Missing were the usual knots of *fan-tan* players in their rings of lantern light, no rattle of dice, no click of dominoes. None of the usual braziers lined the streets . . . no creaking wheels, no slippered feet crisscrossed around her. The shop spaces under the wooden awnings were sucked clean of lanterns and trays. Even the cooking smells seemed muted, fleeting. It was all eerily quiet, yet she could feel the presence of people inside the dark structures, *feel* the attention of unseen eyes just beyond the blank windows, the air charged with the electricity of waiting, of expectation.

She began to listen, straining to hear. What exactly she was listening for she didn't know, but as she turned down Stockton, her ears picked up the faintest buzz—like a distant swarm of bees. She halted. The buzzing grew in volume, but also in scope. It wasn't just coming up one street, but was rushing toward her from several—a swelling avalanche of sound that leapt quickly into a static of angry voices—hundreds of them boiling toward her through the dark. The ground vibrated as they closed in. Cacophonous cries—in a language she didn't recognize—rushed over her. Nightmare bird calls.

It's quite dangerous, you realize . . . gangs always warring with each other . . .

A wavering light—torches in the hands of a mob—slashed up the walls in front of her. Glancing left, right, she looked for sanctuary. None registered. The stampede coming her way would sweep her under its mass and crush her without a thought. She darted forward then back, freezing as a sea of faces bubbled into view, feet churning up the earth like a giant centipede. Her heart thundered. There was no escape. She was going to die right here. In Chinatown.

As she stared into the tide that would kill her, a calm folded around her, an acceptance. Finally, there would be an end to her constant pain.

What yanked her off her feet didn't come from the crowd. Snatched into a darkened, shallow doorway, she was spun by hard hands, shoved against the back wall and crushed there, body to body, just as the mob flashed by with too much velocity to sweep out nooks and crannies such as theirs.

The wave crashed past, chanting and yelling trickling away like draining water. The quiet left in its wake was filled up with the beat of breath, hers and her rescuer's even as relief and fear of a different sort made her push violently free.

"Get off me!"

She broke into the open only to be snatched back, bonnet knocked askew, hard fingers gripping the back of her neck, controlling her, body pressing hers to the wall once again.

"*Caroline?*"

That voice! "*Jack?*"

"My God, it *is* you!"

Hands bracketed her face. It was too dark to see, but she knew that kiss—that hard, hungry, warm vortex of paradise—and she fell into it without grace, without any thought beyond gratitude that he was here and she was whole again because of it.

"You're alive!" she breathed when she finally could. "*You're alive! I thought you were dead!* It almost *killed* me thinking you were gone from this world, that I'd never see you again! Oh, Jack, I'm *so* sorry! I never meant to—"

"Hush! It don't matter now. None of it matters. You're here, I'm here—that's all that counts, and you're never leavin' me again. You hear me? *Never.*"

"I didn't want to—I swear! Louie made me, he—"

"I know, I know. He told me all of it."

"Oh, Jack, I was so afraid, afraid you were going to die and it was all my fault."

"No. No it wasn't." Shoveling her up against him, they wrecked each other with greed—with mouths and hands, their fierce longing finally fed. The sound of a seam tearing filtered through long after the fact, and they fell apart, panting, disbelieving, in the shelter of that small doorway in Chinatown.

"What're you—"

"How'd you—"

"You first—no, wait. Not here, not now."

Holding her away, he stuck his head out of the doorway and looked around. Some of the more usual sounds of life, of people moving around were on the rise, but the alley was still empty. He tugged her closer and tucked her against his side. "Come on. Let's get out of here while we still can. The mob either ran themselves out of steam or into the bay by now. Either way, I don't think this is where we wanna be."

"What was it all about?"

"Who knows? Who cares? I'd rather read about it in tomorrow's paper than get any sort of personal explanation tonight, if y'know what I mean."

Even as they hurried away, hand in hand, they'd break stride to steal a brief hug or kiss, staggering like drunkards. They didn't fully stop until they'd left Chinatown far behind.

In the first empty pool of lamplight, he spun her around. "Caroline . . ." This time his embrace was tender, stroking her back as if reassuring himself she was real and not some specter of his imagination.

Her body curved into his, one hand pressing against his chest for the same reassurance—until she remembered and snatched it back, gasping, "*Oh!* I'm hurting you!"

"No, you're not."

"But your wound!"

"It's fine. It's healed. Listen, we'll talk about it all later. Right now, we—"

"No, no! Let me see," she insisted, reaching inside his jacket and unbuttoning his shirt right then and there.

"We're in the middle of the street," he protested, grabbing at her hands, but she seemed to have more than the usual number and quickly breached his defenses.

"I need to see." Spreading the placket apart, she bit her lip at the dark, jagged pucker, and tears welled. "Oh, Jack! I'm *so* sorry—please forgive me!"

"Hush! Ain't nothin' to forgive." He regained control of his own spiraling emotions by grabbing her and pushing her out to arm's length. "What the hell were you doin' back there? You coulda been killed—you almost were!"

She flowed back against him. "I don't know, I don't care. It doesn't matter anymore. Just don't leave me."

"I won't ever leave you again, I promise. No, don't cry. Please." He kissed her hair, her eyes, her forehead, her cheeks. "*Please* don't cry. I can't stand it."

"I-I can't help it," she protested on a high, thinning note of more tears, and still more, until the sobs wracked her and dampened his shirtfront where her face was buried.

He huffed a laugh this time and began rocking her from side to side—a familiar cajoling—tilting her off her heels until she clutched his sleeves and laughed. "There, that's better."

She wiped her face. "However did you happen to find me?"

"I found you because I been *lookin'* for you—for weeks and weeks. I finally tracked you to the Adelphi where some big guy said I might find you in Chinatown, and told me how to get there. I came at a run. I wasn't even sure I was goin' the right way, but then I spotted you a couple of blocks back—leastwise I *hoped* it was you. Then I lost you again until just before that mob swarmed. Even then, I wasn't sure it *was* you, until—" Grabbing her arms, he gave her a shake. "*You're a fool, you know that?*" Finally, cupping her face, he put his forehead to hers. "These last months have been hell without you," he confessed raggedly.

In unison, they both let out long, pent-up sighs, content to just stand in each other's embrace for the moment.

"It'll be dawn soon," he finally said, pressing a last kiss to her forehead. "You've gotta be tired. I know I am. Let's go back to the Adelphi."

"No. Too many people and I—I share a room. There's no privacy."

"Then let's go to my hotel."

Beyond words for now, they held hands as they walked, fingers continuing to stroke. Neither could quite believe their luck. If indeed this was only a dream, neither wanted to disturb the slumber that conjured it, to jolt awake and be robbed of these moments even if they weren't real.

When he wasn't holding her hand, he was touching, turning her shoulders to point out the dawn's first streak of peach light, or smoothing an escaped curl behind her ear when they paused for a glimpse of the fog-layered bay.

She would smooth his sleeve and smile into his eyes, feeling as if her whole body were lit from within. He could've suggested running down to the quay and into the water, fully clothed, and she would've gone without protest, without question, laughing. She was as God meant her to be in those hours, a woman in love, satisfied with the world. She didn't care where they were going or where they'd end up.

He bought small, exotic oranges from an early morning street vendor. He peeled the fruit and fed it to her, placing each section on her tongue, licking the gleam of juice from the corners of her mouth with his own tongue. Unable to stop there, he left kisses on the crest of her cheek, the corner of her eye, her temple.

Finally, they came to his hotel, but she might as well have been blindfolded for all the attention she paid to how they got there. She had no idea where in the city they were . . . and didn't care.

With his arm around the small of her back, she felt as if she floated up the stairs rather than climbed what must've been the longest flight ever. She wouldn't have been surprised if the door he finally opened led directly into the clouds. Yet she was just as happy to see a plain room with a simple bed and white cotton coverlet, bare wood floor softly shining. There was a single, muslin-curtained window. Jack's bag sat on the floor, sagging against a tall clothes press.

It was the most beautiful room Caroline had ever seen.

They turned to each other without speaking. There was no need. With the perfect communion of love at its brightest and hottest, they rid each other of clothing, then surged together, two forces of need and longing.

At some point, they slept—without willing it, unable to fight it—spooned together under the covers, comfortable in an errant ray of sunshine.

Hours later, Caroline came awake slowly to the affectionate stroke of Jack's thumb along her arm.

"Well, hello. It sure took you long enough," he whispered gruffly.

"I don't want to move."

"Then don't," he said against her skin. "Stay here. With me."

"What time is it?"

He squinted at the window. "Close to five o'clock, I'd say."

"*Oh, no.*" She sighed heavily and pushed up onto an elbow. "I have to get back. Simone's already going to be upset with me as it is."

He rolled out of bed without protest and got dressed, tossing her clothes to her with juvenile enthusiasm.

"Glad to see you're in such fine spirits," she grumbled, getting dressed far more slowly than he did despite her inner monologue to *hurry, hurry!* When her limbs stalled completely, he came and knelt down to help her with her shoes.

"There you go, madam," he said, patting her feet before he rose and offered her a sturdy arm to lean upon. "Let's get you back to Miz Simone's, then we have a lot to talk about."

His hotel wasn't as far away as she'd imagined. They'd only walked a couple of blocks before reaching Kearny, and there was the Adelphi on the opposite corner.

Suddenly, Jack yanked her backwards. "*Whoa, sugar!*"

She swayed and blinked. "What?"

"You almost stepped out in front of that carriage! Are you all right?"

"Of course, I'm—"

And just like that, she went down—not backwards or forwards in some showy swoon, but straight down, legs buckling under her.

Jack hit his own knees on the cobbled street, catching her. Someone nearby lent him a steadying arm, helping him hold her while he regained his feet—then they were gone.

With Caroline limp in his arms, Jack turned a full circle, but no one else did more than glance their way.

Stumbling through gaps in the traffic, he knocked people aside on the steps and backed through the doors of the Adelphi. "You!" he barked at the bartender. "Get a doctor—*hurry!*"

A tall redhead swung around in front of him, sparing a glance for Caroline. "Well, if it ain't Miss La-dee-dah . . . in the arms of—well, hello there, Mr. Handsome!" She offered her best smile, but a closer look at his face made her step back and spin around. "Follow me, honey! Reed, do as the man says and get the doc."

More girls were popping to their feet to stare, and the big burly man who'd given Jack directions the night before met them at the bottom of the stairs and was joined by a heavy-set Chinese man. "It's Caroline," the redhead said, hurrying up the stairs with Jack on her heels, leaving the others to fall in behind or not.

At the end of the hall, she opened a door. "In here. I'm Dee by the way."

Jack swung past her into the room and laid Caroline on the bed. She was starting to come around as he untied her bonnet and tossed it away. Her boots were next, then her gloves. Sitting beside her, he rubbed her hand between his own. "Caroline?"

Her eyes fluttered open. By now the others were hovering, and seeing all their faces above her, she started to cry. "What happened?"

"You fainted—right out in the street. Took a couple years off my life, I can tell you that. But it's all right, love. The doctor's on his way." Tenderly, he stroked damp curls off her forehead. "What's wrong?"

"I don't know. I just—I don't feel well."

"You do look a little green. Uh-oh . . ."

With speed that belied his bulk, Samson tossed flowers out of a china vase and had it down in front of her just in time. When she was done being sick, she flopped back into the pillows with a moan.

Dee brought her a cloth soaked in water from the washstand. "You're okay, sweetie. Chen, go get her a glass of water."

The man who'd been standing silently next to Samson nodded and left.

Minutes later, the door opened again and in walked an older man who put Jack in mind of a pale, washed-out President Lincoln—tall, thin, gaunt, dressed all in gray—even to his tall silk hat. Moving his black bag to his other hand, he stepped forward to shake Jack's hand. "I'm Doctor Fleischman."

Jack felt reassured by the firm, competent handshake. "Jack Transomb."

"Well, well, look who we have here," said a blonde woman just coming into the room. "It's been a long time, Jack."

"Simone," he said with a terse nod, too distracted for surprise.

Over Caroline's head, Samson and Dee exchanged raised-eyebrow looks.

The doctor was already at Caroline's bedside, removing his coat and rolling up his sleeves. "Well, young lady, I understand you fainted. What's going on?"

She murmured something Jack didn't quite catch because just at that moment a man shuffled into the room—coatless, collarless, in a shirt that was badly buttoned and trousers that looked slept-in.

Jack's neck corded. "Atchison!"

Preacher's head snapped up.

"You goddamned, slimy sonofabitch! What the hell are you doing here?"

A distressed sound from Caroline made Jack falter just as he would've lunged for the man. Halting in his tracks, he lowered his voice, but his manner was no less threatening even as the doctor stepped between them. "What the hell are you doing here?" he demanded over the doctor's shoulder.

"Gentlemen!" the physician cautioned.

Preacher's mouth worked a bit, his eyes rounded with apprehension. "I-I live here. What're *you* doing here?"

"Whadaya mean, you *live here? Where* here?"

"*Gentlemen!* I don't know what's between the two of you—"

Jack stabbed a finger toward Preacher. "*That sonofabitch shot me!*"

Caroline had grabbed the vase and was throwing up again.'

"But it'll have to wait 'til later," the doctor continued. "Right now there are more important matters at hand." It was as if he hadn't spoken.

Looking like a dog that expected a kick, Preacher was pointing at the floor with the word "Here," on his lips, but then the word "*Shot?*" came right behind it. "I *shot* you?"

He looked so confused that it confused Jack, which was enough of an opening for the doctor to finally get everyone's attention. "Can someone tell me when this girl last ate? She can't remember."

"Her name's Caroline!" Jack snapped.

"All right. Can anyone here tell me when *Caroline* last ate?" He glanced around at all of them in turn.

Simone shook her head.

Dee giggled and whispered something to Samson. Jack shot her a glare. They both shrugged and fell silent.

Preacher, still frozen near the doorway, glanced at Jack uncertainly before answering. "We had dinner together . . . last night. About six. Here." Again, he pointed at the floor.

"How about you? Anything to add?" Hands on his hips, the doctor looked to Jack.

Raking off his hat, Jack absently fingered the hatband, trying to control the anger twisting his gut. He had to force himself to think, to focus beyond the rising sense of betrayal that made him want to be anywhere but there. Did the little bit they'd eaten hours ago count? "She had a little fruit—an orange—around dawn," he finally answered. None of this was making any sense. *What's happening here? And last night—what was that about if not love? Why, goddamnit, why?* He stepped toward the bed. "Caroline—"

The doctor stopped him with a surprisingly firm hand. "*Later.*" It was an order. The next thing he did was clap his hands together to regain everyone's attention. "Please, if you'll all leave the room now, I'd like to examine my patient."

Crossing his arms high over his chest, Jack stared at the floor. "I'm staying."

Giving him a wide berth, Preacher slunk over to sit on one of the chairs by the window. "I live here," he repeated.

Jack's stare was deadly.

Simone looked between the two of them, brows arched. "Well, I own this place, so if they're staying, I'm staying. Besides, the girl works for me—but you two," she said, indicating Dee and Samson, "get back to work."

They scurried out, exchanging a look that promised gossip later.

"And close the door behind you," she added.

The doctor raised his arms and let them fall in a gesture of surrender that spoke to years of dealing with kith and kin. "Fine, then you," he said, pointing at Jack, "come help me move this screen so this young woman can have some privacy. Then all of you, sit over there together," he commanded, pointing toward the window near where Preacher sat.

After helping the doctor, Jack stalked over and dropped onto the yellow settee. Mouth tight, hands dangling between his knees—knees that were bloodied, he noticed absently—he chewed the inside of his cheek and concentrated on waiting.

Simone just leaned a shoulder against the wall where she was. "Since she and I have the same parts, I'm fine where I am."

The doctor sighed. "Well, at least pour some water in that bowl and put it on the table behind the screen so I can wash," he said, pulling a small cake of soap wrapped in a scrap of leather out of his bag.

"Get *him* to do it," she said, pointing to Preacher. "God knows he doesn't do anything else around here to earn his keep."

Preacher didn't wait, but hurried to do the doctor's bidding with shaking hands.

Jack slanted a look at Simone. She just smiled at him—a wry one tinged with sympathy.

Behind the screen, Caroline moaned and started retching again.

Preacher returned to his seat, and they all waited.

Jack strained to hear anything that was said behind the screen, but caught little and understood less, just brief reassurances from the doctor. It took Herculean effort, but putting everything else aside, he wracked his brain trying to remember if Caroline had felt feverish to him. But in his memory, they'd both felt feverish. And her skin—her soft, milky skin—was unblemished and rash-free, of that much he was certain. He wallowed a bit in remembering the hours they'd just spent together and felt a creeping smile, which promptly drowned beneath a new onrush of suspicion. He cursed himself. Then he cursed her. He wanted to hit something.

He swung a quick glance between Preacher and Simone. They were both staring at the floor. Soon enough, he told himself. Soon enough he'd learn what was wrong with her—probably just a case of those insipid vapors women get, that along with the excitement of last night. Then the doctor would be gone and he'd toss the others out on their ears, so he could get some goddamned answers.

What seemed an eternity later, the doctor stepped out from behind the screen, rolling his sleeves back down.

Jack shot to his feet. "Is she gonna be alright?"

"She needs to eat more, but she's going to be fine—just fine."

There was a faint smile on his face that broadened into a grin as he stepped over to stand in front of where Preacher sat looking up at him. He stuck out his hand.

"Congratulations, son—you're going to be a father!"

Jack's indrawn breath was so sharp it actually hurt.

Preacher gave the doctor a queer, vague look, even as he absently accepted the handshake.

Jack saw none of it. He was blinded with a rage so thick it all but suffocated him. He took a step, lurched sideways, and knocked over something that shattered. Simone came away from the wall, but he pushed her aside and careened out of the room before he could strangle the sniveling bastard, before he gave in to the mad urge to gouge his thumbs straight through the man's neck and crush his goddamned windpipe.

Sixteen

Reno, Nevada, August 1874

The candle was burning low, the gloom gathering closer in the tiny, unpainted room. His hand lifted weakly from the mended coverlet. "*Caroline?*"

Putting down the fan, she took his waxy yellow fingers in her own. "I'm here."

"Talk to me," he whispered.

She smoothed the damp hair off his forehead. The stifling heat made the room nearly unbearable, but he was chilled, so the window would stay closed. *Nothing more to do*, the doctor had said. "What else shall I talk about?"

"Anything." A fit of coughing interrupted, the wracking shudders making her heart twist. "You," he gasped when he finally could, his eyes closed. "Tell me about you."

"You already know about me."

"Family then."

She settled back, hoping to ignore the chair spindles digging into her shoulder blades, and opened her fan again.

"Well, let's see. My daddy, Calvin, was fun-loving—and funny." *And drank a lot.* She glanced over and decided to skip that part. "My mama, Martha, came from French aristocracy way back. She was the backbone of the family. Sweet, but strict. There were lots of rules, but we were loved, Wendall and me, that's for sure."

They were both quiet for a bit until he grew restless and motioned for her to continue.

Tipping her head back, she closed her eyes and started with the first thing that popped to mind. "Know what I miss most? The food. Never was a trip through the kitchen I didn't get a praline or a pecan tart. Makes my mouth water just thinking about it."

There was an answering murmur, barely audible, from the man in the bed, and she leaned over him again. "Do you want anything? Tea maybe?" He moved his head *no*.

She sat back again, searching for a new thread. "And music. Not just recitals in the parlor, but our slaves—they sang often, songs of sorrow and salvation. It would start with a deep hum so low you almost didn't notice it at first, then it would build, sometimes ending up in rounds that could push and pull at you like water waves. I used to fold up small and listen. It was so beautiful. But I felt guilty later—about liking their sad songs. I wanted them to be happy, like me. It took me a while to understand why they weren't, why they couldn't be."

She looked to the man in the bed, at the sheet covering the thin chest. It still rose and fell. "I'm wearing you out."

The squeeze he gave her fingers had surprising strength. "Go on," he croaked.

She rubbed the grit out of her eyes and shifted on the hard seat. She hadn't slept much these last few days. "Sometimes I think we were slaves in our own way back then—to an idea, a way of life. All that time, such a waste of precious lives, such hatred borne of it all."

"Yankees," came the faint suggestion, more breath than sound.

She shook her head. "I don't want to talk about the war anymore, DeForest. It's been over for almost ten years now. It's time to let it go. Jack was right, you can't build—"

That name—*his* name—had dropped off her tongue, slipping through the tiniest of unguarded moments. *Damnit*. It still robbed her of breath, still stabbed her in the heart.

Preacher cracked open an eyelid, the sliver of blue startling her. His lips moved and she had to lean closer, straining to hear. "Go . . . find him. Find Jack."

It was an old topic—another one she was tired of.

"I wouldn't even know where to start."

"He found you . . . You can . . ."

"Why? He's the one who left."

"My fault. Told you. Should've stopped him. Say his baby, not mine. . . but for one. . . selfish moment . . . nice to think . . . being a father. If Helen had . . . lived . . . Go. Find him."

She shook her head. "He could've waited—just five more minutes, that's all."

I'll never leave you.

It no longer hurt, she told herself—then suddenly it did—an awful, howling hurt. It always surprised her that it still had that power. "No, he made his choice."

And there were other topics, too, repeated until they were threadbare.

I still can't believe I shot him . . . Why didn't you tell me? I wish to God I could remember! Dodge is nothing but mud in my head. It's not right. I should feel guilty. Shooting a man down in cold blood shouldn't be something you have to remind yourself of. It should haunt me—God knows, enough other things do.

It wouldn't have done any good to tell you, DeForest. There're so many things we do that, when we look back, we can't believe we were that stupid, that ignorant of our own power . . . that much out of our minds. I can't believe I let Louie bully me into leaving. I should've stayed. I should've gotten myself together and stayed.

You did it to save me.

I could've found another way . . . if only I'd been able to think clearly.

You're too hard on yourself.

And so they forgave each other. They always did.

The hand in hers had grown slack, and dread rushed in to put spots behind her eyes. Chewing a lip that was already salty with tears, she leaned closer and wilted with relief. He was just sleeping. For now.

Rising, she arched her back in a stretch, adjusted the covers, and went to the next room to check on her baby, her son.

Looking down at him sleeping peacefully, his downy hair sculpted from the heat into damp curls around his little face, she heard again the words that always made her grit her teeth.

I'll never abandon them. . . or you either.

No, in this, she was not the guilty one. But it didn't matter anymore. What she had to focus on now was making sure her son got a proper upbringing, something every child was entitled to no matter how many parents it had. Loving him enough wouldn't be the problem—he already had all her heart and more. No, it was the world— her world—of gambling and drinking that had to change. It wouldn't give him the future she wanted for him, the one he deserved.

As she rubbed his tiny, diapered rump—he always slept like that, knees tucked, bottom up in the air—she looked around her. His was the only room she'd painted—yellow. She'd sewn curtains for the window, crocheted a blue rug for the floor beside his cradle, and strung paper cut-outs around the walls, cheerful enough. But it was still over top a saloon.

Never mind that it was hers, something she'd built with her own money soon after she and Preacher arrived from San Francisco. *The Lucky Lady*, she'd called it—not in irony, but hope, a vow that she would never again allow herself to be at the mercy of someone else. (In the end, Simone had wiped her slate clean of debt, but she'd remained adamant they had to leave. And so they went—back over the California border, skirting Indian territory to end up in Reno.)

On the banks of the Truckee River, Reno was good-sized—about a thousand people, she'd been told—and growing rapidly. It had a courthouse, a newspaper, and the Transcontinental Railroad was on its way. Even though named after a Union officer, Jesse Reno, nobody in town seemed to mind that she was a southerner or a gambler, and so it became their home.

She'd built *The Lady*, with their private rooms on the second floor, across from the trestle bridge that spanned the river, and looked out over long fingers of mountain ranges. Something about that view seemed to promise a brighter future—and that's what she'd wanted for her child that was then on the way.

She leaned over and kissed his sweaty, chubby cheek, and went back to sit with Preacher.

He opened his eyes as soon as she'd settled into the chair. "Wish I'd . . . helped more."

Her eyes teared up as she took his hand from beneath the coverlet and brought it to her cheek. "What are you talking about? I couldn't have built this place without you."

It was true.

He drank less—been *drunk* less—while they built *The Lady* than at any other time. In fact, he was the one who'd drawn up the sketches, the layout of the rooms, bent over the lamp for nights at a time, sleeves rolled up, pencil stroking across the paper with skill and confidence.

When she expressed surprise and asked him how he'd known how to do that, he'd looked up with a wide, relaxed smile that reached all the way to his eyes.

"We were always adding to the old place back home. I liked it— the challenge, the satisfaction of seeing something rising out of the ground that had never been there before."

"Truly, you were amazing," she said now, against his bony, wasted knuckles.

The cemetery was on the side of a hill, and the small group at graveside stood under a bright blue morning sky.

Caroline cradled her son, protecting him from sun and wind. The tears striping her face weren't just for Preacher—for DeForest Atchison, who laid at her feet now in the handsomest box she could afford—but for her brother, Wendall, whom she'd never truly mourned.

She could finally face the truth of that now, unlocking that secret place in her heart where she'd harbored the last bits of anger and blame, sweeping out its stale air. Wendall had taken the easy way out and left her to deal with the harsh realities alone. Once she'd dealt with those realities—and survived them—she could finally ache for his loss. *Rest in peace, dear brother.*

"Ashes to ashes, dust to dust."

She closed her eyes as the casket was lowered, its sides scraping the dirt walls, and said a small prayer for her friend, the man who, in many respects, had taken the place of her brother until she could find it in her heart to mourn and forgive him . . . and let them both go.

Accepting murmurs of condolences from the others as they filed out through the cemetery's obligatory wooden arch, Caroline made a point to hand each person one of the mourning cards she'd made herself, complete with black ribbon border and the delicate rosette she'd fashioned from a lock of Preacher's hair. It was the traditional memento.

As with Wendall's funeral, she was the last one to leave the cemetery, closing the small picket gate behind her.

Rocking Jackson for comfort—even though he'd raised not a single howl of protest the entire time—she paused in the middle of the wide street to look off across the valley and through the farthest mountain pass her eye could see, letting the wind rush over her. She allowed herself to linger in the past a bit longer, knowing she'd find her way safely back to the *now.*

She hadn't chosen her role after her parents died, but believed she'd done it well. She'd mended and patched and made do until fate came along to nudge her eyes away from the grindstone.

Change was such a fearsome thing. It was the unknown wrapped in a dark cloak and knocking on your door in the middle of the night, enticing you, daring you, threatening you to step out and off the familiar path. She'd been afraid of taking that first step, but she liked to think she'd done it with courage. And that's when the miracle had happened. Once the responsibilities had dropped away, she began to experience the lightness of freedom, of choice even, for the very first time.

And here it was again. Freedom. Freedom to go and do as she chose. Freedom to live where she chose, to live *as* she chose—she glanced down at her baby—and to care for the *one* she chose. She didn't know where it would take her, but at least this time it wasn't desperation driving her.

She turned around in the street and stared toward the bridge and *The Lucky Lady*. It was a sturdy, decent place, and had served its purpose. Now she needed to figure out how to get rid of it and walk away with her son—with as much money as possible—to start somewhere new. She'd learned a thing or two about business over the years, and now she felt confident enough that she could finally build a successful one of her own as a dressmaker.

"Come on, sweetie," Caroline cooed, gathering her son into her arms, folding the blanket around him, breathing in his sweet baby smell as she tucked him against her shoulder.

He squealed and gave her a drooly grin. "Yes, you're Mama's handsome boy, aren't you? Well, we're going out, you and me. We need lamp oil, yes, we do! And *then*," she said, patting the bottom of the haversack slung over her shoulder, "*then* we'll post Mama's flyers."

He thought that was exceedingly funny and gurgled more of his delight—which made Caroline laugh. He was the happiest baby she'd ever seen.

Once again, she sent a silent prayer of thanksgiving for her son. Without him, she would've felt terribly alone, abandoned and adrift in the months since Preacher's passing.

Jiggling him by habit, she looked out the window at the sulky winter sky. It was a solid gray blanket, and the smell of impending snow hit her nose as soon as she opened the door and started down the long flight of outside steps.

"Maybe we'll have a white Christmas," she said to her son, even though she'd been told the snows here never lasted long or amounted to much . . . and Christmas was still two months away.

Pulling her shawl around them both, she stepped off the last step into the rutted street. No sooner had she done so than the snow began to fall—big, fat flakes spinning lazily to ground.

"Look! Snow!" she whispered to the squirming baby in her arms. "I told you!"

Cautiously, she picked her way across to Murphy's General Store.

The flakes fell faster, and by the time she stepped onto the planked walkway in front of Murphy's, her hair was already dusted white.

The door opened and a man stepped out. She moved aside to let him pass. They glanced up at the same moment, making eye contact, and mutual recognition stopped them both in their tracks.

That face. The last time she'd seen that face, the eyes were blazing with fury. And contempt. Utter contempt—barely a notch below *murderous* contempt.

"*Louie?*"

His stare turned more to the familiar glare as he took note of the infant in her arms.

Instinctively, she turned to shield her son.

He touched the brim of his hat. "Caroline."

She accepted the gesture with a nod, but feeling her sudden distress, her baby reacted with a loud squall.

"*Shhh,*" she whispered against the side of his little cheek. "*Shhh . . .* It's all right."

"How are you?" It was a terse, obligatory question.

"I'm well." *No thanks to you.*

His glance raked the street over her shoulder. "And Preacher? How's he these days?"

She nodded toward the hillside across the road where a couple of headstones were tall enough to be seen. "Buried him the end of August."

Louie's gaze came back to her, sharp and hard. "You have a child." It was an accusation.

"Yes." *And you have a heart of stone.*

His eyes flicked to the bundled infant, then back to her face, curiosity replacing judgment. "What is it? Boy? Girl?"

She looked down at her baby's face, cuddling him closer while she gathered her shredded composure. "A son," she said, feeling both defiant and defensive.

His tone softened unexpectedly. "May I see?"

Briefly, she angled her baby up for inspection. She was just deciding Louie looked far older than she would have expected when his face split into an unexpected smile and much of the added years dropped away.

"What's his name?"

Caroline debated, considering a lie. "Jackson," she finally told him. The truth.

Something flickered across Louie's face at that—speculation, surprise—she wasn't exactly sure, but he studied her face intently for a moment. "Interesting name," he finally said.

Looking down at her son again, she busied herself with tucking the blanket edges closer around him, but a small hand got loose from the swaddling layers and reached for her face. She smiled as she covered the tiny fingers with her own. "We like it, don't we, Jackson?"

Louie stepped closer and reached out with a blunt forefinger.

It was all Caroline could do not to shy away, protecting her infant with her whole body as instinct demanded.

But Louie's face had softened, a crooked half-smile still lighting his blue eyes, his entire face. And her child went from the verge of a fuss to all smiles himself, his own bright blue eyes fixed on this new face so close to his own. Louie grinned and Jackson squealed in delight.

His own delight still shining, Louie turned his head to look up at her. "Healthy?"

"Very," she assured him, allowing herself to relax a little.

They returned their attention to the very active infant between them, imitating the same faces he was making at them. This increased Jackson's glee and the blanket churned with his kicking feet.

Louie laughed outright, knocking his hat back with his knuckles just like Jack used to do.

And that's when Caroline went absolutely still.

When Louie reached for her son, she let him go without a peep of protest. She couldn't take her eyes off him, off the two of them as he pushed his face against Jackson's and rubbed noses with him. Her son squealed his approval. With unmistakable pride, the man tucked the boy close. She couldn't imagine how she'd missed it before . . . how anyone could've missed it. Suddenly, so many things made sense, things that hadn't made sense before. "Does he know?" she blurted.

Louie glanced up, the smile still lighting his eyes.

"Does Jack know you're his father?"

The light drained away from his face until there was nothing left except what the years had left in sadness and regret. "No. I've never been sure of it myself."

"But—"

"There are similarities. Yes, I know."

She struggled not to cry. It was as if the whole world had suddenly cracked open to reveal everyone's pain. "He needed you."

"I know that, too." Carefully, he handed Jackson back to her.

She took him and hugged him to her, rubbing her cheek against the roundness of his small head, giving the comfort to him that she couldn't give his father . . . or his father's father.

Louie pinched the bridge of his nose and shook his head. When he finally spoke, it was to a point on the horizon, to a place far away and long ago. "I've tried to look after him when I could. Mine wasn't the sort of life you could take a boy along. His mother worked in a saloon." Louie glanced at her, then away again. "And there were other men, but she did a pretty decent job with him for all that. If she hadn't died when she did . . ." He shrugged, his voice trailing off as he became snared somewhere in the past.

A sudden gust of wind drove a swirl of snow up under the slanted walkway overhang, reminding them both of the cold and fading daylight.

"Well, no matter," Louie finished briskly, the usual hardness returning to his features. "He turned out alright. We all do—those with backbone anyway. And at least we've been friends."

Caroline bit her lip at that. It took every ounce of willpower she possessed not to ask, not to beg for news. *How is he? Where is he?* This time it was she who shook her head in silence. "Are you staying in town?" she finally managed.

"No, just passing through. Be gone in the morning."

"Oh." That she could experience any kind of disappointment over Louie leaving surprised her no little bit . . . and that he no longer felt like an enemy surprised her even more. "Oh, here." She handed him a flyer from the haversack. "Take this with you."

He glanced down at it. "*'Beat the proprietor...and Win the Lucky Lady'*—what's this?"

"My place. Just up the street there."

He turned and looked. When he turned back to her, he studied her face with a look she knew well. Suspicion. "So why're you using it as table stakes? Still burning bridges behind you?"

She felt her face flame and hugged Jackson for self-comfort this time. "We—Jackson and I—we need a fresh start."

"Why not just sell it?"

"Figure I'll make more money this way. I'm giving up gambling. I plan to open a small dress shop wherever we end up."

Suspicion melted into a nod of grudging approval. "Good for you. You must've gotten pretty good at gaming or you wouldn't have made it this far, but I'm glad you're getting out. You'll have a better life ahead of you—you and the boy."

This was not a man given to praise, so she nodded her thanks.

"Where will you go, d'you know?"

"Not yet. Maybe I'll head back East." She shrugged. "Haven't decided yet."

He looked down at the flyer again. "December third, eh? Well, I wish you luck."

Another blast of stinging snow crystals hit them in the face.

"You've been out in the cold too long. You and the child should get inside."

He was right. Her feet were numb, and she tucked her son's small head beneath her chin to protect him from yet another blast of wind and snow.

"Go on," he urged, opening the door. He closed it behind her, tipped his hat at her through the glass, and walked off.

It was a sunny, breezy afternoon when Louie rattled up the hill in a rented buckboard, following the fence line and the general directions he'd been given in Fiddletown, then more specific ones at the ranch house. Just over the other side, about a hundred yards later, he spotted him.

In a shearling coat, spurred boots, and the wide-brimmed hat favored by cowhands, Jack was working on a portion of the fence, posts and rails on the ground beside him. A horse and wagon waited a few feet away. Looking up and seeing Louie's rig, his stance widened.

Louie reined in and rolled to a stop. He wound the reins around the brake handle, then leaned forward, elbows to knees.

The two eyed each other in silence.

Just inside the front opening of the shearling, Louie saw what looked like a gun belt, the rawhide thong around his right thigh confirming it. He gave a single, short nod. "Jack."

"How'd you find me?"

"Took some doing, I'll admit. Tracked you to San Francisco, then put the rest together from the things you'd jotted down in the margins of this book of yours." He pulled the tattered thing out of his jacket and threw it overhand with enough force to cover the distance between them. Jack let it fall near the fence line behind him. Without a word, he went back to work with the post-hole digger, jamming its spade tips into the ground.

Louie glanced around at the pasture, the rolling hills as far as the eye could see, the copses of evergreen and oak. "Nice place. Yours?"

"Yep."

"How many acres you got?"

Scissoring up the earth, Jack dropped it beside the hole he was creating. "You a tax collector now, old man?"

"Just curious."

Jack didn't answer the question and Louie realized it would be a waiting game. So, he waited, waited and watched him work, grunting with each stab he made into the ground. He'd gotten heavier over the last year. Not fat, just muscle from the look of him.

Jack glanced over his shoulder at him before wrenching the post-hole digger out of the ground again.

"Yep, still here," Louie assured him.

"I got eyes, ol' man."

"You call me *old man* again, I might just come down there and whup your ass, *boy*."

Jack shoved the digger aside. "You think you can take me, *old man*? Come on down here and try." He wiggled gloved fingers in invitation. "*Come on!*"

"You sure? I might be old, but I'm wily. And I cheat." He pointed to the rails. "I might just grab one of those and whack you upside the head."

Jack's eyes flicked between the rails and Louie. "*Shit!* I wouldn't put it past you." He turned his head to spit, but not before Louie saw reluctant humor cross his face.

Climbing down from the wagon, Louie walked up and slapped both his hands on Jack's shoulders—then on impulse, pulled him in close for a quick hug.

Jack's face registered surprise, and he adjusted his hat with a scowl. "Here, make yourself useful," he said, handing over one of the fence posts. He pointed to the fresh hole and picked up a heavy maul that had been lying in the grass. "Drop it in there and hold it steady, but watch your hands," he said as he swung the heavy iron head over his own, and down with a blow that made the older man flinch.

"I got three hundred acres!" he said after another blow that put the post down an inch.

"Good size," Louie said as the maul came down again.

"I buy up more whenever I can afford it!" Another blow, another inch.

Louie wanted to close his eyes at each new swing, but didn't dare. "Sheep or cattle?"

"Cattle! 'Bout thirty head! Half dozen horses! Even got a buffalo. Plenty of deer, too. Turkey, quail." A swing of the maul punctuated each sentence until the post was firmly set in place. Dropping the maul head on the ground, Jack leaned on the handle to catch his breath. "Got a couple ponds, a spring, and a good, deep well. Even got a creek that runs year 'round on the back side of the property. Over that hill there," he indicated with a lift of his chin.

Louie liked the pride he heard in Jack's voice, the clearness in his eyes, his obvious health. "Sounds like you got it all—everything you ever wanted."

Jack didn't respond to that. Instead, he started pitching tools into the back of his own buckboard. "If you need a place to stay, lay low for a couple of days, you can stay here."

Louie brushed his hands together and tucked them into his pockets. "Naw, nobody's on my tail this time. Besides, that Mexican you got working for you ain't too friendly."

"I don't pay Carlos to be friendly. I pay him to cook and help me with the livestock." He walked back for the fence posts and rails, then squinted up at the sky. "He's good with 'em," he said. "Taught me a lot, and his bark's worse 'n' his bite."

"Good to know—and thanks, but I'll pass. Not enough goin' on out here for me. Think I'll head back to Fiddletown—not that there's a whole lot goin' on there either."

Jack looked at him steadily for a moment. "Then why'd you come?"

"I wanted to give you this," he said, digging into a coat pocket. He held out the flyer, which fluttered and flapped in the breeze, flashing its scrolls and fancy lettering. For a couple of heartbeats, Louie thought he was going to refuse to take it.

Finally, he stalked over, took it, and flattened it against the top fence rail to read aloud. "Beat the proprietor and win the Lucky Lady . . . Best saloon and gaming emporium in *Reno, Nevada*? Free beer for the first *hour*? Game starts at seven o'clock, sharp . . . *Please be prompt!*" He snorted. "Where you'd get this?"

"Like it says—Reno. I was through there a couple weeks ago. The day I left, they were posted all over town."

"Who's this proprietor? You know 'im?"

Louie drew a deep breath. "It's not a him, it's a her. It's Caroline."

Jack's head came up, but he quickly looked away, staring out across his sloping pasture for a long moment, a jaw muscle working furiously. "Did you see her?"

"Yep. Talked to her, too. Just so you know, Preacher died a couple months back." He debated whether to tell him about Jackson. He didn't want him going back just for the baby, didn't see any happiness in that . . . then decided it wasn't his call. He liked to think he'd learned a few things over this past year. "Saw her baby, too. Handsome little boy."

Jack finally looked at him. "Why you tellin' me?"

"Just thought you'd like to know."

"Why? So, I can feel guilty about a baby that's not mine?"

"Well, it's *somebody's* baby—and right now, it doesn't have a father."

"So where does this come in?" He waved the flyer. "You expect me to go to her? Last time we talked—what, a year ago—you were pretty pleased at how you'd sent her packin.'"

"I won't apologize for that."

"Don't expect you to. I even understand why you did it, but the law—what there was of it there—could've handled Preacher. Caroline, though. She and me . . . that wasn't your call."

"I know that now. You made that very clear."

Jack stared down at the paper still flapping in his hand like a bird trying to escape, and Louie watched him rub his chest where the bullet had struck. "I don't want a saloon, Louie. I got a ranch, a whole new life. It's back breakin' work, but I like it. I'll die here—in a place I built with my own two hands—not in some flea-bitten hotel or stinkin' saloon. No, you finally got your wish. I'm done with her and the life that goes with her."

"But she—"

"I'm *done*. Ain't nothin' more to say."

Without another word, Jack walked back to his wagon, climbed up, and drove away. He'd crushed the paper in his fist, but hadn't thrown it away. Louie hoped it was a good sign.

Caroline's palms were damp, her stomach jumping. She pressed a hand against the front of her dark garnet dress where it dipped to a point that accentuated her waist—which was almost back to its pre-Jackson narrowness. Despite her nervousness, she felt her lips curve into the smile any thought of her baby always inspired. It was a wonderment that one human being could be so attached to another, she marveled for the hundredth time.

The murmur of voices downstairs was growing. She went to the window and saw the rumps of a half-dozen horses tethered at her rail and a few buggies were lined up across the street. She'd paid Randy an extra dollar to keep the fire stoked high in the grate, greet the players as they arrived, and get them started with a drink.

Would he come? Was he here already?

She pivoted away from the window and began to pace, her silk skirts whispering, her brocade slippers soundless over the carpet. That was the first time she'd fully admitted—even to herself—that she hoped Jack would come, that she *wanted* him to come.

But the odds were against it. Assuming Louie had found Jack—assuming he *wanted* to find him, that he knew *where* to find him . . . There hadn't been much time. No, she was just making it harder on herself with wishful thinking. She was a mother now, responsible for another life. She had no business indulging in romantic fantasies.

The tap at her door startled her. "Yes?"

"Miss Caroline?" It was Randy. "I think all that's comin' is here."

She opened the door, appreciating the rounding of his eyes as he took in her appearance. "My! Don't you look a sight for these ol' eyes!"

He wasn't old in years, but somehow managed to act and sound like he was, muttering to himself as he shuffled around taking care of the place. Barkeep, nursemaid, handyman, and human watchdog, he slept in the storeroom behind the bar, and she trusted him with her life. Jackson's, too. Nothing bad would ever happen to either of them if he could help it.

"Thank you." She took a deep breath, her hand pressed once again to the nervous flutter in her stomach. "I need to look my best."

He grinned crookedly. "Well, not a one of them johnnymarks downstairs'll be able to keep his mind on his cards, 'deed he won't—not with you sittin' across from 'im."

"How many showed up?"

"Eleven."

"All the wall lamps and lanterns over the tables lit?"

"Yup. Not a shadow in the place—just the way you like it. And your table's all set. Locked money box, hankie, unsweetened tea in a whiskey glass, and your chair at the back by the stairs, and me—" he thumbed his green plaid shirt "—for protection. They already got their numbers for the table lottery, and I got me a big box on the bar for everybody's weapons. Figured you'd wanna do that right before the first card cut."

"You've explained all that to them?"

"Yup. Some grumbled, but none of 'em balked."

"Okay." She consulted the little timepiece pinned over her breast. "Let's go."

As she descended the stairs, her eyes swept over her opponents. Before the evening was done, one of them would be her ultimate savior. From work clothes and muddy boots to full dress and fancy shoes, they ran the gamut. Some were introducing themselves, others were walled up in silence. One just spit on the floor, ignoring the spittoon right beside him, which was why she'd never bothered to paint, and why most saloons tended toward the brown-on-brown look. Two men leaned against the bar, drinks in hand. They looked like brothers in height and build, both with dark, bushy mustaches. The rest either stood before the grate warming their hands or lingered near the three tables that had been set up for play, waiting.

Jack was not among them.

Packing away her disappointment, she assessed them individually. That one looked like he came more for the free beer than for play. The youngest one seemed nervous . . . shifty. Another, who allowed no expression to cross his face, his body relaxed inside the old-fashioned frock coat, she labeled a professional. A much older one—dressed as a farmer, but somehow too neatly put together for the role—was probably a rounder. And around she went, deciding—as she always did—that it was best to keep an eye on all of them for one reason or another.

"Good evening, gentlemen!" she said, sweeping into the room with a smile. "Welcome!

"Before we begin, I'd like to thank you all for your interest in *The Lucky Lady*. I trust you've all had a chance to look around the place, and I'm sure whichever one of you wins her tonight, will find her as charming a benefactress as she's proven for me.

"Now, if you'll allow me, I'd like to explain the guidelines for tonight's play. This is Randy—you've already met him. He's explained that he'll be holding all your weapons during this evening's games. So please—if you haven't already—step back to the bar and hand them over for safekeeping. They'll be returned to you right before you leave."

She paused for everyone to comply. "Because of the stakes of tonight's game, security's important. For that reason, as soon as play begins, Randy'll lock all the doors. Once you leave, there's no coming back. If you need to use the privy, several chamber pots have been put in the storeroom for you." She pointed to the door.

Randy harrumphed from behind the bar. "And I sleep in there, so y'all better not miss!"

There was some chuckling at this, lightening the mood some.

"So let's get started. This one is my table and I'll take the first four here. The next four will be there, the rest at that one," she said, pointing. The winners there will move up to my table. Games will be decided at each table. Dealer's choice. One more thing—it's table stakes for each game. That means you win or lose with whatever you put on the table, no IOUs."

"I don't like all these rules!" Free Beer suddenly complained. "I came to play *you*, lady, not all these other fools!"

One of the mustache boys responded. "She can't play all of us at once—no odds in a deck that thin."

"Well, I don't care, I want my gun back. I'm leaving. Don't want this rat hole anyway."

Caroline was unoffended. "Sorry you feel that way." She turned to signal Randy, but he already had the box back on the bar.

Silence reigned until the man stomped out, slamming the door behind him.

"Any other objections?" she asked. "No? Okay, gentlemen, have a seat, make yourselves comfortable. Don't forget beer's on the house for another . . ." she consulted her timepiece again, "forty-nine minutes." She gave Randy the signal to lock up.

Chairs scraped, cards were already being shuffled, and a general murmur of conversation began when the front door suddenly opened and a tall cowhand stepped through.

Randy was locking up the back, so she rose to take care of the latecomer herself.

He'd already shrugged out of his coat and was dropping his hat on top of the coat tree as she came up behind him. "I'm sorry, mister, but the flyer distinctly said—"

He turned around. "Seven o'clock, I know." He dug a gilt watch out of his dungaree pocket and flicked open the cover. "On the dot by my timepiece." He tilted it for her to see, but her eyes never left his now sun-bronzed face.

"You . . ." She felt lightheaded. "You need a new timepiece then."

"Maybe so." He looked around like any potential buyer might. "Still takin' risks, I see. If you wanted to get rid of the place, I'm surprised you didn't just sell it."

Her breathing came faster, driven by the spike in her heartbeat.

His eyes returned to hers—flat, serious, and completely impersonal. "So, you gonna let me play—or not?"

"You arrived before the door was locked, so it's—" she had to swallow "—it's only fair." She pointed to the third table. "Start there. You have to earn your way to my table."

"Only fair," he agreed.

As he walked away, she noticed the rawhide thong around his thigh. He'd obviously gotten more comfortable with guns. "And leave your weapon in that box on the bar."

"Yes, *ma'am*."

Just then, Randy came back through to lock the front door, caught sight of the newcomer, and looked to her in silent query.

She waved away his concern and took her seat, pressing both hands to her face for a moment. Her fingers were icy, her cheeks burning hot. After swallowing a bit of tea, she unlocked her money box, picked up her card deck, and unwrapped it. "Gentlemen," she began, "let's start with some blackjack, shall we?"

She played with scant attention. Oh, she shuffled with the same dexterity, stacked her coins with the same care, played her cards with the same skill. With an iron will, she even managed to control the urge to look over at him. But her mind—and heart—they were at the other table.

Four hours later, she was down to the last three players—the mustache brothers and Jack, who was just taking the chair opposite hers.

She waited for Randy to lock the door behind Farmer and return to his chair by the fire, shotgun cradled across his lap, before she picked up a new deck. True, the last hour of play had been very quiet, very intense, but it wasn't a safety concern that caused her to wait so much as she needed a moment to compose herself before facing Jack head-on.

She watched him stack his money very carefully, very precisely in front of him. It looked like he had a bit more than she did, but then he'd had to vanquish more opponents just to get to her table. The two brothers had less than half that amount between them, both of them hanging on by a thread. Within the hour, one went down, then the other on a split he should never have tried. Each, although dejected, had maintained composure and remained polite, even thanking her for the opportunity as well as the beer.

As soon as the door was shut and locked behind the last one, she offered Jack the cut. They both had triple the amount of money they'd started with, and she knew he was good enough to make it last all night in blackjack. But she had a baby that would need feeding soon. "Let's play poker."

"Just make it a cleaner deal this time," he grumbled. "I keep hearing that top card click."

"Go to hell."

An hour later, they were still neck and neck. He'd win a hand, she'd win a hand.

He blinked and pinched his nose, but she couldn't tell if he was really tired or just trying to sucker her. "One hundred *fifty*," he finally said, moving more money to the center of the table.

She considered her cards and chewed her lip.

"What's the matter? Out of hairpins and stockings?"

Her eyes shot up to meet his, half-expecting to see the glint of humor. Instead, he looked mad as hell. Arming herself with thoughts of everything she'd had to endure alone this past year, she let her lip curl. "You must have a crap hand to use such cheap tactics. *Two* hundred fifty," she countered.

He sucked air in through his nose and shoved the rest of his money forward. "I'll see that—and call. Again." Suddenly, he banged his fist on the table. "*Why won't you fold, damnit? Fold!*"

"*The hell I will!*"

Reaching into a shirt pocket, he yanked out something small and smacked it down on the table between them.

Her silver thimble!

Seeing it took her breath away. *A memento*, he'd called it that Christmas morning onboard the *Quincy*.

"Don't get your hopes up. You'll never win it back."

"What makes you so sure?"

In a single move, he was on his feet, upending the whole table, sending everything on it flying. "*Because I'm done with whatever this is!*"

Randy was on his feet, too—shotgun already leveled. "One more step and you're dead where you stand, mister. Miss Caroline, you might want to move back some."

Jack was standing over her, chest heaving. Eyes on the floor, she was still seated, gripping the sides of the chair. She raised a shaky hand. "It's all right, Randy. Mister Transomb and I, we—we're *friends* of a sort."

"Strange friend—bustin' up things and hollerin'. Ain't no way to act around a lady."

"It's okay. You can put the gun down now."

"You sure? I can have this yahoo outa here faster'n you can say jackanape."

She gave a jerky little nod. "I'm sure. Just give us a moment, will you?"

Slowly, he lowered the gun. "Okay, if you say so—but I'll be in the back room if you need me. Just holler." Throwing Jack one last hot, narrow-eyed glare, he stumped away, grumbling under his breath.

As soon as the storeroom door closed, their frozen tableau broke and Jack raked both hands through his hair, continuing with the same vehemence, but less volume. "Why am I here, Caroline? You sent Louie to get me, but *why*? Because Preacher's gone and I'm some kind of toy on a string to you? Someone to yank on whenever you need me?"

"I didn't *send* Louie—and I don't *need* you."

"Then *why*? And if you're hopin' to hear how sorry I am that Preacher's dead, you got a long wait ahead of you. I don't care. In fact—"

"You said you'd never leave me." Her posture hadn't changed. She hadn't even looked at him, but on those quiet words, she lifted her head. "You *promised*."

They locked eyes, and she watched guilt settle on his shoulders until he sagged under the weight.

"I know." He sounded tired. "I just couldn't stand the thought of you and Preacher . . ."

She allowed herself a small sneer. "Oh, yes, you worked real hard to paint *that* picture for yourself, didn't you?"

"Well, I didn't paint it alone! You were always throwin' Preacher between us. What else was I supposed to think?"

"You were supposed to *wait*—to *ask*—anything to learn the truth. Not just assume the worst and bolt out of the room and disappear. What kind of man does that, Jack? You didn't give me a chance—give *us* a chance. No, you just threw us—both of us—away. You'd said you loved me, so what was *I* supposed to think? That it was just something to say to get one more tumble in bed?"

"Christ, Caroline! How can you—" He floundered, his ragged breathing matching the chaos between them.

Suddenly, he folded to a knee in front of her, grabbing fistfuls of her blood-colored skirt in both hands and pressed his face into the cloth. Defeat and desperation colored his next words. "I don't know what to say, Caroline, what to tell you. *He was livin' with you.* Call me a coward, but I just couldn't bear to hear the words that you loved someone else, that you loved Atchison, that you'd been with him and . . . and were going to have his baby."

The nightmare of their last night in Dodge suddenly burst into her brain, and she lurched to her feet. Dragging her skirts free, she moved away only to whirl back. "You're an *idiot*, Jack Transomb! The only reason he was there was because he couldn't take care of himself anymore. He was hardly ever sober after leaving Dodge, and we only left Dodge because Louie, your *father*, made me, saying he'd hang Preacher if I didn't take him and go."

His face blanked before he rocked back upright. "Who said Louie was my father?"

She flapped that away, a subject for another time. "I should've stood up to him, I know that now, but I was scared out of my mind over you and couldn't think straight." She thumbed her chest. "And I couldn't bear the thought of someone dying because I'd defied a man who maybe wasn't bluffing. *He wouldn't even let me see you, Jack!* I was forced to leave not knowing whether you were going to live or die—do you know how terrifying that was? How much that tore my heart out?" With a hand pressed hard over that very organ that, even now, was trying to beat its way out of her chest, the tears she'd banked for so long began to fall. Annoyed, she dashed them away even as they kept coming. "I was numb with grief, convinced you were dead. It made me want to be dead, too—but then, miracles of miracles, there you were! Suddenly I was the luckiest person in the whole world—but then you were gone *again!*" As if physically grappling with the memory, she curved shaking fingers in the air. "I thought I was angry when Wendall killed himself, but that didn't even come *close* to what I felt when you left me at Simone's. I *hated* you, Jack. *Hated you!* And that helped. So I held onto it, nursed it, wrapped myself in its heat—because that's all I had left of you. *Of us*."

Pelted by her pain, his own face crumpled. He tried to gather her in his arms, but she pushed him away even as he pleaded. "No, please—let me hug you. I need to hug you." He finally got his way, rasping against her temple. "I wish I could take it back—all of it. But I can't. I want nothin' more'n to make it better, but I don't know how. I don't even know where to start, but being without you has left an empty, achin' hole in my heart."

Despite her anger, despite everything, she gradually melted into his embrace. She couldn't *not* because she badly needed this as well.

They stood together like that for a long moment, a silent testament to the healing power of love.

"You're the only man I've ever been with, ever loved," she finally confessed into his shoulder.

"You once told me all you felt for me was *lust*."

"If you really believed that . . ." She sniffed back the last of her tears even as he ground the heel of one hand into his own eyes. "Why'd you come halfway across the country to find me?"

"'Cause you—you were always the best part of me, that's why. And I loved you. *Still* love you . . . never *stopped* loving you."

A sudden stillness stole over him then just before he gripped her shoulders and pushed her out to arm's length. "Wait. So the baby was *mine?* How—"

"*Is* yours, and what do you mean *how?* That last night in Dodge, *that's how!*"

Watching him absorb that, she could almost see the wheels in his head break free of the rust and begin to turn. He looked around—as if suddenly expecting to see a baby squirreled away somewhere.

She finished drying her cheeks with the backs of both hands. "Do you want to see him?"

Looking both alarmed and slightly dazed, he nodded and she took his hand to lead him up the stairs.

Moments later, they stood together gazing down at her baby—*their* baby.

Jack pressed a hand to his own chest, moving it in a tight circle as if easing the pain of that long-ago wound. "I can't believe it. I can't believe *him*. He's perfect."

She beamed. "Why shouldn't he be?"

"What did you name him?"

"Jackson."

The look he turned on her at that was almost too painful, too nakedly emotional to bear.

"You *sure* he's mine?"

One eyebrow winged up. "Well, not entirely—he's half mine. Of course he's yours, you lunkhead!"

His attention swiveled back to his son. "Will it wake him if I pick him up?"

"Probably, but I think it's high time, don't you?"

"'Deed, I do."

Watching him lean over and scoop Jackson into his arms and cuddle him close, nose to nose, made her glow with pride and happiness in a world finally made complete.

Jackson came awake with tiny fists waving and a lusty cry of protest, but quieted unexpectedly as Jack jiggled him expertly.

"*What?*" he demanded at her surprised look. "I seen mothers with babies before."

"Where? In the *brothel?*"

"Sure." He began rocking Jackson from side to side, soothing him back into a peaceful doze. "Babies popped up ever' now and again."

"And they continued to *live* there?"

"No, they were given away."

She couldn't imagine which was worse—being born into a brothel or being given away like puppies. "But not you, why not?"

"Dunno. Guess they liked me better 'n' the rest." He grinned at her in such a way all she could think was *how could they not*? And it hit her then just how much she *didn't* know about this man who'd been—absent or present—at the heart of her life for a very long time.

By now, Jackson had fallen back into that limp-baby slumber, his head on Jack's chest. It took both of them to carefully transfer him back into his bed.

"He's going to wake again any minute, hungry," she whispered.

"Then let's not waste time," Jack whispered back. Taking her arm, he pulled her as far away as the small room would allow. "I'm sorry, Caroline, *so* sorry. I was a jackass to make you go through all this by yourself. If you give me another chance, I swear I'll do my best every single day for the rest of my life to make it up to you, I *swear*. Can you do that?"

Steeping herself in his contrition, weighing it, she didn't answer right away. She had to be careful, to *think* her way through this. There was more at stake than just her heart, her love for a man—even *this* man. There was her child, and *he* mattered most of all.

"I can't make you forgive me," Jack said, filling in the silence. "All I can do is ask—but I'm here now. Least lemme *try* to make it right. For both of you." When she still didn't answer, he wilted, voice hoarse with dread. "*Please, Caroline.*"

Finally, she held up a single finger. "Once more. I'll take one more chance on you, but this is the last time, Jack. If you *ever* leave me again—"

"If I'm ever stupid enough to try that, just shoot me. Better yet, have that man with the shotgun do it—he looked like he wanted to anyway."

Throat locked, she nodded.

Full surrender.

It took a second for each one to realize it, and it sapped the last bit of pride from them both. He crushed her to him, and joy—pure, buoyant joy—made his hands shake as he kissed her hair, her temple, her cheek, her mouth. And that taste of her, so long denied, ignited greed. He shoveled her up against the wall—hands in her hair, mouth sliding the dizzying swoop from her ear down to the tiny dish of her collarbone. He cupped her into the thrust of his hips, taking her weight on his thighs, bracing her legs apart as he dragged her skirts up and tugged at ties with blunt fingers. "*Help me.*"

She did, their fingers fumbling together in sudden urgency. As soon as his palms found bare flesh, his frenzy stilled, and he could finally draw air again. Filling his nose with her scent, his need to savor finally slowed him down.

That's when her greed took over.

Finding him behind his buttons, gripping his hard length in her hand, she impaled herself on him, and they were both lost to time and place. Legs wrapped around him, she gave herself over to his hard thrusts, biting her lip to stop her own cries as that glorious, longed-for tension ratcheted up with every stroke—a rhythm that rocked over and over, sweeping away every thought but one, every restraint but this one . . . final . . . release.

When the room stopped wheeling and her senses sifted back, she didn't care that she was still spread, half-naked, and arched into him in what her mind's eye knew had to be the most wanton display. No, she didn't care a whit. Truth was, she felt she could've remained that way, not thinking, not caring. But it was Jack, breathing hard, who finally eased her back to her feet, steadying her until her legs would hold her.

Brushing her hair back, he framed her face with his new, work-rough hands and spoke to her cattail eyes. "I've missed you, Caroline Cooper, and I love you. I *need* you in my life. Can we get married?"

She cried. She hadn't meant to, hadn't known she was going to, but her heart just cracked open, and she couldn't do anything else. Her whole body spasmed as all the despair, rage, and regret left her in a dam-breaking gush. Locked together with her, he absorbed her wracking hitches with his own frame.

Gradually, the storm subsided. After a deep sigh in near-perfect unison—a synchronicity that made them both huff a quiet laugh—they separated enough to clasp hands just as Jackson woke, wailing as only a hungry baby can.

In a small, straight-backed chair, with Jackson snugged in the shawl she kept knotted into a sling for him when he nursed, and Jack folded contentedly at her feet, his head against her knee as he told her about the ranch and his dreams for it, Caroline finally knew perfect contentment.

Even Wendall lay peacefully on her heart at last. While his death had been a tragedy, she also knew it was what had finally set her free to create a different life for herself, and for that, she was grateful.

Jack turned his head to kiss her knee. "Was that a happy sigh?"

She touched his hair. "It was."

"Good, I'm glad. I wanna give you lots more of those. And you *will* marry me, I hope."

She only smiled.

"Now is my greedy son finished yet?"

"Since he's starting to nod off again, I'd say so."

Jack was already on his feet and scooping their sleepy baby out of her arms, offering her a hand up as soon as she righted her bodice. With Jackson locked in his arms, he headed for the stairs, speaking over his shoulder. "We'll hafta raise him right, of course. Not in a gamblin' hall. No, not in any ol' drafty gamblin' hall, will we?" he cooed at his son.

"No, so I'll sell it now," she said, following them down.

He shifted the baby to a shoulder so he could reach back and take her hand. "You mean *I'll* sell it. I had the winnin' hand."

"You never showed me your cards, so I think not, sir."

"Bah!"

"Raising sheep these days, are you?"

"*Moo* then," he amended, making her laugh. "I think you and Jackson'll love your new home."

As they reached the last step, she felt another wave of happiness.

"It ain't a huge cabin," he was saying, "but there's a long front porch that faces west. I'll put another rocker there and we can watch the sunsets together. The bedroom—our bedroom—faces east, so it gets first light." He turned to her then, Jackson between them, and kissed her with feeling. "I love you, Caroline Cooper. Now let me tell you about the kitchen . . . and the land. Livestock, too—oh, even though you never answered me, we *are* gettin' married—right?"

She smiled and linked her arm with his. "Of course—but on one condition. You *must* stop saying *ain't*. A child needs to be reared hearing proper grammar—and I'll help you."

He made a face. "I bet you will. All right. I'll do my best. Now tell me again that you'll marry me."

"I'll marry you, Jack Transomb."

"Good! Oh—and remind me later to re-set my watch, will you?"

THE END

Epilogue

It was Caroline's favorite time of day, that last peaceful hour before sunset. The shadows were long, the grass cool, and the days' work was finally done. She was stretched out now on ground that sloped gently from their recently expanded cabin on the hill. A short distance away, Jackson was chasing grasshoppers and butterflies, whatever flitted around him. His deep-throated chuckle, a sound too big for his stubby-legged body, always delighted her.

Behind her, she heard Jack's boots chuffing down the hill as he came to join them. The smell of grass, horse, and hard work enveloped her as he leaned to kiss the top of her head before settling down beside her, bracing himself back on both arms.

His exhale was loud, long and satisfied. "*Done*. The new pasture fence is finally finished."

"I knew you'd get it done before the new stock arrived. Maybe now you can rest for a few days?"

"'Fraid not. Always more to do."

She nodded. It was true.

"Tired?" she asked, keeping one eye on Jackson, who was stumbling toward her with a dandelion blossom.

"Yeah, but it's the good kind of—*whoa, boy*!" Jack's arm shot out to shield Caroline even as he caught his tilting toddler with an outthrust leg. "Careful of your mama!"

Caroline laughed, and steadied her son before pulling him down beside her.

As Jack's arm relaxed, his hand came to rest, as it often did, on her rounded belly.

"Baby!" Jackson declared, laying his small hand beside his father's big one. "Careful!"

Jack nodded. "That's right. We have to be very careful of Mama, don't we?"

Jackson nodded vigorously before getting to his feet and going off in search of his next new discovery, and Caroline met her husband's eyes with a smile.

He pushed a wayward lock of hair off her face. "Still happy, Mrs. Transomb?"

She pursed her lips. "I prefer the word *content. Happy* seems fleeting to me, like a once in a while thing, but a person can be content for much longer. When life is running smoothly," she made a long, horizontal wave with one arm even as Jack slid down to fit alongside her, "it's like icing on a cake."

"Cake? Is there cake?"

"Maybe." Amused, she looked away, then grew serious. "You ask me that a lot—am I still happy. Why?"

He kissed her temple. "Dunno. Guess I just worry you might be regrettin' your choice and missin' the excitement, the games."

She shook her head. "Never."

"Never?"

"Never *again*. I had that once and was satisfied with it, but times and games change."

"So this is your game now? Right here? Not very exciting—just the land, cows, me and our little ones. Oh, and don't forget, Louie's coming soon, an' he just might be stayin' this time."

Nodding, she moved to fit herself more closely into the curve of Jack's body, hug his arm to her and rest her cheek on it. "I hope he does. He and Jackson took quite a shine to each other when he was here last time."

Suddenly, Jackson cannoned into them both. Before his father could scold, Caroline gathered up her son, kissed his sweaty head, and squeezed him 'til he giggled and squirmed. "Here's my excitement."

As she looked back up at her husband, her eyes filled with emotion and her heart suddenly felt near to bursting. "And yes, all of that, all of you, are my choice—my dealer's choice."

"Hey—I'm the only dealer here."

She just grinned and rolled her eyes.

Acknowledgments

Thank you to the following individuals and groups who helped in creating this book:

Alison Moore at the North Baker Research Library of the California Historical Society, who—nearly fifteen years ago now—supplied me with stacks of nineteenth-century photos of San Francisco, as well as the gloves and instructions on how to handle them properly.

Bruce and Carol Cochran, my aunt and uncle, who squired me around to every Kansas historical sight they knew of, and I'm betting that my aunt, as a native, knew them all—including the museum of the sunken-and-miraculously recovered *Arabia*, whose docents not only answered every question I asked during their tour, but volunteered so much more, patiently waiting while I scribbled copious notes on paper I had to bum from them. Also, thanks to David Hawley, researcher and author of *The Raising of the Shipwreck Arabia*.

The preservationists, owner(s), and staff of the Ticonderoga Steamship in Shelburne, Vermont. While not technically a riverboat, as its active life was spent on Lake Champlain, its gracious interior informed me and my story of similar passenger vessels of that era.

The Gold Bug in Alamo, California, for their extensive supply of historical maps.

The Ford County Historical Society for their detailed article and old photos of the history of Dodge City, Kansas.

To the uncredited author(s) of the wonderful article, "Delano's Colorful History," for only there would I have learned of the (*ahem*!) magnificent Running of the Doves—thank you!

To Raylene Nickel, for both the guts to do it, and the generosity to write about it in "Starting a Beef Herd from Scratch."

To the editors of and contributors to the wonderful Time-Life Series, *The Old West,* most notably (but not solely) *The Gamblers*, I remain eternally grateful.

To my cousin, Barbara E. Brennan, for volunteering her talent and skill to paint the original cover for this book.

And lastly, to all the dreamers, gamblers, and builders of these United States.

ABOUT THE AUTHOR

Mayo Lucas began her writing journey at age twelve, creating fan fiction inspired by the TV western, *Wagon Train*. An avid reader of Victorian literature and American classics, she was particularly influenced by Margaret Mitchell's *Gone With the Wind*, which spurred her to write her own stories.

Encouraged by her eccentric Great Aunt Evelyn, Lucas later inherited her aunt's desk, typewriter, and original stories, reigniting her passion for writing. At twenty-eight, she wrote her first novel, *Matters of the Heart*, which secured a deal with Avon after placing fourth in the national Golden Heart Contest. Her second book, *Camelot Jones*, followed shortly thereafter.

After a creative hiatus, Lucas returned to writing. Her latest novel, *Dealer's Choice*, received a five-star review from Readers' Favorite. Not yet on the market—but coming soon—are *Amelie*, historical women's fiction, and *Conversations*, a contemporary rom-com.